** DID I READ THIS ALREADY? **

Place your initials or unique symbol in a
square as a reminder to you that you have
read this title.

R. M				*Once*
IL				

REGRETS ONLY

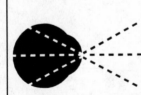

This Large Print Book carries the
Seal of Approval of N.A.V.H.

REGRETS ONLY

M. J. PULLEN

THORNDIKE PRESS
A part of Gale, Cengage Learning

GALE
CENGAGE Learning·

Farmington Hills, Mich • San Francisco • New York • Waterville, Maine
Meriden, Conn • Mason, Ohio • Chicago

Pub 31-

GALE
CENGAGE Learning

Thorndike Press® Large Print Women's Fiction.
The text of this Large Print edition is unabridged.
Other aspects of the book may vary from the original edition.
Set in 16 pt. Plantin.

LIBRARY OF CONGRESS CATALOGING-IN-PUBLICATION DATA

Names: Pullen, M. J. (Manda J.), author.
Title: Regrets only / by M. J. Pullen.
Description: Large print edition. | Waterville, Maine : Thorndike Press, 2016. | © 2016 | Series: Thorndike Press large print women's fiction
Identifiers: LCCN 2016004965| ISBN 9781410489999 (hardcover) | ISBN 141048999X (hardcover)
Subjects: LCSH: Single women—Fiction. | Middle-aged women—Fiction. | Large type books. | GSAFD: Love stories.
Classification: LCC PS3616.U465 R44 2016b | DDC 813/.6—dc23
LC record available at http://lccn.loc.gov/2016004965

Published in 2016 by arrangement with St. Martin's Press, LLC

Printed in Mexico
1 2 3 4 5 6 7 20 19 18 17 16

This book is dedicated to
the memory of my parents
and to my wonderful husband and sons.

I don't regret a single day with you.

And then, after a quarter of an hour's conversation, let the lady release the gentleman from further attendance, by bowing to him, and turning to some other acquaintance who may not be far off. She can leave him much more easily than he can leave her, and it will be better to do so in proper time, than to detain him too long. It is generally in his power to return to her before the close of the evening, and if he is pleased with her society, he will probably make an opportunity of doing so.

— ELIZA LESLIE,
The Ladies' Guide to True Politeness and Perfect Manners; or, Miss Leslie's Behaviour Book

1

Atlanta, Georgia — March 2015

Suzanne Hamilton toyed with a cherry stem while she waited for her date to arrive at the restaurant. She'd ordered a cosmopolitan on a whim after getting a message that Rick would be late, and wolfed it down far faster than she intended. *Never more than one drink with dinner,* her mother's tinkling Southern drawl reminded her. *And for heaven's sake, Suzie, order a salad. Men don't want to marry a girl who eats like a wild boar.*

She caught herself clicking her shoes together under the bar and hurriedly changed positions. The new Beverly Feldman pumps had been special ordered from New York and had to stay scuff-free until at least after the Dylan Burke benefit at the High Museum. It wasn't the three-hundred-dollar price tag that concerned her so much as having to admit to her assistant, Chad, that he had been right, that she should save them for the gala.

The bartender approached her. "Can I get you another, Barbie?"

She shook her head, ignoring his attempt at humor. Tall and thin (and tonight with her long platinum blond hair in a ponytail), she knew she was supposed to be flattered by the comparison to the doll, but she wasn't. He returned to drying glasses and talking about football with a large man in a suit at the other end of the bar. Restless, she pulled out her phone and dialed Marci.

"Hey," her best friend greeted her after two rings. "What are you doing calling on a Friday night? Don't you have a date?"

"First of all, six thirty is not Friday night. It's happy hour. And I do have a date; he's just running late."

Marci did not answer immediately, and Suzanne could hear Marci's husband, Jake, whispering in the background. "Right . . . okay," Marci said finally, sounding distracted.

"Hello?" Suzanne said.

"Sorry, honey. Jake says hi."

"Hi, Jake. Look, Marce, you've got to keep talking to me until he gets here. Sitting alone at the bar is just so *pathetic*." Two seats away, a man writing in a spiral notebook shot her a withering look. "Sorry," Suzanne mouthed to him.

"So who are you waiting for? Is it the basketball player? What was his name?"

"Damian. And, no, I stopped seeing him weeks ago."

"Oh, no! I liked him!" Marci protested. Then, to Jake, "She broke up with Damian."

In the background, Suzanne heard Jake's familiar voice, sounding disappointed. "Aw, man. Ask her if I still get my tickets."

"No!" Marci squealed, in that flirty way girls do when they are pretending to rebuff the attention of an attractive man. Suzanne heard a soft smacking sound that she could only guess was Marci hitting Jake in the chest or shoulder, followed by rustling and giggling. "Ow, Jake, quit it. I am trying to talk to Suzanne. STOOOOP."

Ugh.

Suzanne held the phone away from her ear and stared up at the track lighting over the bar. *Fucking newlyweds.* You would think after three years of marriage they'd be past this intolerable stage by now. Finally, she said in her least sincere sweet voice, "Alrighty then. I can hear that you guys are busy, so I'll just let you go."

"No, Suze, I'm sorry. I can talk." Marci sounded genuinely apologetic. "I'll banish

11

Jake to the office. What happened with Damian? He seemed so great."

"Nothing happened. He's too young for me, for starters."

"Oh, come on. He adores you. And he was only, what, five years younger?"

Thirty-three minus twenty-two . . . "Nine. Wait, no! Eleven."

"Oh, really? And playing professionally already? Well, I still think you should've held on to him."

"Thanks for your input." Suzanne was colder with her best friend than she intended. She was thrilled, of course, that Marci and Jake were finally together after all these years. But it was beginning to feel more and more important to them that she, too, should be happily paired off. "Trust me, it wasn't going to work out with Damian."

"So who is it tonight, Alex Rodriguez?"

"Oh, I'm working my way through the entire Yankees roster tonight. That's why I have to start so early."

Marci's laugh was real, and Suzanne smiled, too. "Actually, his name is Rick, and I met him at that big conference I planned last month. He's in medical sales. We've only been out a couple of times, but he's very cute."

12

"Awesome," Marci said. "Can't wait to meet him."

"Yeah, I think he has potential," Suzanne said in a noncommittal tone. "He's so different from anyone I've dated recently. I mean, he does have a little of that aging frat boy quality about him, but it's not terrible. He's just a little laid-back. But smart and funny."

"Mmm-hmm," Marci muttered, obviously not listening.

"So for our third date, we're going to get hammered and get matching tattoos," Suzanne said. "I'm thinking about a full sleeve with a *Wizard of Oz* theme. Munchkins everywhere. Do you think I can still wear a strapless gown to the gala?"

"Sure, sounds fun."

"MARCI!!"

"Oh, God, Suze, I'm sorry. Jake just . . ."

"It's okay." Suzanne lied. "Rick is here, so I need to run."

"Okay, sweetie, I'll talk to you —"

She ended the call and set her phone on the bar. The guy with the notebook rolled his eyes. Before she could respond, the phone rang almost immediately. "No, Marci, I am not mad at you," she answered.

"That's a relief." Chad sounded less than amused. "I have the Friday wrap-up before

13

I go. I'm off tomorrow, right?"

"Yep. Big plans tonight?"

"No. Just some party David is dragging me to. But, of course, thanks to you, I don't enjoy parties anymore. I'm always noticing that the drinks are watered down or the cocktail napkins don't match the theme. God, I *have* to get another job."

"Love you, too, Chad," Suzanne said. After four years together, they both knew the only thing Chad liked more than working for her was complaining about working for her.

He let out a deep sigh. "So, anyway. Betsy Fuller-Brown called about meeting next week. She wants to go over the schematics for the Firefly Gala on Monday afternoon. Your calendar was clear, so I told her you were available. Meeting at Rathbun's at four."

"Perfect. Thanks." Suzanne loved that Betsy, the hummingbird-sized development director at the High Museum, always wanted to have their lunch meetings at a steakhouse.

"Couple of potential new projects. UPS is having some formal thing at the aquarium; they apparently really liked what you did for them last year."

"We," she corrected.

14

"Hey, you're the face of this operation. I'm just the hired help. Anyway, the other one is an Internet company I've never heard of, doing an IPO party. Have we ever done that before?"

"Eh," Suzanne said. "I have. Those things are so hit-or-miss. Sometimes they get a little theme crazy. We'll look up their executive team. If there's anyone exciting, we'll send them a high bid and make it worth our while."

"Cool. Your mom called," Chad went on. "To ask whether you were going to ride with her to the League Annual Meeting or drive separately. I thought you weren't going?"

"I'm not. It's the day before the gala. I told her that."

"She called me Christopher again," he whined.

"Sorry," Suzanne said, waving at Rick as he entered the restaurant. He wore dark-colored khakis and a slightly sweaty yellow golf shirt. She wrinkled her nose. To Chad she said, "Look at it this way: at least she's moved on from calling you 'that nice gay boy who works for Suzanne.' That's progress."

Rick approached, reaching for her, and Suzanne held up a finger. "Um, sure," Chad said, unamused. "Last thing. That girl

15

Penny called again about internship opportunities. What do you want me to tell her?"

"Oh, right. I forgot about that," Suzanne said. "What do you think? Do we want an intern?"

"By 'intern,' you mean some clueless person who would follow me around all day asking stupid questions and getting in the way?"

Suzanne laughed. "Probably. Though she might be good for some of the grunt work."

"Not worth it," Chad said. "This office is small enough already."

"Fair enough," said Suzanne. "Okay, I gotta run. Call her back Monday and give her our sincerest regrets. Don't worry about Mom; I'll handle that one myself."

"Yeah, you *seriously* don't pay me enough for that one."

"I don't pay me enough for that, either," she said, and hung up. She kissed Rick on the cheek and followed him to a table.

During dinner, Rick talked about work while Suzanne toyed with her Cobb salad. From what she could tell, he really seemed to love his job. A particular type of personality was required to be successful in sales — bombastic, friendly, guileless — and Rick fit the part. All this, along with a seemingly genuine interest in every single word she said, had drawn her to him when they met a couple of weeks before. He was such a gentleman that he had even pretended, briefly, to be surprised when she suggested they go back to his hotel room just a few hours after they met.

He chatted easily now, telling stories about fishing trips and golf games with clients between bites of an enormous burger. *Such kind, lively eyes,* she thought. *And he's mature. Not some self-absorbed kid.* Rick was age-appropriate. He was focused. Down to earth. He was . . .

A little loud, though, isn't he? Out of the corner of her eye, Suzanne imagined she saw people at a nearby table looking over at them. *You're imagining things. Focus. What a cute face. Remember those first kisses?*

Rick was describing a party he'd attended on a boat for some work function in Miami. Something about a thirty-five-foot yacht and scoring a key nursing home account over a game of poker. *Is that barbecue sauce on his chin? Should I let him know?*

Suzanne fidgeted with her napkin and tried to ignore the sauce. She knew very well her reputation as a serial dater. Her friends had teased her about it for years, and she'd never taken it seriously. But lately the teasing felt more like criticism. Like there was something *wrong* with her.

There's nothing wrong with me. I am perfectly capable of making a relationship work long-term. She forked a cherry tomato and put it in her mouth. *Did he just say "irregardless"?*

As the yacht story wound to its apparently hilarious conclusion, she faked a brief laugh, and Rick honed in. "So, how about you? I remember that you grew up here. I've never asked — do you have family in town?"

"Yes, my parents live in Peachtree City."

"Isn't that where they have all the golf carts everywhere?"

"Yes."

"That's pretty cool. Are you close to your parents?"

"Define 'close.' "

"Well, uh, I guess, do you see them a lot?"

"Not really."

Clearly this was a closed door, so the salesman changed tactics. "Well, at least they're nearby. My parents moved down to Florida a few years ago, and I only see them a couple of times a year. It's a good thing Dad and I have an annual fishing trip in the Keys. We go out on this great little boat . . ." And he was off again. Suzanne watched his face as he talked. A little doughy, perhaps, but with kind eyes. She imagined that being on the road all the time meant he didn't eat as well as he should. His dark brown hair was still full and thick, in need of a trim — it curled up just a bit over his ears. Overall, she decided, he was attractive but approachable.

"That sounds really nice," she said at an appropriate pause in his monologue about the fishing trip. *He does seem to have a thing about boats, doesn't he?*

Soon Rick was boasting happily about a swordfish he and his dad had caught several years before. Suzanne wondered whether she could ever successfully decorate a room that included a six-foot-long mounted fish. *It would have to be a nautical theme . . .*

Stop it, she chided herself. *You are not marrying this guy* or *his fish. We are having a grown-up conversation and being open to the possibility of something more. This is what people in their thirties do on dates.*

She smiled broadly at him, remembering to show her teeth the way she'd been instructed before beauty pageants as a child. She could almost taste the Vaseline her mother made her rub on her top teeth to ensure they didn't get smudged with lipstick. *Smile. Be open.*

Rick returned the smile with warmth. He also seemed to notice he'd been talking about himself for too long. "So tell me how you got started in the party-planning business."

Suzanne recounted briefly how she had been an art history major at the University of Georgia, desperately wanting to work as a museum curator, and how she'd taken the job on the event staff at the High Museum right after college. "Originally, I hoped the foot in the door at the museum would land me a job in procurement or something, but it never happened."

"Oh, I'm sorry," Rick said sympathetically.

Suzanne shrugged. It turned out she had a knack for event planning. Something about the combination of creativity and crisis response. After a couple of years at the High, she had been hired away by a large event-planning agency. She stayed there for a few years before creating her own boutique agency. Now she had one of the most successful, prestigious agencies in the city. People were often shocked to discover she and Chad were the only permanent staff. "We actually won an award last year," she told Rick.

"Sounds like you are quite the little rock star in the event-planning world," he said.

"Or do you just plan events for rock stars?"

Normally very discreet about her clients, Suzanne couldn't resist the opportunity to brag a little. "Actually, I am doing a benefit in a couple of weeks for Dylan Burke. Of course, he's more a *country* star . . ."

"Seriously? I was kidding about the whole rock star thing."

A Southern lady is always modest, her mother's voice chided her. "Well, it's not that big of a deal," Suzanne hedged. "It's at my old stomping grounds at the High, which is probably why I got the job."

"Don't sell yourself short," Rick countered enthusiastically. "That's awesome. He's totally famous."

She waved away the words with a manicured hand, but Rick was undeterred. "Seriously, you should be really proud of yourself. That's a huge deal. Obviously, you've earned quite a reputation for someone like Dylan Burke to choose you."

His eyes held hers sincerely. *Okay, Rick, ease up. We've already slept together. You can dial it down a tad.*

"Really, his manager chose me. I haven't actually met Dylan yet. We'll see how it turns out," she said, and pretended to be engrossed in the highlights of spring training on the TV over the bar. "How do you

21

think the Braves will do this year?"

A few hours later, Suzanne awoke suddenly, unable to breathe. She gasped for air in the darkness, desperately trying to move, to figure out where she was. There was no light anywhere. Her chest tightened painfully, heart pounding, lips dry. As she struggled to move, she heard Rick groan softly nearby and roll over, releasing her from his grasp. She was in his hotel room, she remembered, and relaxed a little. When his breathing was soft and steady, she moved again to slide out from between the crisp sheets.

I can't do it.

She found the clock facedown on the floor. Almost 4:00 A.M. She crept into the bathroom and shut the door before finding the unpleasantly bright light. She splashed water on her face and breathed deeply. After a few moments with her hands steadying her against the sink, she looked in the mirror. *Jesus, I look like crap.* Mascara was smeared beneath her eyes, her formerly perfect hair was a rat's nest behind her head, and the evening of cocktails had weathered her face like a sailor's. Suzanne looked and felt much older than thirty-three. She made a mental note to have Chad schedule a facial before the benefit.

Silently, she began gathering her things. The hotel room was pitch-black, so she scrounged in her purse for the tiny key-chain light, shaped like a pig, that Marci had given her years ago. The expensive pumps had been kicked off near the door. Skirt and blouse were in a heap nearby. After a few moments of searching, she located her bra hanging off the desk lampshade across from the bed. Her panties, however, had gone completely missing.

She covered the room with the tiny pig several times, freezing periodically when she heard Rick shift or grunt in his sleep. Opening the blackout curtains a fraction gave her enough light to shimmy into the rest of her clothes and make one more sweep of the room. She kicked herself for wearing her favorite pair of La Perla underwear, as they were about to become the casualty of an early-morning getaway.

Sorry, girls.

She decided to add "Leave favorite underwear at home" to her list of dating rules. The rules were sort of Suzanne's cross between Emily Post and Julia Roberts in *Pretty Woman,* mostly resulting from her own bad experiences: Never bring a man back to your place. No emotional talk during sex. Never get naked with the lights on.

23

Always undress yourself. No dating guys with kids or dogs. No sex in cars. And so on. She thought one day she could publish these rules and make a fortune.

She closed the curtain and crept toward the door. She was nearly out of the room when she lost her balance and bumped against the closet door. It rattled loudly. Rick stirred behind her. "Suzanne? You okay?"

Damn.

"Yes, I'm fine." Her voice was sheepish despite her best efforts. "I just need to get an early start today."

"But" — his voice in the darkness was slow and softened by sleep — "it's Saturday."

"Yeah, I just have so much going on with this benefit; I really need to get home. Thank you for dinner and . . . everything."

She waited as she heard him fumble for the lamp and got it turned on. "Um, sure. You're welcome?" he said, looking around, befuddled. In the sudden light, his bare chest looked a little pudgier, and furrier, than she remembered. He ran his hand through the thick brown hair standing up all over his head.

"Okay, well . . . bye, Rick," she said, as sweetly as she could. She turned back toward the door.

"Wait," he said softly.

Please don't make an ass of yourself, she willed him. *Please just hate me and let's be done with it.*

She didn't have to worry. As much as he liked her, Rick the salesman knew a simple, cardinal rule of all relationships: never beg. He simply asked the exact question to which he wanted the answer. "This is ending right now, isn't it?"

Suzanne noticed that there was neither hope nor despair in his tone. Obviously, he genuinely liked her, and yet the question only sought to confirm, rather than to convince or retaliate. She hesitated only for a split second. "Yes."

She hovered there momentarily, waiting for the usual barrage of questions or arguments to commence, but Rick just nodded slowly and said, "I'm sorry to hear that. It really was very nice to meet you, Suzanne."

Her face flushed. The stark contrast between this courteous ending and last night's very primitive activities embarrassed her, as did standing in her professional clothes and heels with no underwear. "You, too, Rick. Take care, okay?"

She hurried out, made her way down the stairs, and exited the side door. She had the phone number to the cab company on speed dial.

2

"You look awful," Chad said when she got to the office Monday morning, handing her a cinnamon latte. He was right. She'd barely slept all weekend.

"Thanks," she replied. "I would say the same for you, but I have to say you actually look great in jeans. I didn't know you owned any."

He pretended to be offended. "Hey, just because I don't dress like a homeless person every day doesn't mean I can't pull off casual when it's appropriate. You just never get to see me on my days off. Except *today.*"

The snarl was tiny but hard to miss. Typically their office was not open on Mondays, because the nature of event planning required them to work so many weekends. But the gala was coming up in less than two weeks, and Chad had been bribed with the promise of a week's paid vacation and several free dinners to work three Mondays in a row in preparation. It was a raw deal for Suzanne and she knew it, but Chad was indispensable to her and the thought of his being unhappy was more than she could handle. She considered it an investment in her own sanity.

"Thank you again. Your sacrifice has been duly noted."

Chad gave her a tight smile and walked deliberately to his desk, about ten feet away from hers. They worked in a converted loft space in West Midtown with floor-to-ceiling windows; brightly painted, exposed pipes; and red brick along the outside walls, original to the building from its days as a textile mill. Normally neat as a pin, today the office was cluttered with event paraphernalia. Two hundred goody baskets with tiny guitars hot-glued to ribbons hanging from the top. Silent-auction items ranging from original artwork to an autographed pair of boots. Piles of pop culture magazines and music-industry trade publications, from which Suzanne and Chad had tried to glean everything possible about Dylan Burke before the benefit.

Suzanne took the latte to her workstation and began retrieving voice-mail messages: seventeen since she'd checked in on Saturday. The routine questions and confirmations from vendors she forwarded to Chad. She'd have to handle herself the several semipanicked messages from Dylan Burke's squeaky manager, Yvette. When anxious, Yvette had the shrillest voice Suzanne had ever heard. She groaned as she jotted things down on several sticky notes, lining them up in order of priority as she went through the voice mails. Yvette apparently never slept, never took a day off, and never stopped worrying about her young boss's desires and reputation.

Dylan Burke, twenty-six, was the quintessential small-town Tennessee boy made good. Known for his gritty persona and anthem-style country-rock, he had become country music's latest rising star. He'd had several chart-busting hits in the last two years, including "Country Rules" and "Sticking Up for the Sticks." Each of these featured plays on words, guitar solos, and rhythms that seemed to have been designed with line dancing in mind. His most recent hit, "Duct Tape Fixes Everything," was a cutesy ballad-type song that featured a young boy trying to repair his parents' broken marriage. Suzanne, not a country fan, had never listened to it, but the mere mention of the song sent Marci weeping.

Women loved Dylan Burke for his winning smile, tight jeans, and ever-present faded camouflage baseball cap. The mainstream media loved taking pictures of him and his acoustic guitar in beauteous settings, gossiping about his endless stream of busty young girlfriends, and chronicling his fairly predictable rebellious behavior. The tabloids loved his large and conspicuous family most of all.

The Burkes were Nashville's take on the Brady bunch. Dylan's rough, outspoken mother had moved to Nashville from a rural Georgia trailer park, hoping to make it as a singer and dragging her two young daughters with her. While waiting tables at a diner, she had met and married Dylan's father, a divorced music producer who had two teenage daughters of his own. Dylan and his younger sister, Kate, had come along shortly thereafter. By the time Dylan was eight, Donna Burke had abandoned her own hopes of a singing career in favor of her talented only son.

It seemed to Suzanne — as she and Chad pored over articles, researching their famous client together — that after Dylan's career began to take off, his family had a competition to see who could ride his famous coattails farther while embarrassing him the most. Every other week it seemed that his mother or one of his five sisters said or did something ridiculous, and nearly always there was photographic evidence to document it. Dylan must have a terrible publicist, because he not only seemed unfazed by their behavior but also continued to be seen with them at even his most prominent award ceremonies and press opportunities.

She suspected that the gala in Atlanta was designed to soften all of that — as well as to demonstrate Dylan's more urbane side. Even before reading *People,* Suzanne knew that Dylan was making a foray into acting, having been recently cast across from Reese Witherspoon in a romantic comedy set in Atlanta. The benefit at the High was supposed to show his sophisticated side, while subtly promoting both the movie and his current album, *Fireflies.* A tall order, but Suzanne had every confidence she would be able to pull it off.

The evening was a "cowboy meets culture" kind of event, and the biggest deal to hit the High in a long time. The guest list was loaded with an eclectic mix of celebrities — everyone from Jason Aldean to Ryan Seacrest, along with Dylan's verbally uncouth mother, well-connected father, and the more attention-hungry of his five sisters. And, of course, several other artists from country music's freshman class of wild boys would make appearances, accompanied by a gaggle of aspiring starlets. These last were mostly the stick-thin, silly types who wore sunglasses indoors and carried tiny dogs in their purses. It promised to be an entertaining evening.

Naturally, several local and national media outlets had representatives attending, pretending to be focused on style or the arts but primarily awaiting the inevitable spectacle bound to occur when black ties and boots met vast quantities of booze.

This was why Suzanne had been hired, in fact. The High didn't have the internal staff to handle all the intricacies of dealing with the event itself along with the press, agents, handlers, and celebrities. Suzanne's insane dedication to perfection and diplomatic skills, along with her experience at the museum, made her the perfect choice. When Betsy Fuller-Brown had called Suzanne personally to request a bid, she'd suspected they were pretty desperate to hire her and put in for twice her normal project fees to test the waters. To her shock, they had not batted an eyelash, much less tried to talk her down.

Three months later, Suzanne realized she had already earned every penny of her fee and then some. Apparently, Dylan Burke and his staff knew he was the hottest thing going and planned to make the most of it by being the highest-maintenance celebrity entourage ever. Starting the first week after she'd taken on the project, Suzanne had received reams of faxes from Yvette every week detailing special requests for the event. (Apparently, Yvette didn't trust e-mail with Dylan's personal information.) A boot-shaped ice luge that dispensed Southern Comfort into chilled shot glasses. Mason jars full of live fireflies as centerpieces — promoting Dylan's *Fireflies* album. Several large suites at the Four Seasons for Dylan's family and friends, as well as a VIP lounge area at the museum. As Yvette enthusiastically described Dylan's apparently very specific vision over a breakfast meeting, Suzanne thought, *This is why I don't do weddings. The brides.*

Today's crisis had apparently been brewing over the weekend. Yvette's high-pitched voice was especially grating. "Suzanne, it's Yvette. Listen, we are having some major issues here with the seating arrangement. Donna Burke is insisting that she needs a table near the stage, but you already have the VIP tables full for the major donors and the partner sponsors. I also need a press table on the right side of the stage so that the photographers can capture Dylan's left profile for the pictures."

Suzanne dialed back Yvette's number and, of course, reached her voice mail. *If this is so important,* she thought, *answer your damn phone.* "Hi, Yvette," she trilled as sweetly as she could. "Suzanne here. Just got into the office and got your messages. I totally appreciate your concerns; thank you for voicing them so well. Why don't you just buzz me back and we'll talk?"

"Ick," Chad said, putting a file on her desk as she finished her message. "Just promise me you'll never talk to me like that, okay? If I annoy you or something, just tell me. Don't do the whole sweet Southern girl, smile-through-your-teeth-while-you-stick-the-knife-in-my-back routine."

"You're annoying me," she replied flatly. He grinned and turned back to his desk.

"You told her about the problem with the press table?" Chad called over his shoulder.

Shit. Suzanne knew she probably should've left that on the message so Yvette could talk to Dylan before getting back to her. Otherwise, they'd have another long, exhausting conversation to come to a mutual decision that would then be overturned by Dylan anyway. She picked up the phone again.

"Hello?" A man's voice. She paused.

"Oh, I'm sorry. I must've dialed the wrong number." *Wait, didn't I just hit redial?* She was about to hang up when the voice returned.

"Not if you were calling Yvette Olsen, you didn't. Can I, uh, can I help you?"

Suzanne thought she remembered Yvette mentioning that she had a new assistant. Maybe she had started trusting him with phone duty. "Well, is Yvette available?"

"I'm sorry. She stepped out. Is there something I can do for you?" She heard voices in the background — other men — and for a second she thought she heard suppressed laughter.

"Well," Suzanne sighed. "I'd just left her a message a few minutes ago responding to some concerns she had about the benefit —"

"We were actually just meeting about that, so your timing is great." His voice sounded farther away now. *Had he put her on speakerphone? Who else was in the room?*

"Okay," she started tentatively. "I just remembered that I had an additional question about the press table, so if you'll just have her call me when she gets back, that

35

would be great."

"Why don't you just ask me the question?" he said.

"Well, it's complicated."

"The question is complicated, or the reason you can't ask me is complicated?"

Wow. She thought *Chad* was a nervy assistant. This guy was bordering on rude. If this was what the music industry peons were like, she was going to charge more to plan their ridiculous parties. "The question is complicated. It's about the press table."

"I don't think we should have one. Let the vultures stand." She heard more laughter in the background. *Man, was Yvette going to be pissed when Suzanne told her about this.*

"Well, that wasn't really the question. Obviously, there are enough major outlets planning to attend — I think we have to accommodate them. It was just a question of how to keep them separate from the Burkes —"

"Afraid one of those hillbillies will make a scene and ruin the whole event?"

"Well, yes, frankly. Those are the kinds of things we have to be concerned about — the comfort of the attendees, the reputation of the museum . . . You know what? Just have Yvette call me, if you don't mind."

36

"I do mind, as a matter of fact."

Suzanne was completely taken aback. "I beg your pardon?"

"I realize, Miss Hamilton, that my family may not have the blueblooded heritage that yours does. We may not be conventional, exactly. But we're good people."

"My family?" Holy shit. Suzanne collapsed into her chair, mouth gaping. *Oh God, oh God, oh God. Tell me this isn't happening.*

She now realized why the assistant's masculine twang sounded familiar. She had a sudden — and belated — memory, crystal clear, that Yvette had mentioned her new assistant's name was Lisa. She'd been talking to Dylan Burke. For the first time. *Holy shit.*

"Mr. Burke, I —" She stammered, gripping the phone in panic. Across the room, Chad's eyes went wide in shock as he put it together, too. "Please accept my apologies. I —"

But it was too late. "Yvette," she heard Dylan call to the murmuring room behind him. She heard a static rustle as he presumably tossed the phone to her. Yvette made a startled, squeaking noise as she fumbled it. From farther away, she heard country music's golden boy say, "It's for you."

3

"My career is over. Over. Ooooover," Suzanne said, staring into the bottom of an empty martini glass. "That doesn't even sound like a real word anymore. Over. Over . . ."

"Over and out?" came a cheerily snide suggestion from across the table.

"Shut up, Rebecca," Marci said. "Can't you see she's upset enough?"

It was the first time the four of them — Suzanne, Marci, Beth, and Rebecca — had been out together in months. Marci had been holed up with some major copyediting project for the last several weeks. Beth had been busy with her family: she was president of her kids' PTA or something, and her husband, Ray, was starting his own car-repair shop. Rebecca traveled constantly in her new job as a flight attendant; what's more, she had basically been on friend probation for the last few years, since she had made a not terribly subtle attempt to become the next Mrs. Jake Stillwell in Marci's place.

Though she had done nothing overtly mean-spirited, Rebecca had flocked to Jake's side when he and Marci had broken their engagement for a time. Rebecca had never hidden her feelings for Jake very well and had obviously tried to take advantage of a painful situation to get closer to him. When this backfired, she had lost her position as a bridesmaid at their wedding, and Marci had scarcely spoken to her for the first year she and Jake were married.

As time went on, however, she had dogged the three other women with so many invitations and solicitations of friendship that they had let her back in the circle out of sheer exhaustion from the effort of keeping her out.

Now, Suzanne glared at her with one eye through the distortion of the martini glass. "Is it me, Rebecca," she slurred, "or has your head gotten really tiny since the last time I saw you?"

"Suze, I think you've had enough to drink," Marci said.

"I have not haved too much," slurred Suzanne. "You've haved too much."

"I haven't had anything, actually," corrected Marci.

"See? So I have to drink for both of us. That's the tradition."

Rebecca snorted. "The tradition? What tradition?"

"The 'I humiliated myself in front of a major superstar and can never go out in public after tonight' tradition," Suzanne said. She followed this with a dreamy contemplation of the ceiling at the bar. "I wonder if I'll be happy living in Fiji. Or is it Fuji?"

"I think Fuji's a camera, hon," Beth said, patting her hand. "Let's get you hydrated, okay?" She signaled to the waiter for water.

"Did he actually fire you?" Rebecca asked.

"No, but he will, obviously," Suzanne said. "Actually, he'll probably have Yvette fire me — I've never actually met him in person. God, I'm dreading that conversation. That woman sounds like a deranged chipmunk when she's upset. I'd —"

"What I want to know," Beth interrupted, patting Suzanne again in apology, and turning to the group significantly, "is why isn't Marci drinking?"

"Don't be silly," Suzanne said, "of course she is. That's a Coke and . . ."

"Coke," Marci finished. Even in the dim lighting of the bar, Suzanne could tell she

40

was blushing.

"Spill it, Marcella," Beth said.

"Well," Marci said slowly, "we hadn't planned to tell anyone yet, but —"

"I knew it!" Beth squealed. Beth never squealed. "You're pregnant!"

Marci scarcely had time to nod before Beth had jumped up and run around the table to her, almost tackling her in an embrace. "I'm only ten weeks," Marci was saying to Suzanne and Rebecca over Beth's bouncing shoulder. "We just told our families this week."

The announcement should have made her happy, but it felt as though someone had kicked Suzanne in the chest. She plastered on a happy face. Marci addressed the group but gave Suzanne an apologetic look as she reiterated, "Like I said, we hadn't planned to tell yet, so if you guys could keep it to yourselves, that would be great. I haven't even been able to tell Nicole and Ravi yet."

Beth, meanwhile, seemed oblivious to any tension. "So who is your OB? Where are you going to deliver? Have you thought about names yet? Are you going natural? Oh! I have so many books you can borrow!"

For the next half hour, Suzanne stared into her water glass and listened to Beth and Marci get lost in their own little world

41

of impending motherhood. She tried to sober up, to insert appropriate remarks into the pregnancy conversation, and to put the incident with Dylan Burke out of her mind. She failed at all three endeavors.

She glanced over at Rebecca once or twice and thought their expressions must be pretty similar. Rebecca's feelings about Jake, right or wrong, were no secret, but she seemed to have rallied in the last year or two and made a genuine effort to win back Marci's friendship.

Tonight, Suzanne observed, it was obvious Rebecca's feelings for Jake had not lessened — at least if her current disposition was any indication. Suzanne did not feel sympathy, exactly; she was still royally pissed about how Rebecca had treated Marci during that horrible time. But as she watched Rebecca trying to muster the same dubious smile she herself wore, it occurred to her that other people's happy moments were sometimes a very sad place to be.

The next day, her head throbbed like she'd been hit by a truck, and her stomach turned every time she thought about food. She'd basically told country music's biggest star, not to mention her most famous client to date, that his family members were idiots.

This was big.

Suzanne and Chad spent the day reviewing the contracts she'd signed with Yvette and all the vendors, to make sure they couldn't legally ditch her for another event planner and leave her stuck with all the commitments. It seemed okay from what she read, but that was only a tiny piece of the problem. An offended client could ruin her reputation in Atlanta forever.

The situation had been so upsetting that Suzanne had even resorted to calling her mother to ask for advice, which she hadn't done in a decade. She'd been pleasantly surprised by her mother's noncritical support. "Everything is fixable, sweetie. Just smile and show them what you're made of." This might be owing, in part, to the fact that her mother hadn't the faintest idea who Dylan Burke was or what a big deal it was.

Finally, nearly thirty hours after her unintended conversation with Dylan Burke, Yvette called back.

"So you heard what happened?" Suzanne asked nervously.

"Yes," Yvette replied coldly. "I happened to come back in the room for the tail end of the conversation. We were at the beginning of an all-day meeting with the promoters, and I had stepped out to use the ladies' room."

"Yvette, I'm so embarrassed. I —"

"You should be," she said, the squeaky edge returning to her voice. "When we hired you, I assured Mr. Burke that you were the epitome of discretion. Your comments and behavior reflect on me as much as they do you."

"Of course. I understand. I'm so sorry. I wish I knew what to say." Suzanne hated dealing with women in situations like this. With a man, she could have turned up the flirty, feigned helplessness, and she would soon have forgiveness. And, more often than not, a date for the evening. She wondered idly what the chances were that Yvette was a lesbian.

"Well, I'll be honest, Suzanne. I seriously considered contracting with Events by Emma to finish out the benefit."

"Of course."

"But, given our short timeline, I think the benefit will be better if we keep our current team intact. That's the best thing for the museum. Don't you think?"

"Well, yes."

"And, naturally, you understand that I'm doing you an enormous favor by keeping you on . . ."

44

"Yes, and I'm so grateful." *Uh-oh.*

"So I would really appreciate a favor in return."

"Sure, Yvette, anything."

"Well, Mr. Burke, as you know, is a big Atlanta Braves fan."

"Of course," Suzanne said. Pretty much everyone in the Southeast was a Braves fan, except those transplants who had brought fierce loyalties from other cities when they arrived.

"Well, he's decided to come in from Los Angeles a few days before the benefit to meet with a few old friends. They'd like to go to the game next Wednesday evening. I believe it's the opening series."

"It is. But I think I can arrange it," she said, scribbling a note to Chad to call their contact at the stadium. Suzanne knew the stadium would be crowded during the first week of hometown baseball, but for Dylan Burke, she was sure she could get some decent seats. "How many tickets?"

"About twenty-five."

"Wow," Suzanne said carefully. Calling in every favor she was owed probably couldn't swing her twenty-five good tickets, especially not together.

"They'll need a box, of course. Catered with an open bar. And a chartered bus to take them to Mr. Burke's lake home in Tennessee afterward."

"Oh, Yvette, I'd love to help, but —"

"Great. I'll send you the details via fax." *Click.*

Suzanne held the phone to her ear numbly for a few minutes after Yvette hung up, trying to process everything. Under normal circumstances, Suzanne could throw a party in a box at Turner Field in her sleep. But with barely a week to plan, three days before her biggest event of the year, and with everyone in the city champing at the bit to get back into the baseball season? She flashed a desperate look at Chad, who closed his laptop with a snap and whisked himself to her desk.

"What do we need to do?"

"Get out the Rolodex. We need a miracle."

They spent the next three hours combing through Suzanne's extensive contact list, begging and even threatening everyone they could reach. Even Chad had to cash in a favor with an old boyfriend who waited tables at Fat Matt's Rib Shack, persuading them to cater at the stadium. "I might have hinted that he'd get to meet Dylan," he told her. "I guess we'll cross that bridge when we come to it."

Suzanne tossed him a grateful smile as

she dialed yet another of her corporate clients, looking for someone who could give up a box.

Eventually, she found him.

Barry Consuelo was the vice president of human resources at CleanMark Appliances, who employed about four thousand people fifty miles west of the city. Suzanne had planned CleanMark's corporate retreats for years, and Barry was her primary contact. She knew they had a box at Turner Field for entertaining big clients and for rewarding the highest-performing middle managers. She also knew that Barry desperately wanted to sleep with her.

"Hi, Barry. How are you, honey?"

"Suzie Q! Is it time for retreat planning already? You're getting an early start."

"Oh, no, sweetie. We've got weeks before we have to start on that. But I do have some really exciting ideas for y'all. I know you're going to love it. Chad and I have been talking about CleanMark nonstop."

Chad rolled his eyes dramatically, and she threw a pencil at him. She swiveled her chair around to avoid his eyes. "In the meantime, I need the world's biggest favor, and you might be the only one who can help me."

"Oh, really?"

"Yes. I have a very high-profile client, and

I wish I could tell you who it is, who needs a box at the TED next Wednesday night."

"Ah . . ." Barry sounded disappointed.

"Of course, I'd make it up to you," she threw in hurriedly, before he could give her a reason why not. "We'll take twenty percent off your planning fee for the retreat this year. Think how that will save your professional development budget."

"Hmm. There is a conference in California I would like to go to, I guess . . ."

"See? Perfect! If anyone deserves to go to California, it's you, Barry. You can bring me a bottle of wine to thank me."

"I thought I was giving you the box at Turner Field to thank you," he said, a little snarky.

"Oh, right," she trilled innocently. "Well, I guess we'll have to share the bottle of wine, then."

"Yeah?" His voice had a little smile in it now. "Well, I guess that wouldn't be the worst thing in the world. We'd better make it two bottles, though, because my coworkers are going to be pretty pissed that the box is not available that night."

"Barry, you're the best. Thank you so much. Chad will stop by tomorrow to pick up the tickets."

"Not you?"

"Oh, sweetie, I can't. But let's have coffee in a couple of weeks to get started on the retreat."

He sighed. "Okay, Suzie. No problem."

When she swiveled the chair back around, Chad was shaking his head. "You're shameless."

"I know," she said, letting her forehead hit the desk dramatically. "I know. This benefit had better be worth it."

4

The Wednesday afternoon of the game, she made her way to the stadium early, wanting to avoid rush-hour traffic and to make sure everything was in place well in advance. She was exhausted from all the last-minute details for the big event, but it was getting to the point at which there was very little left to do until the day itself. Normally around this time, she took an evening to herself and dragged Marci out for massages and pedicures. Then she'd shut off her cell phone, have a glass of wine, and watch an old movie to get her mind off the stress of the event and start fresh the next day.

Tonight, however, she was going to be awkwardly hanging around a baseball game with a major celebrity whom she'd offended and twenty-four of his closest friends. Suzanne never minded a little schmoozing — it was part of her job — but ass kissing was something else entirely. She vowed to go,

50

get everything set up, make sure it ran smoothly, and then leave after the third inning.

She parked in one of the premier lots, near an exit, calling her stadium contact, Meredith, to get her in before the gates officially opened. Meredith met her at the south gate, and they made their way through the deserted minicity that was Turner Field, up the escalators, to the CleanMark box. A quick double-check to see that everything was in order, and then Suzanne followed Meredith to her office. She signed an outside-vendor agreement on behalf of Fat Matt's and reviewed the beverage orders for the open bar while Meredith chatted easily about her boyfriend and how much she hoped he was going to propose soon.

Suzanne tried to listen and hoped her *mmm-hmm*s didn't sound too distracted. She hoped Chad remembered to confirm with the florist and to order the credit card machine for the auction.

". . . and it's not like I'm one of those girly girls who has just always been dying to get married. Look at me — I'm a total tomboy, and I work in sports."

It took Suzanne a moment to realize Meredith was fishing for reassurance. "Oh, no, you're not a tomboy: you're gorgeous!"

Gorgeous might be pushing it, she thought. Meredith had a pretty face but was at least thirty pounds overweight and constantly wore polo shirts with khakis.

"Oh, thanks," Meredith said, obviously gratified. "Gregory says the same thing, but you never know with your significant other whether they are being honest or just kind."

"No, no, sweetie," Suzanne said. "Gregory is most definitely right."

Meredith blushed. "So do you think you'll be available, if he does ask me?"

"For what?"

"The wedding? You are an event planner, right?"

"Oh, honey, I'm so sorry. I know your wedding would be the *most* fun to plan, but I just don't do weddings."

"Why not?"

"I just don't. It's a lot of things. The hours, the family drama. Working every weekend. You know."

"But weddings are so romantic, don't you think?"

"Sure." *Of course. What kind of monster doesn't like weddings? If you don't like weddings, they take away your Girl Card or something, right?* Suzanne looked closely at the vendor contract, pretending to be confused by something there.

52

"I bet you're going to be the most beautiful bride when you get married," Meredith said, rather dreamily. "I mean, you're so pretty and always so . . . put together. I'm sure your wedding will be flawless."

"Well, I don't know about that," Suzanne said. "I actually have never really wanted to get married."

Meredith seemed shocked. "I thought you had a boyfriend or something?"

Suzanne snorted, remembering how she'd slunk out of Rick's hotel room the other night. "Not exactly . . ." She flipped a page she'd already read and pretended to look for a pen. She desperately wanted to change the subject but was having trouble thinking of a work-related question to which it wasn't obvious she already knew the answer.

When she looked up, however, Meredith was looking at her with an intense sort of concern. "Suzanne, I'm sorry. I just assumed — I didn't know."

It was as if she'd just told Meredith she had a terminal illness or something. Her voice cracked a bit as she answered. "It's okay." To her utter surprise, her eyes were filling with tears. *What the hell?*

She stood and straightened her skirt. "Well, I'd better go check in with Chad before all those boys start showing up. Can

53

I connect to Wi-Fi from the box?"

"Of course," Meredith said with genuine, kind eyes. Suzanne wanted to punch her just a little bit.

By the time Dylan Burke entered the box, the game was in its second inning. The box was already almost at capacity, because in addition to the twenty-something friends for which Suzanne had planned, there were about the same number of attractive young girls, and she couldn't believe it hadn't occurred to her they would also be there. They were slurping down margaritas like water, and the Fat Matt's staff had already had to call back to the restaurant for more barbecue. She was pretty sure she owed that restaurant about a zillion favors by now.

Dylan sauntered in with three additional girls in tow, fished a beer from one of the icy tubs, and made his way directly to Suzanne, reaching out to shake her hand. Considering that she was in the corner of the box farthest from the door, she found this impressive.

"It's certainly my pleasure, Mr. Burke. How'd you know it was me?" She tried to say this with an ingratiating, saucy smile, but their first conversation was burned on her brain and made her too nervous to flirt.

"I have my ways," Dylan said, looking her over, smiling.

Suzanne reddened. "I guess I'm the only girl here not dressed for the game." She had originally planned to wear a khaki skirt and red cotton blouse with her Braves cap and cute earrings — standard uniform for events she planned at the stadium. But considering how she'd gotten off on the wrong foot with Dylan, and on the off chance Yvette would be in attendance, she decided to play it more conservatively with a gray pencil skirt, white blouse, and black pumps. No one was going to add "unprofessional dress" to her list of transgressions.

Dylan smiled at her three-inch heels. "Well, there is that. But I was just thinking: you are the only one not having fun."

"I'm having a great time, Mr. Burke. And about the other day, please accept my most sincere —"

He dismissed her apology with a wave of his hand, turning slightly toward the field. She was losing him. She touched his arm lightly with her fingers and leaned microscopically forward, but enough so that her cleavage was almost visible from his vantage point.

"Well, I just want you to know that I am usually the soul of discretion with all my clients," she said, making her voice just the tiniest bit husky and drizzling the Southern accent like warm butter. "Last week was exceptional."

"Really, forget it," he said to her blouse. "I know my family's not what you'd call traditional."

"No," she conceded, ignoring his leer. "I guess they're not."

He redirected his gaze after a minute back to her eyes. He seemed to assess her, his youthful green eyes sparkling with surprising intelligence. Suzanne couldn't tell what conclusions he was drawing about her, but his mouth curved up just for a split second. "Anyway," he said louder than before, drawing the nearby partygoers into their conversation. "What you need to do is loosen up a bit. Enjoy the game. I realize it's not squash or water polo or whatever you high-society types enjoy down at the country club, but it *is* America's pastime."

She smiled at him through gritted teeth. *You little jackass.* Clearly, Dylan had picked up on her desperation to keep him as a happy client and was now exacting his revenge for her behavior on the phone the other day.

He threw his arm around a petite blonde in a pink baseball cap and impossibly tiny camouflage shorts. "See, Miss Hamilton, you can't always judge by appearances. Now look there." He pointed at the field and squeezed the little blonde closer simultaneously. "That's my buddy Jesse McCreary in right field. He has a six-million-dollar contract, but he ain't afraid to get his hands dirty. I've been fishing with him, and he can clean a bass faster than you can fill up one of your expensive teacups. But I guess that wouldn't mean much to you, would it?"

He looked expansively around at the crowd, grinning smugly. They were eating it up. She wanted to kick him in the balls and storm out. Nothing was worth this.

"No, I guess it wouldn't," Suzanne replied softly, feeling her face go red again. She refused to break eye contact, despite her embarrassment. The two thoughts most present in her mind were that she wanted desperately to smack Dylan in the face and that she wished like hell she had not chosen to wear her mother's pearls today. She'd been aiming for professional and refined, but to Dylan Burke's circle she came off as stuffy and aristocratic.

Dylan was clearly enjoying his advantage. "See there? I sure hope you learn, Miss Hamilton, that" — here he broke into a loud clear melody — *"scruffy don't always mean stupid."* A murmur of laughter and smattering of applause rippled through the box's crowd as they recognized the lyric from one of his early hits. He winked at her and turned toward the field, the tiny blonde in tow.

Screw it. Let him fire me. "Actually, Mr. Burke," she said, calling him back with the most sugary-sweet tone she could manage. "The reason I am not impressed by Jesse McCreary's fishing prowess is that it seems to detract from his performance on the field. No offense to your friend, but he's way overvalued. Sure, his batting average will stay in the three hundreds until the end of May or so, but he's not clutch. His stats go down every year the closer we get to October, and his percentages with runners in scoring position is just pathetic. Those high-profile home runs might be fun to watch, but they won't be enough to get us to the World Series unless he can do it with runners on base. I admit I don't know anything about bass fishing, Mr. Burke. But in baseball, runs matter."

The group in the box didn't know how to react to this unprecedented speech, but she certainly had their attention. A few of them were smiling and exchanging looks of amazement, while others looked to Dylan

Burke to gauge his response before reacting. With nothing left to lose, Suzanne went on. "And as long as we're on the subject of appearances, perhaps you shouldn't assume that a Southern girl with blonde hair and three-inch heels doesn't know baseball, especially here in Atlanta."

Dylan said nothing, his expression momentarily frozen in surprise. The girl under his arm stared daggers at Suzanne. A sudden piercing giggle broke the silence as Yvette Olsen rushed over. "Oh, my! Isn't she just a spitfire? Dylan just *loves* all this witty banter. Suzanne, could I steal you away to consult about the beverage service, please?" She put both hands on Suzanne's shoulders and steered her firmly toward the bar at the back of the room. "Drink up, everyone! Enjoy the game!"

Being hustled away by the squeaky manager, Suzanne managed a quick glance over her shoulder. The partygoers were all returning either to their previous conversations or to the game itself. She heard the loud pop of a bat and the corresponding gasp of the crowd, followed by a collective sigh. A pop fly, perhaps, or a close foul ball.

At the back near the bar cart, Yvette was nearly apoplectic. She couldn't, however, seem to find the words to express it. "Do you — how can — I've never —" she sluttered. Then, finally, "Do you treat all your clients this way?" The khaki-clad bartender looked around uncomfortably and pretended to need something on the other side of the room.

Keep smiling, no matter what, Suzanne's mother commanded, like an angel on her shoulder. If shoulder angels wore vintage pearls and shopped at Nordstrom. Suzanne obeyed, fashion aside. "What do you mean, Yvette?"

Yvette stammered for a moment, trying to put her finger on exactly what Suzanne had done wrong. In her midforties, Yvette had worked her way through the ranks of several B- and C-list singers, and landing a huge star like Dylan Burke a few months back had been the opportunity of her career. Hiring Suzanne had been one of her first major decisions since coming on as Dylan's manager. She knew managers and agents who'd found themselves suddenly unemployed for much less than this kind of disrespect. How could she make this young, thin *Steel Magnolias* cast-off understand?

"I think everyone is having a good time," Suzanne offered, to fill the silence. She gestured at the roomful of people talking, laughing, and, most important, drinking. As she did this, she thought she saw Dylan glance her way with a smirk.

"Yes," Yvette replied tentatively, gazing around. Her beady eyes narrowed as she returned her gaze to Suzanne. "Just keep in mind, please, that your performance is a direct reflection on me. I take that very seriously. Okay?"

Suzanne's phone buzzed in her purse. Probably Chad — a glance at the clock reminded her she'd promised to check in half an hour ago. She flashed a final winning smile at Yvette. "Of course, Yvette, I understand completely. Could you excuse me, please?"

She took the call on her way out the door. "This is Suzanne."

But it wasn't a complaining Chad who greeted her. "Suzanne? It's Rick."

Her heart sank. She let the door to the luxury box close behind her and kicked herself for not checking the number before answering. "Hi, Rick. How are you?" Her voice was an octave too high as she tried to summon dignified politeness.

"I'm okay," he said. "Listen, I feel kind of weird calling you about this, but I have . . . something you left in the hotel room the other day."

The panties. Suzanne felt suddenly, oddly

vulnerable.

"Oh, you can just —" She hesitated. *Throw them out. Burn them. Whatever.*

"I thought maybe we could meet so I could get them back to you?" He sounded mildly embarrassed. Whether it was because of the undergarments or his transparent attempt to see her again, she couldn't tell.

"Oh, Rick, I'd love to, but — it's just . . . I am so busy. The gala is a few days away and —"

"Of course. I understand. I'll —"

"Could you mail them?" she asked quickly. Asking him to throw them out left too much room for creepy doubts. Besides, they were two-hundred-dollar underwear.

". . . hang on to them until —" he was saying simultaneously. Then, "Oh, right, mail them. Of course. I'll be happy to."

"Thanks, Rick. My office address is on my business card. Do you still have it?"

"Er . . . no."

"Well, it's on my Web site. I'll have my assistant send you a check for the postage, okay?"

His voice switched from seemingly embarrassed to firm. "Suzanne, please don't insult me. I'll pay the postage. Take care of yourself."

Before she could respond, the line had

gone dead.

The next evening, she and Chad sat on the floor of her apartment, sticking customized labels on five hundred auction programs and folding in a sheet with last-minute additions to the auction. A half bottle of wine and a bowl of popcorn sat on a tray between them, and *My Fair Lady* was on the television.

"I love this song," Chad said, as Rex Harrison's "I'm an Ordinary Man" resounded from the TV. "Pretty much sums up my whole philosophy. At least about women."

Suzanne snorted. "Just you wait, Chad Gwynn. Just you wait."

He laughed and took a gulp of wine. "I will say that if I were ever going to be with a woman, Audrey Hepburn would make the cut."

"Other than being dead, you mean?"

"Hey, it's not like we're talking reality here anyway."

"True," she said. "I don't know, though. She seems like she'd be high maintenance."

"Well, that wouldn't change my life much," Chad sneered.

His partner, David, who was — Suzanne had learned over time — actually a very sweet man, was a bit prone to dramatics.

More than once, Chad had slept on Suzanne's couch or at the office after they had an argument, after which David would invariably whisk Chad away somewhere for a few days to make it up to him.

When Chad first started working for her, Suzanne had worried that he might be in an abusive relationship, but after spending time with Chad and David, she decided it was just how they worked. She was pretty sure they'd been together since early college, nearly ten years. That was about a hundred and twenty times as long as Suzanne's average relationship, so who was she to judge?

"I'm going to open another bottle," he said, getting up to go to the kitchen. "Need anything?"

Suzanne shook her head. She took the opportunity to stretch her back, though. She and Chad often hung out at her apartment to do last-minute drudgery before a big event. It was more comfortable than the office, and if Suzanne provided the wine, Marci could typically be persuaded to lend a hand. But tonight Marci was too tired to join them. Jake had called at 7:30 to report that she'd fallen asleep on the couch after dinner, and he couldn't even convince her to move upstairs to the bedroom.

Suzanne supposed it was just the beginning. With pregnancy now and children next, Marci's time would no longer be her own — or Suzanne's, for that matter — for a while to come. She remembered how long it had taken Beth to rejoin them socially after she and Ray had kids; when she did rejoin them, it still seemed to be on a limited basis.

She and Marci had often joked about it, swearing that they would have children at the exact same time of life, so neither of them would feel left out. Of course, that was before Marci had moved to Austin, and certainly long before Jake had called in their college pact to marry each other when both turned thirty. Even now that they were having a baby and she saw them so happy together, she still found it hard to believe sometimes that the old promise had held out for so long. Maybe she *was* missing something.

"Suze?" Chad was looking at her incredulously, the ringing she hadn't noticed almost drowning out Rex Harrison on the TV. "If you insist on being the last person on earth with a landline, the least you can do is answer it."

She hoisted herself off the floor and checked the caller ID on the ringing phone. *Rick Sayers. Damn.* "I like to screen my calls. The machine can get it."

Chad shrugged and went back to labeling. Suzanne, too, returned to her pile of programs. Soon the voice echoed out into the living room. "Hey, Suzanne, it's Rick. Look, I wanted to apologize for being rude yesterday. It was kind of a stressful week at work, and that's no excuse, but . . . anyway, I just wanted you to know that I really like you, and when I found your underwear in the hotel room —"

She sprang for the phone, knocking over her wine in the process and trying to ignore Chad's rolling laughter behind her.

"Hi, Rick . . . it's fine. No, really, it is. Thank you. Yep, I appreciate it. Okay, no, I have to go. I'm sorry, I'm . . . working. I'll call you."

Chad teased her as she sat back down. "Flavor of the month? Sweetie, you go through more men than Swinging Richards on a Saturday night."

She ignored him. "Ugh. That *guy.* He's nice enough, but he doesn't seem to know how to take no for an answer. I can't shake him."

"What is it with you?" Chad asked. "Guys beating down your door, interns calling at all times of day and night trying to work for you. I'm pretty sure Barry Consuelo would

66

leave his wife for you if you asked him —
that guy talked to me about you for like
fifteen minutes when I picked up the tickets.
Just sad. No offense, but I don't get it."

"Maybe if I looked like Audrey Hepburn,
you'd feel the same way," she teased.

"Honey, no offense, but you're no Audrey
Hepburn. You're gorgeous, and I love you.
But no Audrey."

"Fair enough," Suzanne said, smiling.
They went back to working in companion-
able silence, and she resisted the urge to ask
Chad exactly what he meant.

5

Suzanne's day-before-event ritual had been the same for years.

She woke at 4:00 A.M., did her favorite yoga video, showered, and spent the rest of the morning at the office running through every possible scenario. What if the keynote speaker didn't show? What if the power went out? What if the big auction item or a key volunteer fell through? Her dad taught her this lawyer's trick, back when he had hoped she'd follow in his footsteps. *Be brutal when you cross-examine yourself, sugar. Then nobody can catch you off guard.*

By the time Chad arrived to triple confirm all the vendors and pack all the large plastic bins they would take tomorrow, Suzanne had a legal pad listing items for him to gather or handle, all in response to the imaginary catastrophes she'd created in her head that morning. They'd go over it, and then she'd hand things off to him and head out for a massage and manicure, so she'd look fresh and rested the next day.

Chad looked critically at the pad. "A hundred battery-powered candles?"

"In case the lighting doesn't work for the tents."

"Six bags of peppermint candy?"

"Registration tables. Oh, and get three good-sized glass bowls to put them in. Nice bowls. No acrylic crap. Remember that volunteer at the car show with the horrifying breath?"

Chad wrinkled his nose briefly to indicate that he did remember as he scribbled "3 glass bowls" on the list. "Eight rolls of red and white duct tape?" he asked incredulously.

"Well, it fixes everything, doesn't it?" A smile twitched at the corner of her mouth.

"Oh. My. God," Chad said, staring at her, working something out in his head. "You *like* him."

"What? No," she said quickly. Then, trying to sound more casual: "No. He's a little too Hank Jr., for me. And not especially nice."

Chad closed his mouth but still eyed her suspiciously. Suzanne flicked her hand at him in dismissal. "Oh, please. Like I need that train wreck in my life right now. I thought the duct tape might be cute around the centerpieces at the VIP tables, if I can do something artsy with them."

Whether the doubt in his face related to her ability to make duct tape artsy or to Dylan Burke himself, Suzanne couldn't tell. But thankfully she had to run to her spa appointment, and she left Chad to his pile, waving her cell phone at him as she exited. She called Betsy Fuller-Brown at the High on her way to the spa, to answer any last-minute concerns. She ignored the call from her mother, who, Suzanne knew, would whine about attending the Junior League luncheon alone. *Catch you on the way back, Mom,* Suzanne thought. Her mother invariably called her after league events to gossip about who was there, who was missing, who made what dishes, and who — gasp! — tried to pass restaurant food off as her own creation.

Massaged and coiffed, her nails painted, and having heard all the latest gossip, Suzanne returned to the office at four. She ran down the usual lists with Chad and let him go home early to rest. She spent the next hour or so cleaning up the office, neatly piling the bins for the event near the door and then straightening, wiping, and polishing the rest of the space. There was nothing she hated more than returning after the excitement of an event had subsided to find that she had to spend the first day back reclaiming the office, instead of gearing up for the next project. She found that her nervous energy was better put to the useful task of cleaning now so that she and Chad could start refreshed on Tuesday.

As she wiped the granite counter in the studio's modern kitchen — which served primarily as a place for coffee and extra storage — she noticed something hanging from the blown glass chandelier far above her. The chandelier was a smallish but colorful Chihuly piece with violet-red tendrils and horns escaping every which way, lit from within to display its beautiful form even while it served the function of lighting part of the room. She had saved religiously for more than four years to buy it, after seeing a Chihuly display at the Atlanta Botanical Garden. It was her prized possession.

But tonight there was something dangling into view on the far side. *A string?* She dropped her sponge and walked around the counter to the other side. It looked like a stray bit of blue ribbon — one of the pieces she and Chad had recently spent hours hotgluing to tiny guitars for the goody baskets.

71

She debated for a moment whether she should bother with it or just do the logical thing and wait for Chad to get it on Tuesday. *It'll be the last thing I think about before I go to sleep tonight,* she thought.

Shaking her head at her perfectionism, Suzanne went to the storage closet to retrieve her ladder, wondering how she or Chad had managed to fling a ribbon so far up. She tried to remember what they'd been talking about while they were hot-gluing. Chad was not usually one for dramatic gestures and elaborate hand motions, unlike his partner, David, for whom telling a good story was aerobic exercise. It had just been the two of them working on the baskets this year, though, and she couldn't remember anything in particular happening that day.

Suzanne kicked off her shoes and started to climb toward the warm light of the chandelier, realizing she should've brought the feather duster while she was up here. She was almost at the top of the six-foot ladder, stretching to reach the ribbon, when she felt the aluminum step beneath her creak ominously. She had no time to react, and her feet refused to accept her brain's panicked signals to move down to the step below. Yet somehow she was able to take in vivid and detailed pictures of everything around her — from a small dust-free patch on the chandelier to the brightly painted industrial pipes running across the ceiling — before the creak evolved into an unpleasant metal scraping sound and she plummeted backward toward the hard, painted concrete floor below.

One ambulance ride, four X-rays, and $1,500 later, Suzanne stood in her bedroom closet with Marci, who had driven her home. It was seven o'clock on Saturday morning. They had dropped Jake off at the office to drive Suzanne's car back, though it would be little use to her for several weeks. Suzanne now wore a black cast — *it goes with everything,* one nurse had joked — on her left arm, where she had fractured it in the fall. Other than that, she had only painful purple bruises on her left side to show for her accident.

Considering the height from which she fell and the hardness of the floor, everyone at the hospital had insisted that Suzanne was lucky not to have been hurt worse. But "lucky" wasn't a word Suzanne felt inclined to use just now. She had been up for twenty-seven hours straight, with just over twelve hours left before the biggest event of her career, and had lost the use of one arm.

What's more, the new cast created a wardrobe problem that had not been outlined in Suzanne's contingency-planning session the morning before.

She and Marci had tried draping every scarf Suzanne owned over the cast in various ways, but none of them seemed to work. Had it not been for a very useful painkiller prescription and an all-night pharmacy, Suzanne might have been tempted to have a nervous breakdown. Whoever had invented those big white pills was a hero in her book. The severe pain in her arm had dulled to an ache, and she stared foggily past Marci into the depths of the closet, periodically having to be reminded to pay attention and give her opinion on the alternatives Marci suggested. The opinion, invariably, was *ick.*

None of the scarf or shawl options seemed right for gracefully masking an enormous plaster arm cast, so they took a break for breakfast when Jake arrived in Suzanne's car. "Why don't you call your mom, babe?" Jake suggested, rubbing Marci's shoulder affectionately. "She's good at this stuff."

Elaine Thompson arrived thirty minutes later, hugging all three of them as though she hadn't seen them in a year. She embraced Suzanne last and longest, rubbing her cast gently. "Sorry about your accident, sweetie. The good news is, I brought the BeDazzler!"

Only Mrs. Thompson would know how to combine a black plaster cast and hundreds of tiny rhinestones into an enviable accessory. She chattered happily while she worked, refusing to allow Suzanne to help with her right hand. "Don't be silly, sweetheart. You have enough to do to get ready for today, I'm sure."

She had to concede this was true, so she pulled out tonight's speeches to make a few last-minute corrections. She would make brief welcome comments at dinner, thanking all the sponsors, pushing the auction, introducing the High's executive director, and, finally, welcoming Dylan to the stage. She'd written his speech, too, of course. They certainly couldn't risk his getting up there and talking about bass fishing for fifteen minutes. She'd been toying with the verbiage for days now, trying to sound appropriate to the occasion and still authentically Dylan.

Despite her good intentions, however, letting Suzanne work in quiet was not in Mrs. Thompson's wheelhouse. Suzanne had been scribbling for less than five minutes when Mrs. Thompson piped up, "You're looking forward to the baby?"

"Absolutely," Suzanne said reflexively. "So excited for them."

"They'll be great parents," Mrs. Thompson said. Then, more softly, she added, "Jake does a nice job balancing Marci out, don't you think? He'll keep her on the right track."

Suzanne nodded. "Definitely."

"And, of course, you know Nicky and Ravi are pregnant again, too. My grandbabies are tripling!"

She hadn't known this, but it wasn't surprising, either. Marci's little sister and her husband were surprisingly natural parents with their daughter, Ayanna, who was amber-skinned, intensely cute, and completely spoiled. Suzanne had never doubted they would make more babies. She squelched the pang of jealousy — jealous of what, she couldn't say — and smiled at her best friend's mother. "It's wonderful, Elaine."

She knew what would be coming next. The same thing had happened when Jake and Marci got engaged (both times) and for the entire month before and after their wedding. Well-meaning aunts, neighbors, friends — even her own mother — had joined together in a constant refrain. *So, when will we hear the good news about you? Haven't you found a nice boy yet? You're so pretty —*

76

don't keep them waiting too long.

One officious relative, Marci's venerable great-aunt Mildred, had gone so far as to squeeze Suzanne's breasts like bicycle horns at a wedding shower, saying something about every melon having an expiration date. Suzanne had been mortified.

But when Mrs. Thompson spoke, it was something equally unexpected. "Have I told you lately how proud I am of you?" she asked. Her tone was so motherly and intimate, Suzanne glanced up to see whether Marci had returned from the grocery store with Jake and was standing behind her unnoticed. But they weren't back yet.

"I hope you don't mind my saying so, but I've always thought of you as my third daughter, Suze. I've watched you grow up, and I'm so very proud of who you have become and everything that you have accomplished. Arthur and I read the Style section every weekend, looking for pictures of you at all those charity functions."

Suzanne's cheeks burned. She felt herself squirming under Mrs. Thompson's gaze. "Oh . . . ," she muttered, staring intently at the neat rows of rhinestones building from the front of her cast. "All I do is get dressed up and plan parties for rich people. It feels like such a silly job sometimes."

"Maybe it does, but just think of all the real people you have helped. You may not have met them in person, but all those charities would flounder and die without the support of silly rich people." Elaine was smiling now. "Besides, I know what you do behind the scenes is damn hard work."

"Thank you, Elaine." There was a break in Suzanne's voice. She could not pinpoint the emotion that washed over her, exactly. Perhaps it was the painkillers or sleep deprivation, but she felt for a moment as though she could pour herself into Mrs. Thompson's lap like a child and weep for hours. She desperately, absurdly, wanted her best friend's mother to reach out and stroke her hair or touch her cheek. With the same intensity, she wanted to pull back her immobilized arm and run away, to plunge herself into a task that would require her complete focus.

Either Elaine did not notice this or she was kind enough to pretend to be absorbed in her work. The only further acknowledgment of their conversation came a few moments later, when Elaine had finished applying the rhinestones and gently squeezed Suzanne's manicured fingertips, sticking out of her cast.

6

Chad Gwynn's phone blared "The Bitch Is Back" at nine on Saturday morning, three hours before he was supposed to meet Suzanne at the High. David looked over the top of his newspaper, scowling. "I thought you weren't on duty until noon?"

"I'm not." Chad had been reaching instinctively for the phone but paused under David's glare. Elton John stopped singing, and the phone was silent.

"She has no right to call you now. It's Saturday morning, for Christ's sake. The only day we get to sit and have coffee together. Isn't it enough that you're giving her twelve hours later today?"

Chad hesitated. David was right, of course, but the phone on the table between them might as well have been on fire, for all he could ignore it. As if reading his thoughts, the phone dinged again with the voice-mail notification. Chad tried to go

79

back to the crossword puzzle he'd been doing, but he could only stare at the same two
clues. He wondered what Suzanne wanted.

Fifteen minutes went by and the phone
rang again. David rolled his eyes and looked
accusingly at Chad, as though somehow he
had made it happen. Chad knew it was difficult for David to understand what working for a high-profile event planner really
meant. David had gone for his paralegal
certificate within months after they left college and had found a job in the wills and
estates division of an enormous firm less
than a year later. He walked or biked seven
blocks to work from their Midtown apartment every morning at eight, was free to do
whatever he liked at lunch, and was generally home cooking dinner or out having
cocktails with coworkers by six.

Chad's schedule, on the other hand, came
in waves. At times it seemed he worked
around the clock, especially if he and Suzanne were doing several events in the same
week or a major event like this gala. Then
there were slower times, particularly the
hottest parts of the summer, when he would
work less than twenty hours a week, ten of
them spent cleaning out storage closets or
being dragged around on tangential errands
with Suzanne.

In July or August, it was not unusual for Chad to find himself halfway through a pitcher of margaritas by three in the afternoon after touring a new conference venue or golf course. Or he would start his day poring tediously over their client files, only to be unceremoniously dismissed by Suzanne midafternoon if the weather was nice. These were the days he would wander to the farmers' market to get fresh ingredients for dinner or surprise David by cleaning the apartment before he got home.

David, however, did not seem to agree that those days balanced out moments like this one. He had a strict dividing line between his work and personal life and seemed to view it as an affront when one intruded on the other. But as systematized and efficient as Chad and Suzanne had become, the big events never seemed to lend themselves to automation. Chad often felt that he was on call for Suzanne the way a surgeon might be for a hospital. David had scoffed at this comparison.

Still, there was the phone on the table between them, singing defiantly into their unspoken conversation. Chad's fingers itched to answer it. "It *is* the biggest event we've ever done," he offered gently. "Maybe I should at least see what she wants."

"I'll do it," David snapped, snatching the phone off the table. Now it was Chad's turn to glare. On the one hand, David's protectiveness of their time together was sweet. On the other, his partner's tendency toward the dramatic was sometimes misguided.

"Come on, we've talked about this. You knew when I took this job —"

But his protests were futile. David answered in a huff, standing to move out of Chad's reach as he did. "Suzanne, it's David. Do you see what time it is? Do the clocks at your house say noon for some reason? Because you have some nerve calling Chad three hours early —"

Anger and embarrassment rose in Chad's throat as the rant continued. When the occasion presented itself for the three of them to be together, Suzanne and David normally got along fine. In fact, they had matching temperaments. Today, however, was not a good day. Dylan Burke's event was the biggest thing they had done so far, and if it went well, it could mean more high-profile jobs for her and maybe a raise for Chad. He was planning to get an MBA in a couple of years, and some extra savings would come in handy during graduate school. David just didn't seem to understand that.

"Mmm-hmm," David said following a

short silence, and stepped outside on the balcony. Chad couldn't read his tone. *Shit.* He wanted to follow David outside and snatch the phone back from him, but he knew from experience that he would rather have Suzanne mad at him than the love of his life. He could get another job if need be, but there was only one David.

After a minute or two, David came back in, put the phone on the table, and sat to read his paper in silence. Chad stared at him. "Well?"

David lowered the paper, looking sheepish. "You'd better get to the office," he said.

The anger Chad had been suppressing transformed into a smile that crept over his face. He worked to hold it back. "Why, David?" he asked in mock innocence. "Surely you don't mean to say there was a *reason* my boss called me at nine o'clock on Saturday morning, do you?"

David was indignant. "Sometimes she calls for ridiculous reasons; you at least have to give me that!"

"I do give you that," Chad said mildly. "What about today?"

A tremendous sigh. "It seems," David said with reluctance to the coffee cup in front of Chad, "that Suzanne fell off a ladder last night and broke her arm. She needs you to

83

come early because she can't lift anything."

"And?" Chad said, sensing there was something else. He felt bad for Suzanne but was enjoying David's rare moment of embarrassment.

David's face morphed from indignant to sheepish as he paused before admitting defeat. He pressed his lips together. "And . . . I'm coming by later to help out, as well."

Chad laughed. David kicked him under the table. They stared at each other, half smiling, half confrontational, until Chad got up and kissed David on the forehead. "How about next time you have a problem with my work, let me handle it, okay?"

David pulled him close and nuzzled Chad's stomach with the top of his head, nodding. Chad rubbed David's close-shaven skull in response and then pushed him back gently when he began to feel more emotion than he had time to handle today. "Fine," David muttered. "But we're going to Bacchanalia for dinner next weekend. And you're leaving that damn phone at home."

"Deal," said Chad, and left the room to get dressed.

The next few hours at the High Museum were annoying, to say the least. With Suzanne injured, there was additional work to do, and she anxiously barked orders at both Chad and Jake, and later on at David, as well. It was nice of Marci's husband to help out, but he and Chad had almost nothing in common, and Suzanne kept forgetting who she had asked to do what. Jake spent most of his time trying to figure out what he was supposed to be doing. Marci was around, too, though she wasn't doing much in the way of physical activity.

Still, the day moved quickly, thanks to all the bustle. The rental company had hoisted three enormous tents and a temporary stage in the museum courtyard the night before. The minute the High's admissions door closed for the evening, workers in matching lime-green T-shirts materialized from nowhere and swarmed beneath the canopies like ants. Soon, as if by magic, the tented areas were filled with tables, chairs, lights, and equipment. David showed up in his best suit, and Chad allowed himself a thrill of pride before putting his partner to work.

Chad oversaw the decoration of all the tables, including linens, flowers, duct-tape centerpieces, and mason jars full of artificial fireflies they'd special-ordered online. Despite his initial objections when Suzanne pitched the idea, the whole effect was actually quite charming. He and Jake hung seventy-five alternating strands of tiny mirrors and white Christmas lights behind the stage. Larger white lights crisscrossed above the tables, creating the illusion of a summer that, in reality, was still a couple of months away.

Chad set up the registration tables, supervised the arrangement of auction items and bid sheets, and helped Suzanne brief each group of volunteers. Before he knew it, the first gowns and tuxedos were emerging from cars at the valet stand.

All things considered, he thought, Suzanne seemed to be holding up reasonably well given her lack of sleep and what must be a painful injury. She flitted about in her stunning size 6 black mermaid gown and sparkly cast, with her long blond hair wrapped in an elegant chignon, solving problems and patting everyone on the back with her unbroken arm. She had a beauty queen's smile, and, more important, she knew how to make every person she encountered feel as though the smile was just for them. Chad had tasked himself with learning that concentrated charm from her before he left this job.

Marci had given him a strict schedule for Suzanne's pain meds, so when he glanced at the clock and saw it was nearly seven, he made his way to the registration table, where Suzanne had stashed her cosmetic bag full of crucial supplies. Unlike the rest of the well-organized supplies and cosmetics, the pill bottle had been tossed carelessly on top, with the lid only half screwed on, so that when he picked it up, half the big white tablets fell out, leaving the whole bag a chalky mess. *Marci.* He knew it was kind of her to help out Suzanne, presumably for free, but the girl was always just a little careless. She didn't have the attention to detail that was so vital at big events.

He arrived at the registration table just in time to overhear a confrontation brewing between an irate donor and a volunteer named Iris — a sweet middle-aged woman with a soft voice and wispy brown hair pulled back in a bun. The expansive man apparently didn't like his seating assignment and was making it well known.

Chad made his way over to listen from a couple of feet away, to determine whether it required intervention. Iris was nearly in tears, trying to appease the donor, who was pressing his point forcefully and getting louder by the minute. "What do you mean, you don't know how to help me?" the man fumed, face turning red.

That was his cue. But before Chad could step in, Suzanne glided up, smiling broadly. "I'm sorry to interrupt," she said sweetly to the frazzled volunteer, putting her hand on the woman's back. "Iris, it looks like we need your expertise over at the credit card machine. I'll take care of this. Chad, Iris will help you."

Chad extended his hand to the stunned-looking woman and guided her to the other end of the table. He got her a cup of water and helped her sit, keeping one ear on Suzanne as she pumped up her Southern accent for effect. "Now, what can I do to help here?"

The donor, who turned out to be a small-plane mogul from Savannah, was quite purple in the face as he rounded on her. He literally spit as he demanded, "Who are *you*?!?"

Chad cringed for her, but Suzanne seemed unfazed. She extended her uninjured hand lightly in a way that suggested the man could either shake it or kiss it. "I'm Suzanne Hamilton, the event coordinator. I'll be happy to help any way I can."

"The first thing you need to do is fire that woman," he bellowed, jerking his finger toward Iris, who let out an involuntary little squeak in response.

Suzanne kept her eyes smiling on the man in front of her. "Well, Mr. — ?"

"Basille."

"Mr. Basille, Iris is volunteering her time to support the children's programs here at the museum, so even if I wanted to fire her, I couldn't. But I do want to make sure you're happy with your experience tonight. What seems to be the problem?"

"For the tenth time, I made it quite clear earlier this week that my date and I wanted to be seated near Mr. Burke's table. That was the whole reason we bought tickets. We were assured by someone in your office that would happen, and if we can't sit near him, I want a refund!"

This last bit was so loud that several guests waiting in line for registration turned to look, murmuring. Chad's ears perked up, wondering whether he would be called in to the conversation. He was the only "someone" in Suzanne's office, and knew for a fact he had made no such assurance to Mr. Basille, but how should he say that if Suzanne called on him?

Suzanne listened intently, but from where Chad was standing, her gaze seemed to travel from Mr. Basille's eyes to his hands, feet, and, finally, to his date. She placed a hand on the man's forearm as Chad had seen her do countless times with angry patrons. She dipped slightly at the knees so she could look up at the rather squat man. "Now, Mr. Basille," she trilled. "Please don't leave us! Let me find out what's going on. It'll take two seconds. What are you two drinking?"

She directed this question at Mr. Basille's date, who replied with a haughty, "Pinot Grigio."

"For you, as well?" She turned to Mr. Basille, who nodded reluctantly.

That was his cue. Chad stepped forward. "Chad, honey," Suzanne said. "Go grab the seating chart for me, and ask Ramon to get Mr. Basille and his date a chilled bottle of their best Pinot Grigio, immediately. Tell him to add it to my tab."

"Now, that's not —" Mr. Basille started.

"Of course it is. It's my pleasure." Suzanne's eyes twinkled up at him, almost flirtatious, for a long second. Finally, he smiled awkwardly in return, and his date shifted her weight behind him, irritated. Chad slid off to get the seating chart, stopping a passing waiter to send over the wine.

By the time he returned, Mr. Basille seemed far more at ease. His date, on the other hand, seemed anything but amused, despite the fact that she had already drained her glass. Chad handed Suzanne the seating chart, and she pretended to study it intently. She gave several *hmm*s . . . while she looked at it, and Chad noticed that she bit her lip suggestively as she thought. This had the desired effect: Mr. Basille was clearly entranced.

"There's no other way," she announced to Chad finally. "There's obviously been a big mistake in our office, and we didn't properly assign Mr. Basille to VIP seating. Let's move the Bickersons to another table, here in the back, and put Mr. Basille and his date here. Mr. Basille, please accept my apologies for the inconvenience and enjoy ten free casino chips on me."

She fished a sachet of casino chips out of her handbag and gave them to his date rather than Mr. Basille. The former smiled perfunctorily and tucked them away in her clutch.

"Thank you," Basille said, unable to find any continued reason to be angry. "I didn't mean to yell at you. It's just —"

"Not at all," Suzanne stopped him, polished fingers brushing lightly across his arm once more. "Just have a wonderful evening, and do make sure you bid on something fun for me at the silent auction, okay?" She glanced back at Mr. Basille's date, who looped her arm through his and squeezed territorially as she looked down her nose at Suzanne.

"How do you do it?" Chad asked her as the couple walked away.

"That's what the Bickersons are for," she answered with a shrug. "You know that."

Of course, Chad knew the Bickersons didn't really exist. They were the fake couple assigned seating at every event, usually in or near the VIP section, in order to provide wiggle room for just such emergencies. "That's not what I meant. I mean, how do you . . . how do you turn them around so quickly? That guy was livid when I got over here."

Suzanne looked at him, her eyes tired but sharp. "Well, it's all about what you can learn about people just by paying attention. Start with his tux. Expensive, but didn't fit perfectly. New money."

Chad glanced at the retreating Mr. Basille and confirmed that his jacket hung off his shoulders just a bit. Suzanne went on. "His shoes were black leather, conservative. No scuffs. I'm thinking he's not a Dylan Burke fan. You'll notice there are many tuxedos wandering around with snakeskin boots underneath, but Mr. Basille isn't that type. His date, on the other hand — too much makeup and a cheap spray tan. That dress was too low cut for an evening at the High. She's more the right age, too. For Dylan, I mean . . ."

Suzanne looked a bit dreamy for a second in spite of herself. *Don't like him, my ass,* Chad thought.

She snapped out of it quickly and went on with her tutorial. "He had a pot belly and bags under his eyes. There was still a little indentation on his left hand, where a ring used to be. So I figure: recently divorced, newly rich entrepreneur type trying to impress his younger date, who is a big fan of Dylan Burke. A guy like that wants to appear powerful. It didn't matter that he didn't talk to anyone in our office; he wants her to see him make a big deal about getting the best. He wants to show her that he can get his way. For her."

"So that's why you made a big deal about not wanting him to leave."

"Right."

"But, why the . . . well, please don't be offended, but the fairly obvious flirting?"

Suzanne grinned. "Rivalry. Quickest way to a woman's heart. If that guy doesn't get laid tonight, it won't be my fault. Plus, now he's all pumped up to bid high on the auction items."

Chad had to smile. She was brilliant, in her way. This was what David didn't understand. She knew that happy people spent more at the auctions and the bar, and she knew how to make them happy and set them free to spend. It's why she was the best event planner in the city.

Two volunteers from opposite ends of the museum arrived almost simultaneously, each brimming with a separate crisis. One of Dylan's sisters had brought three people who weren't on the guest list, and there wasn't enough table space available. Elsewhere, the bathrooms on the main floor of the museum had all been inadvertently locked, and no one could find a member of the cleaning staff to unlock them. Suzanne was walking away to deal with the second issue when Chad remembered and called her back.

"Don't forget these," he said, extracting the two pain pills from his pocket and pressing them into her hand. He caught a passing tray and grabbed a goblet of wine.

"Already?" Suzanne said absently. "God, I swear these things are bigger than before." She popped the pills into her mouth and swigged from the wineglass in one smooth motion as she headed off in the direction of the main building. Chad watched in admiration before returning to the seating chart to try to solve the extra-guest problem.

"Hey," came a wheezing voice behind Chad, and he turned to see Marci looking flushed and out of breath. "You found her pills?"

"Yeah, right in the bag where you left them."

"Huh," Marci said, leaning against a chair for support. *If that girl's not pregnant or something, she'd better start working out more,* Chad thought, trying not to stare at Marci's robust figure in a pretty royal-blue dress that was perhaps a half size too small.

She inhaled deeply. "That's better. Whew. It's just, I looked in her bag a little bit ago and couldn't find them. I just ran out to the car to see if they were there."

"You looked in the cosmetic bag? Black-and-white stripes?"

Marci nodded.

"When?"

"About twenty minutes ago."

"Well, they're in there now. Maybe you just missed them?"

"I guess," Marci said, still looking perplexed. "I have been sort of spacey lately. But I could've sworn they weren't there when I looked."

Chad looked after the rapidly retreating

form of his boss, which had reached the main doors to the museum and was graciously holding one of them open for a cluster of partygoers to enter. Something wasn't right, but he couldn't put his finger on it. He put a hand on her arm the way he'd seen Suzanne do with Mr. Basille. "Don't worry about it. She got her pills, right? So we're all good."

7

Whoever invented those lovely white pills knew quite a bit about pain relief, Suzanne decided, but not nearly enough about navigating the world in four-inch heels. She had been walking in heels on a regular basis since she was eleven, after months of practicing in her parents' hallway with a book on her head, under her mother's watchful eye. In recent years, heels had become such an integral part of her wardrobe that she didn't feel fully dressed without them.

Tonight, however, she felt wobbly — more like Bambi on ice than Ginger Rogers onstage. Her head was spinning a bit, too. Perhaps her lack of sleep was finally catching up with her. The normally soothing lights of the High Museum seemed oppressive and glaring. Having solved the locked bathroom crisis with a call to Betsy Fuller-Brown, she had made her way up the circular ramps to the third floor of the rotunda, where she took off her shoes and sat on the floor at the top of the deserted ramp.

From here, she could look down to the other two floors and hear some of what was going on below without being noticed herself. She rubbed her tired feet and called Chad over the radio to talk about accommodating the three surprise guests at the Burke table.

"Are you okay?" he asked when they'd solved the problem.

"Sure. Why?"

He hesitated. "Um . . . no reason. Why don't you come sit down for a bit? You're exhausted."

"I am sitting."

"Okay, good," he said. His voice sounded oddly far away and a little too sweet. This was not the usual Chad.

"Why are you talking like that?"

"What do you mean?"

"You know what I mean. Like you're the grown-up boss of me, instead of I'm being the boss of you." This did not come out the way she intended, so she repeated the main point. "You know what I mean."

Now it was Marci at the other end of the radio. "Suze, why don't you tell me where you are and I'll have Jake come for you?"

"Marce, I'm fine. Quit being so overprotective. You're the one who needs protecting. You're prego! Pregnant. With child. Con bambino. Pregno-protecto!" This last bit sounded very funny to Suzanne. Like Harry Potter.

"Shh . . . Suzanne, that was a secret, remember?"

"Oh, sorry!" Suzanne said. She meant it, too. Though at this point she was having trouble holding on to what she meant. "Sorry, sorry, sorry." Her thoughts and words seemed to be slipping through her fingers. Out they went, almost as though she could see them, through the white metal grid separating her from the empty air beyond the railing and down, down, down to the ground below. People — lots of people — were down there, milling around. She could see the tops of their heads and black suits or bare shoulders, depending on gender. *Holy shit, I'm far up. How have I never noticed how high up this is? Has anyone ever fallen from here?*

"Well, if it isn't my favorite Southern belle." Another voice came through the radio, surprisingly crisp and audible. That was odd. She held the radio out from her face to examine it.

A good-natured laugh sounded from her left. "I'm over here, Miss Scarlett." She

99

turned to see her most famous client standing a few feet away from her on the landing.

Even had she felt her normal clarity, it might have taken a moment to recognize Dylan Burke. He wore the perfectly faded blue jeans and black boots that were his standard uniform, of course, but with a pressed white shirt, soft charcoal vest, and a wide, tasteful maroon tie. The most surprising thing, though, was seeing him for the first time without his trademark camouflage cap. His hairline was *slightly* receded, as she had wondered, but the rest of his hair was thick and had been expertly tousled into a sun-streaked, light-brown mess on top of his head. He wore glasses — round black frames that were thick on top and thin as wire on the bottom. In spite of her addled state, she couldn't help noticing that he looked amazing. Sexy, even.

"Looks like you've been busy since I saw you last," he said.

This brought her out of her reverie, and she realized she'd been staring at him. "What?"

"Your cast," he said, nodding at her arm. She'd almost forgotten it. "What happened? Some other poor bastard question your encyclopedic knowledge of baseball?"

"Accident," she said. "Weird, though,

because I'm not the accident-prone one. Marci, though, Marci is a klutz."

"And Marci is . . . ?"

"My best friend," Suzanne said, sounding annoyed that he didn't already have this information. "Do try to keep up."

"Yes, ma'am," he said. His smile broadened, but Suzanne got the feeling he was smiling *at* her rather than *with* her. "Listen, can I walk you back down?"

"For the last time, I don't need anyone to walk with me. I'm fine!"

"It's not for you," he said. "It's for me. If I walk down there by myself, I'll be drawn into a hundred different conversations and requests for autographs, and I'll never make it to my table. I'm hungry. You're my event planner. Walk with me."

She stood, still rather wobbly, and he extended his arm. Suzanne took it, feeling ridiculous. "Thanks," he said benignly.

Walking seemed to help her confused state a little. "I can't figure you out," she said to the young country star as they slowly descended the curving ramps to the main floor.

"What's to figure out?" he said. Then, with a wry smile, he added, "I'm just your average Tennessee boy with a crazy family and a private jet."

"I don't know," she said, ignoring the joke. Somewhere in the deep recesses of the medication fog, a tiny but reasonable voice screamed at her to be quiet. Be professional. *Shut the hell up before you say something stupid.* "Honestly, I don't want to like you."

"Thanks," he said drily.

"I mean, I don't love country music in general, especially that oversimplified hokey stuff about farms and tractors. No offense."

"None taken," he said with a surprised laugh.

"And you seem so obnoxious in the press. *And* in person."

"Again, thanks," he said. "Do I have to pay you extra for all this honesty?"

"You're a womanizer, too," she said accusingly.

"Ah," he said. They had reached the bottom of the last ramp, and he stood back to let her enter the lobby first.

"But you know what's weird?" she asked over her shoulder.

"I bet you're about to tell me," he said.

"I like you anyway." She turned to face him momentarily. She couldn't tell whether he was amused or annoyed. "I don't want to, but I do."

He opened his mouth to speak and then closed it again. He seemed to be trying to decide something. After a moment, his puzzled look changed to concern. Only when he grasped her elbow did she realize she'd been teetering dangerously to one side. "Don't take this the wrong way," he said, "but you don't look so good. I really think you should sit down."

Suzanne, thinking that Dylan was probably right, was searching for an appropriate response when the tiny bleached blonde from the baseball game, now in a skintight fuchsia cocktail dress, came from nowhere and flung her arms around him. She leaned close and cooed in Dylan's ear, "Come on, baby. You promised you'd buy me something from the auction before you go onstage." Suzanne must have made an involuntary noise, because the girl wrinkled her nose. "What's the matter with *her*?"

Focusing on the girl's face was difficult, swimming as it was in Suzanne's vision, with the stark white walls of the main lobby behind her. But she tried to smile anyway. "Oh, nothing," she heard herself say. "I'm fine. You guys enjoy the auction. Have a great time."

Dylan looked unconvinced. "You need to sit down, Miss Scarlett," he said. "I'm going to get you some water. Misty, stay with her."

They sat on a bench, and Suzanne tried

to apologize to the girl in fuchsia for the disruption of their evening. "I'm so sorry. I don't know what's happening," she started.

But Misty was in no mood for conciliation, apparently. "Listen," she said harshly, in a far more country-sounding accent than she had been using moments before. "I know what you're doing, and you can just go ahead and give up. No matter what kind of stupid game you're playing to get his attention, there's no way I'm letting him go. Besides, if you were half as smart as you think you are, you'd know that Dylan *never* dates older women."

"What?" Suzanne said, thoroughly confused. Before she could defend herself, however, Dylan had returned with a bottle of water, and suddenly Misty was dragging him away.

When they were out of sight, Suzanne stood, threw away the water, and flagged a passing waiter. She downed a flute of champagne in seconds. She heard it: the tiny warning voice screaming that this was a bad idea, that something was seriously wrong and she ought to find Marci and a place to lie down. But the voice was so muted that it seemed to come to her through ten feet of solid concrete. She talked to herself instead. *Head up. Keep smiling. On with the show.*

It took some time to get to the main tent area. Suzanne was so dizzy that she had to stop once or twice to sit down. By the time she got there, she was sweating and her dress clung to her. To avoid being pressed into problem-solving service by her staff, she veered along the edge of the seating area against the white canvas to the back, where she could check the status of the event undisturbed.

The Christmas lights and tiny mirrors Jake and Chad had so painstakingly draped as a backdrop to the stage had been worth every minute of their time. They twinkled behind Dylan, sitting on a leather-and-chrome bar-stool with his guitar, singing something soft and low. Among the soft lights, the jarred fireflies, and candles scattered around the tent, the whole place looked magical, and everyone seemed rapt by the performance.

The song sounded familiar, and she strained to allow it into her brain and connect it with a title. Eventually, she realized it was Eric Clapton's "Wonderful Tonight" and that Dylan's twangy voice gave it a rough-hewn sound that actually made it even more elegant. Several couples were slow-dancing near the stage. She was proud that things were going well. If only she didn't feel so dizzy and restless.

A sudden wave came over her, and Suzanne was overwhelmed with an urge to be *out*. Away from the tent, the crowd, the lights. Anywhere but where she was. Her feet simply could not stand in that spot another minute. She staggered back toward the exit of the tent, feeling dizzier by the minute. She couldn't help stepping on several coats and purses as she went. She excused herself as quietly as possible as she passed behind people, trying to avoid bumping into anyone with her wavering gait and hard-shelled arm.

It seemed to take forever to get out of the tent, and it was especially difficult to get the canvas out of her way. Her clothes were too tight, the six-hundred-dollar dress scratchy and uncomfortable. Even though she was the same perfect size 6 she'd been for years, she'd had to use the best Lycra had to offer to make sure the lines were smooth beneath the satiny dress. Now she regretted it, because she could barely breathe as she made her way out to the museum lawn. After tonight, she vowed never to torture herself with a bustier and seamless biker shorts again.

The rest of the evening came to her in flashes. The humid night air. The feel of damp grass. Marci and Chad calling to her from far behind. Thinking Marci and Chad were hilarious. Feeling suddenly elated, free. Running. So much running. A funny house. Water. The smell of men's deodorant. And the bright, ominous flash of cameras. Then darkness. Sleep.

8

"Are you ready?" Marci said, handing Suzanne a mug of hot coffee.

She had been staring out the kitchen window of Jake and Marci's home in Alpharetta, examining with detached criticism the blankness of the nearly empty yard, unremarkable wooden fence, and the pale-neutral backs of the houses behind theirs. Jake and Marci lived in a four-bedroom home, with a basement, in a recently constructed neighborhood in the far-flung suburbs — the last place Suzanne had expected them to settle.

Under the circumstances, they really ought to try to make the rear of the houses look as nice as the front, she thought uncharitably. *That would at least improve the aesthetics a little until the trees grow in.*

"Suze?" Marci prompted.

"Yes, I'm ready. Sorry." Suzanne colored, embarrassed by her thoughts. Who was she to judge anyone?

Two days had passed since the debacle at the High, and, except for her second emergency room visit in a twenty-four-hour period, she had been hiding out like a fugitive at Jake and Marci's ever since. They had put her up in the spare bedroom; Marci had confiscated her phone and kept her away from the TV and newspapers. She'd even written an e-mail to Chad on Suzanne's behalf, giving him a script to follow for incoming calls from clients and the press. Both Stillwells had been kind enough to ignore the occasional sobbing that emerged from the guest room.

Suzanne had no siblings, but if she had, she could not imagine they would do better for her than Jake and Marci. Yet, to her shame, instead of appreciating their generosity, she was scrutinizing their neighborhood. What's more, if she were very honest, Suzanne would have to say that she resented just about everything about Marci and Jake's happy damn life and couldn't wait to leave later that day. *What a horrible, ungrateful friend I am.*

As usual, her best friend seemed to read her mind. "You're being hard on yourself," Marci said gently. "Come sit down."

On Jake and Marci's kitchen table were

109

piled several local and regional newspapers. In the wee hours after the event, a friend who worked for the Style section of *The Atlanta Journal-Constitution* had tipped Suzanne off via text message that her "episode" had been recorded in both picture and video format by all the press on hand. The association with Dylan Burke had launched the event onto gossip pages nationwide.

Now that it was Tuesday and she'd had time to stabilize, Marci was going to allow her to look at the papers. With one quick glance at the Sunday edition of the *AJC,* Suzanne had to agree that Marci had made the right call to hide them from her. The sight was horrifying.

Above the masthead on the front page of the paper — the same paper that had landed in her parents' driveway for forty years — was a tiny picture of Suzanne from the torso up, bare breasts pixilated for decency, being restrained from behind by someone in a tuxedo jacket whose face was out of frame. Her hair was wet on one side, falling out of her elegant updo in stringy chunks. She seemed to be yelling at someone far away, trying to break free from whoever was holding her. The teaser headline next to it read CHAOS AT DYLAN BURKE GALA, PAGE 6A.

She flipped to 6A, where her name had

long been associated with glamour, celebrities, and charity, to find a photo-essay of humiliation. Thirty-two pictures filled the page: blurry images of Suzanne looking crazed, stripping out of her dress and shoes, running across the front lawn of the High. In one shot, her six-hundred-dollar dress hung off her arm cast like a garbage bag, and in the next it was gone. The pictures showed her in the black bustier and Spanx, hiding gleefully behind Roy Lichtenstein's famous *House III* sculpture while Marci and Chad approached from either side, trying to hem her in.

Clearly, Suzanne had escaped, however, because the next series of shots showed her on the run again, still trailed by Chad and Jake, the latter of whom had evidently replaced Marci in the worst game of tag ever. It was difficult to make out much, but Suzanne distinctly saw the flash of her mother's antique pearls around her neck, verifying beyond doubt that this crazy person really was herself.

"I'll say this," Jake said, laying a hand on her shoulder. "We had a hell of a time catching you. You could have a career as a running back if you wanted."

Marci glared at him to be quiet. *Oh, right,* Suzanne thought. *That would be a sore subject because my* actual *career is obviously over.*

The remaining pictures followed the spiral of her life going down the toilet: Suzanne running barefoot toward the main plaza with several security guards joining the chase, losing her bustier while trying to crawl under the registration tables for some reason, Atlanta PD arriving on the scene, Suzanne grinning maniacally before flipping backward over the black chain ropes and then landing in the inch or so of water in the reflecting pool next to the museum's front windows. She rubbed her bruised tailbone as the picture brought back the memory.

There it was. Just before the final shot of Suzanne strapped to a gurney being lifted into the ambulance was the full version of the picture from the front page. The former homecoming queen stood topless, wet and angry, apparently having a loud disagreement with the police officers on the scene. It was as if an episode of *Cops* had been filmed at a highbrow museum fund-raiser. The tuxedo holding her back belonged to a security guard, whom she had hired personally. She remembered doing his background check. And just behind them, expression unreadable, was Dylan Burke himself.

"I guess this means there's no chance he didn't see anything," Suzanne said despondently.

"It's a good thing he was there, actually," Jake said, ignoring his wife's signals to be quiet. "He talked them out of taking you to jail."

Suzanne swallowed hard and took a deep breath. She had to face this sometime. "I need to get a shower," she said. "And I'm ready for my phone back."

She got to the office just after ten. If any part of her was hoping for a miracle, praying that people wouldn't notice the story or recognize her in the pictures, the disappointment came as soon as she saw Chad's face. Of the fifteen or so events they had slated for the next year, twelve had already called to cancel. These included longtime clients who had followed her from her previous agency. The remaining three could not be far behind.

Still, Suzanne followed up dutifully with each and every one. She got her standard cinnamon latte for courage and spent the morning returning phone calls with the most cheerful voice she could summon. But no one wanted to be associated, publicly or privately, with someone who'd made the

Sunday paper the way Suzanne had. Her clients had all paid nonrefundable retainers for her services — a practice she adopted from her father — but for the ones more than a month out, she had offered refunds anyway. No one accepted. They all sounded sympathetic and embarrassed.

"Of course, if it were up to me, we'd keep you on. It's just the board of directors . . ."

"Our company has this morality and behavior clause, and while you're not *technically* an employee . . ."

"The management is concerned about our image. If we didn't already have so much negative publicity from that EPA fine two years ago . . . Well, of course, you understand."

Of course.

A few had even offered advice.

"Don't worry, sweetie, it will pass. You'll be back in the game in a couple of years."

"My brother went to this great rehab facility in Malibu. I'll send you the name."

Possibly the worst of these was Mrs. Banks, the co-owner of a small family-owned mailing house who had contracted Suzanne to do their holiday parties for a couple of years running. She was also the wife of the company's president. "I'm sorry, dear, but our employees and customers have

114

certain expectations of us," she said, singing the same refrain as many of the previous conversations.

"Of course," Suzanne said, launching into the polite speech that she had recited all morning. "I completely understand. I'm very sorry and embarrassed about what happened. Although it was an honest mistake involving my medication, naturally I understand that the last thing you need when planning a major event is for the event planner herself to be a distraction."

"Poor dear," said the woman. "I know at times like this, I always turn to my faith."

"Yes, ma'am," Suzanne responded distractedly. She appreciated the sentiment, but this sort of platitude felt hollow coming from a virtual stranger. She was already opening the file of her next client, when Mrs. Banks surprised her completely.

"You know what the Bible tells us, dear: 'For the wages of sin is death, but the gift of God is eternal life in Christ Jesus our Lord.' Suzanne, do you believe in Jesus?"

Seriously? Today?

Suzanne had no idea what to say. Yes? No? I don't know? She had never understood why some people, who would never dare ask whether you colored your hair or had your teeth whitened, were perfectly comfortable asking total strangers about their deepest religious beliefs and the state of their souls.

Thinking quickly, she dropped her can of pencils on the concrete floor. It had the desired effect of a loud clang and scattering sound. "Oh, my! Chad, are you okay?" she called. Chad rolled his eyes. "I'm afraid we've had a little accident here at the office, Mrs. Banks. Thank you so much for your kindness, and we'll be in touch."

She hung up and put her forehead on the desk. Suzanne barely recognized herself. Six weeks ago, she had been at the top. She knew basically everyone in Atlanta, and there wasn't a major party or charity event that she didn't either plan or attend. She'd dated professional athletes, been the president of the Atlanta Junior League. She'd played tennis with Elton John, for heaven's sake.

Now she was a social pariah with a broken arm, faking clumsy accidents to avoid talking to people. Not that any mishap would be unbelievable after the past week. "I'm like the Mr. Bean of party planning," she said out loud.

Chad laughed sardonically. "Except that there's a chance he'll be working this year."

She flinched. Normally, she prided herself

on being able to handle his little jibes, but not today.

"God, Suzanne, I'm so sorry. I didn't mean —"

"Don't worry about it," she said. "You're right."

He shuffled papers for a moment and then ventured softly, "You okay?"

"No," she said truthfully. "But I have to be. Right?"

He nodded and went back to his desk to sort through bid sheets from the silent auction. One silver lining of Suzanne's seminude encounter with the reflecting pool was that people attending the event had stayed much later than anticipated, buzzing about what they'd seen and trying to get themselves interviewed by the media. In a fantastic display of leadership under pressure, Chad had enough foresight to keep the bar open and extend the silent auction for thirty extra minutes, during which many of the high bids on the auction items had doubled. Financially, at least, the event had been far more successful than anyone could've hoped.

Whether Dylan Burke and his people would see it that way, however, was another matter. Every time the phone rang, Suzanne expected it to be Yvette, bringing the ax down. So far, however, the hottest thing in country music was one of only three clients from whom they had not heard a word. Maybe Yvette was having an attorney draft a letter instead of contacting her personally. The thought gave Suzanne heartburn.

She and Chad worked silently into the afternoon and all the next day, writing the usual thank-you notes and filing receipts, just as they always did. A few stray calls came in here and there, but they had talked to most of their clients except Dylan, and a high-profile corruption trial downtown was now occupying the attention of the local media.

By late Friday, their event-related tasks were done and the phone was quiet. She had nothing left to do but call Yvette, who naturally did not answer her phone. Suzanne left the most chipper message she could manage, casting it into the universe the way her grandfather had cast fishing lures into the Chattahoochee when she was a little girl.

She shrugged at Chad, who shouldered his messenger bag to go. He stopped halfway to the door, hesitated, and spoke.

"Um," he said.

"Um?"

"Well, I don't know how to say this exactly, but . . ."

"That's unusual," she remarked, attempting a teasing smile.

"You know how much I like you." He said this as though he were telling her she had a terminal illness. "Like working for you, I mean."

"Jeez, don't start getting all mushy on me, okay? I can't handle that. Don't worry about it. I'm fine, really."

"It's not that. I mean, I was wondering . . ."

Realization dawned. "You're wondering whether you need to find another job," she said softly.

"Yes. Suzanne, please don't be hurt. It's just that David knows someone who has an opening for an executive assistant in Midtown, really close to our apartment, and —"

"I think you should take it."

"I mean, normally I wouldn't even consider it. I love working for you, but I'm planning to start graduate school —"

"Take the job, Chad."

"Of course, I can come back if . . ." He trailed off, and they looked at each other for a long time. "If things get better."

You mean if a miracle happens, and I am resurrected from the dead, she thought. Her eyes welled. "Write the best recommendation you can for yourself, and I'll sign as many copies as you want," she said.

He nodded, took a step toward the door, and then spun and crossed the room, his face contorted with uncharacteristic emotion. He embraced her awkwardly. "This sucks," he said, wiping his eyes and speeding away. When the door closed behind him, the silence in the office was oppressive.

That night, Suzanne had a bottle of wine and a can of spray cheese for dinner while watching *Gone with the Wind.* She fell asleep on the couch and stayed there for a long, restless night. Her broken arm still ached and itched, but she had refused to take any painkillers since Saturday. She woke often, and when she slept, she dreamed of Scarlett O'Hara, trapped inside an antebellum mansion that was somehow sculpted by Roy Lichtenstein — all bold lines and primary colors. Scarlett flitted from window to colorful window, screaming wordlessly for help that would never come, while Atlanta burned.

9

Suzanne spent the weekend in her pajamas with the ringer off, feeling sorry for herself and filling her kitchen counter with food-delivery containers. By the following Tuesday, she had to force herself to go into the office. She had little to do, but she watered the plants and walked around with the feather duster, trying to be cheerful. Chad had called to say he had an interview with a law firm today, but had promised to stop by afterward to see whether she needed anything. No word from Yvette.

The mailman came around noon, delivering a check from the museum for her fees for the event. Well, at least Dylan's people hadn't been angry enough to refuse to pay the museum her fee. A pink sticky note stuck to the top of the check bore Betsy Fuller-Brown's elegant scrawl.

S — Call me in a couple of months when

everything has died down and I'll see if I can help. Chin up. — B

She opened her business accounting database, added the check, and did a few calculations. With the cash on hand before the event and one or two clients who had not accepted refunds of their deposits, there was enough money to pay Chad for another week and keep her afloat until the end of July. *Then what?*

Suzanne pulled up her résumé on the computer and stared at it. She couldn't remember the last time she actually sent a résumé out looking for a job. Somehow, the jobs had always found her — through a client, a league connection, whatever. The prospect of sending out cover letters was daunting.

Her desk phone rang shrilly. She glanced at the caller ID before answering. "Hi, Mom."

"Hello, honey." Her mother's phone voice was somehow both warm and formal, with her thick, parlor-Southern accent. "What are you doing?"

"I'm working," Suzanne replied. "I'm at the office."

"Do you have time for lunch Thursday? We could meet at the club."

"Thanks, Mom, but I promised Marci I'd have lunch with her on Thursday. Rain check?"

As she spoke, Suzanne opened her e-mail and typed *Lunch Thursday?* to Marci and hit send. She hated lying to her mother but didn't think she could handle lunch at the club just yet.

"Certainly, sugar. It's just that there was something I wanted to ask you."

"Okay," Suzanne said slowly. "Can you ask me now?"

"Well, I know how . . . *rough* it's been for you this past couple of weeks, and I was wondering if Daddy and I could lend you some money? Just until you get on your feet again."

"Daddy wants to lend me money?" Suzanne was surprised.

"Of course, honey," her mother said nervously. "I mean, you know how proud we both are of you."

"Does he know you're calling me?"

"Not exactly, but your father has been so busy. I didn't want to bother him with a little thing like this. I feel certain he won't mind a bit."

Busy, right. If she were a lawyer and this were a small law firm she'd started, maybe he'd think it worth rescuing. "How is Daddy doing with all of it?" she asked cautiously. Imagining how he'd reacted to seeing his baby girl in what seemed a compromising position in the papers was not pleasant.

"Oh, sweetie. You know your dad. He'll be fine. Now, I'm writing you a check for, say, ten thousand dollars. That should cover your expenses for a while. You can buy some sensible suits and start interviewing for jobs. I don't think the ladies at the league will be too hard on you, especially once we explain —"

"Mom," Suzanne said through gritted teeth. "I thought the loan was to help me rebuild my business."

"Oh, come on, Suzanne. Don't you think this little venture of yours has run its course? All those events with alcohol and celebrities." She said *alcohol* and *celebrities* with distaste, as though she were saying *flatulence* and *defecation.*

"I love what I do, Mom. I'm not going to let a little setback knock me out of the game."

"Of course. I just hate seeing your college degree go to waste. I think I heard that Bolton Academy is looking for an elementary art teacher; you'd be perfect —"

"Hold on, Mom. I have another call." It was true. The red light on her second line was blinking rapidly. "Suzanne Hamilton," she said, switching to the other line without waiting for her mother's reply.

She was surprised to hear the chipmunk voice of Yvette sounding stiff and awkward. "Hello, Suzanne. I hope you have recovered from your, er, sudden illness?"

Her tone indicated that Suzanne's recovery was not at all among her chief concerns. In any case, she didn't wait for a reply. "I'm calling with a message from Mr. Burke. I just want it noted for the record that I have advised Mr. Burke against this course of action," she said. Suzanne held her breath.

"Mr. Burke wishes me to ask whether quote-unquote hillbilly weddings are in your repertoire? His sister Kate is getting married Memorial Day weekend at Dylan's mountain cabin in Tennessee, and he'd like you to plan the wedding."

"I don't do weddings," Suzanne replied reflexively. It had been her mantra ever since she went into event planning. Marci and Jake's wedding had been the only exception, ever.

"Of course not," Yvette sneered. "You have your reputation to consider. That's what I told Mr. Burke."

"Even if I did, six weeks isn't much time to plan a whole wedding."

125

"I agree," said Yvette. "Though Kate is quite set on the date. Her fiancé has a professional commitment in two months, and they want to be married beforehand. Still, I told Mr. Burke I thought it would be better to hire a *real* wedding planner. And as there will be some media attention, I have suggested we hire someone . . . less inflammatory? Of course, you can't disagree with that."

Suzanne could not disagree. And yet she wanted to, desperately.

The red light was still blinking on line 1, where her mother waited for her to accept help and get a regular job like everyone else. Here on line 2 was a woman she didn't like, representing a man she was too humiliated to even consider facing again, with an opportunity to do something she had always hated. It was a no-brainer.

"I'll do it," Suzanne said in a rush.

At the other end of the line, Yvette was quiet. Suzanne continued, assuring herself as much as Yvette. "I'd be honored to help Kate Burke plan her wedding. Thank you and Mr. Burke so much for the generous opportunity."

The squeaky manager recovered from her apparent shock, and her tone was composed and polite when she finally answered.

126

"Lovely. E-mail me a contract, and I'll get you the basic details. Kate is out of the country, but she has some preliminary ideas gathered that I think you'll find useful. I can have someone on our staff get them to your office on . . . Monday? Is that soon enough?"

"Sure," Suzanne said numbly.

She heard a shuffling of papers as Yvette went on matter-of-factly. "You'll meet with Kate when she gets back from Prague. Let's see, she's flying in Sunday, April twenty-sixth. How's that following Tuesday? I assume you have no other clients beating down your door right now?"

Suzanne could almost hear the smirk at the other end of the line.

"No, I don't," Suzanne said. "Thank you so much for taking that into consideration. Tuesday the twenty-eighth is fine." She hung up without waiting for a response.

When Jake and Marci arrived at her office before for lunch on Thursday, they found Suzanne researching Dylan Burke online. "Obsessing much?" Jake asked, and then recoiled from the look Suzanne sent his way.

"Jake," she trilled as sweetly as possible. "I need your wife for a few moments. Could you make yourself useful and water the plants?" She gestured to the row of ferns hanging high along the enormous wall of windows.

Jake came around the desk and rubbed Suzanne's shoulders playfully. "Anything for you, my dear," he said. As he headed back to the storage closet to get the ladder and watering can, he called over his shoulder, "There's nothing like having *two* wives. Some guys aren't even lucky enough to have one."

"Well, I guess that makes you twice the husband, honey," Marci called after him, winking at Suzanne. She then turned to look more closely at the computer, where Suzanne had an article pulled up about Dylan and his family — one of few Suzanne had found that mentioned his younger sister Kate. Most articles focused on his mom and her other daughters, Sherrie and Amber. "What are you doing, really? Dylan Burke fired you, right?"

Suzanne shook her head and launched into the story about Yvette's call and Kate Burke's wedding. She was just getting to the part where she had stupidly agreed to do a famous person's wedding in just a few weeks — with the bride herself out of the country for a third of that time — when Jake called to them. "Guys? Can you come here for a second?"

They obeyed, exchanging looks of confusion, and found Jake standing in the enormous storage closet behind the loft's bathroom, scratching his head. At first glance, Suzanne didn't see anything amiss. The closet was tidy and organized, as usual.

"What's wrong?" she asked.

He pointed. "Is this the ladder you fell off before Dylan's party?" She had forgotten until now that it was broken.

"Um, yes. Sorry, I forgot that you can't use the top step, but I think you are tall enough —"

"No, Suzanne," Jake said, with no trace of humor in his charming face. "I think maybe you should consider calling the police."

Officer Frank Caputo of the Atlanta PD was polite and thorough, if not overly helpful. He had arrived about twenty minutes after Suzanne called. He jotted down the details of Suzanne's fall from the ladder, including the time of day she'd gone to the emergency room and the name of the doctor she'd seen. He took a picture on his cell phone of the broken ladder and of what Jake had just discovered: the tiny metal shavings on the floor underneath it.

They looked like silvery-black pencil shavings and were in a small pile next to the baseboard of the closet. Once Jake pointed them out, Suzanne was surprised she hadn't noticed them when she pulled the ladder out originally. Jake had noticed them, though, which led him to look more closely at the broken step. A single jagged point of metal stuck out where the top of the step had remained connected to the side; the rest of the break was clean. Someone had sawed almost all the way through the step before Suzanne had stood there. Her fall had not been an accident.

Officer Caputo had agreed with this assessment. Beyond that, however, he seemed to have little to offer.

"How many people have keys to the office?" he asked, sounding bored.

"Just me; my assistant, Chad; and the landlord."

"Your assistant? Any problems there?"

"None," she said without hesitation.

"Is there anyone your landlord might have let in recently? Like to do service on the unit?"

"No, I don't think so," Suzanne said, thinking. "The last time was a broken toilet, but that's been . . . more than six months ago. There have been some vendors here dropping things off for an event recently,

130

but Chad always meets them here with the key."

"Have you filed any other reports recently?"

"Well, my tires were slashed a few weeks ago," Suzanne said. "There was someone in my spot, so I had to park on the street. I was here late; I just assumed it was some neighborhood kids — there's been some vandalism lately."

"Vandalism. Any other issues in the neighborhood? Disputes with your neighbors?"

"No."

"Recent breakups? Boyfriends?"

Marci snorted, and then recoiled under Suzanne's glare. Officer Caputo gave her a questioning expression.

"There have been a few . . . I've dated a good bit recently." She tried for her usual Southern charm, but it sounded instead like a bad imitation of Amanda Wingfield in *The Glass Menagerie*.

I declare, sir, I have had a good many gentleman callers.

"Anyone you may have rejected?" the police officer asked. "Maybe someone more interested in you than you were in him?"

Suzanne bit her lip.

Marci interjected. "That pretty much describes *all* of them."

The officer gave Suzanne a look she couldn't read, and she stared down at her feet, reddening in response. The elbow she aimed at Marci missed by inches.

"Ma'am, I'll file a report, but there's not much we can do for you unless you have some idea who is doing this." He handed her a photocopied page with a blurry title across the top: "Ten Tips for Stalking Victims." *Stalking.* Shit.

"You might want to make a list of boy-friends, or, um . . . *dates,* you've had in the last year or so." Suzanne could tell the word "dates" made the young officer uncomfortable, and she suddenly felt inexplicably dirty. "Maybe even further back, if you can think of anyone who might be upset with you. Are you ever here alone?"

Suzanne thought about Chad's new job with a lump in her throat. "All the time," she said softly.

"You should have an alarm installed here and maybe at your residence. You live alone?"

"Yes."

"Well, try not to get too worked up about it. Use common sense — don't walk alone at night, stay in touch with your family and friends, lock your doors. Don't open the door to anyone you're not expecting. Two-thirds of stalkers are someone you know; the other third are strangers. Either way, awareness is your best weapon.

"I'd suggest taking pictures with your phone if anything happens or you see a suspicious car. You can call us with the license plate. We'll file a report and that will help, if you get a protective order later."

"Protective order?" Suzanne couldn't believe the words coming out of her mouth. "Will that help?"

The officer's tone was professional, emotionless. "Sometimes it does, if whoever did this to you is afraid of being arrested. Of course, it doesn't matter until you know who it is."

"So there's nothing you can do?" Marci demanded.

"I'm sorry, ma'am, there's not. Not until we have more information." He turned to Suzanne, and her face must have looked as colorless as it felt, because he softened a bit. He put a large, rough hand on her shoulder. "Make your list. Keep your eyes and ears open. If you get any evidence of who might have done this to you, call us."

10

Three hours later, Suzanne and Marci sat in the kitchen of Suzanne's large Buckhead condo, waiting for brownies to finish baking. From the adjacent living room, they could hear Jake snoring on the couch. He had fallen asleep watching basketball.

"I don't think anyone will bother you tonight," Marci said. "Jake snores like a bear with hay fever. That should scare people away."

Suzanne was silent, washing out the bowl of brownie batter in the sink.

"They smell amazing. It was a good idea to make them," Marci went on. "Remember when we used to do this in high school? And we'd add all those weird ingredients? Basically anything we could find at my house."

Suzanne laughed. "I remember. You always wanted to add cherries to *everything.*"

"Hey!" Marci said defensively. "Maraschino cherries are good! Besides, they're fruit, so they're healthy. Mmm . . . you don't have any, do you?"

"Yes, I do," Suzanne said. "I keep them right next to the giant pack of hot dogs and frozen chicken nuggets I always have on hand in case an elementary school takes a field trip to my apartment."

"No need for sarcasm," Marci said. She rubbed her belly thoughtfully. "I probably will have that stuff on hand before long."

Suzanne could see that Marci's already-soft waist was beginning to thicken and protrude more than usual. She felt wistful, wishing she could feel more excited for her best friend about the new baby. She wanted to reach out to her, but she knew nothing about pregnancy and even less about babies. What could she possibly offer?

"Just don't bake those horrible Dr Pepper brownies for your kids. Remember those?"

"Oh my God! What were we thinking?" Marci rolled her eyes. "Didn't we put vanilla pudding in those, too?"

Suzanne nodded grimly. The results had been disastrous — a soupy, frothy mess that had been completely inedible, even with spoons and teenage determination. Marci's mom had sent them to the grocery store early the next morning to replace all the ingredients they'd wasted and gently suggested that they find a hobby other than baking to occupy themselves on Friday nights.

"So should I go through what we have so far?" Marci suggested. On the kitchen island lay a legal pad covered with names and notes.

"Sure," Suzanne sighed.

"Okay, Rick, we got — and personally he seems the likely candidate to me. Dated for three weeks, broke up a month ago. Reason . . . did I get a reason for him?"

"Do we have to write the reasons?" Suzanne protested for the third time. "Really, does it matter?"

"Yes, I think so," said Marci. "You never know what might help narrow it down."

"Fine," Suzanne said. Marci seemed to enjoy her role as junior detective a little too much. "He talked about himself too much. His vocabulary was atrocious. He was . . . sort of barbaric, I guess."

"Barbaric . . . vocabulary . . . ," Marci muttered as she wrote. "Got it. Okay, what's he doing now?"

"He's in sales, and he travels all over the state. I don't know whether he's dating anyone. He — he had to mail me my underwear."

"Underwear . . . ," Marci repeated, writing. Suzanne waited for the inevitable joke, but none came. "Okay, before that was Damian. Pro basketball player, dated three months — hey, that was pretty good, Suze!"

"He was out of town a lot," Suzanne answered drily.

"Broke up because . . . ?"

"We've been over this. He was too young for me. He always had girls trying to follow him back to his hotel room. I couldn't compete with that."

"So he cheated on you?"

"No, I don't think so," Suzanne said thoughtfully. "But it was only a matter of time, right?"

"Riiiiight," Marci said, with no small amount of sarcasm. "Any chance it could be him?"

"Doubt it," Suzanne said. "He's busy all the time, and he wasn't really too upset when I ended it. Besides, he's not here that often. He has an apartment here during the season, but his family is all in Chicago, so he spends most of his time there."

"Hmm . . . not upset. Are you sure?"

"Well, he sent me some free tickets the other day with a nice little note. I have them here somewhere. I was planning to give them to Jake, but in all the excitement I forgot."

"Sent . . . free . . . tickets . . . ," Marci repeated and made a contemplative noise. Suddenly she was Columbo, apparently.

"So your theory is that the professional basketball player, who could have just about any girl he wanted, was so devastated by our breakup that he is taking time out of his busy game schedule to slash my tires and sabotage my office ladder? And he's sending me tickets to a game where twenty thousand people will be watching so that he can . . . what? Kill me at halftime?"

Marci chewed the end of the pen. "Perhaps not. Who's next?"

"Kenneth."

"Kenneth, stockbroker, dated six weeks. Broke up because" — Marci peered more closely at her notes, as though she had not been Suzanne's sole confidant for each and every turn of these events — "because he had a hairy back — ew — and was 'weird about kids.' What does that mean?"

"You remember this, don't you? He wanted kids a little too much?"

Marci flipped a couple of pages. "Two years ago, you broke up with Xavier because he *didn't* want kids."

"I know. I'd like to have the option, I guess. But Kenneth was more interested in the kids than in the grown-up part of the relationship. Like he was just looking for a womb."

"Womb . . . got it. Now, Brad Number Two."

"Brad Two was too outdoorsy for me. A little too Grizzly Adams, you know? Plus, he had smelly feet."

Marci lowered her voice. "Don't tell him I told you, but Jake's feet are smelly, too. Yuck! Okay, Timothy . . ."

"Got into a fight at a bar on our third date."

"Matthew?"

"Mommy issues. Remember?"

"Oh, yeah. Who was that guy who didn't wash his hands after pooping?"

"Reggie." Suzanne made a face. The two of them shuddered and giggled. The timer dinged, and Marci got the brownies out of the oven before going back to the list.

"Okay, what about Frank?"

"Public relations guy. Dated three weeks. Too . . . polished. He seemed like the kind of guy who would make you iron his underwear."

"Manuel?"

"He's a chef. Owns the Mexican restaurant down the street. We weren't dating so much as hooking up after closing some nights. He'd give me free margaritas, and

139

we'd talk business for a while, and then . . . you know. It just never turned into more than that. I'm not really sure why."

"Down the street? So he might be able to follow you?"

"I guess," Suzanne said slowly, thinking. "But I don't know why he would. I'm pretty sure he's dating someone now. I think he would've told me if he were mad at me — stalking doesn't seem like his style."

"Hmm . . . You put a star by this one. Who is William? Oh, wait . . . *that* William?"

"Seriously, Marci. I know you lived in Austin back then and everything, but pay attention."

"It was San Francisco, actually, before I moved to Austin," Marci corrected. "Speaking of paying attention. And of course I remember now. The New Year's Eve party." She shook her head sadly.

"Yeah, I thought he should go on the list, even though it was so long ago. I dated him the longest, actually. Almost a year. Aren't you proud?" She said this with a bleak smile.

"So why, again, did you say no?" Marci asked.

Here was a question everyone Suzanne knew had asked her over and over at the time, and her mother still asked about twice a year. She had never come up with a satisfactory answer. "I just . . . wasn't ready."

William Fitzgerald was the boy Suzanne had dated the longest, and she had tried very hard to fall in love with him. He was also the boy who had asked her to marry him in front of their parents and nearly everyone their parents knew at the country club's New Year's Eve party. And in front of more than three hundred people, all half blitzed and ready to celebrate good news of any sort, Suzanne had been forced to say no.

"Where is he now?"

"I have no idea."

The brownies had cooled enough by now not to burn the roofs of their mouths, so they set the notes aside and cut into them with a spatula, eating them warm, straight from the pan. For a few minutes there was no conversation, all of it lost in the smacking sounds of eating gooey chocolate.

"You know what's weird?" Marci said. "There are so many guys on this list I've never met."

"Well, you lived out of state for a lot of this time," Suzanne said, reaching for another brownie. Marci had moved away shortly after college and only returned three or four years ago. Suzanne had always hoped she would come back; things weren't the same without her. In the end, it had been their college friend Jake who'd brought her best friend back to Atlanta, with a love none of them had fully realized existed until then. Suzanne would always be grateful to Jake for bringing Marci back.

"Yes, but even in the last few years, when I was here, there are guys you dated that I never met. Don't get me wrong; it's fine. It's just . . . weird. I feel like you know everything there is to know about me, and yet there are all these people who were important in your life that I never even met."

Suzanne waved away the idea. "It's not that I didn't want to share with you. It's just that . . . well, I don't want you guys to get attached to someone until I know I have something worth attaching to."

"Oh, come on. Don't you think Jake and I could handle it?"

Suzanne hesitated. "Well, to be honest . . ."

"What?"

"Well, you met Damian twice, months ago, and you're still asking about him."

"Teasing. We're teasing. Jake thought it was neat that you were dating an athlete, because he works in sports. That's all."

"But it's not just him. There were a couple

142

of others, like Tanner. And Brad Number One, who you got all upset about when things didn't work out."

"I didn't get all upset. I just think sometimes you're a little capricious about letting guys go."

"Capricious?" Suzanne repeated, slightly offended.

"Well, yes," Marci said. She gestured to the legal pad. "We have four pages of guys there, four pages of nice guys, for the most part, and your reasons for breaking up with some of them are downright silly."

"So I should stay with someone who's not right for me? Someone I don't want to be with?" She felt defensive and angry. Now that she was happily settled, Marci had apparently forgotten how hard single life could be.

"Of course not. That's not what I meant —"

"It's exactly what you meant. You've always been this way about the guys I've dated, but ever since you and Jake got together, it's been so much worse."

"Suzanne, what the hell are you talking about?"

Suzanne knew she should stop talking. She should apologize, hug her best friend, and eat another brownie. But the events of the past couple of weeks boiled inside her, out of control. "You think just because you got your fairy-tale ending that means everyone else has to have the same thing. You are always pressuring me to be with someone, anyone. Like our friendship would be better if I were part of a couple instead of just me."

"That's not true. I —"

"I'm happy for you, Marce. I really am. I'm happy you and Jake finally figured things out and you're married now, and I'm happy for you about the baby, too. But I'm not there yet. Maybe . . . maybe I will never be there."

"That's ridiculous. Of course you will. You just have to stop looking for perfection. You dump these guys for idiotic reasons, and then you complain about being alone."

"When have I ever complained about being alone?"

"Well, maybe you don't complain out loud, but —"

"Oh, so now I complain in silence? Or is it just that you can read my mind? Now that your life is so perfectly worked out, you're clairvoyant, too, I suppose." Suzanne could hear her ugly tone, and it made her wince. But she was so angry. This had been building for a long time.

"It's not that," Marci said. Angry tears

were streaming down her face, too. "It's just that you are always moping around, especially when Jake and I are together. We're sort of afraid to be happy around you sometimes, like it's an insult to you."

" 'We,' huh? So you guys are sitting around talking about me and how pathetic I am. How I'm in your way. Well, you shouldn't bother."

"No, that's not true —"

"Maybe I don't want the cookie-cutter house in Alpharetta and a minivan and soccer games. Maybe I'm looking for something extraordinary. Just because I haven't settled like you did, maybe I am still looking for someone who is perfect for me . . ."

Marci's anger turned to a rage Suzanne hadn't seen since middle school. Her face was nearly purple. "I. Beg. Your. Pardon. *Settled?* You're saying that I *settled* for Jake?"

"No, that wasn't what I meant. I meant 'settled' like 'settled down,' not —"

"For your information, that man in there asleep on the couch is ten times any man you've *ever* been out with. He's a good person. No, he's a great person. He loves me and I love him. And maybe his feet are smelly and our house is boring and our relationship looks humdrum to you. But he would *die* for me, and I for him. Can you honestly say that about any of the men on this list? Have you ever cared about anyone more than you care about yourself?"

Struck dumb by her friend's rage, Suzanne could find nothing to say.

"Of course not," Marci said. Her voice was softer now, but Suzanne knew it was just the deceptive blue core of the flame. "You think we're judging you, Jake and me? When we say something nice about a guy you obviously like, or at least liked enough to sleep with? Or we show an interest in you and your life, you think that's selfish somehow?"

Suzanne shook her head. It was all going wrong. None of this was making sense.

"Meanwhile, have you asked once how I'm feeling? Have you wanted to see sonogram pictures? Have you offered to throw me a shower?"

"Shower? I thought that would be . . . later? Of course, I'll —"

"Do you even care that we're having a girl?" Marci was sobbing now.

"A girl," Suzanne said softly, almost to herself. Of course, it was a girl. She didn't even know they knew. Her tears flowed freely again. She reached for Marci, who shrugged her off.

146

"Well, probably. It's not a hundred percent at this stage, but I had an early ultrasound last week."

"What? Why? Is everything okay?"

"It's fine. It was . . . just a precaution," Marci said, softening. "I had some bleeding."

"Oh my God." Suzanne felt like she'd been slapped.

"It's fine," Marci said quickly. "But with everything you've had going on, I didn't want to worry you. At this rate, though, she'll be in college before your life is together enough to care about my boring existence."

"That's not fair," Suzanne said. "Sit down. Come on."

"I'm sorry," Marci said. "But I just can't do this right now. I need to be away from you for a while. Jake will be around if you need anything or if you're . . . in trouble."

With that, Marci whirled around and stormed out, dragging a half sleeping and very confused Jake behind her. "What's going on, babe?" Suzanne heard Jake ask on his way out the door, but she could not make out Marci's mumbled answer before the sound of the door slamming reverberated off the walls around her.

She sank to the kitchen floor, despondent

tears wetting her face. She couldn't remember the exact time, but she knew it had been years since she and Marci had fought this way. As close as they were, they could both be horribly stubborn, which meant a real fight could last a while. Still, somewhere in her mind a seed was planted. It boded Easter hats and sundresses and pink frills, in all of which Suzanne would delight and Marci would need convincing was necessary. Princess clothes. Dress-up parties. Barbie dolls. *A girl.*

11

There hardly seemed any point in going to the office the next day, as Suzanne had only one client and wasn't meeting with Kate Burke for a couple of week. In fact, she called Yvette and asked her to send the materials to her condo on Monday instead of the office. Brave as she tried to be about it, the fact that someone had been in her office and tampered with the ladder was too creepy for her tastes. She'd relocate here for a few days. Decision made, she put on her most comfortable pajamas and curled up on the couch to watch bad TV. She picked up the phone but couldn't bring herself to call Marci. No surprise that Marci didn't call her, either.

Friday evening, she turned down an invitation to play tennis with Rebecca the next day and ignored a call from her mother. Saturday, she cleaned the entire condo from top to bottom, including scrubbing the baseboards and dusting the ceiling-fan blades. Sunday, she reorganized her closets and makeup drawers, which, even with her vast quantities of personal-care items, only carried her partway into the afternoon. She called her mother back and pretended to be on her way out the door so they wouldn't have to talk about her prospects.

After surfing through various reality-TV programs for the next couple of hours, Suzanne finally turned off her phone and went to bed early. There, her frustration mounted as she tried to sleep but couldn't. Her mind raced, and her body went from hot to cold to hot again. By 2:00 A.M., her pink satin sheets were a twisted mess and she could barely keep her eyes closed for more than a minute or two. She gave up trying to sleep and went back to the living room.

Listless, she picked up the pad where Marci had written all the notes about her previous relationships. She smiled at the stars and arrows Marci had used to indicate who she thought were key suspects. As she flipped through the pages, she glanced more than once at the door to make sure it was dead-bolted.

This is ridiculous. Hamiltons do not live in fear. Tonight it was her father's voice in her head; she could hear him as though he were standing right there with her, helping her with her homework. *It's a problem to be solved, sugar, that's all it is. You just got to figure out which tools you need to solve it. Follow your strengths.*

She stared at the yellow pad. Her strengths had always been an eye for beauty, calm in a crisis, and a strong sense of organization. Beauty didn't seem to be serving her well just now, and while she certainly had enough crisis to go around, it seemed calm had failed her, too. That left organization.

Suzanne went to her closet and dug out the poster board, markers, and rulers she kept on hand for emergency event signage. She poured herself a glass of wine and spread out in the middle of the living room floor. She was not even sure which problem she was trying to solve: the stalker, Marci, or maybe her whole damn life. She knew only that it called for straight lines and color coding. In two hours, she had taped several sheets of poster board to her dining room wall; neat grid lines and symbols brought order to the chaos. She went to bed and slept soundly until the sun was high in the sky.

Suzanne got up just after noon, showered, and made fresh coffee. She had spent the wee hours of the morning putting all the guys she'd dated since high school into a well-organized, color-coded grid — thirty-four of them, she was a bit embarrassed to discover. She had painstakingly listed each one in chronological order, documenting next to each guy his occupation, length of time dated, and the reason they had parted ways. She was hoping that if it didn't lead her to the identity of her stalker, it might at least help her figure out why she couldn't seem to find the right guy.

Marci was right, Suzanne thought, though she was not ready to admit it out loud. For one thing, when you looked at it in black and white, Rick seemed the likeliest candidate to be the stalker. This in itself was a little calming. At least being able to picture Rick with his pudgy white belly in the hotel room made him seem less threatening. Suzanne thought she could call him, confront him, and maybe get him to back off, or at least threaten him with a protective order.

Marci was also right that some of Suzanne's reasons for ditching the men she had dated were frivolous at best. This didn't mean that she should have stayed with those men but maybe that she never should have dated them in the first place. Suzanne, wanting so desperately to feel the soul-crushing love other people seemed to have, looked for it everywhere. Even in the places that her instincts told her she'd be unlikely to find it.

The answer was William, she thought, sipping her coffee. Or, at least, William was the question that would lead to the answer. If Suzanne could figure out what went wrong with William, she might be able to figure out what had derailed her entire love life, which in turn had led her to meaningless sex, fighting with her best friend, and a crazy stalker.

Suzanne could have pictured herself with five guys — *maybe* — on this whole list. And one, just one, whom she could honestly say she'd loved. William Fitzgerald. If she could find him, if she could figure out what went wrong, maybe there was hope for her after all.

The doorbell interrupted her reverie and reminded Suzanne that someone was coming to drop off Kate's wedding stuff today. She glanced down and realized she was still in her silk camisole and pajama bottoms, even though it was afternoon. Without time to get dressed, she pulled her faded cotton robe over her shoulders and went to the door. *Oh, well, I guess whichever messenger drew the short straw gets to see me at my best.*

She was relieved to see the UPS man standing there, rather than a member of Dylan's staff. With amusement, she thought that only Yvette would consider the entire UPS system part of her "staff." She opened the door and signed for the package with a brief nod to the driver, who politely looked up at the ceiling rather than at her state of undress.

The package was long and narrow — oddly shaped for what she had been assuming would be a couple of binders full of wedding information. She opened it to find a similarly shaped box inside with a florist's logo on it. *Flowers?* Suzanne opened the interior box curiously and found it filled with gorgeous white calla lilies, her favorite. She could see a card shaped like a smiley face attached. *Maybe this was an apology from Marci?* It wasn't Marci's style, really, but so few people knew her favorite flower.

Ouch! Shit! She jerked back her hand from the box, and blood began to drip from her finger onto the box and the chair where she had dropped it. She stuck her finger in her mouth and looked more closely at the flowers, seeing shards of glass intermingled among the calla lily stems.

154

Her finger was bleeding profusely. The cut did not appear very wide, but it was deep enough to create searing pain and quite a bit of blood. Suzanne ran to the sink to wrap it in a damp paper towel while she found a bandage — a process complicated significantly by the cast on her other arm. The doorbell rang again, and she began to wonder whether she might still be asleep, having a very strange nightmare. When she looked through the peephole to see Dylan Burke standing there, she was sure.

"It seems like every time I see you, you're in some kind of trouble," he said, once she had opened the door and he saw her wounded finger. He put the binders — exactly as she'd pictured them — on her kitchen table and followed her to the sink. "You really are Scarlett O'Hara."

"It's okay," she said. "I'm fine. Just a little cut. Please excuse my . . . my appearance."

It was too late to do anything about it now, but her robe had fallen to one side as she rushed about, and one shoulder was exposed, along with a good bit of unharnessed cleavage. *Why hadn't she at least slept in a T-shirt or something?*

"It's quite all right," Dylan said, not bothering to hide either a lecherous stare at her breasts beneath the lacy pajama top or a sideways grin at her predicament. She tried to cover herself, but the casted arm wouldn't cooperate. Dylan reached out and helped her get the robe back up. She could feel herself going blotchy with embarrassment, a rare state for her. At least, it had been rare until these last few weeks. Lately, it seemed she had spent half her life in a state of humiliation.

"Thanks," she muttered.

"Ma'am," he said, in a mock-cowboy tone, tipping his hand to the bill of his camouflage cap in a salute. "Can I help you with the bandage, too?"

Suzanne nodded, and Dylan reached out for her injured hand. His playful tone disappeared. "Jesus, what happened?"

"It's a long story," she said.

"I'm not busy," he said, rolling the gauze around her finger with practiced skill. "Just running errands for my baby sister and playing nurse to accident-prone event planners, as you can see."

"I have to say I was wondering about that," Suzanne said, grateful for a potential subject change. "I am delighted to see you, of course, but I'm surprised that you are the staff member Yvette assigned to deliver Kate's wedding binders."

"I'm the highest-paid errand boy in Atlanta." He smiled. His soft Tennessee accent was different, more casual than her dramatic Georgia drawl. "Nah, really, I have a few weeks off before the summer tour, and I always like to spend time in Atlanta. I have an apartment here, actually. It's nice to get lost in the city."

"Really?" Suzanne asked, surprised.

"Well, that and Kate didn't trust any of my guys with her stuff. I don't blame her, honestly. They're good guys, but I don't see them having a deep understanding of why fabric samples and magazine clippings would be so important to a girl."

"And you do have this deep understanding?"

He laughed. "I have five sisters. I had all kinds of feminine mysteries revealed to me very early on. Pounded into me, some of them. Trust me. I get it."

Suzanne could tell he was remembering something fondly. His eyes were on his work, taping her finger tightly, but they seemed distant. "So you're an expert on women?" she asked.

"Come on, now," he said. "I'm not stupid enough to claim that. Any guy who knows anything about women knows better than to pretend he knows about women."

She laughed in spite of herself. "That

sounds like one of your songs."

He grinned. "It does, doesn't it? I should write that down. Wiggle your fingers."

She did as he instructed. He frowned slightly, took back her hand, and made an adjustment to the tape. "Seriously, though, I have been fully initiated into the female realm."

"That seems kind of unbelievable to me. You seem like such a guy's guy. You know — camouflage, guns, girls . . ."

"I keep telling you not to judge people on their appearances. Go ahead, test me."

"What?"

"Test me. Send me to the store for tampons. Ask me to braid your hair. Cry on my shoulder about some guy who broke your heart. I'll be back from the store before you can say 'Ben and Jerry's.' "

She laughed loud this time, and he chuckled in response, pleased at having entertained her. His crooked grin was infectious beneath a day's worth of stubble. *I can see why people are so captivated with him.*

This realization reminded her suddenly of who he was: a client. Her only client. A wildly famous one at that. She had to be careful not to fall under his spell, not to believe that his charms were meant for her any more than they were meant for the millions of other weak-kneed girls who obsessed over him. One of the many pictures she'd seen in *People* with a young starlet on his arm flashed suddenly across her mind.

"Well, Scarlett, you probably ought to get a stitch or two in there," he said, looking finally satisfied with his handiwork on her finger. "But that should hold it for now."

"Thanks," she said, pulling her robe tighter to her. He was looking her in the eye now, rather deliberately, she thought. "Is there any message?"

"What?" he asked.

"With Kate's binders. Is it all self-explanatory?"

"Oh, that. Yeah, I think so. She'll be back in town next week. Did Yvette tell you?"

"Yes. Prague, right?"

"Yep. Church choir tour of Eastern Europe."

"Really?" Suzanne wasn't sure why this should surprise her, but it did.

"Yeah. Kate's a better singer than I am, actually. She's been going on that choir tour since we were kids. Of course, now she's a chaperone. She loves working with the teenagers."

This wasn't what Suzanne had expected. In the press, most of Dylan's sisters were portrayed as entitled, self-centered brats.

"That's so nice," she said.

"She's a lot nicer than I am, too," he said with another lop-sided grin. "What's all that?"

Following his gaze, Suzanne wished she could melt into the floor. He was pointing at the poster board along the dining room wall. In her astonishment, she had almost forgotten it.

"It's, um . . . I'm embarrassed to say this, but it's a list of people I've been involved with. Romantically."

He let out a long whistle. "Damn. And people say *I'm* a player."

"Well, it includes people all the way back to college, and I am a few years older than you."

Stop, she commanded herself. *For heaven's sake, stop. You are making it worse.*

"Are you?" he asked absently. He had walked to the wall for a closer look. "So do you keep records in case they make dating an Olympic sport or something?"

There was nothing to do but tell him the truth. "Well, it seems that I might be being . . ." She couldn't bring herself to say the word "stalked." It would make this too real and too scary. "It seems like one of them might be trying to hurt me, or at least scare me. Maybe someone I rejected. The

160

police suggested I make a list."

He turned to face her, his expression darkened. "Someone is stalking you?"

"Well, yes. It seems that way. But don't worry. I've been in touch with the police, and I am trying to figure out who it is. I have no reason to believe it will interfere with your sister's wedding." As she said it, Suzanne realized she was not at all confident of this. She had no idea what might happen next.

Dylan crossed back to the box of flowers and looked at them more closely. "This is how you cut your finger."

"Yeah," she conceded.

"You've called the police?"

"Not yet. I mean, not today. Not for this."

"I'll hang out until they get here."

"Really, that's not necessary —"

"I'm not busy," he said again. His tone left no room for argument.

After another second's hesitation, she went to the bedroom in resignation. She found Officer Caputo's card, called to tell him what happened, and changed into jeans and a T-shirt. When she returned to the living room, Dylan was out on the balcony, talking on the phone. He was still there when the knock came on the door. This time it was a squat black female officer, with hair swept into a tight, neat bun on the top of her head. She gave her badge number when Suzanne got to the peephole and instructed her to verify it with the Atlanta PD dispatch before opening the door.

"You always want to do that," the policewoman said, once the door was open. "Anytime someone comes out here, you get their badge number and confirm it before you open the door. Even if you called us, okay? I'm Officer Bonita Daniels. I'll be taking over your case."

Dylan came in off the porch. Officer Daniels eyed him with suspicion until Suzanne introduced him. "This is . . ." She hesitated. *What was the protocol here? Should she use his real name? Explain who he was?*

He saved her the trouble. "I'm Dylan Burke. A friend of Ms. Hamilton's."

"I recognize you," said Officer Daniels seriously. Then a controlled smile spread across her features. "I have a fifteen-year-old daughter. We're both fans."

Dylan smiled warmly back. "Thank you for coming so quickly, Officer Daniels. I'll let Ms. Hamilton show you the package she received." He waited a beat and then added, "Would your daughter like an autographed CD?"

162

The police officer's professional demeanor broke temporarily as her eyes lit up. Suzanne could tell she was imagining the reception she would get at home if she walked in with an autograph from Dylan Burke. "Oh, Mr. Burke . . . that would be great. Thanks."

"I'll just go out to my truck. Ms. Hamilton probably doesn't have a CD handy. She's not a big fan of my work." He winked at Suzanne on the way out the door. Officer Daniels eyed her reprovingly before she began asking about the box of flowers. Clearly, Suzanne had been diminished significantly in the officer's good opinion.

Dylan returned from the truck with a new CD, signed it for the officer to her daughter Chrysaline. She returned to asking Suzanne questions, though her cold professionalism had softened slightly.

"Can you describe the driver who delivered your package, Ms. Hamilton?"

"Suzanne. Please."

"Okay, Suzanne. You can call me Bonita, then." The officer smiled slightly and waited.

Suzanne didn't remember much about the driver, but she said what she could recall: white, midtwenties, physically fit. He seemed to have the right uniform, and he did not look familiar.

"So it's unlikely that it was him. I'll check into it. In any case, don't open your door to any deliveries until we get this resolved, okay? Just tell the carrier company you want to pick things up at their local station."

"That's going to be a pain," Suzanne said.

Behind her, Dylan snorted. "Well, ladies, I think you can take it from here."

He ducked out with an imaginary tip of the hat to Suzanne and a brilliant smile for Bonita Daniels. The policewoman returned his smile and then stayed with Suzanne for half an hour — longer than Suzanne had expected — reviewing the tips for stalking victims and encouraging her to stay calm.

Easier said than done.

12

If you have a ruined reputation, a broken
arm, a sole client (who is out of the country), and a stalker of unknown whereabouts
or identity, it's nice to live in a building with
a rooftop pool. Suzanne had begun spending hours there each day, trying to balance
the claustrophobia that frequently plagued
her inside the condo. The only other places
she went were to the Starbucks and the tiny
grocery store on the bottom floor, and even
those made her feel unnerved because they
were open to the public.

By Friday afternoon, she had gone
through Kate's wedding binders twice, making notes and jotting down questions.
Although she still was not looking forward
to planning a wedding, Kate at least seemed
to have decent taste, not the showy and
ridiculous stuff some of the Burke girls
seemed to favor. Maybe it was possible this
wouldn't be the worst experience of her life

after all.

Suzanne had also spent many bleary-eyed hours at her computer, searching online for traces of William Fitzgerald, the man who had once loved her enough to ask her to marry him. She was determined to find him again and figure out where things had gone wrong. The process was slow going, with one hand in a cast and a finger on the other hand throbbing painfully beneath a tight bulb of gauze and tape. Typing seemed to take forever, and errors were frequent.

William did not have a large online presence, which made him even more of a mystery to be solved. No Facebook page or blog. She found scant, outdated entries about his father's law practice and about his brother, who was apparently married and teaching economics at Georgia Southern, down in Statesboro. She had found William's parents' old number; they were apparently living in the same house he'd grown up in. She had almost worked up the courage to call them.

Now she was sitting by the rooftop pool, which she had to herself because even in late April, it was still a little chilly for mid-afternoon swims. In a few weeks, the seats around her would be constantly flooded

166

with the building's young professional tenants, skipping out on Friday afternoons to get a head start on the weekend, going through papers in their reclining beach chairs while they tried to acquire a glow for the bar scene later in the evenings.

Even if it had been warm enough, she couldn't swim today with her cast and sliced finger. She had opted against getting stitches, hoping Dylan's bandage job would do the trick. Days later, it still throbbed painfully but was now beneath a simple bandage rather than the original big gauzy mess.

She stretched out in her cargo shorts with her laptop and phone beneath the glare of the sun and city around her. She picked up the phone and stared at it for a long time. William's parents' number was in her pocket, but those weren't the digits she was tempted to dial right now. This was the first time in years she and Marci had gone more than a day or two without speaking on purpose. She felt as if a part of her was missing.

She dialed Marci and then hung up before the first ring. *Can you honestly say you ever cared about anyone more than you care about yourself?* Suzanne had always thought she did care about others. Wasn't half her life spent in service of charity organizations? *Paid service,* her brain reminded her. She volunteered a few times a year at a women's shelter, too. But was that the same as truly caring?

These musings were interrupted when the phone in her hand buzzed suddenly, startling her almost off the pool chair. "Miss Hamilton?" said a soft, unfamiliar voice. "This is Kate Burke."

"Oh, hello, Kate," Suzanne said. "I thought you were out of the country?"

"I am," Kate said. "I'll be flying back Sunday. We're in the hotel today, though, and it's raining, so I had a few minutes. The kids are all watching movies downstairs."

"Ah," said Suzanne. Then, uncertainly, "What can I do for you?"

"Oh, um, I just wanted . . ." The voice was sweet and a little nervous sounding. "I wanted to just say how much I am looking forward to meeting you and to thank you for planning our wedding at the last minute. I know it must seem like such a small event by your standards."

"Don't be silly," Suzanne said reassuringly. "I'm very happy to be doing it, and I'm honored that you chose me."

"Thank you," Kate said. "Um, I talked to my brother earlier, and he thought it would

168

be good if we met at the cabin, because that's where the wedding will be? There will be lots of people there this week, music people, planning for the summer tour, including my fiancé, Jeff. Jeff Wendell. He's Dylan's promoter — did Dylan tell you? Anyway, it could be fun, if that's convenient for you?"

"So, would you want me to come up for a day?"

"Well, you can stay for a few days, if you want," Kate said. "It's a very pretty place."

Suzanne hesitated. Of course, there was nothing keeping her in Atlanta at the moment, no reason she shouldn't leave town. But something about being thrown into Dylan's world and being stuck there made her uneasy. Still, it seemed ridiculous to refuse.

Before she could answer, however, Kate jumped back in. "I'm so sorry. I told Dylan it would be better for me to come to you in Atlanta, Miss Hamilton. Please don't feel obligated to come all the way to Tennessee. I'm sure you are busy."

"Not at all, Kate. I'd love to come. I was just . . . checking my calendar. Can someone e-mail me directions?"

"Dylan said he can send a car for you, Miss Hamilton."

"That's okay. I'll drive myself. And Kate?"

"Yes, ma'am?"

"Please, call me Suzanne. 'Miss Hamilton' makes me feel about a hundred years old."

The tinkling laugh on the other end of the line sounded genuine, if a little marred by transatlantic static. "Sure thing, Miss — um, Suzanne."

"I'll see you next week, Kate. Safe travels."

She returned downstairs to the condo, where she paced several miles around her living room, until she summoned the courage to call William's parents to ask about him. Her heart pounded as she dialed, blood echoing in her ears while the phone rang on the other end. It turned out to be anticlimactic, however, when she got the Fitzgeralds' answering machine and William Sr.'s long, rich drawl asking her to leave a message.

She did so, with a bit of hesitation, trying to sound as chipper as possible: "Hi, Mr. and Mrs. Fitzgerald. It's Suzanne Hamilton. I was just — I was just thinking about William and wondering how he was doing. I thought I would call to say hello. If you could just pass on the message at your convenience, that would be great."

She left her number, thanked them, and

hung up. She could only guess whether they would relay the message and, if they did, whether he would call her back. Ten years was a lot of water under the bridge, but Suzanne's mother had gathered over the years, through the club grapevine, that resentments were still going strong.

13

By Friday evening, Suzanne was seriously contemplating whether she might actually go insane in her condo. After being cooped up alone all week, her desire for human interaction was beginning to outweigh her fear. What was she going to do? Stay locked in her apartment forever? She remembered years ago, she and Marci had sneaked into a scary movie, in which Sigourney Weaver played a woman with severe agoraphobia who couldn't leave her apartment. Even then, it had sounded like the worst kind of hell to Suzanne. She didn't even like wearing the same pair of shoes for too long, and she had not left the building in five days.

She had received an e-mail from Yvette with directions to Dylan's cabin in Tennessee, along with a nondisclosure agreement with dire warnings if she were to reveal its location to any member of the media. The e-mail had suggested she arrive around three on Tuesday afternoon to meet with Kate at four.

"Dinners at the cabin are informal," Yvette had written. "I think you will find that jeans and a comfortable blouse will be sufficient and appropriate. You may wish to bring a sweater, considering evenings in the mountains can be chilly. Shorts and T-shirts are acceptable for daytime wear. You'll have a room in the guesthouse. Please plan to stay until as late as Friday."

Yvette had missed her calling as a tour organizer, Suzanne thought. She suddenly had a clear mental image of the mousy little woman hustling tourists on and off an enormous bus, reminding them that they had two hours on their own before a buffet lunch and a stop at the gift shop.

Staying "until as late as Friday" was longer than Suzanne anticipated staying at the "cabin," which apparently was large enough to have a guesthouse, and she thought about telling Yvette this. Under what normal circumstances was a wedding planner required to spend days on end with the family of the bride in Nowhere, Tennessee?

These aren't normal circumstances, she thought. *Be gracious. Maybe you can get the plans taken care of and sneak out of there by late Wednesday.* She made a mental note to have Chad call her a couple of times with pretend emergencies to give her an out if she needed it. He'd called a few times to see how she was doing, sounding almost as listless and lost as she was. Maybe Chad's doing her a favor on a coffee break from his new job would make them both feel better.

A mixture of fear and relief washed over her when she heard a sudden, emphatic knock at the door late in the afternoon. She took the phone with her to the door and peered nervously through the peephole. Never in her life had she been so happy to see the face on the other side.

"I hope you don't mind the intrusion," Rebecca said in her usual haughty tone. "But I know given your . . . er, circumstances . . . I thought maybe you wouldn't mind."

Normally this kind of jab from Rebecca made Suzanne's blood boil. After the past few weeks, however, she was too beat down to be bothered by condescension. She could accept an offer of friendship from wherever it came. "I don't mind, Bec. Come in. Please."

Rebecca looked surprised at this reception but smiled broadly as she entered. "Suzie," she said with intensity, gripping Suzanne's hands. "How. Are. You?"

"I'm okay, really," Suzanne said. "Mostly just bored."

"That's why I'm here," Rebecca trilled. "I talked to Marci, and she mentioned your little . . . tiff. I do hate seeing best friends fight so. I'd love to help get you two back together. But you both have always been stubborn as mules."

This much was true. In part, Suzanne could tell, Rebecca was enjoying the fact that the rift between her and Marci left a space for Rebecca to become more important to both of them. She did seem a little sorry, though, for their sadness. Suzanne wondered vaguely what Rebecca did with herself when there was no drama to keep her busy meddling.

Come to think of it, she was actually surprised Marci had confided in Rebecca, after Rebecca's attempt to claim Jake for herself a few years before. Marci must've been pretty lonely, too.

"How is she?" Suzanne asked.

"Okay," Rebecca said. "She seems like she has more energy this week. Not as tired as the early part of the pregnancy. She misses her best friend, though."

"Yeah," Suzanne said, looking at the floor. "I bet she's giving Jake fits."

"Probably," Rebecca muttered. "I don't know."

When Suzanne glanced up, she saw that Rebecca had now looked away, feigning interest in something in the kitchen. Her face was red and blotchy, an appearance Suzanne recognized from her own countenance of late. For the first time ever, it occurred to Suzanne that Rebecca might actually have been in *love* with Jake. It didn't excuse her behavior, of course, but it did make Suzanne sad for her.

"So what brings you over today?" she asked cheerily, hoping that a subject change would help them both.

"Marci told me what happened. I thought you could use an evening out. Maybe a reason to shower?" She glanced at Suzanne's disheveled hair and sloppy clothes with an attempt at a teasing smile.

Suzanne had to admit she didn't look her best. Normally meticulous in the extreme about her appearance, she had been letting things slide since her self-imprisonment began. Going out was certainly tempting, but . . .

"You can't hide here forever, Suzanne." Rebecca's tone was matter-of-fact and firm. Motherly. "The Suzanne I know is many things, but a coward isn't one of them. I've never seen you let anyone bully you before, and I don't see why this guy should get the better of you."

Immediately, she knew Rebecca was right. She had not realized until that moment that she had been hiding out, cowering in her pajamas and self-pity. This wasn't like her.

"Give me ten minutes," she told Rebecca, and headed off to the shower.

They went to the Mexican restaurant down the street. In her heart, Suzanne knew that Manuel was not on the list of stalker suspects, but she wanted to face him anyway. They had not seen each other much at all since they stopped hooking up a few months ago — when he started dating his new girlfriend — and when she did go into the restaurant, she always chose a time when it was crowded so he wouldn't feel pressure to make polite conversation. If he noticed her, he'd wave politely and comp her drinks, but that was all the communication they had.

Tonight, she and Rebecca got a table close to the bar, and Suzanne did not request a change. The place was crowded, but Manuel gave her a nod as he poured tequila shots. She smiled back as she and Rebecca took their seats. *No way it's him.* She was almost positive.

"So you come here a lot?" Rebecca asked, not missing the silent exchange.

"Yeah," Suzanne said. "It's close by. And the food's good."

"I could see that," Rebecca said lightly, with an appraising look at Manuel. He was a good-looking guy, Suzanne conceded. He was smart and funny, and their occasional hours together had been enjoyable, if a bit on the primal side. A memory floated to the surface: following him, tipsy and giggling, hand in hand, to the cramped office in the back of the restaurant. So why hadn't they ever actually dated? Something told her Manuel would have been open to the idea, but he had never approached her with it.

The two women ordered a pitcher of margaritas, chips, and dinner. Rebecca chattered happily about her job as a flight attendant. She was always name-dropping about the people — hip-hop artists, producers, actors — she met in first class on the well-traveled route from Los Angeles to Atlanta. As distasteful as this was to Suzanne, she listened, smiling and even gasping in awe when appropriate. It was good to get out, whatever the reason, and it was nice to have something to think about other than her wretched life.

They were halfway through dinner when

Manuel stopped by the table, surprising Suzanne completely. "Hi, ladies. Everything all right?"

"Fantastic," Rebecca said. "This green chili sauce is heavenly."

"Thanks, it's house-made," he said to Rebecca. He turned with feigned casualness to Suzanne. "Haven't seen you around in a while, stranger." He pushed a foot gently at Suzanne's chair, like an adolescent flirting in the school cafeteria.

"I know, I've been . . . busy," she finished lamely. "Did I hear correctly, though, that you're off the market? Dating someone special, are you?"

"Engaged, actually," he said, and appeared to be watching Suzanne for a response. She held onto the big smile she'd plastered across her face, so he turned to Rebecca conversationally. "Getting married in December."

"Congratulations," Rebecca said. She raised an eyebrow at Suzanne, calling attention to the fact that Suzanne should say the same.

"Oh!" She came to herself. "Of course, congratulations, Manny. That's wonderful. Really."

She stood abruptly and wrapped the restaurant owner in a warm but awkward

179

embrace. The smell of him was familiar and oddly comforting. She found that while her happiness for him was genuine, there was a twinge of sadness, too. *Sad for what?* she asked herself. *You're going to miss having sex behind the bar of a deserted Mexican restaurant at two in the morning?*

"Thanks," Manuel said, guiding her gently back to her seat. "I'm very happy. It's good to get married."

He looked at Suzanne when he said this. She saw an intensity in his soft brown eyes that she had never noticed. In the space of a heartbeat, she realized three things: One, that Manuel had loved her once. Two, that the door on such an opportunity was solidly and irrevocably closed; he had moved on. And, three, that Manuel was absolutely not her stalker.

"Cross that one off the list," she muttered under her breath, after Manuel had politely taken leave and informed them that their entire check was on the house.

"The list?" Rebecca asked.

"Nothing," said Suzanne dismissively. She filled each of their glasses to the rim from the pitcher of margaritas. But Rebecca's inquiring look remained. Suzanne shook her head. "You wouldn't understand."

Rebecca lifted her glass in a salute, took a

sizable sip, and put it down again. "Try me."

They staggered back to Suzanne's apartment arm in arm, singing. Barely 10:30, it felt like the end of a long night drinking and dancing. *We* are *getting old,* Suzanne thought.

"I was wondering what this was!" Rebecca said, swaying in the dining room in front of the grid.

"Mmm-hmm," Suzanne answered, digging in her pantry for something chocolate.

"So is this just a list of people who might be stalking you, or everyone you've ever dated?"

"Well," Suzanne answered from deep inside the pantry, disappointed to find that what she had thought was a bag of Oreos was actually a blue bag of potato chips. "It started as just potential stalkers, but the police said people I'd dumped would be the first people to consider. Then, when I started making the list, I decided to include everyone. I thought it might help me figure out what I want in a relationship."

Rebecca seemed to consider this for a while, scanning the grid and muttering the names of guys and reasons Suzanne had stopped seeing each one, like a spell. She waved away Suzanne's proffered potato chips and looked at her. "Did you figure it out?"

"What? The stalker?"

"No. What you want."

"Oh, that. No. I guess I found a long list of things I don't want, so that's a start, right?"

"Is it?" Rebecca asked.

It had not occurred to Suzanne to question this reasoning. "Well, how else do you figure it out, besides trial and error? Eliminating what doesn't work."

Rebecca made a noncommittal sound.

"And on the positive side, there's William," Suzanne said. "All this led me to think maybe I made a mistake letting go of him."

"Isn't he the one who proposed to you? The country club guy? I thought you turned him down and he never spoke to you again."

Suzanne reddened, trying to ignore what she thought might have been a note of satisfaction in Rebecca's voice. "Yeah, but I hope that's water under the bridge now. I mean, it's been so long."

"You hope? You haven't *talked* to him yet?"

"No, I can't seem to track him down yet, but I did find his parents, and I think —"

"Suze," Rebecca said. "How on earth do you know you made a mistake breaking up with him if you haven't even *seen* him? What if he's married now, or gay or something?"

"He is *not* gay," Suzanne said emphatically. "That was not the problem."

Rebecca laughed. She crossed the big open room to the couch and flung herself on it with a deep sigh. "You know what? I always resented you."

This was a sobering change of subject. Suzanne had felt it over the years, of course, and had never been Rebecca's biggest fan, either, but hearing it stated so plainly was a little jarring. Rebecca's face clouded as she concentrated on her words in a way that only a very drunk person can. "I never told you this. No, I didn't. Never said it outloud–out loud. You know? But I felt it. I always felt like you had everything I wanted — a name people respect, money, connections. All handed to you. It was like you were born into the life *I* was supposed to have."

Rebecca's lip curled into an unattractive snarl as she said this last bit, and she was staring at the floor with a deep, absorbing bitterness. She seemed temporarily unaware Suzanne was still in the room. A thought flickered into Suzanne's head: *Could it be Rebecca? Is it possible that I've just gotten*

183

smashed with someone who tried to kill me and brought her back to my apartment, alone on a Friday night?

As though sensing Suzanne's thoughts, Rebecca turned to her. "I've always liked you," she said baldly. "But I kind of hated you, too. You could have been a legacy at the sorority I'd always dreamed of being in, and you didn't even rush. Your mom had to *drag* you kicking and screaming into the Junior League, where you skipped provisional status somehow. Meanwhile, I had to scrounge for a sponsor to get me in. Plus, I've been stuck on the thrift shop committee for three years . . ."

"I didn't realize —" Suzanne started.

"It's okay," Rebecca said. "I just need to say this to you. After all these years, I want you to understand. My dad was a mailman in a small town; my mom was a housewife. My parents were *pissed* when I called to tell them that I was staying in Atlanta. They could care less about the Junior League. They said I was acting like I thought I was better than them."

They had known each other for more than fifteen years, and yet Suzanne felt she was somehow seeing Rebecca for the first time. "I don't fit in anywhere. When I go home to Alabama, I'm a snob. And here, I'm nobody.

184

Even with you and Marci."

"That's not —"

"No, it's okay. I know I'm not easy to be friends with," Rebecca said, nodding in vigorous agreement with herself and wiping tears with the back of her sleeve. "And I don't want pity. It's actually a relief, tonight. I've spent so long trying to be you and wishing I had what you had, and now . . ."

Suzanne turned to look at the dining room wall, where Rebecca was pointing with an expansive wave of her arm. After a moment, it dawned. Suzanne concluded for her. "Now you realize I'm just as fucked up as the next person."

Rebecca nodded, wiping more tears. "No offense."

Suzanne sat down hard on the floor, right where she was, and began to laugh. Rebecca looked at her hesitantly and then began to chuckle through snot and tears. The soggy noises that resulted struck them both as funny, too, and soon they were both helpless to stop — Rebecca rolling on the couch; Suzanne, on the floor.

When the laughter subsided, neither of them had much else to say, and a small measure of their usual awkwardness returned. But Suzanne flipped on the TV to *Project Runway,* plopped on the couch next

185

to Rebecca, and rumpled her hair.

They watched in companionable silence as the contestants tried to make evening wear out of the contents of a recycling bin. When Suzanne stood a little while later, she covered the snoring Rebecca with her favorite throw before wobbling to her own bed. Drifting off easily, Suzanne realized it was the first time in years she had let anyone other than Marci sleep over at her place.

14

Following the instructions Yvette had e-mailed to her, Suzanne set out from Atlanta at 10:00 A.M. and arrived in the surreal little vacation town of Gatlinburg, Tennessee, a little more than four hours later.

The sudden hustle and bustle of the packed little tourist town was overwhelming after the long, peaceful drive through the Great Smoky Mountains National Park. She had to pee by then but didn't see a convenient place to pull over. Gatlinburg appeared to be one of those places where tourists parked their cars for the whole day and crowded into store after store, buying trinkets and ice cream and T-shirts for hours on end. There seemed to be nowhere to pull in for a minute to use the restroom in exchange for a bottled-water purchase. Yvette had mentioned that the cabin was closer to Gatlinburg than anywhere else, so Suzanne opted to wait, rather than pay to use a parking deck and search frantically for a public restroom. Perhaps there would be someplace clean along the way.

Dylan's cabin, in fact, was a solid twenty minutes into the mountains from Gatlinburg, in an area where her phone never got a signal strong enough to support her GPS. Suzanne cautiously followed a series of long and curving two-lane roads that scaled gradually and consistently upward. They were not well-signed, which led her to constantly question whether she had missed a turn or was on the wrong road altogether. She even turned around once to go back to the last intersection and make sure she had followed the directions correctly. Her cell phone had only spotty reception up here, and as she passed hand-painted signs warning dourly against trespassing, she wondered what she would do if she really did become lost. Or when her need to pee became a true emergency, as it shortly would.

The route eventually narrowed to a seemingly endless high-country lane surrounded by dense forest on either side. Houses — or at least mailboxes and gravel driveways leading into the thick — popped up every quarter mile or so, becoming more spread out as the road became rougher, and civilization seemed increasingly farther away.

To Suzanne, every grove of trees looked like a rest stop at this point, but there was hardly any shoulder on which to pull off to get out of the car. Even if there had been a place to stop, something about peeing in the woods on her way to see a celebrity bride just didn't seem right. So Suzanne danced in her seat, deeply regretting the choice to pass up an earlier gas station that didn't look very sanitary on the outside, and prayed that Yvette's directions would not steer her wrong.

The mailbox at the top of the cabin's driveway was unremarkable, but the street number was clearly signed, and the gravel drive freshly maintained — wider than most she'd seen. She followed it for thirty yards or so to a large, sturdy iron gate that crossed the drive at a creek. The gate was open, the tiny guardhouse empty. She wondered whether it had been installed just for Dylan or whether he had purchased the cabin from someone else who valued his privacy. As she crossed the creek, thinking almost exclusively of her overinflated bladder, Suzanne realized that keeping the press and other interested onlookers at bay for Kate's wedding would be her responsibility. *Sheesh.*

She was not sure if the driveway was *actually* ten miles long or if it simply felt that way to someone in urgent need of a bathroom, but it twisted and turned up through the mountain woods for quite some time. Eventually, it left the larger trees behind, emerging into the clear top layer of the mountain, where bare rocks were numerous and only scraggly little trees had a foothold. Finally, the path crested over a rise, revealing the house tucked snugly into the side of the mountain on the other side amid a few trees and returning her gratefully to civilization.

It turned out that the place Dylan and his entourage referred to as a "cabin" was actually more of a lodge, and a big one at that. At least two stories from the front side, the gray wood was trimmed in white, and lots of big, clean windows added to the striking first impression. Both the ground floor and the upper level had wide wraparound porches where ceiling fans turned lazily in the mountain breeze. She would later learn that there was even more to the house than that, including an enormous terrace level beneath the first story, built into the side of the mountain, and a back deck the size of her condo that jutted over the slope of the mountain behind the house.

But she could be amazed by all of it later. For now, all she could do was leave her car in front of the house and skitter up to the front door. Yvette answered her knock promptly — *thank God* — and showed her to the closest powder room with an air of reluctance, as though someone without enough foresight to manage her urinary tract was obviously a poor choice to plan a wedding.

When she emerged from the bathroom, feeling as if she might float away with relief, Yvette led her into the den, which was actually a two-story great room with polished wood walls, a double-sided stone fireplace, and a full wall of windows looking over the green mountains beyond. Several people were in the den, lounging on assorted couches watching TV or playing checkers, and two guys were picking softly at guitars in one corner, murmuring to each other.

She recognized one of these last two as Dylan, but he was absorbed in conversation and did not notice her. Some of the others looked familiar from the Braves game and the night at the High. She spotted Misty, sprawled on one of the couches, painting her nails and looking bored. Next to her were two women Suzanne recognized as a pair of Dylan's older sisters. Her humiliating experience at the High came back to her in flashes. Suzanne's stomach churned, and she fought hard against the fervent desire to turn and run back out the door.

"Wait here," Yvette murmured softly, leaving Suzanne to stand uncomfortably on the edge of the room. A girl with long light-brown hair was curled into an overstuffed chair on the opposite side of the den, near one of the colossal windows. She had a blanket pulled over her and was reading a well-worn leather-bound book. Yvette touched the girl's shoulder, and the she looked up to meet Suzanne's eye and give her a broad, endearing smile.

Suzanne waved awkwardly and followed the girl's beckoning motions to meet her in the next room. As she made her way across the back of the den, she glanced at Dylan, who nodded perfunctorily in acknowledgment of her presence. As he turned his gaze back to his fingers working on the acoustic guitar, she thought she saw the corner of a crooked smile.

15

The kitchen was open and sunny and had soft yellow walls, glossy white cabinets, and light wooden furniture. The room was at the back corner of the cabin, which meant large windows let in daylight on two walls. Kate and Suzanne sat across from each other on stools at the breakfast bar, going over the binders and Suzanne's notes. Yvette flitted in and out, asking periodically whether they needed anything and pausing to look at whatever Suzanne was writing.

It struck Suzanne as odd that a soft-spoken, sweet girl like Kate would command so much power over an established professional in her forties like Yvette. Certainly it was not owing to any outlandish demands on Kate's part. As they went over Kate's expectations together, Suzanne found that Dylan's younger sister was meek about her opinions and preferences almost to a fault.

"I don't know, Suzanne, what do you think?" Kate was saying for the hundredth time in the past hour.

"Well, it's really up to you, sweetie," Suzanne said. "Personally, I think with an outdoor wedding it's better to go with the nicer white plastic folding chairs rather than the ones with fabric covering. That way, if it rains . . ."

"Of course," Kate said. "That's so smart. It's the kind of thing I would never think of."

Suzanne put a hand gently on Kate's to get her attention. "Sweetie, ease up on yourself, okay? I wouldn't have thought of it, either, except that I had a hundred and fifty black velvet chairs get soaked right before an annual meeting once."

"Really?" Kate said.

"Really," Suzanne said. "It was a nightmare."

"What happened?"

"This advertising firm wanted a black-tie meeting slash celebration, but outdoors. We had a tent over the dance floor and music and stuff, but the president wanted to give the speech under the stars for some reason — some 'reach for the stars' theme or something, I forget . . . Anyway, we were all set up, and there was a sudden rainstorm. It only lasted ten minutes, but that's all it takes. My assistant and I spent thirty minutes trying to fix it with hair dryers, until we realized the velvet chair covers were ruined. We only had two hours until the keynote speech, the chair rental place was closed for the night, and it was supposed to be this big elegant deal . . ."

"What did you do?" Kate asked, her eyes wide, as though Suzanne were telling her she'd been present for the Cuban missile crisis.

Suzanne laughed at the memory. "It sounds crazy, but I had just done a huge event the weekend before called Couches for Kids, where people donated their old sofas to a children's-shelter thrift store. It was sponsored by a big furniture company, people got a coupon for donating, yadda yadda . . ."

Suzanne could feel herself becoming animated as she recounted it. Something about an impending crisis had always energized her. She was at her best in those types of situations, and her resourcefulness under pressure set her apart from other event planners. "Anyway, I called my contact at the shelter, and it turned out there were still a ton of couches on one of their trucks. So Chad ran to a fabric store and bought every yard of black fabric he could find, while the guys from the shelter brought all the couches out to the venue and set them up instead of chairs. We even put some floor lamps around and hooked them up to extension cords, right in the middle of this field."

"How funny!" Kate said.

"Yeah, and the effect was actually pretty spectacular," Suzanne said, grinning in spite of herself. "It actually made the *AJC*. There was a wave of outdoor couch parties in Atlanta the whole summer after that. The firm's president was so happy with the publicity of his event he made a big donation to the children's shelter."

"That's awesome!" Kate said. "Sounds like it worked out even better because of the rain."

Something about the sweet twenty-four-year-old's unadulterated admiration checked Suzanne's own enthusiasm. Last week, both the children's shelter and the advertising firm had fired her, very politely and apologetically.

A reputation takes years to establish, Suzanne's mother reminded her, *but only one night to ruin forever.* Of course, Mom had been talking about one night in the backseat of a Buick, not a public debacle at a hallowed institution of art, but the principle still held.

"That's exactly why I recommended her, sis," said a voice behind Suzanne. "She's kind of a creative genius, at least for a blue-blooded city girl."

She turned to see Dylan entering the kitchen behind her. Without his guitar, she could see that he was wearing old jeans with paint splatters on them and a beat-up Ramones T-shirt. "I know she'll come up with something as unique as you are." He walked behind Kate and tousled her hair affectionately on his way to the refrigerator.

Kate threw an elbow at him in an unconscious gesture of playfulness. Suzanne imagined this was the same basic interaction they had been having since they were kids. Dylan fished a few beer bottles out of the fridge and gestured toward Suzanne on his way back to the den. "Hey, when you ladies are done in here, I need to talk to you for a second."

"Me?" Suzanne asked.

"Yup."

She and Kate exchanged shrugs. "Well, I guess let's get back to it," Suzanne said when he was gone.

"Yeah, Jeff will be back soon," Kate said. "We're going to town for dinner. Trying to get all the time we can before the summer tour starts."

"So he travels with Dylan?"

"Yes. Basically, as soon as the wedding is over, they're all hitting the road. It's a short tour this year, though, which is nice. We're taking a honeymoon in September."

"Why not get married then?" Suzanne asked. "I'm sure it's lovely here in the fall, with the leaves changing on the mountain."

Kate went scarlet. "It's a long story," she said, fidgeting with a scrap of lace.

Suzanne instinctively changed the subject. "It must be hard, having him away so much."

"Well, yeah, it is. But I have my parents and my older sisters. Half-sisters. You know, Dylan and I are full siblings and then there are two older sisters on each side."

"Yes, I'd heard that. I saw two of your sisters at the —" she hesitated, watching Kate's response. "At the gala a few weeks ago."

If Kate knew about the incident, it didn't show on her pretty features. "That was probably Sherrie and Amber. They're both here now, actually. They're the single ones, the ones you usually see . . . in the limelight."

The ones making asses of themselves and

getting plastered all over the tabloids, Suzanne corrected mentally. But then, who was she to talk?

"I love them and everything," Kate said. "They're Mom's kids and they lived with us when I was young. But I'm actually closer to my other sisters, Francine and Carla. They're both married with kids. I have great nieces and nephews!"

"Dylan mentioned you do the choir tour as a chaperone. You must really like kids," Suzanne said conversationally.

Kate nodded. "Well, those are big teenage kids, and they're great, but I like the little ones more."

"Do you get to see them much?"

"Francine lives in Memphis with her husband, so I see her little boys pretty often. Carla teaches at the American School in Madrid — her husband is Spanish — so I don't see her and her family as much. I'm spending a few weeks with them this summer, though. I'm really excited."

Kate's face, however, did not reflect that excitement. At least not at this second. Her pallor was suddenly pale and green, especially in contrast to the deep blush from just moments ago. "Kate? You okay?"

"Yes, I'm fine. Would you excuse me, though? Can we talk again later? Or tomorrow?" Without waiting for an answer, Kate rushed out of the room. Suzanne heard quick footsteps on the stairs and the rapid slam of a door above.

Had it not been for Marci, she might not have put it together. Having recent experience, however, watching morning sickness in action — which did not at all confine itself to mornings and therefore had a stupid name — Suzanne thought she knew why Kate did not want to wait until fall to get married. She smiled to herself and collected the materials back into the binders, making herself a note to look up all the foods pregnant women weren't supposed to have, so she could keep them out of the wedding meal.

When she had everything neatly stacked on the counter, she wandered out to the den looking for Dylan, and found that almost everyone had vacated the large room. Yvette alone sat on the abandoned couch, working away on her laptop, with three phones and several manila file folders lying next to her. She smiled perfunctorily when Suzanne entered.

"Um, I think Dylan wanted to see me?" Suzanne said.

"They went downstairs," Yvette said, closing her laptop. "I'll take you down there. I

200

might as well give you the tour and show you to your room while I'm at it."

"Great."

The house was as spacious on the inside as Suzanne had imagined from the outside. The second story was in the shape of a fat U, wrapping around the open den downstairs with a landing railed by solid polished pine. Six guest bedrooms were upstairs, each pair taking up one side of the house and sharing an adjoining full bath between them. Yvette opened the door to an empty room at one end of the hall, saying, "Dylan's parents will stay here when they arrive tomorrow, so I'll just show you this one so you get the idea."

Large for a guest bedroom, especially in a cabin, the picture windows looked out on two sides toward the wilderness beyond. The furnishings were rustic but pretty, and the walls boasted pictures of Dylan and his five sisters at various ages. In one corner was a pet bed, and Suzanne remembered that Dylan's mother had a small dog she took with her everywhere. This was obviously the room his parents always stayed in.

"Do you spend a lot of time here?" Suzanne asked curiously.

"Well, sometimes," Yvette said. "Dylan comes here for a week or two at a time at different times of the year. It's a good place to get away and work. Quiet, but room enough for lots of people. The guys wrote the entire *Fireflies* album here. My room is in the guesthouse with yours. I'm not always with them when they're here, but when they need me, it's easier to be on the premises than at a hotel in town."

For the first time, Suzanne wondered what kind of personal life Yvette had. What did she do when she was off the clock? Was she ever off the clock?

Yvette cocked her head to the side, listening, and Suzanne thought she discerned what *might* be the sound of vomiting from the bathroom door. *Kate.* Suzanne coughed loudly to try to cover the sound and then put her hand on Yvette's shoulder. "What about the master?" she asked, searching for a distraction.

"It's downstairs," Yvette said. "Though obviously we can't go in *there.*"

Obviously.

Still, Yvette had taken the bait and led Suzanne back downstairs. They covered the den, an office/library, and what was clearly intended as a dining room but was used to house an assortment of music equipment. "This can all be out before the wedding," Yvette said. "Between the two main rooms and the library, I think you could seat forty-five inside easily. The longest part of the back deck will accommodate two ten-by-twenty tents, I believe, which would be another forty. I think Kate is only planning to invite a hundred people, so . . . Well, you're the expert; I'll let you do your own measuring."

Suzanne had to admit she was impressed with Yvette's attention to detail. "That's great. Thank you for your thoughts."

As they passed the door to the master bedroom, which Yvette indicated by a quick wave, curiosity about it struck Suzanne. How did he decorate his bedroom? Did he even do it himself? Was it neat or messy? Did Misty have her suitcase full of tiny shorts in there, too, or was she in one of the bedrooms upstairs? How did Dylan's parents feel about her being here?

You're a fine one to judge, she scolded. Still, these thoughts made her surprisingly uncomfortable, and she pushed them away with a furrowed brow.

They were going out the back door onto the deck, which was actually more like the deck of a cruise ship than a house, much less a cabin. At least twenty feet wide from the house at the narrowest point, it wrapped halfway around the house on one side and tapered off at the garage on the other. Several bikini-clad bodies lay facedown on chairs at the sunnier side of the deck, where a radio played music Suzanne couldn't distinguish.

The deck also had a couple of narrow piers — it was the only way Suzanne could describe them — that went several yards over the mountainside to end in smaller observation decks above the trees. Both of these satellite decks had benches around the sides, and one even had a little gazebo overhead. It reminded Suzanne of the movie *Crouching Tiger, Hidden Dragon,* where people walked in the treetops.

"You can see the guesthouse, where you and I will stay, from here." Yvette led her to the side of the deck next to the master bedroom and pointed down to a small cottage a hundred yards or so from the main house, tucked neatly into the woods.

As they turned to go back inside, Suzanne kept her eyes away from the master bedroom windows, afraid that either Yvette would think she was nosy or that she would see something she didn't want to see. An intrusive image appeared in her mind of Dylan, tangled in a white sheet and nothing else, snoring peacefully, sprawled across an old-fashioned bed made of pine logs.

No, no, no, she said to the Dylan in her head. *This is inappropriate. You're a client, and I won't think of you that way. Go away.* She willed herself to concentrate on Yvette, to hear the words she was saying. ". . . didn't think you would mind staying with me out in the guesthouse. I hate to intrude on the kids' fun, don't you? It's very roomy, and at least we won't be kept awake at all hours."

She returned to reality as the implication of Yvette's words registered. The chipmunk-like little manager considered herself and Suzanne peers, while Dylan and his bandmates and friends were a younger generation. *But I'm barely thirty-three,* she wanted to protest, realizing that this would have been incredibly offensive to Yvette if she said it out loud.

"I know Dylan wants to see you," Yvette said, "so we'll just stop in down there first and I'll have someone get your bags to the guesthouse. Okay?"

"You have servants here?" Suzanne asked. It felt as if she was in a Jane Austen novel.

The response was a high-pitched, nasal laugh that Suzanne had learned meant Yvette thought you were an idiot. "Of course not. Don't be silly. We have a cleaning service, of course, but no. Dylan's road manager is here, though, and he's very nice. Considering his job is getting thousands of pounds of equipment from one place to the next every night, I thought maybe he could handle your little bags."

"Right, of course. Sorry."

Yvette opened the door to return inside and then turned back, leaning close to Suzanne and whispering confidentially, "Just don't tip him, okay? I'm sure that's what *you're* used to, but he would find that insulting."

Suzanne supposed she deserved that one. She nodded obediently, resisting the urge to respond, and followed Yvette back through the den and down the stairs to . . . Guy Heaven.

Nearly as big as either of the other stories, the basement had a bar area, pool table, workout room, rehearsal space, and even a small recording studio. More couches and overstuffed chairs were scattered about, plus four or five flat-screen TVs. Sliding glass doors opened out to a shady concrete patio beneath part of the huge deck upstairs. On one half of the patio, there was a large grill and two wooden picnic tables. On the other was a screened-in porch housing a ten-person hot tub, with a sliding window so that someone at the bar in the main room could hand drinks directly out to the soak-ers. No wonder Dylan came here as often as he could.

Yvette led Suzanne around, poking her head into various rooms, but they did not find Dylan. The rest of the band were play-ing around in the rehearsal space, with a few girls Suzanne didn't recognize looking on and giggling wildly as the guys changed the lyrics of popular songs to raunchy parodies. Three or four other guys were playing video games in the main living area, and Suzanne noticed that at least two of them had cups of spit-out dipped tobacco. *Ugh. Disgusting.*

In the workout room, one of Dylan's sisters was on the treadmill, yelling at someone on her Bluetooth headset. They found another sister outside in the hot tub, with the guy Suzanne recognized as her date at the museum, and, of course, Misty. All three were drinking the same kind of beer Dylan had brought out of the kitchen earlier, and there was a fourth bottle on the ledge near Misty.

"Hi, Sherrie. Seen him?" Yvette asked. *So Amber was the one in the workout room,* Su-zanne noted to herself.

Sherrie shook her head just as the guy next to her dived elaborately between her floating breasts and nuzzled wildly. "Roger!" she squealed. "Stop, my bathing suit is coming off!" Although most people who faced this unfortunate situation would probably duck back into the water to hide themselves, Sherrie apparently thought the best remedy was to *stand and hop* away from Roger toward the side of the hot tub nearest the house, holding her useless bathing suit top in her hands as she did.

Suzanne glanced and saw that the guys inside had paused the video game to watch this little production with wide grins. When Sherrie took refuge from Roger by wedging herself behind Misty, using the petite blonde's enormous breasts as a shield from him, the guys inside forgot about their game entirely and began nudging one another and pointing.

Maybe Yvette is right. Maybe I am too old for this.

With an almost imperceptible eye roll, Yvette retreated from the porch and Suzanne followed. "Kids," she muttered. "Well, at least I can show you your room, and we'll come back for him."

That, however, turned out not to be necessary, because they were halfway down the stone path to the cottage when they ran smack into Dylan. Suzanne noted that he was not in wet swim trunks but still wearing the jeans and Ramones shirt she had seen him in earlier.

"There you are," he said to Suzanne. "I've been looking for you."

"We've been looking for *you,"* Yvette put in cheerily. "I gave Suzanne the tour, so she's ready for whatever you need from her."

The three of them stood awkwardly on the path for a moment, until Dylan reached for Suzanne's elbow. "Let's go sit down."

Yvette moved to follow them toward the cottage, and Dylan stopped her. "Could you wait for us in the main house, please, Yvette? This is confidential."

She looked surprised but said nothing and returned toward the sound of splashing and giggling in the hot tub. Dylan guided Suzanne down the path, and she wondered whether he was going to take her into the cottage and show her the guest room himself. Against all reason, her heart pounded wildly at the thought of being alone with him in a remote cottage in the woods. *Pull yourself together, Suze.*

But these ponderings were irrelevant, because Dylan stopped at a little clearing about two-thirds of the way to the cottage and sat on a large, flat piece of granite. He motioned for her to join him. "Okay, this is

209

totally off the record," he said softly, "but there's something I need to add to the wedding plans."

The wedding plans. Of course. You imbecile.

"Kate asked me to sing," he began. "But obviously I can't do that."

"Why not?" Suzanne asked.

"No way," Dylan said, shaking his head. "Too emotional. I'll cry like a little girl. It'll sound awful. But I want to surprise her with something else."

"You two are really close, aren't you?"

He looked at her for a moment, surprised by the question. "Well, yeah. I mean, I love all my sisters, of course, but Kate . . . Kate is special to me. We've always been the closest of the siblings. She's the best person I know. Definitely the best person in my hillbilly family."

Suzanne blushed. Even a joking reference to their first encounter still made her feel ashamed. She started to say something, but he stopped her with a hand on the arm. "Relax, Scarlett. I'm just giving you shit. I think you can be done apologizing for that now."

He was grinning at her. "Anyway, the thing I need your help with is that I've arranged for Pat Green to be here and sing to Kate and Jeff as a surprise. Kate's a huge fan, and he's a friend of mine. Anyway, I can get him here, and I have a place lined up for him to stay, but I need your help figuring out how to include him in the wedding without ruining the surprise."

She could see that he was trying to contain his excitement, like a little kid with a secret. It was endearing. Just then, there was a feminine squeal from the house beyond, followed by a loud crash and the sound of breaking glass. *"Idiots,"* he muttered, getting up. "I'd better go see what that was. Thanks, Scarlett."

Suzanne decided settling in to the guesthouse was more appealing than watching whatever drama was happening up the hill unfold. She continued down the path and went in. The house was simple and quaint, particularly compared with the luxury resort above. Two bedrooms with spartan furniture flanked a tiny kitchen and a modest living area. Yvette's room was the one closest to the house, easy to spot because of the crowded desk in the corner, overflowing with papers. Suzanne found her bag at the foot of the bed in the other room, which was cool and shaded by the surrounding pine trees. The quilt underneath was clean and soft, and she collapsed into it face-first, suddenly exhausted.

She awoke in pitch-black. It took a few moments to figure out where she was, with no moonlight coming through the window. Someone, presumably Yvette, had covered her with a blanket. Otherwise, she was exactly as she'd been in the afternoon, except ravenously hungry. She fumbled for her cell phone and saw that it was 1:30 A.M. *How had she slept so long?* Her recently healed arm ached from being in the same position for several hours. She rubbed it absently and padded out to the tiny kitchen, trying to be as quiet as possible.

She found nothing in the fridge except a few ancient condiments and Yvette's weight-loss shakes. Suzanne debated briefly whether she could simply go back to sleep hungry and then exited the cottage as quietly as she could and made her way up to the main house. The lights were still on downstairs, and strains of rock music contrasted with the peaceful nighttime wilderness. She could smell charcoal and cigar smoke.

As she got close to the house, she could see the silhouette of a couple alone in the hot tub, locked in what had apparently gone beyond a simple embrace. As she passed the screened area, she heard soft moans from the water but didn't dare look more closely to figure out who it was.

The main room of the basement was complete disorder. Plastic cups were everywhere, along with greasy paper plates and wadded-up napkins. Sherrie and Amber were singing inebriated karaoke while one of Dylan's friends recorded them with his phone. *That* would be on YouTube by morning. A few of the girls who'd been admiring the band earlier were now cheering on the singing sisters, while a couple of others were passed out in various states of dishevelment on the couches. Two of Dylan's bandmates were in the rehearsal room, playing guitar with surprising sobriety. She noticed one of them wore a gold wedding band and wondered what it must be like to be married to one of these guys.

No one seemed to notice her as she picked her way to the stairway and up to the den on the main floor. This was where the cigar smoke originated. Several large windows were open to the night air as Dylan and four other guys sat around a folding table in the middle of the den playing poker. Not wanting to disturb them, she crept around the back of the room to the kitchen. She had nearly made it when Dylan's voice called out, "Miss Scarlett, in the kitchen, with a butcher knife."

She stopped and turned toward the poker table, putting on her best gracious smile. "Good evening, everyone."

"Good evening," one of the guys echoed back at her, with exaggerated affectation. He made a ridiculous bow to the friend next to him with a flourish of his hand.

The guy next to him joined in, laughing. "I trust this night finds you well, sir? Do you have any Grey Poupon?" For the hundredth time since she'd met Dylan Burke, Suzanne felt her cheeks get hot.

"Don't pay any attention to them, Miss Hamilton," said a man Suzanne recognized as Dylan's drummer. "They're just being assholes because I've taken all their money tonight."

Suzanne smiled at him. Dylan, who had not looked up from his cards, said, "There's a plate in the fridge for you. Hope you like chicken wings, because it's either that or Pop-Tarts."

She was so hungry, wings *and* Pop-Tarts sounded heavenly. She realized she had skipped lunch on the drive up and slept through dinner. "Thanks," she said.

"Don't thank me. Kate's the one who made a plate for you. But if you like the wings, I grilled them myself."

"And if I don't like them?"

"Then Eddie made them."

"Hey," Dylan's drummer retorted, "don't go blaming your culinary disasters on me. I'm a vegetarian."

Suzanne left the room to a chorus of the guys ribbing Eddie for being vegetarian, which was apparently the next best thing to wearing pink footie pajamas as far as they were concerned. She went to the kitchen and found a large plate with several chicken wings, potato salad, baked beans, and a roll, all set out neatly beneath plastic wrap. She saw the sticky note on top with "Suzanne" written in neat, feminine script. Suzanne sent a silent murmur of thanks up to the ceiling to Kate, whom she hoped was sleeping comfortably.

She popped the plate in the microwave for a few seconds and sat at the table to eat, losing herself in the simple joy of satisfying hunger. It was not long, however, before Dylan called to her. "Hey, Scarlett, no need to be antisocial. I know this ain't the country club you're used to, but we don't bite in here."

"Unless you want us to," called the Grey Poupon guy. A loud thud was followed by, "Ow! Shit, Dylan, that hurt."

She picked up her plate, hesitated for a second, and then retrieved a beer from the fridge. *When in Rome.* She settled onto the chair she'd seen Kate in earlier in the day and finished her dinner, watching the five of them play. Eddie won the next hand and spent several minutes taunting the others while Dylan went to the kitchen for more beer.

The guy she'd heard the least from tossed his chips into the center of the table. "I'm out."

"Come on, Jeff," someone said. "We won't tell your wife if you stay another hand."

"Hey," Jeff said. "She's not my wife yet, and if I don't get up there, she might change her mind about it. Then I'd be stuck married to you jerk-offs for the rest of my life."

He clapped Dylan on the shoulder. " 'Night, brother."

Dylan gave him a nod. "We'll look at the tour schedule at lunch tomorrow."

It struck Suzanne how enmeshed everyone's work and personal lives had become in this world. Jeff was Dylan's drinking buddy, promotions manager, and future brother-in-law all at once. The seriousness of running a business that sustained several families was entwined with the debauchery and abandon going on downstairs. It was little wonder that so many musicians succumbed to this lifestyle.

216

"What about you, Miss Scarlett? You play?" Suzanne looked up to see Grey Poupon gesturing to Jeff's empty seat.

"Oh, no, thank you. I'd rather just watch."

"What? They don't play Texas Hold'em at the Junior League soirees?" Dylan's crooked smile was baiting. He'd done his homework on her.

"No, we ladies prefer the classic five-card stud. You know, while we're drinking tea in the drawing room, talking about beauty magazines." Her accent dripped with exaggerated condescension, and she batted her eyelashes for effect. The guys laughed in approval.

"We can do that," Eddie said, patting Jeff's empty seat in invitation.

Why not? Suzanne thought. *What else am I going to do in the middle of the night, in the middle of nowhere?*

She won the first two hands easily, feigning beginner's luck and shock at winning. By the third hand, however, the guys had figured out she knew what she was doing. For years as a little girl, she had hidden in the butler's pantry of her parents' large colonial home and watched her father play poker with lawyers from both sides of the aisle, judges, and even a senator or two. It was a better education than all the charm classes her mother had dragged her to put together.

"Careful, boys," Eddie said as they began the fourth round. "I think we have a shark on our hands."

"I'll bet you have a professional poker player on that list of yours, eh, Scarlett?" Dylan said, sounding drunker than he had a few minutes before. He looked around seriously at the other men at the table. "See, what y'all don't know about Suzanne is, she's dated just about every kind of guy there is to date. She's got a big list of 'em. Which one of them taught you poker, Scarlett?"

Her chest tightened painfully, and she fought hard to bury the anger and hurt welling up inside. "Actually, I learned from my dad," she said, working hard to modulate her voice. She kept her eyes on his. They were a soft green, if a little red around the edges at the moment. Some emotion was behind them, but what it was, she couldn't tell.

The other guys at the table were all looking down at their cards in intense concentration, not wanting to meet either Suzanne's or Dylan's gazes. After an uncomfortable minute of silence, Dylan looked down at his cards and then dropped them facedown on the table. "I fold," he said.

"Read 'em and weep," Eddie responded, laying out a straight flush.

Suzanne didn't need to look at her cards. She knew she had a royal flush and could take the fourth hand and probably the game. "I'm out, too," she said, tossing her cards in facedown. She got up, stretched, and took her empty beer bottle toward the kitchen. "Thanks for letting me play, boys."

When she got back, Dylan had disappeared, presumably to the bedroom where Misty waited for him. The rest of them murmured and dispersed. Eddie must have had the privilege of one of the guest bedrooms, because he went upstairs. Suzanne followed the other two down to the basement. Quiet now, the three picked their way around sleeping bodies and party debris: the guys, to an air mattress that waited for them in what served as a community bedroom, and Suzanne out to the back patio to the cottage path.

The hot tub lovers were gone now, and she wondered vaguely whether they had gone their separate ways or were curled up somewhere together. Given the scene inside, she was now officially grateful to Yvette for sticking her in the guesthouse.

She was halfway down the path, using her

cell phone for a flashlight, when something made her look over her shoulder. Most of the lights were out now, but there was a faint glow coming from the master bedroom. From this angle, she couldn't tell much about the room except that it appeared to have a large poster bed, of which she could see a single ballast.

Then she noticed him, an outline in the dark, leaning against the railing next to the open bedroom door. She waved nervously and Dylan returned it, not moving otherwise. She continued on, feeling his eyes on her until she had closed and locked the cottage door behind her. When she glanced out the window a moment later, the master bedroom light was off, and she could see no one in the inky-black night.

16

Suzanne was utterly surprised when she awoke again, this time having put on pajamas and climbed under the quilt, that only a few hours had passed since she returned to the cottage. Her phone had informed her it was 3:26 A.M. when she set her alarm, and it was just after seven when she awoke. Oddly, she felt fine and was up and into her yoga pants almost immediately. Yvette must be a morning person, because she'd left a note in their tiny kitchen that she had gone into town and would return in the afternoon.

With nothing to do or eat down at the cottage, Suzanne made her way back up the hill, hoping that Kate might also be up early and that they could even finish their wedding work before noon. Suzanne was surprisingly eager to get home. Her life in Atlanta may not have been anything to be excited about, but the sense of disconnect from all reality up here at the party lodge was unsettling in its own way.

In the morning light, the lowest level of the house made for a pathetic scene. Litter was everywhere, glass was shattered by the hot tub, and an empty plastic vodka bottle floated on the water. Although some people had clearly made it to bed during the night, accompanied or otherwise, others had simply slept where they'd fallen — bodies were strewn across the floor as well as the available furniture. She was surprised that no one had curled up on the pool table.

One sad little couple had apparently passed out while attempting to make a last-ditch mistake together before the end of the night. The girl, who might have been twenty, lay on the couch with her blouse unbuttoned to reveal a lacy pink bra. The guy slept with his close-cropped head on her bare stomach, legs hanging off the end of the couch, and the little soldier who had failed to report for duty still dangling out of his open fly. Suzanne suppressed a giggle at this as she sneaked past them to the stairs.

The main floor was silent, too; without all the carnage of the night before, it was more peaceful. All the doors were still closed, so Suzanne tiptoed to the kitchen to look for Pop-Tarts and discovered that someone had already made coffee. Yvette maybe? *I seriously need to do something with my life so I can hire someone like her,* she thought as she poured a cup and went outside.

Dylan was sitting at a small patio table on the observation deck at the end of one of the piers, his back to the house. A coffee mug was standing sentinel next to him, and what looked like a legal pad was nearby, but he seemed to be simply staring into the distance. She tried to slip back into the kitchen so as not to disturb him, but there was a beer bottle she hadn't noticed at her feet. She kicked it by accident, causing a clatter on the boards. Dylan turned, put his finger to his lips dramatically, and waved her over.

"Have a seat," he said, when she got to the end of the platform. "Best one in the house." It really was breathtaking. Although you could see the mountains in the distance from nearly any window in the house, the little decks were far enough out that they gave you the feeling of floating above the forest, far from the solid ground just a hundred yards or so behind you. The view from here was nearly a full circle, and in the morning light it was a lovely combination of soft pastel sky and blue mountains covered in a deep gray mist.

223

"That's why they're called the Smokies," he said, following her gaze, without a hint of his usual condescension. "Beautiful, isn't it?"

Suzanne nodded. Her family had spent some time in the mountains as a child, but she didn't remember them being quite this awe-inspiring. She took the seat across the table from Dylan and sipped her coffee in silence.

"I owe you an apology," he said suddenly, just as her mind was drifting far away.

"What?" she stammered.

"For last night. The comment I made about . . . you know."

"Oh, that," she said, going pink at the ears. "It's fine. Late-night poker game, everyone had been drinking . . ."

"No," he said firmly, turning to look at her. "That's no excuse. Whether you meant to or not, you trusted me with something personal about yourself, and I betrayed that. I should have apologized last night, in front of the guys, but I was ashamed. I just ran away. I am really sorry. I'm going to talk to them today."

"That's not necessary." She meant this. His apology seemed genuine, and frankly the last thing she wanted was to have that brought up again.

"Yes, it is." His tone brooked no argument. Then he apparently decided the topic was closed and moved on. "How's the coffee?"

She made an approving noise.

"Good," he said. "Everyone complains that I make it too strong."

They were silent again for a while, watching the mist slowly evaporate from the mountains into an increasingly crisp blue sky. Suzanne had never been the type to get starstruck — she'd known enough powerful people in her life to recognize that people were people, famous or not. But it did strike her as surreal, sitting in midair over a mountain, casually drinking coffee with someone she barely knew, who sold out stadiums when he performed in concert.

"Can I ask you a question?" she said, breaking the silence.

"Sure. If I can ask you one back." The crooked little grin again. Her insides fluttered. She ignored them.

"All right. What's with the camo hat?"

"What do you mean? You don't like it?"

"No, it's not that. It's just . . . such an interesting choice. I wondered how you picked that as your thing. You know, your trademark or whatever."

" 'Interesting choice' sounds like a nice

way of saying you think I look like an idiot," he said, grinning.

"It's not that . . ." She fumbled for the right words. "It's just, I think you look so nice without it, like now. I wondered why you always wear it. I mean, you have great hair."

He laughed now. "You thought I was bald under there, didn't you?"

"No!" she protested. But she *had* wondered that, before the gala.

"You're not doing some kind of secret interview for *Vanity Fair* or something, are you?" Then he considered her for a minute and answered his own question. "No, you're not. You'd be a terrible spy."

"Never mind," she said flatly. "Let's just drink our coffee and look at the mountains."

"Relax, Scarlett, I'll tell you." He leaned back and clasped his fingers behind his head. "But you're going to be disappointed."

"I'll be the judge of that."

"It was, I don't know, five years ago, maybe? We were still playing dive bars and high school dances, all of us kids trying to break into the business. Couple of those guys are inside now. Eddie is the only one still playing with me from back then, but we've all stayed tight. Anyway, we got this chance to play at a big festival up in Virginia

Beach, a huge break. Another band had to cancel last minute, and my dad knew someone who knew someone . . . you know how it goes.

"So we went up the day before and, like a bunch of idiots, got hammered and went out to the beach looking for girls. We didn't find any girls, as I recall, at least not any that were willing to talk to us, but I did fall asleep in the sun. I had sunscreen on, but my head wasn't covered, so by the time those idiots had the courtesy to wake me up, my scalp was totally fried. Hurt like hell. I had to have a hat for the festival, because it was outside, but we stayed up so late the night before I had no time to go to a real store. So we went to a convenience store and my choices were FEMALE BODY INSPECTOR, VIRGINIA IS FOR LOVERS, or the plain camouflage one."

Suzanne smiled. "Gotta go with plain camouflage on that one."

"It's funny," he said. "These days, I probably would've chosen VIRGINIA IS FOR LOVERS and sort of worn it ironically, but my sense of humor wasn't as sophisticated then as it is now."

She snorted in response. He grinned sideways and went on. "Anyway, that festival turned out to be our big break. Somebody

227

from Nashville reviewed the festival and raved about us, and he mentioned the hat, so I kept wearing it for the next few shows. When things start going well, you're scared to change anything. Like you might break the spell. Next thing you know, it was like people thought it was part of me. Girls started coming to our shows wearing camo hats and tank tops and —"

"And those itty-bitty camo shorts," she finished for him.

"Really? I hadn't noticed those."

She had nothing to throw at him, but made a face. "So that's how it became your trademark."

"Yeah," he said. "And at first I wasn't too thrilled about it. I don't like being pigeon-holed to a certain identity, and when you're from the foothills of Tennessee trying to make it on the national scene, you don't want people assuming you're just a dumb redneck."

"Not that anyone would do that," Suzanne said sheepishly.

"Of course not," he said. "But you know what? I find it works to my advantage. When people don't think you're all that smart, it's easier to stay a step ahead of them. I went through three business managers before Yvette, all of them trying to take advantage

228

of me, one of them blatantly stealing. They thought I wouldn't figure it out, but I keep an eye on things."

"I can actually relate to that," Suzanne realized aloud. "You know — dumb, helpless blonde. People treat you a certain way based on their assumptions . . ."

"And then you take them to school with your baseball knowledge and poker skills."

She raised an eyebrow. "Oh, that's just the beginning of my résumé."

His eyes widened. "Jesus. I don't know if I'm looking forward to finding out what that means or not."

The flirtatiousness of their conversation seemed to occur to them both simultaneously. An awkward silence threatened, but Dylan sidestepped it. "Is it my turn?"

She gave him a blank look.

"To ask a question? I get one, right? I mean, assuming my answer was satisfactory."

"It was. What's your question for me?" She couldn't imagine.

"What took you away from wanting to be an artist?"

Suzanne was flabbergasted. Marci and a couple of others knew this had once been her dream, but she hadn't talked to anyone about it in years. "What do you mean?"

"At the High. You told me you always wanted to paint."

"I did?"

"Yep. While I was helping you down those circular ramps. Man, that museum would *not* be good for someone with vertigo."

Suzanne laughed. "Well, yeah, I guess I did used to want to be an artist, especially a painter. But my parents wouldn't pay for four years at school for that. Art history was the closest thing I could convince them was actually an investment. They'd heard of art dealers who weren't living in their parents' basements, I guess. So that put me on the path to the High, and I found event work, and . . . well, I just don't have time to paint these days."

"Wow," Dylan said. "My parents are pretty crazy sometimes, but I can't imagine what it would be like if they didn't support my music. Speaking of which, why don't you like my music?"

She burst out laughing. "When did I say that? I think I said I didn't *know* your music. But I actually did go out and buy a couple of albums the other day."

"And?"

"I like it," she said, unsure what to add.

"Well, now, *that* was convincing. That's what my dad used to say when Mom came

230

home wearing a hideous dress."

"What do you care what I think?" she said. "I'm just the stuck-up Scarlett anyway, right?"

He grinned. "Hey, you're avoiding the question. I thought we were having this nice, honest conversation out here."

"Well, okay. Country isn't really my genre. Honestly, I've never cared for it much, and I only listen to it when my best friend, Marci, forces it on me." She cringed at the mention of Marci's name. She'd almost forgotten they weren't speaking. "So, I don't have any frame of reference, and it's not exactly my style, but I did really like what I heard. Truly. You're very talented. Obviously." She felt ridiculous.

He didn't seem fully satisfied with this. "Well, if country isn't your genre, what kind of music do you like? Classical?"

"Right. It's either honky-tonk or Mozart. You do see things in black and white, don't you? Actually, I like a lot of things — folksy stuff like Sheryl Crow, Carly Simon, James Taylor. I still listen to a lot of the same stuff I loved in college, like Radiohead and Widespread Panic. It probably sounds lame, but my favorite songs haven't changed in a long time."

"Why would that sound lame?" he asked.

231

"I'm the same way. So what's your all-time favorite?"

"Ugh! I hate that question. It's too hard to choose." She heard voices from behind. The day had grown bright around them and the house was waking up.

"Just choose for right now. *Vanity Fair* won't hold you to it."

"Okay, but you can't laugh."

"Fine."

"I've always loved 'Fire and Rain,' by James Taylor. Ever since I was a little girl. I think it's because it has my name in it. You said you wouldn't laugh!"

Footsteps sounded on the planks behind them. Dylan turned slightly and muttered something under his breath she couldn't hear. She glanced back and saw Misty, wearing a tight white T-shirt and tiny pink pajama shorts. "Dyyyyylan," she whined. "I'm hungry. Where have you been?"

"Right here," he said.

"With her?" Misty said accusingly at Suzanne.

"No," Suzanne said immediately. "I just got here a minute ago." She picked up her coffee, and the cold cup belied this statement.

Misty seemed to appraise her briefly and then turned back to Dylan. "Baby, I want

232

breakfast. Let's go get pancakes."

"I don't want to go to town today. There's cereal in the kitchen," he said. Suzanne wanted to get out of there, but Dylan was looking in the other direction, and, after their long conversation, it felt odd to just vacate the deck without saying anything else to him.

"Please?" Misty put her arms around his neck and hoisted a bare, tan leg over him to straddle his lap. Suzanne saw that her shorts had juicy written across the back. She began kissing Dylan's neck, imploring him between each kiss. "Please, baby, please? I really want pancakes. I'll make it worth your while."

Awkward did not begin to describe it. Dylan kept his hands resolutely on the arms of the chair as Suzanne stood stiffly, knowing that the only reasonable thing to do was to walk away, but she was unable to go. She felt as if she was gaping at a traffic accident: she wanted to look away but couldn't.

"Misty, stop," Dylan said as she nibbled his ear. "You're being rude." He did not look at Suzanne.

Now Suzanne wished more than anything that she had already walked away, because Misty turned to her and spoke. "I'm sorry, Susan," she said lightly, thrusting her hips

233

downward as though giving someone a lap dance in front of a stranger was a perfectly ordinary thing to do on a weekday morning in the mountains. "But unless there's anything else you need? I think Mr. Burke and I would like some privacy right now."

"Of course," Suzanne heard herself say, and then she made her way numbly back to the house. She met Kate in the kitchen.

"Hi," Kate said, unmistakably glowing. "Are you okay?"

"Yes, I'm fine," she said. Then, without having planned it, she continued. "Listen, Kate, something's come up, and I need to get back to Atlanta a little earlier than I'd planned. I think I've . . . seen what I need to see here. Can we wrap up by phone later?"

"Sure," Kate said, taken aback. "But you're not leaving now, are you? Everyone is going down to the river to go inner tubing."

Suzanne had an image of Misty straddling Dylan, except soaking wet in a bathing suit. "I'm so sorry, Kate. I just can't. We'll figure everything out, though. Please don't worry."

The girl's eyes filled with tears, stopping Suzanne's progress toward the door. This family was going to be the end of her. "Kate, what's wrong?"

"Nothing. I'm — please don't judge me, but I need to tell you —"

"Oh, honey," Suzanne said gently. "I know about the baby. And, believe me, I am the *last* person to judge you. It will be fine."

Kate's relief was palpable. "You know?"

"Well, yes. My best friend" — the name stuck in her throat — "Marci is pregnant, and I recognized the symptoms."

"Congratulations," Kate said. Suzanne nodded numbly. Nearly two weeks had gone by since she'd talked to Marci, which was unprecedented in their relationship, even during the years when Marci lived thousands of miles away. She wanted desperately to talk to her best friend, but her shame and anger had been holding her back.

Suzanne had no idea where to start with Marci, but at least calming the bride to be in front of her was a doable task. She took Kate's hand and used her best motherly tone. "Listen, Kate, don't be so hard on yourself. You certainly won't be the first blushing bride to walk down the aisle with a little passenger on board. There are way, way worse things in life than putting the cart a tiny bit before the horse."

Kate gave her a shy smile. Suzanne went on. "And as for the wedding, we can totally work with it. We'll get sparkling grape juice for the champagne toast and make sure you've had plenty to eat so you'll feel good walking down the aisle."

As small and demure as Kate was, Suzanne was still caught off guard when the girl threw herself at her in a sudden, forceful hug. "Oh, thank you, Suzanne!"

17

When she got in the car and found her way to the highway, Suzanne called Marci's phone, which went straight to voice mail. She hung up without leaving a message — it was too weird to apologize via recording. She was about to dial Jake's number just to make sure Marci was okay, when she suddenly remembered where they were: Marci had mentioned weeks ago that they were going to Tempe for Jake to do some filming for Arizona State's spring athletic programs and that his parents were coming along to make it a family minivacation. They wouldn't be back until Friday. She had completely forgotten. *Marci's right,* she thought bleakly. *I* am *totally self-absorbed.*

After that, Suzanne drove with her phone off and the windows down. She stopped only once for gas and water and was so absorbed in her thoughts that she barely noticed the four-hour car ride. For the first fifty miles, she flipped restlessly through the scattered radio stations, eventually turning the damn thing off when two of the three stations she could get were playing Dylan's songs. What the hell was going on?

This is crazy, she told herself. *You're Suzanne Fucking Hamilton. Pull it together. This world, this celebrity garbage — it isn't real. You've dealt with famous people and attractive men before. Just calm down; do your job and live your life, like always.*

On a whim, she took an early exit once she arrived in Atlanta, stopping by an art supply store. For the first time in years, she needed to paint.

For the next two days, Suzanne stayed locked in her condo in sweats and a T-shirt, paying no attention whatsoever to time. She painted, she slept, she ordered takeout, she painted some more. While she painted, she put Dylan out of her mind and thought about William Fitzgerald instead.

Her father had introduced them the summer after she graduated from college. She was trying to break into the art world and he was clerking at her father's firm. They didn't start dating for another year, because Suzanne kept deflecting his advances. He was attractive, but she saw him as a symbol of her father's continued need to control her life. He couldn't force her to be a lawyer, so maybe getting her to marry one was the next best thing.

Still, William did have his charms. He was smart and funny and had a strong sense of right and wrong that Suzanne found admirable. He had a quiet persistence, too, which finally paid off at a Fourth of July barbecue at the country club. They were both several beers in to a long holiday weekend with their parents when they ran into each other in the hot dog line. They had started out arguing about condiments and ended up on a deserted hillside near the seventh hole, sharing a contraband flask of bourbon.

Until William, Suzanne had consistently chosen men who were either unattainable or unsuitable in the eyes of her family. Her picks were all about the challenge — from the punk band leader with a nose ring to her married art history professor in college. She had taken pleasure in defying expectations, but she had never considered what would happen if she tried to meet them instead.

William was a chance to find out what it was like to be the good girl. He also happened to treat her well, which was nice, if not necessarily thrilling. After a few months,

William began hinting at their future together. Suzanne felt conflicted but told herself it was probably normal to feel that way in a relationship that lasted more than a couple of months. It might be scary, but would it really be so bad? Marriage, kids, the whole suburban dream?

The more the relationship cycled toward commitment, however, the more she noticed about William that she didn't like. He had no fashion sense. He slurped his spaghetti like an eight-year-old. He said "it's all good" way too often. She began to notice every little thing she hated about him, and with each item, the feeling that she was trapped in an ever-shrinking box increased.

By mid-December that year, she decided it had to end. But the holidays were approaching, and there were plans and parties that would be ruined if they broke up now — not just for herself and William, but their families, too. She'd wait until January.

To her horror, William did not intend to wait that long at all. At the New Year's Eve party at the country club, he had gone onstage just before midnight, borrowed the microphone from the band, and proposed to her. It had seemed everyone in the club was watching, sighing collectively and turning to kiss their own spouses in celebration of how fucking romantic it was. Suzanne had wanted to die.

No such luck. So she had gone to the stage, pushed from behind by her mother, and when the crowd began to cry out for her to answer him, he held the microphone to her mouth. She shook her head, begging him with her eyes not to make it any worse.

"Don't be shy, honey," someone nearby said. William grinned and held the mike in front of her.

So when she whispered, "We need to talk," it was broadcast not only to the immediate onlookers but to everyone within hearing distance. William had stood as gracefully as he could, handed the mike back to the singer, and left the room through the back door. His face had been a horrifying combination of shock and hurt that she never wanted to see again. Suzanne followed him, but he ran into the men's locker room near the golf course. Part of her had been relieved to have an excuse not to go in after him. He had never spoken to her again.

That was the day Suzanne started making her rules for dating. She never wanted to get that close to someone again, only to hurt them. Instead, she tried to figure out as soon as possible what might not work about a relationship and make a decision early on, before things got too serious. She had more or less decided then, though she had never uttered it aloud, that she would most likely never get married. And dated accordingly.

Now, out on her balcony, slapping paint on the canvas in a messy but therapeutic abstract, she thought perhaps she had been too hasty when she rejected William. Or maybe she just hadn't been ready back then. Immature. He had loved her — that was absolutely clear. Maybe he still could. Why shouldn't she have the beautiful marriage Marci and Jake had? What was so scary about sharing your life with someone who wanted to be there for you and take care of you? She'd been basically single for more than a decade, and she had nothing to show for it except a ruined career and a stalker. Of course, a stable relationship didn't solve *everything,* but at least it would mean she wasn't battling all this alone.

Her reverie was interrupted by the sound of a phone in the distance, and after a moment she realized it was her phone, inside. She barely got through the sliding glass door fast enough to catch it before it went to voice mail. She hoped it was William.

"Oh, hey," she said when she heard the voice on the other end.

"Wow, it's been a while since a woman

sounded so disappointed to hear from me," Dylan said. "I'm having flashbacks to tenth grade."

"No, no, of course not." She tried to recover her usual graciousness. "Don't be silly."

"You left the cabin in such a rush," he said.

This time, she heard her dad's voice. *Never explain; never apologize. Let them come to you.* "Yes."

"Well, anyway, you left a scarf at the cabin on Wednesday. Yvette found it and asked me to bring it to you because I'm in Atlanta tonight for a meeting tomorrow. It's light green with a blue pattern on it. Kinda wispy." Her father had given her that scarf for college graduation.

"Yes, it's mine," she said, about to suggest that he mail it to her, when the thought of Rick and the stray panties gave her pause.

"I was thinking we could meet for a beer later and I'll return it to you. If that's convenient for you, of course, Scarlett."

Was Dylan Burke asking her out? No. It wasn't possible. Her first impulse was to say no. But why? He was a client; that was all. She was free, and there was no reason not to meet him.

"Sure," she said.

"I'll e-mail you the address," he said, and hung up.

Suzanne reconfirmed the address of the bar in front of her against the printed e-mail several times before finally turning off the car and going inside. She was somewhere west of the city, away from the populated areas with trendy nightclubs, but not yet into the clean, predictable suburbs. The bar was in a shopping center between a non-descript nail salon and a check-cashing store. The storefront was darkly tinted glass with a simple neon OPEN sign near the door and a handwritten sign taped to the door: THIS IS A SMOKING ESTABLISHMENT. NO ONE UNDER 21 ALLOWED. PERIOD. She took a last glorious gulp of fresh air and went in, thinking she should have had Dylan mail the scarf.

To her relief, however, the inside was not nearly as sketchy as the view from the parking lot. Beyond a cold, dark entryway, there were warmly lighted tables and booths surrounding a clean, polished wood bar. A couple of pool tables and dart boards were occupied in a back corner. A garage band was performing a passable rendition of a Smiths song on a crude wooden stage in the other corner.

It took a moment to find Dylan, who was tucked into a booth on the music side, wearing a frayed Braves baseball hat pulled down low, a crisp blue Oxford shirt, and the glasses he'd worn at the gala. When he noticed her, he waved to get her attention just as her recognition was sinking in.

"What, no camouflage today?" she said.

"Nope," he said, smiling. "It's my night off."

"I like the glasses," she said. "They make you look . . . mature."

"Thanks," he said. "I always feel a little self-conscious in them. But my contacts were hurting my eyes."

A waitress came by, and Dylan ordered them each a pint of Guinness, raising an eyebrow for her approval as he did. She shrugged and glanced around for her scarf.

"It's in the truck," he said, following her gaze. "I didn't want to get it all smoky. Or for you to get hammered and forget it."

"I'm not planning on drinking tonight, Mr. Burke."

"Whoa. What's with the sudden formality, Scarlett?"

Suzanne had decided on the drive over to bring things back to a safer, more professional level with Dylan — for the sake of her reputation and her sanity. But it was meant to be a subtle change, and she didn't expect him to notice. "Sorry," she said. "Dylan. Have you been here before?"

"Yeah, I like this place. It reminds me of a bar we used to play in outside Knoxville, you know, in the early days."

She nodded and looked around, politely taking it in. The bar was fairly busy but not crowded, considering it was a Friday night. There seemed to be a good mix of people, of various ages and races, which was somewhat unusual for a dive bar in Atlanta. The walls were adorned with liquor and beer ads, with a few British travel posters and some Union Jacks thrown in. She noticed a random stuffed sheep on one wall next to a flat screen with a soccer game on. The more she looked around, the more she liked it.

"The owner is English," Dylan said. "He's from Newcastle, I think. I came here pretty late one night after a rehearsal and had a few beers with him. Didn't know who I was until the fourth drink. That's what I love about being in Atlanta."

"Being anonymous?"

"Sure, sometimes," he said. "I mean, it's fun when people like you and tell you how much they like your music and all. But other times it's nice just to be a regular person, talking about sports and eavesdropping on bar conversations. I can't exactly do that in Nashville."

"So you're an eavesdropper?" she asked.

"Oh, like you don't do it, too," he said. "Bar conversations are better than soap operas. I get great ideas for songs that way sometimes. Not that you would know, seeing how you don't like my work . . ." He nudged her under the table with his foot.

"Oh, get over it already." She scowled playfully. "Oooh, *one person* doesn't own every song you've ever made. Poor little rock star!"

He grinned. "I know, I know. I'm a narcissistic asshole. But you're not *'one person,'* you're . . . you."

She was unsure how to respond to this, so she took a big swig of Guinness. He looked at the table, toying with a paper coaster. "Speaking of you being you . . . ," he began awkwardly. "This doesn't have to mean more than it does, but I'm really sorry about what happened with Misty the other day."

Suzanne's face flushed a bit. The Guinness, surely. "No, no. It's not a big deal," she said dismissively. "I can understand why she would feel territorial. It must be hard dating a superstar." She attempted a sideways grin like the ones he gave her sometimes.

He rolled his eyes. "Well, we weren't exactly dating. And she probably *was* feeling territorial and pissed off for other reasons." He looked at her as though waiting for some kind of response, but she had no idea what to say.

He went on. "Anyway, it was totally inappropriate and childish, whether we were dating or not. I told her that when you left. And I made her leave, too."

"You did?"

"Yeah. It was overdue. You were just a catalyst."

"I'm sorry," she said.

"Are you?" he asked.

"Shouldn't I be?" This conversation reminded Suzanne of an old movie, but she couldn't place which one.

"Well, this conversation is really going places," he said. "Anyway, I apologize."

"Apology accepted," she said definitively.

They were quiet again then, but with less awkwardness than before. She drank her Guinness and bopped her head a little to the sound of the band, watching them do a version of an old Clash song she loved but couldn't remember the title of. Dylan turned to watch them with her, and she saw that his hair was getting just long enough to make a little ducktail at the back of his hat.

"They're pretty good," he said appreciatively.

"I wouldn't have thought this was your kind of thing," she said.

He nodded as if he was expecting this. "Yeah. Actually, I like all kinds of music. Good is good, as far as I'm concerned. I mean, sure, my roots are country, especially the old-school stuff, but I think you always benefit from keeping your horizons broad. Some of my favorite artists aren't anything close to country."

Suzanne nodded, still watching the band. They all seemed to be in their early twenties, wearing black, with longish hair of varying artificial colors, a variety of piercings, and black fingernails. She wondered how they would feel if they knew that one of music's biggest stars was watching them right now. Would it change how they played? Would they scramble to play the twangiest thing in their repertoire, something he could relate to? Or would they think a mere country star irrelevant to them? She had joked with Dylan about being the only person who didn't know his music, but she could hazard a guess that most of these guys didn't, either.

"So have you had any more problems?" he asked after a while. "Any creepy deliveries since the last one?"

"No," she said. "I've been trying to pay attention, and Bonita calls me every couple of days to check in. She's really going above and beyond."

"She's good people," he agreed. "But you're no closer to figuring out who this jerk is?"

"No, I'm not. But I haven't been trying, except . . ." She broke off.

"Except?"

Oh, why not? He'd been honest with her, and it was nice to have someone she could talk to, especially with Marci not speaking to her. "Well, it's not really related to who is stalking me, but seeing all those names up there — as you so graciously pointed out, there are lots of them — made me think about whether I am doing something wrong. Like maybe I've let some people go I shouldn't have."

"What do you mean?" He seemed genuinely perplexed.

"Well, I know it sounds silly, but I'm thirty-three, and I've never really wanted to get married, but I'm starting to get concerned that I haven't had a relationship last for more than a couple of months since . . ."

"Since when?"

She hesitated, and then told him. About

William and his proposal. About her conflicted feelings, and how she was now
searching for him to try to understand it all
better. She didn't mention the part that was
so far just a glimmer of something in the
back of her mind — the hope that finding
William would not just be insight into why
she pushed men away but that a rekindled
relationship with him could be an answer in
itself.

"So this guy was the beginning? After him
you started chewing men up and spitting
them out?"

"You make me sound like a monster."

"Not a monster. Maybe a praying mantis,"
he said. She kicked him under the table.
"Ouch!"

The waitress brought another round, and
Suzanne licked the foam of the fresh Guinness off her top lip. "I don't chew men up
and spit them out. I'm . . . picky. You don't
know what it was like to let things get that
far and then hurt him so badly. I never want
to make that kind of mistake again. So I
don't stay in a relationship unless I feel
really sure about it."

"I know," he said. "I saw the list. Poor
bastards."

"What about you?" she fired back accusingly. "You're not exactly living like a model

of monogamy yourself."

"True," he said, "but I think girls know what they're getting into when they're with me."

"That is such a typical male way of seeing things," she said, her Southern accent becoming thicker with her slight buzz and sense of outrage. "It's such a fucking double standard."

He laughed and pretended to back away from the table, holding his hands up in surrender. "Whoa, there, Scarlett."

"Well, it is. You can do what you want, and you're a playboy; I do the same thing, and I'm a slut. How is that fair?"

"I don't think you're a slut," he said seriously. "I would never call you that."

She had hit a nerve. "Sorry," she said, though why *she* was apologizing to *him,* she wasn't sure.

"I have five sisters, remember? I don't do that word. The guys around me don't use it, either." His face was full of conviction, and then he added more playfully, "Besides, now that I have a feminist friend in my acquaintance, I have a feeling there will be plenty of other politically incorrect words I'm not allowed to use anymore, either. I'm assuming you'll provide me with a list or something? Or will I just have to run into

252

each one as I go?"

She smiled. No one had referred to her as a feminist in a long time. It was a mantle she had taken up in college with some amount of seriousness but somehow pushed aside as the years went on. Could you still be a feminist if you were in the Junior League and flirted with men to get discounts on facility rentals for a living?

Then something else struck her. Feminist *friend.* Dylan considered her a friend, and she realized that she thought of him that way, too. How odd. *If someone had told me two months ago that my newest friend would be a twenty-six-year-old country superstar with a high school diploma and friends who still got drunk and played video games . . .* It felt like the weirdest dream ever. Maybe none of this had actually happened and she was still passed out on her couch with her arm in a cast having painkiller dreams.

The lead singer came to the mike as they finished a song Suzanne didn't recognize. "Thanks," he said to the smattering of applause. Sixty or seventy people were in the bar now, about ten or fifteen of whom seemed engaged with the music. "We're Rickenbacker's Revenge. Taking a break for beer; we'll be back in ten."

"I get it, I really do," Dylan said, grasping

her hands across the table. "I think it's admirable that you're trying to figure out why your relationships haven't worked so far. But maybe, just maybe, you ought to consider that you're an exceptional woman. Why would you want to settle for someone who doesn't deserve you?"

Her heart lurched. *What was he saying?* She looked down at their hands, linked on the table between them. His grip was warm and firm, but not necessarily romantic. She met his eyes, and he held her gaze with sincerity. She felt as if she was in a staring contest with Marci back in middle school and had to fight the totally inappropriate urge to giggle.

Dylan broke the spell, laughing good-naturedly. "I fold. Again," he said, standing to exit the booth. "I definitely wouldn't pass the Suzanne Hamilton perfection test. Poor bastards."

He signaled the bartender as he left the table, who glanced at Suzanne and nodded. She watched him walk to the restroom at the back of the bar, shaking his head theatrically as he went. It was remarkable how her conversations with Dylan, whom she had known for just a few weeks, could be so like her conversations with Marci, whom she had known nearly her whole life.

Marci. It was Friday night, and Marci was home. Suzanne pulled out her phone and sent a text:

This is stupid. I'm a jerk. I love you and I'm SO sorry. Can we be friends again? PLEASE?

She wasn't expecting an answer. Marci had probably gone to bed a couple of hours before, but maybe she would see it in the morning. To her surprise a text appeared just a few moments later. The response had come not from Marci, but from Jake.

Suze, it's Jake. M's asleep. Please come over tomorrow. Take her for a pedicure or something. My treat. She's driving me insane.

Suzanne laughed. She looked up when another round arrived at the table, but it was only her beer. The waitress took the other one directly to Dylan, who was standing across the room, where the band was taking their break by the pool tables. She watched him shaking hands with a couple of them as they returned from a smoke break outside. All wore broad smiles, and, as they talked, she watched Dylan sign autographs for one or two of them, who looked grateful and a little sheepish.

She couldn't hear what they were saying, but once or twice the whole group laughed. The lead singer was showing his guitar to Dylan, who showed appropriately polite interest. He looked over at her and waved but did not seem to be inviting her over. She pulled her phone back out and played Tetris while she waited.

Then a cold chill ran over her suddenly, as though someone had scratched their nails on a chalkboard directly behind her. Almost imperceptibly, her mood changed and her muscles tightened. She had the faint but distinct feeling that she was being watched. She glanced at Dylan, but he was engaged in conversation and did not look up to meet her gaze.

She pretended to stretch and did a casual sweep of the bar and tables behind her, half expecting to see Rick there. Or perhaps someone hiding behind a strategically placed newspaper. Nothing. She saw two men in Vietnam veterans' hats having a lively debate of some kind at the bar. A robust girl in a short black dress and striped knee-high socks with inky black lipstick and pigtails the same color, talking to a tall bald man who was facing away from Suzanne. The bartender, busy with the remote control, a nearby customer in a polo shirt and khaki shorts advising him on locating something specific on TV.

Next to the bar at a long table, there was a group of young black women — one of whom wore a glittery tiara and wispy veil that were the trademarks of bachelorette parties — laughing at a shared joke with one of the waiters. A middle-aged couple in leather Harley-Davidson jackets making out in the corner booth. Four college-age guys apparently having a drinking contest of some sort.

One man was sitting alone, diagonally behind her. She did not recognize him at first glance but chanced a second look. He was about her age, give or take a couple of years, with wild black hair and glasses. He wore a short-sleeve button-down plaid shirt and a wedding ring. A plate of half-eaten food was in front of him, and most of a light-colored beer. He was writing in a small spiral notebook. *Was that a popular thing to do in a bar? Sit alone and write?* She had seen someone doing that recently but couldn't remember when. Yet neither the man nor the notebook looked familiar.

She decided to get a closer look. She stood and walked toward his table, her heart pounding, pretending that she was actually looking out the window behind him. When she was a few feet away, he looked up at her, returned the polite twitch of a smile she'd sent his way, and went back to his notebook. No nervous response, no blushing, no involuntary sign of recognition crossed his face.

"I thought I'd left my lights on," she mumbled as she pretended to crane her neck to look out into the night, half to herself, but so he could hear. He gave another polite smile in acknowledgment and returned to the notebook. She could not see what he had written there, but it appeared to be a flow chart of some kind, or something with basic shapes and lines. She turned around and went back to her table.

Shortly thereafter, Rickenbacker's Revenge made their way back to the plywood stage, and Dylan came back to the table with one of their CDs and his now half-empty beer. "Here you go," he said, handing her the CD, grinning. "I had them sign it for you."

He didn't, however, sit down. "Would you excuse me for another minute?" he asked, patting her shoulder as though she were an elderly relative.

"Sure," she said, confused.

He walked to the stage and stepped up,

smiling awkwardly as the lead singer handed him an acoustic guitar. *Oh my God. He's going to* play. *Just a regular guy, eh?* He smiled at her as he hoisted the guitar strap over his head. The lead singer stepped back and squeezed in next to the bassist, but still called the count for the band to get started. After a few bars, Suzanne recognized it as a very sped-up cover of Sheryl Crow's "The First Cut Is the Deepest."

Dylan's usual twangy sound was more gravelly and interesting on fast-moving rock, though he kept the strong Tennessee accent that made him recognizable. He sang close to the microphone, with barely a couple of inches between the well-worn bill of his cap and the top of the mike. His face was largely hidden this way, but he grinned at the band when he fumbled through a couple of lyrics.

Even though he fibbed a little through the words and the timing, the lack of rehearsal didn't take away from the polished quality of his voice. In this setting, it was more obvious, not less, that Dylan made his living singing. His pitch was spot-on, as far as Suzanne could tell, and sounded more authentic than it had on her iPod. She decided that Dylan was one of those singers who was more hurt than helped by all the editing and studio mixing that go into an album.

It took the ever-growing crowd a few minutes to process the change in lead singer. Some people did not notice at all. But near the end of the song, Suzanne could see a few whispered conversations and people nudging one another as they realized, or suspected, who Dylan was. He caught her eye and winked at her from beneath the baseball cap. He was having fun.

The song ended, and the band moved smoothly into a slow, familiar tune. Suzanne was just realizing what they were playing when Dylan's voice began the lyrics, as familiar to her as the worn sweatshirt she'd had since her freshman year of college. "Fire and Rain" was her favorite song. He'd remembered and was now singing it with almost velvety softness, the garage band accompanying unobtrusively.

He did not look at her as he sang but gave a crooked little smile at the mention of her name in the second line. No one had ever sung to her before. Suzanne felt a flush spread from her belly up to her cheeks, and down, too. *Jesus, no wonder all those girls throw their panties onstage at him.* She brought her hands to her mouth, smiling so wide behind them that her cheeks began to ache.

The folk song was closer to his usual genre, and by the time it was over, almost everyone in the bar had figured out who he was. Applause greeted him as he ended. Dylan gave the room a polite wave and turned around to restore the guitar to its rightful owner.

The lead singer of Rickenbacker's Revenge tossed a dark black mop of hair out of his eyes as he returned to front and center. "Thanks to our new friend," he said to the crowd, gesturing at Dylan with an open palm. Dylan returned to his seat across from her with a polite "we're done here" sort of wave at the crowd. Most people got the hint and turned back to their drinks and conversations, while a few continued to gaze at Dylan with broad smiles, hoping to catch his eye. The band, meanwhile, launched into a raucous version of the Ramones' "I Wanna Be Sedated," bringing the attention back to themselves.

"Show-off," Suzanne said.

For a split second, he looked hurt. "But it was beautiful, thanks." She put her hand on his. "Really."

She opted not to mention the eerie feeling she'd had that someone was watching her, or the man with the spiral notebook who gave no evidence whatsoever of being menacing. Still, she felt off-kilter for the rest of the evening and had trouble staying focused on their conversation.

"You okay?" he asked finally. "I didn't embarrass you, did I?"

"No, of course not," she said. "I'm just really tired, that's all."

In illustration of this point, Suzanne shook her head vehemently when the petite waitress stopped by to ask whether they wanted another round. "Together or separate?" she asked.

"Separate," Suzanne said firmly, giving Dylan her best uncompromising look. He opened his mouth to object and then rolled his eyes, muttering something about stubborn feminists.

The waitress returned with a check for each of them and an extra bit of receipt paper, on which she had scrawled a phone number. "I don't mean to be too forward," she said, looking at Suzanne. "But if y'all aren't together — ?"

Suzanne shook her head no. Then she realized what was happening. *Did girls really do this?*

"Okay, good," said the waitress. "Well, Mr. Burke, I'm a *huge* fan, and I don't know how long you're in town or anything, but I'm off in an hour and some friends and I were going out to have a good time. If you're interested, we'd love for you to join us."

"That's really nice, sweetheart, but I think I'm going to make sure my friend here gets home all right and then go straight to bed. Maybe some other time, okay?" He left the number sitting on the table where she'd put it. The waitress looked a little crestfallen but clearly not ready to give up.

"Don't be silly," said Suzanne. "I'll be fine. You should go. Have a good time."

Dylan raised an eyebrow at her, which the waitress obviously took as an encouraging sign.

"Yeah, seriously, you should, Mr. Burke. How can you turn down a bunch of hot girls who know how to party?" Suzanne thought the poor little waitress sounded like a bad commercial for a phone-sex line. Apparently, though, she thought the reason Dylan hadn't scooped up her number was that she was *too* subtle. She licked her lips, leaned over, and began whispering in his ear.

Suzanne couldn't hear what was being said, but she saw Dylan turn bright red. "Wow," he said, when she had pulled back and stood waiting for a verdict. "I tell you what, sweetheart, I'll put your number in my pocket, and if I think I can handle . . . *that,* you'll be the first one I call."

Taking this as a potential acceptance of what was obviously quite an offer, the waitress scooted off, arching her eyebrows as she looked back over her shoulder at him. Dylan reddened again and turned back to Suzanne.

"I didn't think you would embarrass so easily," she said.

"Embarrassed? Hell. Try *terrified.*" Dylan looked at the disappearing form of the waitress and shuddered. Suzanne noted, however, that he did not take the number out of his pocket.

In the parking lot, he looped her missing scarf around her neck and lingered at his truck for a moment, considering. "Will you be offended if I offer to follow you home? I have only honorable intentions." He made a little mock bow.

"What, you think I can't handle myself? I need some big, strong guy to protect me?"

"Not you," he said. "You don't seem like the type who needs rescuing, Scarlett. I'm more worried about the poor idiot who's stalking you. But I know you don't need some macho asshole running your life for you. I'll see you around."

He started to get in his truck, and she thought about the guy with the spiral notebook with a slight shiver. She put a hand on Dylan's arm. "Um, actually," she started.

"Yeeees?" he said.

Why did this guy insist on needling her all the time?

She spoke deliberately with no exaggerated accent or batting eyelashes. "I would really appreciate it, Dylan, please, if you would follow me back to my condo and make sure that no one is there before going home."

He bowed again and tipped his baseball hat. "Ma'am, I am at your service."

Dylan not only walked her to the door when they got to her condo, he followed her inside, making an elaborate show of checking all the closets and even the balcony. Suzanne couldn't tell whether he was serious or still making fun of her, but something about having another human being here with her was comforting.

"Do you want anything?" she asked, getting a bottle of water from the fridge. "I have beer, or I can make coffee."

"That's okay," he said. "I think I'd better go."

You mean you really came all this way just

to check my closets? "You sure? I hate for you to have come all this way for nothing."

"You took your posters down," he remarked, looking at the dining room.

"Oh, yes," she said. *Because I decided to track down the guy I was almost engaged to fifteen years ago.* The thought struck her suddenly as completely ridiculous.

"Here," she said, handing him a chilled bottle of water. "For the road. If you decide to call that little waitress, it sounds like you'll need to be hydrated."

"Thanks," he said, taking it. If she had been hoping this conversational bait would lead him to illuminate his further plans for the evening or to deny that he might call the kinky little waitress, she was disappointed. He looked at her with a curious expression and then surprised her with a kiss on the forehead. "I gotta go, Scarlett. I'll, um . . . I'll call you."

She closed the door behind him and sank against it until she reached the floor. She sat there for a while, wondering about the mystery that was Dylan Burke. She realized it was the first time a guy had told her he'd call and she was neither sure if he would or, more important, whether she wanted him to.

18

"Now you know how we *normal* girls feel," Marci said. "You know, those of us who aren't a perfect size-six blond bombshell with a line of guys around the block waiting to fall at our cute little feet."

"Oh, shut up," Suzanne countered. "I seem to remember a time in the not-so-distant past when you had your pick of at least a couple of different guys. Didn't He Who Shall Not Be Named drive all the way from Austin to try to win you back? *Asshole!*"

Suzanne said, "Asshole!" in this ritual way every time she referred to Marci's old flame Doug in conversation, the way superstitious old women sometimes spit to ward off ill luck.

"That was an exceptional situation," Marci said. "That kind of stuff happens to *you* all the time."

They were sitting in massage chairs at Fab

Nails III, a small salon around the corner from Marci's house in Alpharetta, soaking their feet in warm water with some kind of blue stuff in it. Suzanne had followed Jake's suggestion and driven to his and Marci's house first thing that morning, bearing a gift of blueberry bagels with honey cream cheese, Marci's favorite.

Their reconciliation was quick and tearful. It began with hugging and crying and ended with both of them swearing that they couldn't remember what they were fighting about but that they were each positive it had been her own fault entirely.

Jake had watched this scene with bemusement. *"Chicks,"* he said, shaking his head as Marci bawled and Suzanne rummaged in her purse for tissues.

They had both glared at this misogynist utterance, which apparently reminded him that he had some footage to edit in his basement workspace right away. He dug in the paper bag until he found his favorite everything bagel and ran away with this and a large thermos of coffee. Suzanne noticed as he rounded the corner heading for the basement that Jake was not yet showing any signs of sympathy weight gain from Marci's pregnancy. He still looked great, even in loose jeans and a ratty old T-shirt.

"Ahem," Marci had said, clearing her throat and arching and eyebrow. "That one's mine, remember?"

Suzanne stuck her tongue out at Marci, laughing. "Don't worry, no danger there. Jake was the only guy I could never win over, remember?" She put her hand lightly on Marci's little belly bulge. "He was meant for much better things."

This had prompted a fresh round of tears and hugging; so it was another hour before they had managed to get to the nail salon, where Suzanne was catching Marci up on all that she'd missed during their time apart.

"Anyway," Marci was saying, as she obediently lifted her left foot out of the water for the pedicurist, "it sounds like you have nothing to worry about. He obviously cares about you."

It might as well have been twenty years ago: the two of them spending a Saturday together, talking about boys. "Maybe, but . . ." Suzanne said. "I don't even know if I *want* more from him."

"Yeah, that would suck," Marci said, her voice dripping with sarcasm, "to have an attractive, sweet, rich guy who can sing like an angel show an interest in you."

"An attractive, sweet, rich guy who's featured in *People* every week, with a family who's in the tabloids every other week, who goes on tour for months at a time and has girls *literally* throwing themselves at him. You should've seen that waitress last night. She might as well have just given him a blow job right there at the table."

The small Asian woman working on Suzanne's feet looked up sharply. "Sorry," said Suzanne. "But seriously, Marci, she basically offered him at least a threesome, if not more than that, while we were paying our checks. Right in front of me."

"Yeah, but obviously he didn't take her up on it," Marci argued. "Did he?"

"I don't know," Suzanne admitted. "He still had her number in his pocket, as far as I know, when he left my place. Who knows what he did next? He can do what he wants. He's Dylan Burke!"

The other pedicurist, now using what looked like a cheese grater to exfoliate Marci's feet, looked up now. "Dylan Burke?" she said, and Suzanne was instantly embarrassed that she'd been assuming the woman didn't speak English. "I love his music! What is that song, with the little boy?"

Suzanne shrugged. The nail tech turned to the woman working on Suzanne's feet and said something rapid in Vietnamese.

The latter shook her head, obviously not a Dylan Burke fan. She turned back to Marci for help. "Come on, you know, the little boy, his parents are splitting up . . . Ugh! Makes me cry just talking about it."

"Duct Tape Fixes Everything!" Marci squealed.

Then she began to sing, "And when I sat him down to tell him, I'd be moving out for good, he brought that silver roll to me and said he'd do all that he could . . ."

Now the little pedicurist *and* the customer in the chair on the other side of Marci joined in. "He said, 'Daddy, don't you worry, Daddy, don't you cry. I'll tape you back together. It's gonna be alright . . .' "

Other people at the salon were watching now, as big tears rolled down Marci's cheeks. *So that's pregnancy,* Suzanne thought. Then she noticed that the other women looked misty-eyed, too. *Jeez.*

"Okay," she said quietly, once the singing and resulting female bonding had died down and the other women moved on to a different conversation. "You see? This is exactly my point. Look at the effect that stupid song has on you and all these other women. Can you imagine dating the guy who sings it? How would you feel if women were crying and swooning at Jake's football

271

videos?"

"I've cried several times at his work," Marci said defensively.

"Of course," said Suzanne. "Me, too. But that's not the point."

Marci looked ready to argue this, so Suzanne added quickly, "Anyway, I've been trying to track down William."

"William who?" Then Marci gasped. "*William?* Why on earth would you do that?" As always, Marci did not bother beating around the bush.

"Well, I've been thinking about what you said about how I've dumped all these men for stupid reasons and then I complain about being alone . . ."

"I never said that!" Marci snapped.

"Yeah, Marce, you did. Though I think you might have said 'idiotic' reasons. And you know what? You were right. I looked at the list of all the guys in my past, and I realized that I did have ridiculous reasons for breaking up with some of them."

"Now, wait. You can't take that seriously. I'm hormonal; I was upset . . ."

"You were *right*," Suzanne repeated. "I can't keep going along, waiting for true love, thinking the next guy might be perfect. Maybe not everyone is meant to have the fairy-tale romance like you and Jake."

"Our romance was not exactly a fairy tale, either," Marci corrected. Their relationship had definitely been rocky, including — at one point — a broken engagement.

"See? That's my point. Not everything can be singing doves and rainbows, right? I've had so many opportunities to be with guys like William, who are great and would make good partners, but I've dumped them for practically no reason."

"I thought you weren't really in love with William."

"I don't know. I did love him; I did care about him. Maybe this whole 'being in love' concept is just an amplified version of that. For some people, it happens all at once, with chemistry and fireworks; for others, it's a slow build, through commitment and mutual respect. You and Jake had a slow build."

Marci bit her lip, considering. "Well, yes and no. It took us a long time to get together, yes, but I think we always felt fireworks for each other. I know I did."

"*Always?* Marci, come on." Suzanne knew for a fact there were times in Marci's life where Jake Stillwell had been far, far from her mind. She didn't say this out loud, but she wondered whether the happiness of their marriage now was causing Marci to take a rosy view of their past. "Even when you were so involved with Doug? *Asshole!*"

"Well . . . ," Marci started, and then held back. She seemed to be trying to figure out how to say something and then evidently gave up. "Well, anyway. This isn't about me. So you found William?"

"Not yet. But I left a message at his parents' house a week ago, and I'm hoping he'll call me. He could be married or something, so I'm trying not to get my hopes up."

Marci nodded and was quiet for a while, watching intently as the pedicurist who was a Dylan Burke fan painted her toes a deep red. Eventually, Suzanne broke the silence by asking about the plans for the baby, which launched them into a conversation that lasted the rest of the pedicure and halfway through a trip to the mall before they returned to Marci's house.

"I still can't believe you had dinner with Rebecca *alone*," Marci said as they entered the front door with shopping bags. "Jake! We're back!"

"It wasn't that bad, actually," Suzanne said softly.

Marci gave her a quick skeptical look. "Well, it wasn't," Suzanne said. "I mean, it wasn't like having dinner with you or anything, but Rebecca . . ."

"What?" Marci demanded. Suzanne was astonished how quickly her best friend had rounded on her. Whether it was bitterness about Jake, jealousy of Rebecca's spending time with Suzanne, or just pure pregnancy hormones coursing through her veins, Suzanne decided that their makeup was too fresh to risk on this particular point.

"Nothing," she said. "It just wasn't the same without you. That's all."

Marci looked dubious, but seemed placated. "Staying for dinner?" she asked, in a way that assumed the answer was yes.

Truthfully, Suzanne wanted to get back home to paint and obsessively monitor her phone for signs of William, but neither of these seemed like a valid reason to bail on Marci after she'd been missing her so much the past few weeks. "Sure," she said.

They found Jake on the back patio, firing up the grill. He wore a Georgia Bulldogs apron and held a bottle of Bud Light in one hand, grilling tongs in the other. "I have burgers and chicken," he said, and, when Marci made a face, "and veggie burgers just in case meat didn't sound good to you."

Marci kissed him on the cheek before plopping onto a deck chair, shopping bags falling at her feet.

"I'll get those," Suzanne said. She scooped up Marci's bags and carried them in with her own, pulling her phone out of her purse to check it before putting it away. Apparently, she had forgotten to turn it back on after the nail salon, because there were two voice mails.

The first: "Hey, Suzanne, it's Chad. I was just calling to see how you were doing. I was thinking about stopping by the office next week for lunch if you're free. Have you remembered to check the voice mail on my line? I bet you haven't. You always forget stuff like that. Maybe I'll check it now. Anyway, let me know about lunch next week."

That's nice, Suzanne thought, and she was making a mental note to call Chad back tomorrow afternoon when the second message started. "Hey, Suzanne, it's Dylan. I know you debutantes probably stay busy on Saturday nights, but I wondered if you might happen to be free for dinner tonight. Call me."

An involuntary shiver ran down Suzanne's spine. Simultaneously, she wondered whether it would be prudent to ignore his message and call him back in a couple of days so he wouldn't think she had no life and whether it was too late to back out of dinner with Jake and Marci without being amazingly rude. She decided to split the difference and call him back immediately to tell him she had plans.

"Hey," he said, picking up on the first ring.

"Hi there. How was the rest of your evening?" She kicked herself for being unable to resist asking. *What do you care?*

"Good. I caught up with that waitress and her friends," he said. "I'm pretty sure more than a few laws were broken."

"Oh," she said stiffly. *I don't care. I don't care. I don't care.* "How lovely. I look forward to seeing the pictures on TMZ."

He chuckled. "Just messing with you, Scarlett. I went straight to my place and went to sleep. Protecting you from bad guys wears me out."

Her laugh was thin and brittle, like a sheet of ice. He didn't seem to notice. "So did you get my message about dinner? There's a pizza place in Midtown I really like, but if I go alone I'll have to spend the whole time fighting off well-meaning fans." Marci came into the kitchen then, fanning herself and waving apologies at Suzanne for interrupting.

"Rough life," Suzanne said to Dylan. "But I'm sorry, I have plans tonight with friends."

At this, Marci stopped her progress toward

the stairs and perked her ears curiously. "Who is it?" she mouthed.

Suzanne waved her away, but she might as well have told a hungry cat to ignore a small, flightless bird. "That's too bad," Dylan said. "Maybe tomorrow night."

"I thought your sister said you were taking her to a show or something tomorrow," Suzanne said, recalling a conversation with Kate from earlier in the week.

"Dylan?" Marci mouthed, and Suzanne nodded. "Invite him here."

"Oh, yeah. I almost forgot," Dylan said. "Where would I be without you?"

"No," Suzanne said, meaning to address Marci but saying it to Dylan instead.

"Sorry?"

"Nothing, I was just . . . saying something to my friend." She tried not to laugh at Marci, now on her knees in the middle of the kitchen floor, making an elaborate plea in exaggerated mime.

"Oh, okay," Dylan said, sounding put off. "Well, you seem kind of busy there, so . . ."

"No, no. I'm sorry," Suzanne said. She didn't want to hurt his feelings. Or disappoint the pathetic pregnant woman making an ass of herself on the floor. "I was just saying, my friends are grilling out at their house tonight. Would you like to join us?

No hot tubs or anything, but it should be fun."

She stuck her tongue out at Marci. To her surprise, Dylan answered quickly. "Sure. Where do they live?"

"It's up in Alpharetta — do you know where that is? It's kind of a long way from Atlanta . . ." Suzanne had no idea where Dylan stayed when he was in town. Hotel? Apartment?

"I know where it is. That's fine."

She gave him the address, still shocked that the country star had nothing better to do on a Saturday night than to drive forty-five minutes to eat burnt chicken in the suburbs. Perhaps the life of famous musicians was not as glamorous as Suzanne had always thought.

For the next hour or so, Marci went completely insane in the way only a starstruck pregnant woman could manage: alternately cleaning, giggling, and complaining to Jake that she wished their stuff were "hipper." Neither Jake nor Suzanne could reassure Marci that their furnishings were just fine, no matter what argument they made, so they eventually just started ignoring her rants and sat out on the patio together, drinking beer.

After a while, Marci joined them. She was

a bit sweaty and winded from her efforts to tidy up the house, but Suzanne couldn't help noticing with a smile that Marci had changed into a dressier black maternity shirt with laced edges and put on mascara.

Jake noticed it, too. "So what's the plan, Marce? Distract me with a grill fire or something and run away with him?"

"What are you talking about?" Marci demanded. Her tone was indignant, but her cheeks were ruby red.

Her husband did not relent. "I'm just saying, it's been a while since you wore makeup for just me, that's all."

"That's completely unfair," Marci said. "I can't clean up a little when we're meeting a new person? Someone special to Suzanne?"

Suzanne snorted. "Don't drag me into this."

"He's a *famous* special person," Jake said, lifting his beer bottle to Marci. "You can't deny that plays some role in all your primping and preparing. It's not as if you do this every time Suzanne brings home the flavor of the week."

"Hey!" Suzanne snapped.

"Sorry," Jake said.

"Yeah," Marci said, trying to get the heat off herself. "But Suzanne really likes this guy. I can tell."

Suzanne opened her mouth to speak, but a voice behind them cut her off. "I'm glad to hear that."

Apparently, none of them had heard the doorbell, and Dylan had entered through the side gate. He approached without hesitation and kissed Suzanne gallantly on the cheek. "Nice to meet you," he said to Marci, and kissed the back of her hand while she turned a shade of red Suzanne had never seen on a person before.

"It's the pregnancy," she said, fanning her face. "Makes me blush at anything."

"Then I won't have to work too hard," Dylan said huskily. "Thank you for having me in your home." He handed Marci a bouquet of wildflowers and a bottle of wine before turning to shake hands with Jake. Suzanne made the formal introductions without letting her gaze linger too long on Dylan. She wondered how much he had overheard. Could she *never* be around this guy without being completely embarrassed?

Things smoothed out quickly, however, as Dylan asked polite, open questions about Marci and Jake and their jobs, the area they lived in, the house, and so on. He was interested in Marci's copywriting and her side project, "The Temp Girl's Guide to Life." But he connected more with Jake's work, as he was a sports fan and had spent so much time around cameras himself.

At a lull in the conversation, Dylan asked Jake and Marci how they'd met, and all three of the old friends laughed. They told the story in rounds, interrupting one another and disputing details. They argued about the name of their harsh TA in English 101. Marci said Jake had hit on her after a Frisbee game, but Jake said she'd been flirting with him first. They all three vehemently disagreed about whose idea it had been for the two of them to promise to get married when they turned thirty. Dylan laughed at the story in appropriate places, and whether he was laughing at the story itself or the hilarity of watching the friends try to tell it, the response seemed genuine.

They enjoyed a feast of burgers, delicious — not burnt — chicken, grilled veggie kabobs, and microwave brown rice. Marci seemed to recover from her fascination with Dylan and was able to make relatively normal conversation with him. Only once or twice did she sound a little like someone doing an article on a movie star for the high school paper, and Suzanne was able to nip those instances in the bud with a series of tactful, distracting interventions. As the other three polished off a few beers, the evening became more relaxed, and they found themselves playing spades around the kitchen table.

By midnight, Marci could barely keep her head off the table. Because she refused to let pregnancy push her into bed early, Jake was forced to claim that *he* was too tired to stay up any longer, even though he nearly had to carry her up the stairs. They said good night, and Suzanne promised to make sure the downstairs was locked before going home.

Dylan shuffled the cards expertly. "Another game?" he asked. "Gin rummy?"

"Sure," Suzanne said. She knew she should go home. It was a long drive back to Buckhead, and at some point she, too, would have trouble staying awake.

"Let's just hope you don't kick my ass at this like you did at poker the other night."

"I didn't kick your ass," she objected.

"Yes, you did. You kicked all our asses. And then you folded with a winning hand. I looked at your cards when you left."

Suzanne was silent. What could she say?

"Why would you do that?" he asked. His tone was curious, not accusatory.

"I don't know," she lied. "I guess it seemed rude to beat everyone on my first visit."

She had tried to sound light and flirty, but

he eyed her suspiciously under one raised eyebrow. "You don't strike me as the type to pull punches," he said. "I don't know. I've got my eye on you, Scarlett."

"Seems to me you'd be better served with your eyes on your cards," she said, trying to mimic his homespun accent.

He laughed. They played two hands, which she won, and agreed it was time to call it quits around 1:00 A.M. She was debating hanging out to sleep on Jake and Marci's couch, but he held the door open on his way out, and she followed him without thinking. The night was cool and humid. Suzanne realized it was the second time in two nights she had walked out to her car with Dylan Burke by her side. She shivered involuntarily, and he put his arm around her.

"I guess this is ending better than the last time we played cards," she said awkwardly. He looked at her without speaking, and she felt suddenly exposed. "I mean, at least you're not pissing off some busty blonde just by talking to me."

"You realize, don't you, that you yourself are a busty blonde?" he said. "You're always mentioning it, so I thought I would point out that it applies to you, as well."

"Yeah, but it's different. I don't wear those

astonishingly tiny, revealing outfits."

"Hmm . . . ," he said. "I seem to have vivid memories of a silky lace thing that wasn't exactly modest."

"But that wasn't in public —"

"Calm down, Scarlett. I'm just giving you a hard time."

She smiled noncommittally. *He remembers my pajamas.*

"There is something else, about Misty," he said cautiously, pausing at the driver's door of her car and leaning against it. His truck was directly behind her car in Jake and Marci's driveway.

Here it comes, Suzanne thought. *They're engaged. She's pregnant. She's his cousin or something.*

"One reason she was so pissed, and so rude to you, was that I slept in a hammock on the deck that night. After the poker game."

"Ah," Suzanne said. She felt silly that she had no idea how those things were connected.

"Shit," he said, to no one in particular, confusing her even more.

Dylan leaned his head back against the roof of her car, looking up at the few stars visible with all the lights around. He looked brooding and dramatic, like one of his

285

videos. He seemed to be gathering himself for something. "Yes. She was in my bed, waiting for me, and I couldn't . . . I couldn't be with another woman with you on my mind. Couldn't even sleep next to her. I know how ridiculous that sounds. It's why she was completely pissed at me. And why the guys made fun of me the whole next day."

"You told the guys?"

"No, but they knew something was going on. You left so fast, and Misty's not exactly discreet when she's angry."

But what *was* going on? They had flirted a little, maybe. He'd hurt her feelings, and she'd folded her cards. She had walked to her cabin alone, and they spent the next morning talking like old friends. Then he showed up to return a scarf and been a perfect gentleman last night. Now, here they were. One in the morning in a driveway in the suburbs. Like teenagers out past curfew.

He reached up to tuck a strand of hair behind her ear, letting his hand linger there.

"You make me . . . discombobulated," he said. It would've sounded ridiculous from almost anyone, but in his country accent it was even funnier.

"Discombobulated?" she asked, unable to repress a smile. "Well, I can't say I've ever done that to a man before."

"See?" he said. "You're doing it again. Just . . . just shut *up.*"

Before she could express her indignation, he pulled her abruptly into him. The kiss was unexpected and a little rough. Then he softened, bringing up his other hand to hold her head on both sides. She wanted to pull back, to escape the confusion his closeness created. But she wanted to be closer, too. Dylan held her and kissed her for a long moment, leaning against her car, her head captive in his hands. Her heart swelled in her chest, and warmth spread all the way to her toes.

"Sorry," he said eventually, pulling back and breaking the spell. "I didn't plan to do that. *Dammit.*"

"It's okay," Suzanne said uncertainly. *Was it?* She thought of Misty grinding on his lap at the cabin. And in her head, about fifty glossy magazine pictures of him with various women. She had seen them all during her research before the gala, and now she couldn't erase them from her mind. The images spun in front of her: awards shows, parties, concerts, beaches. Dylan coiffed and styled, wearing anything from a trendy tuxedo to carefully ripped jeans to a bathing suit and, naturally, the camouflage hat.

Always with a crooked little grin for the camera, and always a perky pair of double-Ds in easy squeezing distance.

She could not erase these images, nor could she reconcile them with the man standing here, leaning against her car like a lost kid and holding her hand. She felt as though the guy in front of her had . . . not an evil twin, but a famous one. Tonight, he wore glasses, several days' stubble, and a look of frustrated longing, clearly torn by something she didn't fully understand. She could virtually feel his heart beating against hers, entirely and miserably human.

But it is *the same man,* she reminded herself. *You can't pretend that other life doesn't exist.*

"Suzanne," he said, saying her real name with deliberation, sounding tortured. Not Scarlett. He lingered near her neck as though at any moment he might sink into her and lose himself. "I — God — I'm an idiot for saying this . . . but I don't think this is a good idea. Not now, at least."

She'd half expected it, even thought it herself. But hearing him say it stung.

She saw sadness in his eyes as he started to explain. "It's just —"

"Please, don't," she interrupted. No speech. With the exception of Jake, who had spurned her early advances in college before showing a slow-building preference for Marci, this was the first time in her life a man had rejected *her,* and the one thing she did not need was a laundry list of reasons.

"I want to," he said, almost pleading. "I need to say why."

"Why? How does that help?" she fired at him. "Anyway, I know the reasons. I mean, there are so many of them. They could fill up my dining room wall."

He snorted, nodding grimly.

"There are the hundreds of women. No, hundreds of *thousands* of women, out there." She gestured wildly in the direction of what might have been Atlanta. Or New York. But who cared? It was true in all directions. "All in love with you, and all fantasizing about what would happen if they could get you alone for just a few minutes. There's the fact that not only do we work together, sort of, but that your sister is my one and only client at the moment. The fact that you spend half your life on the road, that neither of us could hold an adult relationship together with superglue, our age difference —"

"We're only seven years apart," he protested, raising his head to meet her eyes.

"Whatever. It's enough. And we don't

have to talk about any of it. There's no point, right?" Her surprising anguish was coming out as hostility, not at all what she intended.

"No, we don't have to talk about it, if you don't want to. But" — he put his hand on her cheek and wiped away a tear she didn't realize was there — "age has *nothing* to do with it."

"Only someone your age would think that," she said sardonically.

He smiled ruefully. Suzanne had the sense that neither this evening nor this conversation was turning out as he'd hoped. Their playful flirting over gin rummy felt like forever ago, rather than just a few minutes. He looked tired. Resigned.

"Can I follow you home again? Please? I'll feel better if I know you're safe."

"No, thanks," she said bitterly. He nodded. She tried to follow up more softly. "I'm fine. Really."

"Can I call you sometime?" he persisted. "As a friend, I mean?"

"It seems to me you have more than enough friends, Dylan." Starlets. Groupies. Drinking buddies. Fans. Old friends. Wait, no, only *young* friends. The chasm between twenty-six and thirty-three felt suddenly massive. Especially when twenty-six was active, talented, and obscenely famous and thirty-three wanted to be in bed by eleven o'clock most nights and had Junior League meetings to attend each month.

"Well, yeah, but you're . . . different. I can talk to you."

She could tell he meant it. Looking at him under the mercury orange of the streetlight, she saw not the successful singer who had capitalized on his wild streak and rebellious attitude, but a little boy trapped in a man's body. A man's handsome, deep-voiced, sexy body that she wanted desperately to reach out and touch. *No. He's right. No, no, no.*

"I don't think it's such a good idea." She kissed his cheek, pleased with herself for this gesture of maturity. "I'll see you at the wedding, okay?"

Dylan grazed her cheek with one hand, sighing. "Okay. Good night, Scarlett."

She spent the night on Jake and Marci's couch, rolling around miserably and getting up to leave before they ventured downstairs in the morning. She was in no frame of mind for conversation, even the funny, Dylan-bashing kind that she knew Marci would help provide. Maybe in a couple of days.

On the drive back to her apartment, she

tried to calm herself with reasonable thoughts. She had no reason to be mad, or even annoyed, at Dylan. He had simply said what they both knew to be true. If he hadn't said it, she would have. He had saved her the trouble. She should be grateful. Having an adult conversation about why a relationship wouldn't work was so grown-up, unlike sneaking out under cover of darkness as she normally did. He was helping her grow as a person. *Fan-fucking-tastic.*

By the time she got to her apartment a half hour later, Suzanne had run out of both mature, reasonable thoughts and irrational, angry impulses. The building was silent this early on a Sunday; a light drizzle was keeping all but the most hardcore runners tucked in their beds. Sleep was foremost on her mind as she put the key in her door, exhausted and a little light-headed from the last couple of days. Otherwise, she might have noticed the tiny scratches around the lock or that the smooth retraction of the dead bolt was not quite as solid as usual.

Two messages were waiting on her machine when she got inside. She dropped her purse and keys next to the door. Her heart leapt at the flashing red 2 as a seedling of hope sprouted, despite her best efforts to keep it down. *He had called.* Dylan had called to say that he was wrong and wanted to see her today. Not that seeing him was what *she* wanted, of course. Suzanne knew absolutely that being with Dylan was a horrible idea. And that's what she would tell him if he had called.

But Dylan hadn't called. The first message was from an equally surprising person, however: William Fitzgerald. His deep, rich Southern accent had become more pronounced with time. "Hello, Suzanne. My mother said that you tried to get in touch with me. It's really nice to hear from you. I'd love to catch up. It's funny you called, because I've actually been thinking about you quite a bit recently. Why don't we meet for dinner this week sometime?" He left his number. *Dinner — not coffee or drinks. So he's probably not married, then.*

The next message was not Dylan, either, but Chad. "Hey, Suzanne, call me when you get this. I've been checking my old voice mail, and there's something I think you should —"

The message was cut off by the startling sound of the phone ringing in the present. A quick glance at the caller ID told her it was Chad again. *I'm so tired,* she thought. *I should just let it roll to the machine. Chad will*

understand. What could possibly be so impor-
tant?

Suddenly, it struck her, and a cold shiver ran down her spine. It was not yet seven in the morning. On a Sunday. Her former assistant was not a morning person, and neither was she. They had generally started their work in the office at ten, and even then they barely said two words to each other before noon. If he was calling this early, it must be important.

She had just grabbed the receiver from its cradle to answer, when it was smacked violently out of her hand, sent tumbling to the floor by some sort of object — a stick or handle of some kind. Shock and pain clouded her awareness; on instinct, she tried to bend down to get the phone rather than look at the person behind her who had cast the blow. In seconds, however, there was a strong arm around her throat, and she could no longer move to accomplish, either. A white cloth moved in front of her nose and mouth. In an instant, the world went black.

19

Dylan Burke paced in frustration around the studio apartment his family kept in downtown Atlanta. Just a tiny space with nondescript, corporate-looking furniture, it was designed for his and his parents' sporadic use during layovers, meetings with non-Nashville executives, or social visits to Atlanta. Although the place paled in comparison to his cabin in the mountains or his parents' home in Nashville, lately he'd found himself here more and more often. He loved Tennessee, and it would always be home, but Atlanta seemed to offer him more diversity of culture, more opportunities to reinvent himself and expand his musical sphere of influence.

The place was small, but it had all he needed: kitchen, comfortable couches, a bedroom closet big enough to keep an old guitar handy. A couple of excellent bars and barbecue restaurants were within walking distance, and it was only a few minutes to Turner Field. He had a decent view of downtown, and busy neighbors who either didn't recognize him or were polite enough to pretend. It was one of the few places in the world he could come and go unnoticed. It was as close as Dylan could come to a normal life, and it felt as much like home as anywhere else.

Right now, however, he wanted to tear down the walls.

It was nearly two o'clock on Sunday afternoon. He had been doing laps around the coffee table all morning. He was mad at himself, mad at Suzanne, mad at the damn phone for not ringing.

He had regretted what happened with Suzanne almost immediately after pulling out of Jake and Marci's driveway. His logical brain knew he had been right, that getting into a real relationship with someone like Suzanne — and there was no way he could settle for less than that, *not with her* — was a recipe for disaster. Yet a less logical part of him had wanted, more than anything, to keep kissing her and walk straight into that disaster with his eyes and heart wide open.

He had been about to turn onto the entrance ramp for GA 400 on his way back to the studio apartment when the tide

296

turned in the battle going on inside his brain, and he decided to go back. He wanted to call, but he'd forgotten to charge his phone the night before, and it lay useless in the ancient truck's passenger seat. He guessed she'd probably still be at Marci's house, though, because she had not yet gotten in her car when he'd pulled out of the driveway.

So he'd go to her, knock gently on a window, and tell her . . . what? That he thought he might love her? After one kiss? Impossible. But there was something about her. He needed her to know. The words would come, he reasoned, just as they did when he'd been stuck on a lyric for weeks and they had only hours of studio time left. He'd think of something. He always did.

Maybe she'd reject him right back, as she seemed inclined to do, and reiterate the reasons that things wouldn't work out between them. Maybe friendship would be all they'd ever have. Or maybe, if she'd been telling the truth, she would not offer him friendship even. But he was sure he had seen something behind those eyes. And she was the first new friend, real friend, he had made in ages. Whatever was going to happen, he had to try.

Exuberant with the idea of seeing her

again, and for the first time in years telling a woman the exact truth about how he felt, Dylan sang along loudly with Willie Nelson on the radio. He was heading down a long two-lane road that he thought should lead back to Marci's house, not caring at all that it was nearly two in the morning. The directions to the house were on his lifeless phone, but he thought he remembered the basics and that he would know it when he saw it.

After a while, he thought the scenery looked less familiar and that perhaps he'd gone too far. Alpharetta seemed to be a sea of subdivisions with lots of similar, oversize houses on small lots broken up by upscale strip malls, chain restaurants, and pharmacies. It was difficult to tell, especially at night, whether he was covering familiar ground or not. He came to a cross street with a familiar name and followed it for a while, feeling increasingly confused and frustrated. He passed several subdivisions that looked similar to Marci's and struggled to remember the name on the stone wall he'd seen on the way in a few hours ago. *It was something "ford,"* he thought. *Kingsford? No, that was charcoal. Stratford? Wafford? Wexford?*

He passed a gas station that did not look at all familiar and found himself at another intersection: Kimball Bridge and Medlock Bridge. He was suddenly unsure that he had been on the right road at all. Everything seemed to be named "bridge" or "ferry" in this part of the world. Now, he had absolutely no idea where he'd come from or how to get back. He thought about going into the gas station for help, but what would he say? He didn't know Marci's last name or phone number or even Suzanne's number. And if he had known, they were all probably asleep by now.

There was nothing to do but go home and charge his phone and call Suzanne tomorrow. He went into the gas station to get directions back to the highway, vowing to himself that he would memorize Suzanne's number the next day and buy a car charger for his phone.

After finally getting his phone charged this morning, he had memorized her number as he dialed it, just in case. But so far Suzanne had not answered his calls. He'd tried her cell phone a couple of times before lunch and even managed to get her home number from an irritated Yvette. He knew Suzanne was angry from the frosty way she'd pulled away from him last night, but this kind of avoidance didn't seem like her style. In his experience, Suzanne had always been classy, even under duress. So he paced around the tiny living room, alternating between dismissive anger and an absurd impulse to simply drive to her apartment and confront her in person.

He was in the middle of this very debate when there was a knock on the door. He froze. *Who the hell could that be?* Not Suzanne. She didn't know where this apartment was, and he was not even sure he'd mentioned that it existed. Had she called Yvette looking for him? It wasn't like Yvette to give out his private information, but because he'd called her looking for Suzanne this morning, maybe . . .

The knock came again, more insistent. He crossed to the peephole. *Shit.*

Misty's face had a natural frown to it, which seemed emphasized by her tanned skin — unusually dark for spring. Her white-blond hair was pulled back in a sporty ponytail, and she wore a tight T-shirt and running shorts, which showed off her best features: extra-large silicone-enhanced breasts and sturdy, athletic legs. He marveled at how he could appreciate these things through the peephole and feel no desire whatsoever to open the door.

Misty, however, had other ideas. A duffel bag was slung over her shoulder. "Dylan. I know you're in there. Open up."

He thought about ignoring her, waiting to see if she would just go away, but she persisted more loudly. "I saw your truck downstairs. I'm *not* leaving."

He knew she meant this. Before they'd started seeing each other — if you could call it that — a few months before, he had known Misty most of his life. His sister Amber used to babysit Misty as a kid and sometimes brought her home to play with Dylan and Kate while Amber talked on the phone. As adults, Amber and Misty had stayed in touch and become friends.

So Misty had known him since long before fame and fortune had struck. For this reason, Dylan had found that she was more comfortable — refreshingly so, at first — than most girls speaking candidly with him. He'd also found that it was harder than he expected to extract himself from the relationship once it had begun. They had hooked up after a night of drunken revelry at the mountain house, and she had more or less set up camp at his side ever since.

At first, he hadn't minded this: Misty was obviously attractive. He'd noted with pride how other men's mouths watered when they walked past. The press loved her, too — especially the rose tattoo on her cleavage that she showed to advantage in everything from bikinis to formal wear. She was bold and refreshingly fearless, unlike the hordes of groupies who acted as though everything he said or did was solid gold.

But lately Dylan had been feeling that Misty's demands for attention were becoming more frequent, more expensive, and less polite in their delivery. Amber and Sherrie had also begun hinting in front of the family, to his utter dismay, that Dylan and Misty might be moving toward marriage. He'd pleaded with them to stop adding fuel to that fire, but Amber in particular could apparently imagine no better sister-in-law than Misty.

Seeing her now in the hallway, arms folded across her chest in impatience, Dylan knew there was no getting around letting her in. He owed her that much, he supposed. They hadn't spoken since he dismissed her from the mountain house the week before, and he'd been avoiding both Misty and his sisters ever since. That couldn't last forever. *Might as well take your medicine, Burke. This day isn't going well anyway.*

"Hi, Mis," he sighed as he opened the door and she sauntered in, tossing her bag on the couch.

"Where have you been?" she asked without preface.

"What do you mean?" he asked. He knew it was an insulting question, even for Misty, but he couldn't think of what else to say.

"Dylan. I'm worried about you. I've been talking to your sisters. We're *all* worried about you."

"Why?" he asked, leaning against the back of the leather love seat for support. He was actually curious. Were his sisters really worried about him?

"You've been acting weird lately. Distant. And then, at the cabin, it's like you were a different person. I mean, you were all fidgety, like you couldn't sit still. I couldn't even keep you in the hot tub with me. Or our bed." *Our* bed. The significance did not escape him. She made a pouting face and stepped closer to him, running her fingers along his arm. "That's not like you at all, baby."

"Sorry," he said softly. He looked down at his bare feet. Misty wore a pair of baby-blue running shoes with rounded bottoms that were supposed to tone her leg muscles while she walked. Dylan had mentioned once that they looked ridiculous and incurred her wrath for days. She followed his gaze and slid one foot between his, her tanned leg grazing his rolled up jeans.

303

"You're not attracted to me anymore?" she asked.

"That's not it," he said. It really wasn't.

She took his hands from the back of the couch and put them on her hips. "Then what is it, baby? You don't have a new girlfriend, do you?"

"No, I don't," he said. That much was certainly true. He left out the part, however, where he had kissed Suzanne and then gotten hopelessly lost in Alpharetta trying to get back to her. And the part where he'd been on edge all day, the bottom of his stomach churning, trying to get her to call him back.

But other than that, what was there to tell, really? She wasn't returning his calls; they had both agreed their relationship was a no-go. Was there any reason to rub it in Misty's face?

He should just end it with Misty and get it over with. Maybe be alone for a while and try to sort things out between now and Kate's wedding. He knew it was the right thing to do, and the words he needed were available to him: *I'm sorry, but this isn't going to work.* Walk her to the door, hand her the duffel bag, and spend the next two weeks defending himself from his sisters and hoping to talk to Suzanne.

But he didn't. His feet felt stuck to the hardwood floor. His hands on her hips felt as though they were holding the only solid matter for miles. He did manage to turn his head slightly when Misty leaned in to kiss him, but she seemed perfectly content to kiss his neck instead. Her lips were thin and a little dry, and he wondered how Suzanne's softer, fuller lips would feel against his skin. The familiar warm feeling stirred in his belly, and he sucked in air as Misty sharply bit a small area of skin on his collarbone.

Tell her to leave. Push her away. "No," he said softly to the ceiling. "This is not a good idea." Exactly what he had said to Suzanne the night before. And she had agreed.

"Why not?" Misty whined. "I'm so hot for you." In demonstration of this, she grasped his hand and pushed it down the front of her shorts, where he could feel the truth of her statement, warm and wet on his hand. She held his hand there and began to move her hips in little circles, pressing herself against him. She was familiar and inviting beneath his hands; he felt his body respond to her arousal. He remembered the pain of unlinking himself from Suzanne the night before, how his body had ached for hours afterward while he drove around lost in suburbia. It seemed as if he had used all his

305

willpower to do that, and now he had none left to resist Misty.

No, he thought. *It's not right.*

But why? a familiar voice intoned. It was the voice that had led him all his life toward pleasure and abandon, toward warm touches and good feelings and the impressed laughter of his friends. It had earned him his wild reputation and hosted countless parties that bordered on orgies. *Who is it hurting? Misty and I have been dating. This is nothing new. Suzanne and I are not dating. She doesn't even want to be friends. Hell, she's ignoring my phone calls.* No one *ignores my calls.*

Something burned in him — a combination of lust and anger, wounded heart and wounded pride. And Misty, grinding against his hips and hand and kissing his throat, seemed to sense the change and pounced. "Oh, baby, I've missed you," she groaned into his ear. "Please, please let me show you how much."

Without waiting for an answer, she peeled herself out of her T-shirt and shorts, revealing a lacy bra that was incongruous with her running gear and a tiny white thong that barely covered anything. *She planned this,* Dylan realized somewhere beneath the fog.

But did it matter? Did any of it really matter?

Misty hoisted herself onto his hips, crossing her legs behind him. He instinctively grabbed hold to keep her from falling. "Take me to bed, baby," she commanded in his ear. Whatever his better judgment might be saying, whatever confusion he was feeling, even the faint sound of his phone buzzing softly on the table — it was all left behind as he staggered through the bedroom door and kicked it closed.

20

The face glaring at Suzanne when she awoke was not that of Rick or anyone else from her list. It was a familiar face, she thought, but not one she could place. Round, cherubic, surrounded by inky-black tendrils of hair pulled into pigtails. Pretty, except for, perhaps, wearing too much makeup. Suzanne's vision was blurry, but behind the girl she could see the familiar, if sideways, cabinets of her own kitchen. She was lying on her side in the carpeted area where her kitchen and living room merged with the bedrooms and bath.

Her head ached and her face felt raw, as though she had been dragged across the carpet on her side. She started to reach up and touch her face, to inspect the damage with her fingers, and found she could not move her arms. A rough rope bound her wrists behind her back. The chubby girl, dressed all in black except for striped knee-socks, sat a few feet from her with her legs crossed. As Suzanne tried to wriggle free, the girl spoke in a chirpy singsong voice that reminded her absurdly of Snow White and was in complete contrast with the content of her words. "Ah, ah, ah — no moving, please. I would hate to kill you, but I will."

At the girl's words, she saw the gun. Small and silver, the girl twirled it carelessly around one finger. Suzanne knew nothing about guns, but she felt sure it was dangerous despite the small size. As awareness returned to her confused brain, terror came with it. She looked at the girl again, and a name floated back to her as though from a dream. *Patty? Penny?*

"I'll bet you don't even remember me, do you, you self-absorbed bitch?" the girl said.

Suzanne frantically searched her mental files. The stalker was a *woman*. She'd been making all the wrong lists. "I remember you," she said slowly, trying to keep her voice neutral while she worked to place the familiar face in front of her.

A memory floated up through the muck of her aching brain. "I saw you . . . at the bar the other night." She remembered now, this girl, in striped knee-high socks, standing next to a tall man whose face Suzanne hadn't seen. Maybe *he* was the key? "You

were with . . . um, I can't remember . . ."
She fished, hoping for more information.

"You don't know him," the girl snapped.
"But I think maybe he'd like to get to know
you."

This sent a chill down Suzanne's spine.
She tried to look around to see whether
anyone else was with them, but they seemed
to be alone. "We'll get to him in a minute,"
the girl said. "I told him I'd call when you
woke up. I can't believe you don't remember
me. You really are as narcissistic as I
thought. That actually makes me feel better."

"I'm sorry," Suzanne said. "My head
hurts, but maybe if you give me a minute . . ."

"I've given you years!" the girl shrieked.
"We met at UGA, remember? You came
back for that alumni luncheon three years
ago, and I was your ambassador?"

Suzanne did remember, now. It had been
one of those things she'd said yes to doing
months in advance and then regretted as
the actual date approached because she
didn't really have time to do it. At the height
of her success, right after she had planned
an absolutely stunning rooftop party for a
new hip-hop label and helped organize a
huge charity event for Elton John, the

university had invited her back to be a keynote speaker at a humanities alumni luncheon.

She'd been superstressed about it and almost canceled, until Chad reminded her that would not be good for her image. This girl — the name was Penny, she decided — had been an undergraduate art history student assigned to give her a tour of the new buildings on campus and to introduce her to key faculty before the luncheon. Later, she had been invited to make a substantial gift to the university, as well, and she realized that having spent the morning with one of its hopeful future graduates was supposed to remind her of her happy days in Athens and grease the wheels for a donation.

Suzanne remembered two main things from that day. One was that Penny had been superchatty and fairly annoying and that Suzanne had tried to ditch her at several points in the morning but failed. The other was that after lunch she had located her old art history professor, now divorced and head of the department, and canceled the rest of her day to relive old times with him — this time in his sad little apartment rather than behind the locked door of his office. Their time together had been a somewhat disappointing encounter with someone she'd once thought of as so powerful and sophisticated, but Suzanne had supposed that was a good lesson, too. In the end, people were just people.

Now, lying bound on the floor of her condo, she felt deeply ashamed of that day — how she'd blown off Penny, how she'd refused to even stay for dinner with Dr. Kimball, pretending she had a meeting to get back to in Atlanta. She'd never asked him about his marriage or how he was doing or, until just this moment, considered that maybe the breakup of his marriage had something to do with the fact that he'd been fucking Suzanne during his office hours all those years ago. She hadn't asked because she didn't want to know.

"Of course I remember you. Penny, right?" she ventured, praying like crazy that it wasn't Patty.

Penny brightened, and Suzanne breathed a sigh of relief. The girl pulled her off the floor to a sitting position. "Well, I'm glad you remember that, at least. I *told* him you would know who I was."

"Absolutely I know who you are, sweetie." Suzanne knew she was going out on a limb with "sweetie" but figured she had a better shot with this girl while it was just the two of them. She didn't know who "he" was, and she didn't care to find out. Then her slowly firing synapses put something together. "You've been calling us. About being an intern."

"Yes!" Penny said. "I called for weeks, and I kept getting that awful Chad guy — he's so stuck-up — and I knew if I could just get through to you, you'd remember what you promised."

"What I promised," Suzanne repeated, not having any idea what this meant.

"Yeah, you know, after the luncheon, when you said I had potential because I was so persistent and you'd be happy to teach me the ropes in event planning. You said I'd be great in fund-raising, especially."

"Right," Suzanne said. She did not remember this at all. She met so many people in the course of her work and at the Junior League, it often felt as though she were an actress onstage, delivering lines. Surely, she could not be expected to remember every member of the audience. Maybe Suzanne had said those things, but people said those kinds of things all the time. Surely, this girl hadn't thought it was a job offer?

Penny was tearful. "When you didn't return my calls, it really hurt my feelings. I thought we were friends, and I thought you were going to help me get a job. My parents kicked me out and I waited tables for a while, and every week I'd call you, looking for a way to work with you. I just admired you so much. I wanted to be like you."

"I'm so sorry, Penny," Suzanne said, and meant it. Of course, that didn't excuse the stalking or the kidnapping, and Suzanne was planning to hit her over the head with something at her first opportunity, but still. She did feel a little sorry for the girl all the same. "Maybe I can help you now?"

The girl seemed to go cold at this. She glared at Suzanne. "Oh, you're going to help me, all right."

Suzanne scrambled to soften Penny again, to win her over. She had to find a way out of this. "Of course I'll help you. Maybe you can come work with me now. I've seen that you can be persistent and creative, at, er, problem solving."

Penny laughed, a high, unsettling sound. "You think you're going to offer me a job *now?*" she asked, incredulous. "And they say *I'm* crazy!"

I'd say that's an understatement, Suzanne thought. Not knowing what to say next, she was silent.

"Who are you to offer anyone a job? I've destroyed your career. You'll be lucky if they let you plan kids' birthday parties after how you've humiliated yourself. How I've humiliated you. Just like you humiliated me. I told everyone I was going to work with the great Suzanne Hamilton and pretty soon I'd be on the style pages like you."

"I am really sorry, Penny. Please, just untie me and we'll talk about it. Let's make this right before it gets worse."

"Oh, it might get worse for you, *sweetie.*" She spat back Suzanne's endearment as though it were poison. "But things are going to be fine for me and Gunnar. Speaking of which, he's waiting to hear from us."

Silencing Suzanne's protests with a glare, Penny pulled out a phone and pressed a button. "She's awake," she said simply, and then asked Suzanne, "What's your ATM code?"

"What?" Suzanne asked. Immediately, Penny reached back and slapped her hard across the face.

"Next time, sweetie, I use the hand with the gun in it. What's your fucking ATM code? If you tell us wrong, I'll shoot you right now." Her words were designed to sound cold and aggressive, and they were, but Suzanne thought she sensed a hesitation, like Penny was playing a role for the man on the phone. If that were true, maybe she had a chance.

Suzanne recited the numbers and waited. After a minute, Penny nodded in apparent confirmation that the code had worked and hung up. Gunnar was going to be clearing out her checking account. Well, it wouldn't take as long as it once might have, Suzanne thought grimly.

She decided to try Penny again, feeling she had little to lose and that things could only get worse when Gunnar got back. "So what happens when my money is gone? I assume you have a plan." She tried to sound calm, authoritative, like the person Penny had once seen her as.

"Of course we do. I've done my homework on you, and your parents are well-off. I think once we get you out of here, they'll pay big money to get their sweet, perfect little girl back." Suzanne's first, shameful thought was that Penny might be barking up the wrong tree. Given his background in law and connection to politics, she could almost imagine a scenario in which her dad might say, "We don't negotiate with terrorists."

But of course that wasn't true. In her heart, she knew her parents would have the house mortgaged and the family silver sold in hours to save her if it got that far.

Something like this would absolutely devastate her parents. Her dad especially. This wasn't about the fact that she hadn't gone to law school or gotten married before thirty. No matter what had or hadn't transpired between them, Suzanne had a sudden clarity that her parents' hearts would break if they thought they might lose her. She wouldn't put them through that. She wouldn't let that happen.

She closed her eyes, took a deep breath, and allowed herself one brief moment of absolute terror before she put her fear in a box in her mind and sealed it. She'd allow herself to be scared later. Penny was pacing back and forth in the kitchen, whispering to Gunnar on the phone again, something about which ATM he was at now and how many more he would need to find, to get the bulk of Suzanne's money.

Suzanne tried to mentally size up her captor the way she did an unhappy client or a needling reporter. *Now, you listen to me, you little overgrown mall rat. You caught me off guard and knocked me down. You made me look at the worst of myself and live in fear. But now I am in this fight. I will defeat you. I will make you damn sorry that you picked me.*

She sat up as straight as she could and forced herself to appear calm. When Penny snapped shut the phone once more, Suzanne asked, "How did this happen to you, Penny? You always seemed so sweet. This doesn't seem like something you would do on your own."

"You don't know me," Penny said, defiant. "I can think for myself."

"Well, obviously, you're smart enough," Suzanne said. "I mean, you've been following me for weeks, and surely Gunnar hasn't been with you that whole time."

"No. He hasn't."

"So the ladder, that was your idea? Were you just trying to hurt me or hoping I'd break my neck and die or something?"

"No, I didn't want you seriously hurt," Penny said quickly. "I still hoped then that if you had an injury from the fall that you'd need extra help with the gala at the High. It was supposed to happen a week earlier, but you didn't see the ribbon for a while."

"You put the ribbon on the chandelier? So I'd have a reason to climb the ladder? What if Chad had climbed instead?" As if remembering, her arm began to ache a little. She fought off the rage building inside and tried for outward serenity.

"I thought it might serve the same purpose. Either way, you'd be short staffed. I called a few days before to see whether you needed help, but Chad blew me off, so I knew nothing had happened." Penny said this without emotion, as though she were talking about the weather.

Bless your heart, Suzanne thought with malice. "Still, pretty clever."

"I know," Penny said haughtily. "I don't need you to tell me I'm clever. Not anymore."

"You know what, Penny, maybe you never did."

"Shut up," Penny said, waving the gun at her.

Suzanne's mind raced. This wasn't working. Time to try a different tack. "Can you tell me what time it is?"

"Why?" the girl demanded.

"Um, no reason. Never mind." Suzanne hoped she sounded sincere enough that Penny might take the bait. She thought, absurdly, of Wallace Shawn and Cary Elwes in a battle of wits in one of her favorite movies, *The Princess Bride.* She and Marci had watched it more than a hundred times together since middle school. She fought off a wild urge to giggle.

"Why do you want to know what time it is? What's going to happen?"

"Nothing," Suzanne said. "I was just wondering. It's okay."

Penny came over and pointed the gun directly at Suzanne's face. The urge to giggle disappeared and her stomach lurched. "Tell me why you want to know what time it is. Now."

"Well, it's just that I'm supposed to be meeting a friend here today, but . . ."

"Which friend? When?" Penny demanded. Good, Suzanne thought; she was putting it together.

"Just my friend Dylan," Suzanne said. She strained to see the numbers on the clock over the stove and hoped she was reading them right. She tried to sound dejected. "But he won't be here until one."

"You mean that country singer? Didn't you just come from seeing him last night? He's not coming here. You're lying."

Suzanne wondered how much this insane girl knew about her life. Had she followed her to Marci's? Could Marci be in danger? *Oh, God. The baby . . .*

She stayed silent, partly because she couldn't decide the best way to convince Penny that Dylan would be there within the hour and partly because her throat was choked with rage. It seemed to work. Penny looked nervous again. She probed. "Well, you'll just stand him up. I'll move you to the back closet and put a gag in your mouth. He'll think you forgot about your little date. Or that you were just avoiding him. That wouldn't surprise him, would it?"

This last barb was caustic and pointed, but Suzanne ignored it. She was punishing herself enough for all of that. She didn't need this crazy bitch piling it on. "Actually, he knows about you," she said truthfully. "He was here when I got your *lovely* flowers."

"Oh," Penny said softly.

"So if I don't answer the door or the phone, he'll call the police. We have an agreement about it." It was a total lie, of course, but she hoped it was believable enough.

"Unless . . . ," Penny said slowly. "You call him to cancel."

Suzanne pretended to be horrified. "You can't make me do that. I won't."

Penny leveled the gun at her again, and it made an ominous clicking sound. Suzanne swallowed hard and found she did not have to fake the cracking in her voice. "Fine. I'll call him."

"And I'm going to listen on speaker to make sure you don't say anything . . . funny."

Suzanne cleared her throat nervously. "Of course. We'd better hurry before your friend gets back. Can you untie me?"

Penny seemed to think it over momentarily and then said, "No, I'll dial." She retrieved Suzanne's cell phone from her purse and found Dylan's number saved there. Obviously, Penny wasn't quite as stupid as Suzanne had hoped, but there was still a chance she could get herself rescued before the deranged duo took her to wherever they had planned to hold her for ransom. But now it all depended on Dylan.

He didn't answer, and when his voice mail message started, Suzanne raised an eyebrow at Penny, who nodded. She willed herself to stay calm, and when she heard the beep she gave it her best shot. "Hey, Dylan, it's Suzanne." Her voice was unnaturally high, but maybe that was better. "I had a great time last night, and I was just calling to say I need to reschedule our meeting today. I'm . . . catching up with an old friend, and believe it or not she loves your music almost as much as I do. She's a huge fan. I'll have to give her one of those autographed CDs of yours I always keep on hand."

Penny scowled and waved the gun in a "hurry up" motion; Suzanne knew she was out of time. "Anyway, why don't I call you next week and we'll meet then, okay? Thanks." Then Penny had pressed the END button and Suzanne had nothing left to do but wait.

21

Dylan lay in the double bed, naked from the waist down, listening to Misty talk and staring at the ceiling. The lovemaking, if you could call it that, had been swift and furious. Dylan had been nearly out of his mind with anger and frustrated lust and had been barely aware of Misty herself, which, oddly, seemed only to increase her enjoyment of the event. Now, lying in the sweat and shame of the last hour, he found himself even less happy than he had been that morning. Misty, on the other hand, seemed invigorated by what she obviously perceived as passion for her, and she was rambling on about plans for the summer tour and God knew what else.

Dylan felt restless and sick. Sick of Misty and the inane conversation, but mostly sick of himself. After a few minutes, he was desperate for a reason to get out of bed. He remembered that his phone had been buzzing earlier and mumbled something about it without waiting for her response.

He played Suzanne's message three times, trying to get his head around it. It made no sense whatsoever. Could she be drunk? No. Was she messing with him? Not really her style. Especially after the tense note they'd left on last night. She'd never been a fan of his music, and obviously didn't keep autographed CDs on hand. They'd talked about that when Officer Daniels —

It hit him like a bucket of ice water. Dylan nearly dropped the phone. With shaking hands, he checked the time Suzanne had called. Nearly forty-five minutes ago. If she were hurt, if something happened . . .

No. He wouldn't think that way. He didn't have time. He dialed 911, but before hitting SEND he realized that was bound to be a useless exercise. What would he say? A friend called to say she liked my music? How was that an emergency?

He ran to the bedroom to find his wallet, ignoring Misty's affronted questions about what was so important. Credit cards and other papers scattered to the floor unheeded while he searched, eventually putting his hands on the business card he'd been frantically searching for. He ran back to the kitchen and called Officer Bonita Daniels's direct line.

Fifteen minutes later, he hung up the phone, pulled on jeans, and reassembled his wallet. He told Misty to stay at the apartment. "Where are you going?" she demanded.

"It's an emergency with . . . a friend," he said hastily. Misty made a face.

"What do you expect me to do here by myself?" she demanded.

He had no time to argue with her. "You're welcome to leave, then." He slammed the door without waiting for an answer and barely stopped for red lights on the way to Suzanne's condo.

The police cars were in front of her building when he arrived. Bonita had answered his call right away and believed him without question. But he needed to see it for himself, to see that someone was there, helping Suzanne. He slammed the truck into park in the garage across the street and ran through the revolving doors into the lobby. Two uniformed officers were blocking the elevator doors and a couple of confused residents murmured to one another nearby.

They wouldn't let Dylan up or give him any information, so he made himself sit in an armchair across from the doors and wait.

Just please, God, let her be safe.

After what seemed like an eternity, the doors opened and a group of police officers emerged, leading out in handcuffs a robust girl with black pigtails and a tall, bald white guy who looked menacing even to Dylan. At the back of the elevator, he saw the short, round figure of Bonita Daniels, who gestured for him to join her. He held his breath until the elevator doors closed, and she said, "She's okay."

Bonita led him to Suzanne's apartment, where she was wrapped in a blanket at the dining room table, looking a way he never, ever wanted to see her. Suzanne, being interviewed by a female officer with a tightly wound bun, was speaking softly and wringing her hands on her lap. He could see red marks on her wrists where she'd apparently been tied up. When she looked up and saw him, tears welled in her eyes, and she threw off the blanket to run to him.

"Oh, God, thank you, thank you," she said. "You got my message. I was so scared. Dylan, I was so damn scared."

"I know. I'm so sorry I didn't answer the phone. Oh, Suze. I'm so sorry for what you went through." He held her back, putting his hands on her cheeks, inspecting her like a mother would examine a child who'd fallen off the monkey bars. An angry bruise was starting to show on her right cheek. "Are you hurt?"

She shook her head softly as tears flowed fresh. He pulled her close again, putting his face in her hair and inhaling deeply. She sobbed into his neck. The officer at the table gave him a wan smile as if to say that Suzanne was lucky to be alive. Dylan held her tighter, not wanting to let her go. He wanted to protect her, to erase her pain, to never leave her side again.

The officer cleared her throat, and he led Suzanne gently back to the table to finish the interview. Dylan sat next to her, holding her hand. Bonita bustled in and out, asking questions and giving directions and quiet updates. Radios beeped and crackled on the hips and shoulders of officers who came and went, taking pictures and notes, collecting evidence in little plastic bags.

"So then after you called Mr. Burke and left the message . . . ," the officer was prompting gently.

Suzanne nodded. "For a few minutes, nothing else happened. I knew that Gunnar, the man, was going to several ATMs using my card. The girl, Penny — she seemed to be just waiting for him."

The officer nodded, taking notes. Bonita

had stopped her hustling around to listen quietly as Suzanne went on. "So then he called her, I guess, to ask for the PIN to my credit cards, to get a cash advance. I don't have those codes memorized, and I said that. It sounded like maybe he told her to hit me again. But she said no, that she believed I didn't know the numbers, and she didn't think hurting me more was going to make a difference. They fought for a minute on the phone, and then I said I could look through my filing cabinet to try to find the numbers. I knew things would get worse once he got back, and I was trying to buy some time."

Dylan shuddered. The time she'd been desperately trying to buy to save her life was the same time he'd spent with Misty, ignoring Suzanne's call and trying to erase his feelings for her. He was the worst person on earth.

"So Penny got into my filing cabinet, but we couldn't find any of the information, and when Gunnar called back, he said he was around the corner." She started breathing heavy, he noticed, and he could tell she was reliving the panicked feelings.

"Are you sure she needs to talk about this now?" he asked. Bonita nodded at him, so he squeezed Suzanne's hand and sat quietly waiting.

When she went on, her voice was very small. "When he, *Gunnar,* got back, he had two black ski masks and a newspaper with him. He told Penny to put me on a chair and they put" — she gave Dylan a pained smile — "duct tape on my mouth. He took pictures of me with the newspaper in front of me and made Penny hold a knife to my throat."

She took a deep, rattling breath. The next words came out choked with fearful sobs. "That's when he said that I — I didn't look *scared* enough. That my parents might not believe I was in real danger. So he . . ." She stopped, looking at her lap. Dylan's whole body hurt. It was all he could do to remain seated, holding her shaking hand. For the first time in his life, he wanted to kill someone. Not punch or kick or wound. *Kill.* He wanted that bastard dead.

The officer taking notes wore the neutral expression of a professional: patient and nonreactive. Bonita wore a version of the same expression, one that years of training and witnessing horrible experiences had obviously given her, but he thought maybe her deep brown eyes looked watery.

Suzanne's voice was barely a whisper now.

"So he took the gun and the knife from Penny and told her to take me to the bedroom. She didn't seem to want to. I got the impression that it — maybe it hadn't really been part of their plan. Penny seemed scared, too, actually. She said they had what they needed and shouldn't they go ahead and take me to the warehouse. I guess that's where they were going to keep me while they waited for the money. Gunnar told her to shut her fat mouth and do as she was told. He pointed the gun at her and told her to take me to the bedroom, now."

Dylan felt sick. It must have shown on his face, because Bonita said softly, "Mr. Burke, why don't you step out for a minute? Dylan?" He shook his head. He needed to hear this. It was his fault it happened, and he needed to hear it.

"Penny got me up from the chair and tried to move me toward the bedroom, but my ankles and wrists were still tied, so I fell. Penny tried to carry me but couldn't. Gunnar said never mind, the kitchen table would work just fine. I tried to wriggle away, tried to scream through the duct tape. He said if I moved again, he'd shoot me. Penny put me facedown on the table. He gave her the knife and told her to cut off my skirt and underwear. He was still holding the gun at

331

her, and I think he might have been taking video with his phone." The policewomen exchanged looks.

"I think she was hesitating, because she didn't touch me, and I'm not sure what she would have done next." She looked intently at both female officers and repeated, "I'm not sure what they would have done."

Dylan wondered whether Suzanne was feeling some sympathy for the girl. He did not share these sentiments one bit.

"That's when you got here," Suzanne told Bonita, her wavering voice strong again. "Thank God."

"Ms. Hamilton, you've survived a terrible ordeal," Bonita said. She put her hand on Suzanne's shoulders. "You're going to need lots of support over the next few days." She told Suzanne and Dylan what would happen next — a trip to the hospital just as a precaution; a visit from a social worker, who would talk to Suzanne about trauma and help her find counseling if she needed it; and so on.

"Thank you," Suzanne said. Then she smiled wanly and put her hand on top of Bonita's. "Lately, I'd been feeling that my life had become a series of terrible ordeals. Now I know it was all basically just one. And it's finally over."

Even now, Dylan thought, with tears staining her cheeks and her face crumpled like a little girl's, she was beautiful. He wanted to wrap her in his arms again, but he knew that she needed her space.

Moments later, Marci's unmistakable voice echoed in the hallway. "Let me through, please, she's my friend. Yes, they called me. What is your badge number? That's *right;* you'll let me through."

Behind her, they heard Jake, murmuring apologies as Marci flustered into the room. She was blotchy and pale today, nothing like the rosy glow Dylan had seen two nights ago. She rushed to Suzanne and embraced her. "Oh my God. Are you okay?"

Bonita nodded to the other officer that she could get up and clear the space. Dylan stood, too, to give Marci his seat. He and Jake shook hands awkwardly while Marci tearfully inspected Suzanne for damage the same way he had.

"And you," Marci said, whirling toward him and hugging him hard. He could feel the ball-like hardness of her belly against him, an odd sensation. "You saved her. Thank you so much."

"No," he said, his eyes filling with tears for the first time. He fought down a painful sob trying to escape his tightened throat. "I should've been here sooner. I should've answered my phone."

"What are you talking about?" Marci asked. "That's stupid." She looked behind him then, at someone else entering the room.

When he turned around, he thought for a second he was imagining things. But there she was, standing in the doorway looking lost, wearing the same running shorts and T-shirt she'd had on when she showed up at his door a few hours before. Misty was looking curiously around Suzanne's condo, seemingly assessing both what was happening and the home of her perceived rival. She had followed him. He never should have opened that door.

"Hello," Marci said shortly. "Are you a neighbor?"

Suzanne looked up then, and Dylan wished with every fiber of his being that he could make someone invisible. Preferably Misty, but really anyone would do. "No, I'm here with Dylan," she answered possessively. She bounced over to him and put her arms around his waist. "Is everything okay, baby?"

Her presence here was a big problem in itself, but the feigned concern made him angrier. "Go wait outside," he hissed. Her disappointed gaze moved from Dylan to

Marci, who was glaring at her, and Jake, who looked confused. She slunk back out of the apartment, but the damage was done. Suzanne's head was lowered. He took the seat next to her again.

"Suzanne, I —"

Her words were soft, emotionless. "You were with her when I called."

He wished that she sounded angry. Anger, he could handle. Jealousy, he knew what to do with. Even sadness he might have been able to respond to. But Suzanne's tone was so quiet, so neutral, that he felt as though she had shrunk inside herself like a snail.

There was no reason to add dishonesty now. "Yes, I was." He tried to ignore Jake's and Marci's stares, keeping his eyes trained on Suzanne. The hot lights of the stage were nothing compared with this. "I'm so sorry."

She nodded almost imperceptibly, taking the information in. When she looked up, he saw to his utter shame that she was crying fresh tears. He sank to his knees in front of her. "Suzanne," he started. He wanted to apologize, to explain, to try to make things right. He wanted to take it all back. Anything that would make him not the worst guy in the world right now.

"No," she said, and took both of his hands. Through the tears, she sucked in a deep breath and looked up at the ceiling. "You don't need to explain anything. I owe you my life."

This complacency was the worst thing imaginable. "Suzanne, please. Can't you just slap me or call me an asshole or something? Come on, kick me in the nuts."

She gave him a tired smile. "Maybe some other time," she said.

"Sorry to interrupt," Officer Daniels said gently from the doorway. "Suzanne, your parents are here. The ambulance is on its way, and they can ride with you if you want."

"Oh, God, Bonita, do I have to go in an ambulance? I'm fine. Physically, at least."

"Well, that's protocol, but let me see if I can take you in the squad car."

Bonita stepped back into the hallway and radioed back and forth with someone while Suzanne's parents, looking overwhelmed, went to their daughter. Her mother was blond and pretty, an older version of Suzanne, and her dad was the well-fed pasty type, seemingly too young for the cane he carried.

Suzanne hugged her mother tightly while her father hung back awkwardly. He seemed unsure whether to talk to Jake and Marci or to wait to hug his daughter. Dylan felt like a stranger at a family dinner. After a few moments, his shame and discomfort became unbearable. When Bonita returned to say that the ambulance had already arrived and it might be best if Suzanne simply rode in it, he took the opportunity to duck out quietly.

22

On the Thursday before Memorial Day, nearly three weeks after the attack, Suzanne set out for the cabin in Tennessee with even more discomfort than she'd felt when she left it last time. Traffic was a mess getting out of the city, as everyone else seemed to have the same idea she did of starting the holiday weekend early. The afternoon heat was stifling, and the I-75/I-85 downtown connector was a parking lot.

She fidgeted in her seat while she waited for the cars to move, practicing her deep breathing exercises and trying not to panic. She'd been seeing a therapist twice a week since the attack, which seemed to be helping her regulate her feelings, but she was still sensitive to feeling hemmed in. Mercifully, the traffic began to move after about twenty minutes, and soon she was barreling up the highway toward the Smokies.

Kate had offered, of course, for Suzanne

to back out of the job, with full pay, after what happened. But Suzanne knew there was no way she could hand off the wedding now, especially knowing that anyone who could be found on short notice for a holiday weekend would be likely to take advantage of Kate. More than that, Suzanne was tired of hiding. Now that she knew who Penny and Gunnar were, it was easier to direct her anger at them, and she refused to let them steal one more minute of her life.

Until the incident at the High, she had never failed to finish an event, and she did not intend to let that become a pattern. Neither her attackers nor her feelings about Dylan were going to prevent her from keeping her promise to Kate.

She had barely spoken to Dylan since the attack. He'd called a couple of times to check in on her the first week, during which she stayed with her parents until she could force herself to go back to the condo, but she let it roll to voice mail. The third time, she had answered, and their conversation had been short and stilted. He asked how she was, she assured him she was fine, and then they sat in uncomfortable silence for a few seconds before Suzanne insisted that she needed to go. So many emotions tumbled inside her: anger, gratitude, attraction, betrayal, and . . . something deeper that she did not at all want to acknowledge. She couldn't process all of it. He seemed to get the message, or maybe he felt something similar, because he hadn't called back.

William, however, had called again, that same week. When she heard his voice, she realized she'd completely forgotten the message he left right before the attack. She decided to simply explain what had happened. Their first "date" was actually a long walk around her parents' neighborhood, during which she told the whole story and cried, and William held her hand as though no time had passed since they were together.

Suzanne had apologized for his humiliation ten years before, and he waved it away. "It's in the past," he said with a smile. "Even my parents are getting over it. Besides, it's nothing compared to what you just went through." They'd been out a few times since then, and he had graciously agreed to come up the next day to be her date to the wedding weekend. Crossing the border into Tennessee Thursday evening, she still wasn't sure this had been the wisest choice. But Marci and Jake had plans for the weekend, and Suzanne didn't think she could handle it alone.

■ ■ ■ ■

Friday morning, Suzanne wandered into Kate's bedroom at the cabin to bring her a tray of snacks and found the bride in tears. Thinking it was hormones or prewedding jitters, Suzanne sat on the bed next to her and waited for her to talk. When it seemed all Kate could do was cry, Suzanne prompted gently, "Anything I can do?"

"You can send everyone home!" Kate said wildly. Unlike some of Dylan's other sisters, Kate was not prone to baseless dramatics, so Suzanne began to worry.

"Honey, what's wrong?"

"Everything. Jeff is playing *golf.*"

"And we don't want him to play golf?"

"I told him if he went to play golf, he shouldn't bother coming back because the wedding was off!" Kate hesitated and then went on, embarrassed. "We had a huge fight. I had asked him to stay nearby today, in case I needed him. Then he *informed* me this morning he was going to play golf, by text message. The coward."

"Ah," Suzanne said. She had actually overheard Dylan and his two brothers-in-law convincing Jeff the night before that he should go play golf with them that day. They

341

reasoned that keeping himself out of the way would really be a gift to his bride and that it was his last chance to play golf without needing permission from his wife. Jeff had resisted, but they had teased him mercilessly about his manhood and being "whipped" until he gave in. Suzanne suspected that the primary reason they actually had in mind was that taking the groom to the golf course before the wedding made it easier for them to get permission from *their* wives. But she stayed out of it.

She decided to take a practical approach with Kate. "Do you need him now? Is there something I can do?"

"No," Kate admitted tearfully. "But I just can't believe he would go play golf after I asked him not to. He didn't even *ask* — not that he needs my permission, of course; I know that'd make me sound like a controlling bitch."

"No, it doesn't," Suzanne said.

"It's just so unlike Jeff to disregard my feelings like that, or at least I thought it was unlike him. But lately it seems like we've been fighting a lot."

"Fighting?"

"Well, not knock-down drag-outs or anything," Kate said. "Oh, you don't want to hear all this. Not after everything . . .

everything you went through."

"Of course I do," Suzanne said, pressing Kate's hand gently. "This matters, too."

"Well, we've been talking a lot about the wedding and the, the baby." She reddened on the word baby. "I have wanted to tell our families about it. I just think it would be easier if everyone knew. I'm three months along now, and I have so many questions. I want to be able to talk to my mom and my sisters who have kids, and to tell Dylan."

"They don't know?" Suzanne asked, incredulous. She had spotted it almost immediately a month ago; she found it hard to believe that Kate had successfully hidden this information from the people who knew her best.

But Kate shook her head. "Everyone's been really busy and distracted; we told them I had mono. I think they believed us."

Suzanne had her doubts, especially about the formidable Mrs. Burke, but she stayed silent. "Anyway," Kate went on, "I didn't want a bunch of questions this weekend about why I'm not drinking or when we're going to have kids, and I just feel better when my family knows what's going on. We're close like that, you know? Especially Dylan and me and our parents."

"Jeff doesn't want to tell anyone?"

"His father is a Baptist minister," she explained. "His parents are really conservative."

"And he doesn't think they'll do the math when you have a baby six months after your wedding day?"

"That's what I said!" Kate agreed. "But he said they'll be really upset when they first find out, and he's worried that their disappointment will ruin our wedding. They still think he's a virgin."

Suzanne snorted loudly. Jeff was certainly one of the more wholesome members of the Dylan Burke entourage, but a good-looking music promoter in his late twenties with access to all those girls just dying to meet someone famous? A virgin? *Inconceivable.*

Kate looked surprised for a second and then giggled. "I guess it is kind of silly, isn't it?"

Suzanne searched for something diplomatic to say. "Well, I guess it's nice that they have so much confidence in him and that he wants them to be happy."

"Actually, he says he doesn't care what they think, really, but it's just that they can be kind of harsh and dramatic with their opinions sometimes. He says he doesn't want me to look back on my wedding day and remember that his mom called me a

344

harlot or that his parents refused to pose for pictures."

"Surely they wouldn't?"

"I don't think so. I think maybe Jeff doesn't give them enough credit sometimes. Anyway, that's what we've been fighting about. Well, that and my sisters . . ."

"Amber and Sherrie?"

Kate nodded. "The crazy two. They're my mom's daughters, and before she met my dad, her life was . . . a little unpredictable. I love them, but . . ."

Suzanne smiled. She could only imagine how soft-spoken Kate, so much like her dad, must react to that pair. Suzanne had once seen a picture of the two of them on the front page of some tabloid magazine, both blitzed out of their minds, wearing tiny denim shorts and halter tops and drinking something fruity from yard-long beakers. They were onstage somewhere, dancing around a stripper pole that was probably serving as much to hold them up as it was a prop. Suzanne still remembered the headline: KEEPING UP WITH THE WHITE TRASHIANS.

Kate seemed to know that Suzanne would fill in the blanks, because she went on. "Jeff didn't want them here this weekend at first. He said they're an embarrassment to the family. But Dylan talked to him, and he changed his mind. Still, he barely talks to them. I know what everyone thinks of them, but they're still my sisters. And I'm kind of pissed because Dylan had to talk him into letting them come to our wedding. Why didn't he listen to *me*? I'm starting to wonder what it's going to be like raising a baby with someone who doesn't respect my opinions."

The old Suzanne would've said: *Screw the wedding and run like hell. Obviously, this guy is never going to treat you like an equal.* But she paused; something told her maybe it wasn't that simple.

"Is it normal for Jeff to disregard your opinions like this? Is that how he's always been?"

"No," Kate cried. "That's what's so frustrating! I've always felt that we understood each other so deeply, and now I feel like he's so focused on what everyone else thinks."

Suzanne mulled this over for a minute. "Well, it's your choice. You never have to marry anyone you don't want to marry. And while it is a big decision in terms of this baby" — she gestured toward Kate's belly — "one thing I know for sure is that you can't let the *wedding* make your decision about the *marriage*. If you think you've made a mistake, don't let the people and the catering and the embarrassment bully you."

Kate looked at her, wide-eyed, and nodded slowly. "That said," Suzanne went on, "Jeff seems like a really good guy most of the time, and no one is perfect. From what I've seen, he is absolutely crazy about you. And I just know he's excited about this baby."

"He really is," Kate said, her entire expression softening with affection. "He's going to be a great dad."

Already, Suzanne could tell what Kate really wanted to do. The task now was to help it go more smoothly.

"I think . . . ," she said, giving words to a thought that had been forming since she started making her list of rejected men. "I think it's hard being a guy sometimes. Especially a guy who loves a smart, strong woman like you. People tell them they're supposed to be manly, to wear the pants, to not let their wives and girlfriends drive the relationship. But things are different now, and we women have so many more choices. That's wonderful, but it makes it difficult sometimes for guys to know where they fit into our lives. Their hearts can break just as easily as ours can, but they're not allowed to show it. They want to protect us, and sometimes they can't even protect themselves."

"I never thought about it that way," Kate said.

"Me, either," Suzanne said, smiling. "Not until recently."

Kate started to say something, but stopped; so Suzanne continued.

"Maybe what Jeff needs is a chance to show you that he can protect you and do the best thing for your relationship, without ignoring your feelings. Maybe he just needs a little nudge in the right direction, and for you to be honest with him about what you need. Then let him figure out how to give it to you."

Kate thought this over for a minute. "Honestly? I thought him playing golf was a great idea, once I realized I didn't really need him here. I just wanted my opinion about it to matter to him. It's the same with the baby."

"Easy enough," Suzanne said. "He can fix that. So that's what you tell him."

"But I was so mean to him. I can't ask him to come back now. I'll look like an idiot."

"Tell you what — it's your wedding weekend, and I'm a full-service event planner. I'll go talk to him and get him to come see you. Just this once, though. Next time, you're on your own. He's going to be your husband. You'd better learn how to start these conversations."

Kate smiled sheepishly. "Thanks, Suzanne." She added more softly, "I can see why Dylan is so fond of you."

Now it was Suzanne's turn to blush. "Well, that's what wedding planners are for."

She found the guys not on the golf course a few miles from the house but at a bar on the green called the 19th Hole. They were in a corner booth with a pitcher of dark beer, an empty one next to it. Carla's husband, Guillermo, was talking animatedly about something, gesturing wildly and grinning. Dylan and his other brother-in-law, Spencer, were listening with amused attention. Jeff, who was in the corner hardest to see from the door, appeared to be glumly leaning over his beer glass.

Suzanne took a deep breath before walking over. It pained her a little just to see Dylan. Still, she had a great affection for Kate and knew Kate loved Jeff, so she would have to get past her own feelings.

"Hello, boys," she said, pulling up a chair and sitting backward in it — a gesture that was at once flirtatious and nonnegotiable. Guillermo and Dylan both looked shocked to see her, while Spencer and Jeff each gave her a polite smile. "How did everyone shoot today?"

They each reacted according to their performance, bragging or making excuses, muttering about how little time they had to play or that they were just lucky enough to beat the pants off someone else. *How cute,* she thought, *you think I am really here to ask about your golf game.* But she smiled appreciatively and talked golf with them for a few minutes. Golf was another game she'd learned from her father, and though she seldom played for pleasure now, the basic skills had served her well in meetings over the years.

When the chatter slowed, she got down to business. "How are you, Jeff? You don't look like a guy who just shot two over par on a tough course."

He stared at the table, and the other three made incomprehensible gestures, as though she'd just announced that she had brought his STD results and was about to read them aloud. She continued. "You know, driving over here, I was just thinking how nice it

350

would be for you, marrying into a big family like this one — you already have three brothers-in-law to give you good marriage advice."

Dylan, who had been avoiding her gaze, smirked at the ceiling. Despite her anger and hurt, his approval of her comment was energizing. Guillermo and Spencer, meanwhile, looked appropriately shame-faced and uncomfortable. *That's right, you little bastards. Squirm.*

Jeff spoke next. "You've talked to Kate?"

She nodded.

"Is she . . . is she okay?" he asked.

"I think she will be," Suzanne said brightly, "once she talks to you again."

"Oh, God. Suzanne, I screwed up. I feel so bad. I've never seen her so pissed off."

Dylan's face clouded. Clearly, Jeff had not relayed the fight to the rest of the guys. "What happened, dude?"

"Nothing big," Jeff said quickly. "I mean, I don't think it is. I was just . . . kind of a jerk. I've had a lot on my mind with the wedding and the b—" He stopped himself and corrected, "the band."

Dylan eyed him suspiciously, but Jeff looked at Suzanne. "Do you think she'll talk to me? Do you think I can make it right?"

"I think she'll talk to you," Suzanne said.

"I mean, she did agree to marry you and all."

"How do I make it up to her? What do I say?"

"I have to admit, I don't have a lot of experience with being in love," said Suzanne, trying hard not to look at Dylan in her peripheral vision. "But I think women often appreciate grand romantic gestures at times like this. *Meaningful* grand romantic gestures."

Jeff considered this and then swallowed the last of his beer. "Can you give me a ride back?"

Shortly after she pulled up to the house and let Jeff out of her car, her phone buzzed. "Hi there," said William. "I'm afraid I'm going to be late. I had a case that I thought would be over by now, but it's still going on. I'm so sorry." It was 3:15 according to the clock in her car. Her heart sank. She had hoped he would be here to keep her company during the rehearsal dinner, and there was no way he would make it up in time.

"Are you going to come up afterward?" she asked.

"Well, it's up to you. I know I'll miss dinner tonight, but I could come anyway or I

352

can leave at the crack of dawn and be there to help out all day tomorrow."

"Why don't you just come up in the morning?" she said after a moment. "This place can be hard to find at night, and I have everything pretty much under control. Kate's been a breeze." She was sorry for Kate's turmoil, but in a way it was easier working for someone who had more on her mind than whether the flowers looked wilted or a bridesmaid had gained two pounds.

"You sure?" he asked, tentatively. "I think my GPS will get me there."

"That's okay," she said. "Get some good sleep and I'll see you in the morning."

Suzanne tried to ignore the relieved feeling that accompanied her disappointment. Even though they'd had several dates in the past three weeks, this would have been their first night in a bed together, which made her feel oddly nervous. Not only were they moving at a snail's pace compared with her usual dating pattern, but it was particularly strange because they had slept together many times during their previous relationship a decade before. Still, she was content to push their night together in the tiny guesthouse back one night.

"I'll be there bright and early, then," he

said. "Gotta run, okay?"

The phone clicked, and Suzanne rested her head on the steering wheel for a moment, inhaling deeply. Her heart pounded inexplicably. She took several deep breaths and willed her body to be still. Even though she knew Gunnar and Penny were safely in jail, she still occasionally had to fight off the feeling that someone was behind her, watching. Waiting.

The rehearsal dinner was at a steakhouse overlooking Gatlinburg, about twenty minutes from the cabin. The owners were longtime friends of the Burkes and would be attending the wedding the next night; the dinner was their wedding gift. For Suzanne, this meant no shopping around, no price negotiations, no obsessing over whether the gratuity was included in the budget, no fighting with the restaurant staff to make sure they had use of the banquet room at the right time. She sat at the end of the table and watched things unfold, reminding the wait staff about a few food allergies and preferences, cueing the parents when it was time for them to make toasts. Other than that, she had only to eat and take a few pictures.

After the other toasts were long over,

when the guests were finishing dessert and patting their bellies demonstratively, Jeff stood and tapped a water glass to get everyone's attention. He and Kate had stayed holed up together in their room from the moment Suzanne had dropped him off earlier that day until it was time to leave for the restaurant. Suzanne could see they'd gone a long way to solving whatever problems they had. They both glowed rosily tonight, and she noticed that Jeff kept Kate's hand in his even as he stood to address the guests.

"Kate and I want to thank y'all for coming tonight. Thanks to Mike and Mary for the best steak dinner I've ever had and for being such good friends to this family I'm marrying into. I'm honored to be here with you all, and honored that the most amazing woman I've ever met agreed to be my wife. If any of y'all are planning to question her about her judgment, I just ask that you do it after the ceremony tomorrow night."

A mild chuckle passed around the room. Someone, Suzanne thought maybe it was Amber, made a high-pitched "woo-hoo" sound that was at least celebratory, if not entirely appropriate. Jeff raised his glass in the direction of the disruption and went on. "I want to thank both our parents for being here and for their kind words tonight. For my parents, I want to say how much I appreciate your love and support over the years. I hope that will continue, no matter what the future brings."

Suzanne saw him squeeze Kate's hand. *Ahh.* "And to Kate's parents, and my best friend — my *brother* — Dylan, thank you for trusting me with this precious girl. I promise to take care of her and our little family in a way that will make you proud. And I know it might not be the right time for this, but after today I realize timing is almost never perfect in life. So I'd like to make an announcement."

The last few whispered conversations died out to give the groom their full attention. If he was nervous, it didn't show. Jeff grinned from ear to ear. "Kate and I are very excited to tell you that we're expecting our first child in early January. So this weekend is just making official something Kate and I have known for weeks — that we're already a partnership, well on our way to becoming a family."

A collective gasp at the initial announcement turned into scattered applause and happy chatter around the table. Jeff bent to kiss an ecstatic-looking — and deeply blushing — Kate before they began accepting congratulatory remarks from those around them. Suzanne noticed that Jeff's parents looked shocked but not necessarily angry (at least, not yet), and, more important, she noticed that he was not even looking at them to gauge their response. Jeff could only see Kate. Suzanne wiped away tears, and soon Dylan was standing behind her.

"How long have you known?" he asked, putting both hands on her shoulders. It could have been an intimate gesture, a friendly gesture, or a preparation to strangle her.

"Known what?" she said, feigning innocence. Dylan squeezed her collarbones slightly and she relented. "I guessed it a month ago, when we were up here before."

"I can't believe you didn't tell me," he said.

It had never occurred to her to share Kate's secret with anyone, even Dylan. But now that he said it, she realized it was a little strange that she'd kept it from him, considering how much they had talked about everything else. "It wasn't mine to share," she said honestly.

He didn't seem angry, though, and he let his hands linger on her shoulders as he watched his younger sister across the room.

357

"They're going to be okay, aren't they?" he said.

Suzanne looked at Kate and Jeff, hands linked, now talking excitedly to Carla and Guillermo, who had three children themselves. "I think so," Suzanne said. "I certainly think they have as good a chance as anyone."

The party was breaking away from the table as people gathered their things and began the long process of chatting their way out. Some would return to the mountain house and continue the celebration there. Kate and her sisters, and a few of her close girlfriends, were staying in a hotel in Gatlinburg for the night. Suzanne would stay to pick up stray gifts, cards, sweaters, and sunglasses left behind and deliver them to the house later.

Dylan moved himself to the chair next to her, still watching the bride and groom. "I thought Kate said you were bringing a date tonight?" he asked. His voice sounded artificially casual.

"William had to work late," Suzanne said. "He'll be up in the morning."

"Oh," he said. She waited for him to go on, but he didn't.

Might as well rip the bandage off. "And you're here alone? Misty didn't —"

She was surprised at how the name caught in her throat, bringing back fresh pain from the last time she'd seen Misty, that horrible day in her apartment.

"No," Dylan said firmly. "That's over."

Suzanne was happy to hear it, though she told herself she had no right to an opinion on the subject. Still, she detested that girl, and, even as a friend, she thought Dylan could do better. She was not sure what to say, so they sat in silence for a minute or two, both watching Kate and Jeff make the rounds of the room. When one of the waiters approached with a question for Suzanne, Dylan patted her knee, stood, and quietly faded into a little throng of friends and family.

Later, when everyone had been piled into cars, limos, and taxis bound for various destinations and Suzanne had done three sweeps of the banquet room to make sure she had gathered all the lost things, plus half of an enormous cake, she stepped out into the cool evening to drive herself back to the house. She was exhausted. The quaint little bed in the guesthouse, with its home-made quilt and the window above opened just a bit, sounded like heaven right now. Once again, she was grateful to Kate for being so low maintenance. Suzanne did not have some ridiculous task to do tonight, like putting personalized stickers on tiny bottles of bubbles.

As she got close to her car, her heart lurched. A man was leaning against it, silhouetted by a street lamp behind him so that she could not see his face. She froze. It was too late to turn around and run back to the restaurant. Certainly, at this distance, he could catch her easily, and the front doors were locked. She had been the last patron to leave, and the staff was all busy cleaning up to go home. She had her keys in her hand as always, but her phone was at the bottom of her low-slung purse underneath everything else she was carrying. Her heart pounded as she struggled to breathe and tried to make a decision about what to do.

"Scarlett? You okay?" It took a minute for her to process the voice and the nickname, and for her terrified brain to put together that these things added up to Dylan. He stepped closer into the light, so she could see his face. Relief washed over her, and tears of panic streamed down her face.

"Hey . . . oh my God, what's wrong?" he said. Her heart was still racing, but she managed to wipe her tears on her sleeve as he approached to take the cake box from her arms and put it on the roof of her car. "Darlin', what's wrong?"

She shook her head to clear it. "Nothing, nothing's wrong. I thought you left with Jeff a while ago, and when I came out, I couldn't see your face, and I thought . . ." She couldn't finish.

"Oh God. After everything you've been through, I go and scare the shit out of you again."

"No, it's fine. I'm just embarrassed. I thought I was past it."

He hugged her tightly and kissed her forehead. "Of course you're not past it. It's been less than a month. Cut yourself a break. I am just sorry as hell I scared you. That wasn't my intention."

She managed a few deep breaths and began to feel better. Her heart was slowing now. "It's okay. I'm okay."

He released her from his embrace and helped her get the cake and other items into the car. When she closed the trunk, she turned to him. "I thought you'd be with Jeff tonight? Aren't the guys doing something . . . manly?"

Dylan laughed. "Yeah, I guess so. They're down at Gatty Freight playing pool and drinking beer. I'm supposed to be with them."

"Surely, you're not bailing on your future brother-in-law's last night as a free man?" she asked. She was beginning to feel better, more centered.

"No, I'm going. Someone's gotta keep an eye on those idiots. But I was hoping maybe you'd give me a ride?" He looked around the deserted parking lot and gave her a sheepish grin. "Well, actually, I was kind of *counting* on it. I wanted to talk to you."

She nodded and they got in the car. He pointed to indicate directions, and she waited. For a few minutes, he didn't say anything except "right," "left," and "it's about three miles this way." Finally, he said, "Kate says you've done a great job with the wedding. I wanted to say thank you."

So that's what this was? Professional courtesy? "You're welcome. She's been very easy to work with."

"It means a lot to me that you've been helping her with this. Kate's a sensitive kid, and I think some people would've bullied her into doing more than she wanted, knowing that there was . . . money around."

"I'm happy to help," Suzanne said. "Kate's a wonderful girl."

More silence. They came over a hill and

she saw the sign for Gatty Freight, along with a retired boxcar that sat out front, perhaps fifty yards away. "Is that it?" she asked. Dylan nodded.

She wondered whether that really was all he wanted — to thank her. But he could've done that any number of times: earlier in the evening, tomorrow night at the wedding, on the phone. He looked nervous. "Just park in the back for a minute," he said as she pulled in. She did as he said but left the engine running. No way she was getting sucked into whatever revelry was going on inside.

"I've been wanting to say this for a month," he said finally. "I owe you an apology. For what happened. For Misty."

"No," she said, shaking her head as she had moments before, trying to keep calm. "You don't. You saved my life, Dylan. You don't have to apologize for any part of it."

"But the night before, when we kissed —"

"And then we mutually decided that was a big mistake and that things would never work between us. We were *absolutely* right." Her tone was icier than she intended, but she knew that if she wasn't firm, she might fall apart. She felt vulnerable enough already; she would *not* fall apart again tonight.

"I wanted to tell you that what happened

with Misty; it was —"

"You don't have to explain yourself to me, Dylan. We are friends. I owe you my life, and I hope someday I can repay you for that. But we weren't dating then, and we're not dating now. I'm seeing someone, and you are free to date, *or fuck,* anyone you'd like."

She was surprised to see that he looked wounded. Part of her wanted to scream and cry and tell him how much he'd hurt her. How her chest tightened every time she saw him and the thought of him with Misty — or anyone else — made her physically sick. She wanted to touch his cheek and feel his arms around her and never let go.

But her outward composure of the past few weeks disguised a fragile latticework inside. The events of the spring had revealed that what Suzanne had always believed were her internal pillars of strength were actually elaborate but fragile illusions. The attack had not only disrupted her peace of mind, it had shown her the hollow places in her heart. She had spent the last few weeks trying to re-create herself in an existence that felt safe. If she became vulnerable now, it would all fall apart and she would have nothing left. She would not let anyone do that to her. Not even him.

He stared at her for a moment. "Fine," he said coldly. "I wanted to apologize to you and I have."

"As I said, it's not necessary."

"I heard what you said, Suzanne." The words were white-hot with angry intensity. She could see him seething in the passenger seat, and for a second she thought he might lash out at her. But he seemed to regain himself. "I have to go. I'll see you at the wedding. Thanks for the ride."

The car door slammed, and he walked into the bar without looking back. She forced herself to navigate the dark roads to the mountain house, put the cake away, walk to the guesthouse, and get into her pajamas and under the quilt before she allowed herself to collapse into sobs.

23

Suzanne had to admit that, as much as she hated planning weddings, she did a nice job putting Kate Burke's together. Kate and Jeff got married at sunset on the deck at Dylan's mountain cabin. The lovely — and pregnant — bride wore a soft, flowing empire-waist dress and a wreath made of wildflowers on the crown of her head. Suzanne had decorated the deck with simple maypoles hung with ribbons that would blow in the breeze, along with Mexican-style white paper banners and, after sunset, large white Christmas lights to light the dance floor.

Some of Dylan's friends provided soft bluegrass music, and after the ceremony Dylan made a touching toast that led into Pat Green serenading a surprised, delighted, and very pink Kate. He then graciously sang the couple through their first dance, which kept the crowd mesmerized until the bluegrass band took over again. They served barbecue provided by a favorite local restaurant and buckets of beer at every turn.

It was Suzanne's favorite kind of party, one that focused on the delight and comfort of the guests rather than a show of opulence. The guests were impressed, too, as was William, who had arrived early that morning to help out as promised. Kate looked radiant, of course, and she and Jeff seemed pleased. And married, which was the most important thing. Contrary to Jeff's fears, there was no family drama resulting from their announcement the night before, and in fact elation seemed to be the overriding emotion, even for his parents. When they left for their honeymoon (as a final wedding gift, Dylan had arranged for Jeff to have the first week of the summer tour off), ducking under an arch of sparklers toward a waiting town car, their smiles were genuine and carefree.

With the happy couple gone, the older guests began to filter out, as well, along with Dylan's parents and their friends, who had reserved a block of rooms at one of the nicer hotels in town. As the reception morphed into a party, Suzanne had very little to do except be available to answer stray questions from the caterers and to direct some of the cleaning staff. She found a spot on the edge of the party, in view of the kitchen, where she and William could sit in folding chairs and observe. She took her shoes off and rubbed her feet. After a couple of months without work, she had grown unaccustomed to marathon evenings in heels.

Dylan, who had not returned to the house until half an hour before the wedding, and who had barely said two words to her since, was holding a bottle of Jack Daniel's, dancing with some of Amber and Sherrie's friends. Suzanne noted, bemused, that some of these friends had not been invited to the wedding itself but appeared after the bride and groom left, as though they'd emerged from the surrounding forest, drawn by the scent of an open bar. "You okay?" William asked, following her gaze and rubbing her shoulders a little too hard. He had always done that, she remembered.

"I'm fine," she said firmly, and added, "I was just thinking I need to make sure the bartender has enough Jack. It could be that someone besides Dylan Burke will want some."

"It's still crazy that you know this guy," William said. "Oh, I promised Scott at the office I'd get an autograph for his girl-friend."

Suzanne sighed audibly. The *very* last thing she wanted was to ask Dylan for a favor, especially a stupid autograph. William added swiftly, "I mean, if it's convenient. If not, I'll just tell him I forgot. You know what, let's just say I forgot. What were we talking about?"

She smiled gratefully and patted his arm. "Thanks for all your help today."

"No problem," said William. "I guess now that we're back together, I'll get lots of practice stringing lights and hanging ribbons."

Back together. Shit.

Suzanne quelled the familiar sense of panic. She remembered the words of her therapist, who she'd been seeing twice a week since the attack. "It's all about looking at your old patterns and deciding whether they are still working for you." Running away from nice guys and potentially stable relationships was what she'd done her whole life. Had it worked for her? Hell, no. She leaned over and gave William an appreciative peck on the lips.

When she turned her attention to the dancers out on the deck, she saw that Dylan was looking at her. He gave her a grimace that was supposed to be a smile, took a swig from the bottle, and threw his arm around a petite redhead dancing next to him. *Now on-deck for the visitors . . .*

A little while later, the party began its inevitable descent into debauchery, and Suzanne got up and paid the bartenders so they could pack and go. They left what little booze remained in a box in the kitchen, where Suzanne knew it would not survive the night. She and William helped the cleaning staff break things down, starting at the edges of the party and working inward, pushing the stragglers inside. The poker table was set up in the great room, where they ran into Dylan on their way downstairs for the night.

He lifted his drink in salute to her — he'd re-civilized himself with a glass, she noted — and shook William's hand as Suzanne introduced them. "Nice to meet you, Willie," he said, ignoring Suzanne's glare. "You know, Scarlett, this is a great party. Think you should consider planning weddings for a living."

"I believe we all know by now I'm not a wedding kind of girl," she said without thinking, and William blanched. *Oh God.* She fished desperately for something to say to redeem herself, with Dylan wearing an almost malicious smirk, amused by her discomfort. "I mean, it's really the bride and groom who make a wedding wonderful, not the event planner. Kate looked lovely, don't you think?"

She turned to William, pleading a silent apology for being so thoughtless, but he seemed to have recovered his normal color. He rubbed her back, gently this time, and said, "Well, I think you can do whatever you want and do it well, weddings or anything else."

"Well put, William," Dylan said, lifting his glass again. "Your man here is right, Scarlett, you really can do *whatever* you want."

Suzanne bit back the caustic retort brewing in her mouth and forced a genteel smile. William smiled for real, not catching the covert meaning of the conversation at all. Just then, the petite redhead emerged from Dylan's bedroom and began pulling on his arm, whining. "Dylaaan . . ."

"Déjà vu," Suzanne said quietly. Though he didn't respond, she felt sure Dylan heard her.

"Well, I hate to be an ungracious host," he said expansively, "but duty calls. Will, it was a pleasure meeting you. Hope you've enjoyed my little cabin in the backwoods. Scarlett, you take care of yourself. Nice work. Good night."

He allowed himself to be led into his bedroom, and the door swung shut just a little harder than necessary. Next to her,

Guillermo, Spencer, and a couple of other guys were setting up for poker. "I thought Dylan was playing, too?" she heard Guillermo ask.

"Oh, he'll be out in a few minutes," said one of the guys she didn't know. "Gretchen's not exactly big on foreplay, if you know what I mean."

Guillermo knew what he meant. Suzanne knew what he meant. Half of Tennessee knew exactly what he meant. She took William's hand and practically dragged him down the stairs and outside to the cabin.

"He seems like a good guy," William said, a little winded, trying to keep up with Suzanne on the path to the little cottage. *Servants' quarters is more like it,* she thought bitterly.

"He's a fucking saint," she muttered.

"What? Honey, slow down. There are rocks and roots and stuff out here."

Suzanne flipped on the light, glad that Yvette had a family obligation this weekend and was therefore not in her usual room in the guesthouse. The little bedroom across the cottage from Suzanne's was piled high with tour-preparation materials, though, which she supposed was why no one else was in there, either. Yvette would be in late the next afternoon, along with the rest of the band and crew who weren't here already. The summer tour started midweek, and from there they'd be gone for three and a half months.

She pushed William down on the couch as soon as they got in the door, straddling his lap and kissing him forcefully. "Wow," he said, coming up for air. "Not that I'm complaining, but where did this come from?"

"I don't know," Suzanne said, stripping out of her shirt and loosening his tie. "I just really want you tonight."

"Okay," he said, helping her with the tie and his shirt. "It's been a few years, but I seem to remember that arguing with you is useless."

She didn't want him to talk anymore. She kissed him violently and bit his lip, hoping to work him into a frenzy that would leave words, and everything else, behind. "Ow," he said softly. "Easy." But it was working. She could feel him responding to her, getting hard beneath his pressed khaki dress pants, which was, in itself, gratifying. Maybe not everything about her was broken.

Just her heart.

The words came as William was shifting himself on top of her on the couch, fumbling with the zipper on the side of her skirt. She forced herself to focus on the moon, reflected from the window behind her off a mirror near the door, while he worked at the obstinate zipper. But it wouldn't budge, and he grinned shyly up at her for help. She tried, too, and it wouldn't move. Suzanne let out an exasperated groan.

"Should we just . . . leave it on?" he suggested. She wanted to say, *Yes, that would be such a turn-on. Let's make love with my skirt on like we're in an elevator stuck between floors or I'm your secretary or something hot like that.* But her face contorted with pain, and, to her absolute frustration, tears dripped down her cheeks.

"Fuck!" she said. She couldn't get away from it. Her heart was broken. Whether Dylan had broken it, or Penny and Gunnar, or whether she'd done it herself almost didn't matter. This was the feeling she'd been hiding from her entire adult life, the thing she'd done everything possible to avoid. And now she was in the middle of it with nowhere left to run.

"Oh God," William said. "Did I do something wrong?"

She shook her head. "No, I did. William, I'm so sorry. For *everything.*"

His face softened. Suzanne was relieved to see that he didn't seem to need an explanation, because she didn't know whether she had the energy to give one. "Oh, sweetheart," he said, putting his arms around her and stroking her hair. "I kind of had the feeling that wasn't about me."

She sobbed freely now while William held her. Minutes or hours passed — she wasn't sure — lost in a nameless, shapeless grief for which there was no solution. After a long time, he released her and gently handed her the shirt she'd tossed on the floor, then pulled on his undershirt and sat next to her again. "It's Dylan, right?"

She nodded. "Partly."

"You're in love with him?"

"I think so," she said. "But it's more than that. It's me. My whole . . . life."

William put his hand on hers. "Do you think it's possible that you may be being a little bit hard on yourself?"

She laughed. He was probably right. She'd never known any other way to be: hard on herself, hard on everyone else.

"Come on," he said. "You need some sleep. It's been a long day, a long few months, and you're exhausted."

He led her to the bedroom, where she changed into her pajamas and crawled under the covers. She wanted him to stay so she wouldn't be alone, but she didn't want to be touched. William seemed to get this without having to be told. "I'm going to sleep with all those papers in the other room," he said lightly. "Maybe if I have trouble sleeping, I'll read some contracts or something."

She smiled. He turned to go. "William?"

"Yeah?"

"All those years ago, when you proposed and I . . ."

"Yes?"

"Did I break your heart?"

He laughed sourly. "It was pretty bad, yeah."

"I'm so sorry," she said.

"Hey, no . . . That was a long time ago," he said. "We're not there anymore. Plus, several other girls have broken my heart since then, so you don't get to be quite so special anymore."

"Oh," she said. They hadn't talked much about the years between their original romance and the present day, except in vague terms. She realized that she'd been arrogantly assuming his life had been ruined because of her.

"I'll say this, Suzanne. It gets easier."

"It does?"

"Sure. What's life without a little heartbreak? You know what they say . . ."

She waited for the platitudes. What doesn't kill you makes you stronger. You can't make an omelet without breaking eggs. Rain and rainbows . . .

"Well, they say a lot of shit," he said, a rare curse word coming from clean-cut William. "And in my experience, none of it makes you feel one damn bit better."

She laughed. "Thank you, William."

"Good night, Suzanne."

She woke at dawn to the sound of a zipping suitcase in the next room. Suzanne had expected William to be gone early and decided it was better to stay put and let him leave on his own terms. She could ask no more of him than what he'd already done for her. He deserved not to face her today, if that was what he wanted.

When she heard the door pulled softly closed, she got out of bed to get herself ready for the same hasty exit. The note on the counter read, "Better if I go. Call anytime you need a friend. — WMF." She packed quickly, showered without washing her hair, and slipped out of the cottage before seven, leaving the key under the mat. The house was asleep in its usual post-party chaos, so she sneaked into the kitchen to grab a slice of cake for the road. The coffeepot was cold — obviously, Dylan had not risen early to make it today — so she decided to skip the cake, too, and just stop at a gas station on her way home.

She paused in her bustle to look out the back windows, realizing this could be the last time she'd be in this beautiful place. As quietly as she could, she sneaked out the back door and went to the deck. She was about to wander out to get a better view of the mountains when she saw something that made her smile. At the far end of the deck, sleeping soundly in his favorite hammock, was Dylan Burke. She watched him for a moment, knowing this meant he had not stayed all night, at least, with Gretchen the redhead. It was small consolation, but it would have to do. She grabbed her bag and tiptoed out of the house and out to her car.

24

After the most tumultuous spring of her life, the hot Atlanta summer slipped away in relative quiet. Suzanne spent her time in June and July trying to establish a new order in her life. The experiences of recent months had changed her forever, and she was determined to make sure at least some of those changes were positive ones. She continued therapy twice a week and went to a prenatal yoga class with Marci at least once or twice a week. Usually, they would grab breakfast afterward, and Suzanne worked hard on listening more than she talked. She found that pregnancy was at least mildly fascinating and that she and Marci were growing closer all the time.

She also made it a point to spend more time with Rebecca and to force Marci to do the same. They went out for Mexican food frequently, and they all became spectators of Manuel's wedding plans with his future wife. They oohed and aahed over pictures of cakes and flowers and favors, and Suzanne consistently declined invitations to help them plan professionally. Her parents had her over for dinner at least once a week, and she and her dad would play cards for hours after each meal.

She signed up for a refresher painting course through the Atlanta campus of Savannah College of Art and Design and found that her talents had not atrophied as much as she had thought during the last decade of neglect. By July, she'd sold two paintings just by sending an e-mail out with pictures to her Junior League address list. Normally, she would've been too embarrassed to accept money for her artwork, especially from people she knew, but she couldn't argue with the four months' rent the paintings brought in. She felt the same sense of pride receiving those checks that she had felt when she made her first dollars as an independent event planner.

Her list of men was long gone, and she put it out of her mind for the most part. She had called Rick, however, to apologize for the ungracious way that she'd left him and the unfairness of the way things had ended. In her mind, she also apologized for thinking he was her stalker, but she was too

380

embarrassed to say it out loud. He'd sounded awkward but eventually laughed, told her he was seeing a nice girl from Augusta, a kindergarten teacher. She saw William once a week or so, for a movie or to wander through an art festival. They were just friends now, and she knew the day was coming soon when he'd begin dating someone else and be less available to her. But she enjoyed what she had.

Suzanne wasn't surprised that she did not hear from Dylan. They had not talked since the night of Kate's wedding. When really honest with herself, she thought it was possible she might never talk to him again.

Suzanne did, however, hear from Kate periodically. She had sent Suzanne a sweet thank-you e-mail when she and Jeff returned from their surprise honeymoon, and the two of them had been corresponding off and on ever since. Once Jeff rejoined Dylan's tour, Kate had spent a couple of weeks at her parents' home in Nashville and then flown to visit Carla and Guillermo in Madrid. She e-mailed Suzanne beautiful pictures of her sightseeing trips into the Spanish countryside and mailed her a lovely inlaid-gold bracelet from Toledo "to thank you for all your kindness."

Only once in their e-mail exchanges did

the subject of Kate's brother come up. Kate had been responding to a casual question about the challenges of a long-distance marriage:

It is very hard, definitely, being apart. But it's easier knowing that Jeff's job is with my brother. I know Dylan will look after him and make sure he gets back to me whenever he can. He treats all the guys like they're his family. He treated Jeff that way long before he and I got together. He's a good man, Suzanne. I know it seems hard to believe when you see the parties and the girls and everything, but Dylan is actually very kind, and extremely loyal. He's one of those people who, once you're part of his family, he will do anything for you and defend you at all costs. It's hard to find people like that.

Suzanne had stared at the e-mail for a long time after reading it. She knew or intuited this about Dylan, but had he said something to his sister that he had not said to Suzanne? After a half hour or so, she decided she was simply reading too much into it and responded with a casualness she did not feel:

You are so right. Dylan is one of a kind. :)

Though she resisted contacting him, she looked at the online tour schedule periodically to see where he was: Peoria, Illinois; Lubbock, Texas; Sacramento, California. Sometimes, she imagined what he might be doing or how he was feeling, but she found this led her to a deep sadness from which it took a while to recover, especially when she was alone. Only when she was with Marci or her therapist could she really allow herself to talk freely about him. Even those conversations became less frequent and lengthy as the oppressive summer wore on.

The one time she did see Dylan that summer, it was for a few minutes in August, under tragic circumstances.

Suzanne had been at Jake and Marci's for a couple of days when it happened. Jake was out of town filming for a piece on Olympic fencing, so Suzanne had been at their house keeping Marci company. She still had two months before the baby was due, but Jake felt better if Marci had someone with her. He was so cute and overprotective. But Suzanne hardly needed the excuse to spend entire days with her best friend, taking walks, shopping for the nursery, and evenings eating junk food together in front of reality television.

So they had been doing that Wednesday evening, plowing through a gallon of Edy's and watching *Big Brother,* when a teaser for the ten o'clock news gave them the first hint of what happened. "Atlanta PD officer killed in traffic accident. Details tonight."

Marci and Suzanne exchanged a sad look and shook their heads but forgot about the story when *Big Brother* came back on. At ten o'clock, Marci was half asleep and Suzanne was clearing the spoons and bowls from the coffee table when the news returned. The anchor, a black woman with short-cropped hair and a lavender suit, looked grave as she spoke to the camera. "Channel Two has received confirmation that an Atlanta police officer struck by a car early this morning has died of her injuries this evening at Grady Hospital. Officer Bonita Daniels —"

The bowls clattered to the floor from Suzanne's hands, and Marci awoke with a start, gripping her belly reflexively. "Shit! Suzanne! What's wrong? Suzanne?"

Suzanne pointed numbly at the television, where there was a picture of a younger Bonita in dress blues and her patrol hat in front of a blue background and an American flag. She looked serious and confident, with bright lipstick standing out against her dark skin. The lipstick was different, definitely, but it was the same firm, confident face she had brought to Suzanne during one of the hardest experiences of her life.

"— was struck by a vehicle around two thirty this morning while assisting a stranded motorist. Witnesses described a black or dark-blue SUV, license plate ending in three-eight-four, that veered out of its lane and struck Officer Daniels as she assisted with a disabled vehicle. She was airlifted to Grady Hospital, where she later died. Police are still searching for the driver of the vehicle, asking anyone with information on the car or its driver to contact Crime Stoppers or dial the Atlanta police department directly."

"Oh, Suze," Marci said.

"Shh!" Suzanne hissed. It couldn't be right. There was a mistake. The news had cut to a man in a suit, standing in front of Grady Hospital, with a red cross lit up behind him.

"Thank you, Wanda. I'm here at Grady Hospital, where we were just told moments ago that Officer Daniels had not recovered from her injuries. There is a heavy police presence here, both in an official capacity and, I believe, paying respect to the victim's family. Officer Daniels leaves behind one daughter, who is fifteen, and her mother, who also lived with her. We are told, Wanda, that at one point she was conscious and able to speak to her daughter for a moment before she had to be sedated for surgery. That may be the one bright spot amid what is a horrible tragedy for this family, the police force, and of course the city of Atlanta. Wanda?"

The anchorwoman promised that they would give additional details and updates as they emerged and then moved on to a story about a fire at a grocery store.

They both sat in stunned silence for a while. "Oh, honey, I am so sorry," Marci said.

Suzanne nodded. "Me, too." She wanted to cry, but the tears weren't there. "He called her directly."

"What?"

"When I was attacked. When I was . . . being held, Dylan called Bonita directly because he knew she would believe him and come help me. And she did. And she was right there the whole time with me. She held my hand; she . . ."

"I know," Marci said softly. She touched Suzanne's arm, which grounded her.

"I have to call him," Suzanne said.

"I think you do," her friend replied softly.

Suzanne was only able to reach Yvette that night. Dylan had either been onstage or ignoring her calls, but she found it was easier to break the news to Yvette anyway. Suzanne called her back the next morning when she found out the memorial service would be Friday morning at Bonita's church; Yvette said that Dylan had back-to-back shows Thursday and Friday night, so he probably wouldn't make it.

They were surprised, then, when Friday came and they saw him, standing on the steps of the church in a simple black suit as Jake, Marci, and Suzanne filed in. "Hey," he said sadly, kissing Marci's cheek and shaking Jake's hand. He put his arm around Suzanne, and they walked in together, wordlessly.

The service was one of the saddest and most inspiring things Suzanne had ever seen. Nearly an hour and a half long, tributes came from Bonita's family, fellow officers, friends, and even the mayor. The most moving thing of all, however, was when Bonita's daughter, Chrysaline, went to the podium to speak and found that her voice understandably failed her. She

387

squeaked out "thank you" through a face contorted with pain and nearly collapsed before having to be helped away from the microphone and back to her seat. Dylan put his head in both hands, and Suzanne thought she saw his shoulders shake with emotion.

Afterward, the other three lingered awkwardly on the church steps while Dylan stepped aside to call Yvette. Suzanne would later discover that he was giving her Chrysaline Daniels's name and asking her to set aside VIP tickets for a future concert, to be given at a more appropriate time. His tour would be over in a couple of weeks, but he'd make sure she got to see him next year. He would write a personal note to go with them and let her know he'd been at the service.

He hung up and returned to the other three, face blotchy with the same emotion they were all feeling, and sweaty. Even at eleven in the morning, the August sun was already making downtown Atlanta intolerably hot. Marci looked miserable, in a sleeveless black cotton dress. No one seemed to have any idea what to say.

Dylan broke the silence. "I have to go get back on a plane," he said, his voice strained. "I'm already on thin ice with Yvette for cutting it so close." Suzanne felt herself nod, reluctantly. He hugged Marci, and Jake, too — one of those awkward, male-acquaintance hugs — and then gave Suzanne a tender kiss on the cheek. She shivered, despite the hot Atlanta morning.

"Are you all right?" he asked, looking directly at her.

She nodded. He let his hand linger on hers for a moment, as though he wanted to say something else. The awkward pause lengthened; it was the place in the conversation reserved for endearments or promises to reconnect. *See you next week. I'll call you. I love you.* As they both searched for words and found none, she realized with renewed sadness that it was because neither of them could point to a place in the future where they would be together again.

She wanted to hold on to him, to grasp his hand and keep him close. But nothing would change with another minute, or ten, or maybe forever. She let his fingers drop. "See ya," he said, and walked away. In seconds, he had disappeared around the corner.

Marci gave her a sympathetic look, and Suzanne hugged her tightly, being cautious of Marci's big belly. They linked arms, leaning on one another for support, and the three of them walked to a nearby diner for an early lunch.

"Wow," Jake said as they settled into a booth.

"Such a sad day," Marci agreed.

"Well, yeah, that, too. I mean, obviously," said Jake, opening a menu. "But I was actually just wondering how long Dylan Burke has been in love with Suzanne."

Both women looked at him incredulously. "What?" he said.

"First of all," Marci said, glancing at Suzanne for support. "How is it that I can talk directly to you about my feelings for forty-five minutes, using the *actual words* for the feelings, and you don't catch a word of it, but you see two people saying good-bye after a funeral and suddenly you're Oprah Winfrey?"

Jake grinned. "Oh, were you talking about your feelings the other night? Sorry, I thought we were summarizing an episode of *Real Housewives.*"

Suzanne smiled despite herself, and Jake ducked to avoid a menu aimed at his head. When Marci regained her composure, she continued. "Second of all, where have you been? Dylan's been in love with Suzanne forever. Didn't you see the way he looked at her that night at our house?"

"What?" Suzanne said. Marci was wrong.

She had to be.

The playful smile she'd been directing at her husband faded from Marci's face. "I — you mean? Suze, I thought you knew."

Suzanne looked out the window at the sun reflecting off the nearby buildings and the brilliant blue sky beyond. He'd be up there soon, on his way to wherever he was singing tonight. Maybe Marci was right, and maybe it still didn't matter. Maybe feelings were just a part of the equation, and they could either enhance reality or be destroyed by it. It certainly seemed the case for her and Dylan.

"No," she said quietly. "I guess I didn't."

25

Suzanne knocked tentatively on the salmon-colored wooden door. She fidgeted with the bouquet of flowers and tuna casserole in her hands and shifted her weight nervously from side to side, the wooden floorboards of the aging front porch creaking beneath her. Bonita Daniels's house was near the end of a quaint little street in Reynoldstown, one of Atlanta's older city neighborhoods. The Craftsman houses dated back to around the 1920s, and each was painted a different color. Single-family homes were mixed with duplexes and even a couple of quadruplexes, many with bicycles or scooters parked out front.

The last three weeks had dragged by since the funeral. Suzanne had waited until the initial chaos was over to come to pay her more personal respects to the woman who saved her life. Dylan's tour had been over for nearly a week, and she still had not heard from him. For a woman in her thirties experiencing her first real heartbreak, Suzanne thought she was holding up pretty well. She had resisted the temptation to call him, as well as the very strong desire to let lovelessness and joblessness keep her in bed all day. She was nearing the end of her savings and needed to create work for herself soon, which wasn't going to happen if she was hiding in her bed.

Bonita's mother, Mary, answered the door, pulling Suzanne into a bear hug almost as soon as she'd said hello. "Thank you for letting me stop in," Suzanne said. "I hope you don't mind tuna."

"No, that's lovely. Just lovely," said Mary. "Chrysaline!"

"That's okay. Don't pull her away from anything. I really just wanted to look in on you —"

"Chrysaline! We have company!"

The girl came into the room softly, a sharp contrast compared with her boisterous grandmother. She wore a simple purple hoodie over a white T-shirt and jeans, with her hair braided to each side. "I'm here," she said.

"This is Miss Hamilton," Mary said.

Suzanne held out her hand, and Chrysaline shook it loosely. "Please, call me Suzanne. Your mom helped me when —"

"I know," Chrysaline said. "She talked about you. She liked you. I'm . . . I'm real sorry about what happened to you."

"Oh, gosh, no," Suzanne stammered. "I'm fine, now. I'm sorry for your loss."

Chrysaline looked at the floor. "Thank you. She was a great mom."

Mary set out a plate of cookies, and Suzanne sat at the kitchen table with the two of them. She told them how helpful Bonita had been to her, how comforting. "I could see right away what a great mom she must be to you," she told Chrysaline, who nodded and wiped tears. "And if she was my mom, I'd want to know that she was a hero to someone."

They talked for a while longer, Suzanne probing about Chrysaline's school and interests, Chrysaline asking Suzanne what it had been like working at the High Museum.

"I went there on a school field trip once, and I never wanted to leave," she said, with as much animation as could be expected from a fifteen-year-old who had just lost her mother.

"You like art?" Suzanne asked.

"You kidding?" Mary interjected. "She's so talented. We're hoping she'll get a scholarship to art school. You should show her some of your stuff, Chrys."

"Grandma, stop," the girl objected.

"Oh, no, I'd love to see it. I've gotten back into painting recently myself," Suzanne said. "May I?"

Chrysaline led Suzanne up to her attic bedroom, where she had hundreds of sketches, mostly in pencil, covering every surface. A few were flowers, and some were impressions of buildings; there was a stray seashell here and there. But mostly they were faces. Beautiful, joyful, sad, pensive, and even haunted. All races and ages — from a toothless baby in pigtails to a weathered elderly woman shelling peas in a rocking chair. They were breathtaking.

"Oh, wow. That's all I can say. These are better than anything I ever did, even in my college-level art classes."

"Nah, it's just messing around," Chrysaline said dismissively.

"Hush up," said Grandma Mary fiercely. "Girl, if you can't stand up and be proud of yourself, no one else will do it for you!"

Suzanne began to see how Bonita Daniels had grown up to be such a formidable woman herself. She turned back to the teenager, who was biting a thumbnail nervously. "Chrysaline, you *are* going to art school, aren't you?"

The girl looked embarrassed. "I'd like to, but with Momma gone . . ."

"Don't be silly. We'll find a way," her grandmother broke in again, this time reassuringly. Chrysaline shot her a mild smile, and for the first time that afternoon, Suzanne saw both women's lips quaver.

Suzanne turned her attention to the sketches, not wanting to intrude on their very personal grief. She walked around the hot room the way she had seen so many do at the High, hands behind her back, pointing reverently at some of the more impressive sketches. She made what she hoped were encouraging comments about their beautiful composition and Chrysaline's obvious skill. After a few minutes, Grandma Mary excused herself to go put the casserole in the oven, and Suzanne followed her down the stairs to say good-bye.

Grieving or not, Chrysaline had just started school again, and she probably had homework to do and friends to see. Certainly she had better things to do than talk to a stranger who had been impacted by her mother's work. Suzanne promised to get her a VIP tour of the museum as soon as she could, which genuinely seemed to delight Chrysaline. As she walked to her car, Suzanne thought she would stop in and check on them from time to time. It seemed like the least she could do to repay Bonita.

On the car ride home, however, the seed of an idea began to take hold in her mind. Maybe she could do more than she thought.

26

It was nearly midnight the next day when Suzanne set out for Gatlinburg. She had originally intended to leave earlier, but things had started cascading as soon as she got home from Bonita's house the evening before and started making phone calls, and the activity continued all day. She had been absolutely shameless, phoning in every favor she was owed, and a few she wasn't owed, even from people who had distanced themselves from her after the gala. Betsy Fuller-Brown had been the most help, even making a few calls to connect Suzanne with the right people. But to pull her idea together, she needed more than money and connections. She needed Dylan.

She knew it was probably unwise to get on the road so late, but she had been up late the night before, making notes and doing research. When she finally fell asleep, she'd slept in until 10:30, so even at midnight she didn't yet feel tired. She drove through the twenty-four-hour Starbucks for a Venti coffee with two extra shots just to be sure.

"I'm up all night," Marci said when they spoke around eleven and Suzanne told her what she was planning. "Call me anytime you need to talk. I sleep on the couch because it's too damn hot upstairs, so it's not like you'll be bothering Jake."

But she had not needed to call Marci, and might have been fine without the coffee, but she sipped it slowly over a few hours anyway. Her internal wheels were spinning too fast for her body to want to rest. There were so many things to think about, so many details to iron out. She kept her old voice recorder next to her in the car and dictated to it when things occurred to her. Ideas, people to call, issues to address, and more ideas. Lots and lots of ideas. They seemed to be snowballing on top of her original thought, picking up speed and power as they rolled downhill, taking on a life of their own. It was thrilling.

Once upon a time, it had been Chad who would collect all those stray thoughts and put them into action. Now, it would just be Suzanne. She'd need help, of course, which was why — or part of why — she was driving to the Tennessee mountains as fast as her little car would take her.

Yvette had been confused and a little reluctant to tell Suzanne earlier in the evening where Dylan was. "Look, Suzanne, I'd like to help you," she said, "but I don't get involved with Mr. Burke's personal life. If you want to talk to him, call him yourself, and he'll tell you where he is."

"Yvette, I know it's hard to understand, but this is important, and I don't want to intrude, but I have to talk to him in person. It's a . . . it's a girl thing," she finished lamely, kicking herself for saying it. *Jesus, Suze, who's the stalker now?*

But whatever she'd said had worked on Yvette, or at least made her decide that the potential trouble she could be in with Dylan was likely less than the hassle of dealing with Suzanne any longer. She confirmed what Suzanne guessed, that Dylan was at the mountain house. She thought some band members who did not have families to return home to might still be there, as well, but beyond that she wasn't sure. It was good enough for Suzanne.

She got to Gatlinburg by four in the morning. She checked into a hotel to sleep for a few hours, but found that — whether from the caffeine or adrenaline — her body

would not stay on the bed. She paced fruit-
lessly around the room for a few minutes
before getting back in her car and driving
up the long curvy roads to the cabin.

For the last hundred yards of the driveway,
she drove slowly with her lights off, not
wanting to wake anyone on the front side of
the house. She parked far away and scaled a
good bit of the walk to the house on foot.
When she got to the cabin, only a single
light shone through the window from the
kitchen. Through the window on the side of
the house, she could see that the coffeepot
was on, and this told her exactly where
she'd find him.

She tiptoed to the deck, where the pre-
dawn morning air was chilly and moist. The
clouds that had hugged this part of the
mountain all night were just beginning to
evaporate into the gray light of morning,
which made the whole world look like a
black-and-white film. Fall was almost here,
she realized. She wished she had thought to
bring a sweater. If she had thought much at
all, though, she probably would have come
to her senses and would not be here. All she
could do now was see it through.

He was out on the farthest deck, where
they'd shared a cup of coffee months before.
His back was to the house, and he did not

move as she approached. She walked softly, not wanting to startle him. She couldn't tell whether he was looking out at the mountains or asleep. As she got closer, she saw that he wore a dark knit cap and a hooded sweatshirt.

"You're up early," he said, not turning around. The mountains beyond him hulked like dark purple shadows as the sky surrounding them became a soft bluish pink.

"I'm up late," she said. "I drove all night."

"Yeah?" he said, his tone unreadable.

"Yes." She tried to sound sure of herself. She was anything but.

He hesitated and then said tentatively, "William okay with you doing that on your own?"

She was surprised to hear him come from this angle, until it occurred to her he had no reason to know that she and William weren't still dating. "William doesn't get a vote."

"Oh," he said softly. She still couldn't read him.

"We're not together. I haven't seen him in weeks."

He nodded. "What's that in your hand?"

Until then, she wasn't sure he had even looked at her at all. She had almost forgotten the two little notebooks, which she was mostly holding to help her stay focused. "Well, there are two things I came to talk to you about," she said. "And I brought notes."

He looked at her now, curious. "More lists?"

"Well, yes, sort of," she conceded.

"Okay, Scarlett. I think I can reschedule this meeting for later." He made a sweeping gesture at the mountains in the distance. "You have my attention."

He looked both more boyish and more menacing in his dark hat and sweatshirt. She was struck once more by how unlike his public image he could look sometimes. She had decided that she liked this — that she knew a Dylan that no one else did. Or that few people did, anyway. Suzanne found herself standing there, unable to speak. She was torn between twin desires: one, to reach out and touch him, to press herself into him until he had no choice but to take her in his arms. The other: to run as fast as she could back to her car and never see him or think of him again.

No way through but forward, darlin', she heard her dad say in her head. She took a deep breath. "I've been thinking about all the reasons that we shouldn't be together," she said, trying to control the shaking in her voice.

Dylan snorted. "Yes, that seems to be a favorite topic of yours," he said. She thought maybe it was meant as a joke, but the bitter edge was hard to miss.

"I've spent my whole life cataloging reasons I should or shouldn't be in a relationship. As you know, it never took much to convince me something wasn't going to work. But with you, the list of what won't work is long. I mean, longer than most."

She held up the notebook as illustration. Dylan's expression was one of scientific curiosity, rather than emotion. "For example?"

Suzanne felt awkward and childish, as though she'd brought him her diary to read. "Well, some we have already talked about. I'm older than you; you're on the road all the time; the incredible volumes of women hanging on you at any given moment. But it's more than that. Sometimes I'm ashamed of who I am and what I've done. I know how I feel when I know you've been with someone, how I feel when I think about Misty —"

"Suzanne," he interrupted. But she shook her head, wiping a couple of stray tears.

"No, let me finish. It hurts me so much to think of that, and I know it would hurt you to think of that horrible list on my dining room wall. I think underneath all of this" — she gestured at the house behind her, thinking of the parties she'd seen there — "you're kind of a traditional guy. One day, you're going to want a traditional girl and marriage and babies. I've never wanted to get married, and I've always wanted to have a career.

"And I love kids, but I have always felt like the world is a damn scary place to bring innocent children into. It even took me a while to get excited about Marci's pregnancy. My own best friend. Plus, you're still so young and on the road all the time, and . . ." She flipped through the notebook, trying to decipher her writing through the blurring of tears. "Well, I think maybe some of these are just Journey lyrics . . . Anyway, I think you get the idea."

He chuckled. "So you came to explain why we shouldn't be together?"

She shook her head. "No. I need to tell you something, but please don't feel like you have to answer me now. It's just something I need you to hear from me, face-to-face. Okay?"

"Okay," he said seriously.

She held up one of the notebooks. "I made this stupid list this summer because I thought it would help me feel better about being away from you. It's all true, and things probably would never work between us. There are a million reasons we shouldn't be together. But I don't want me being a coward to be one of them.

"Dylan, I drove all night to tell you that I'm in love with you. I have been for months. I don't think I've ever said those words out loud before. I don't know if that will mean anything to you at this point, and it's okay if it doesn't. I know we've hurt each other, and I'm sorry, and that we don't make any sense together. If you don't feel the same way, or if too much has happened, I will understand. No matter how you feel about me, I'm just grateful to have the chance to say that to another person."

Suzanne forced herself to stop talking. Dylan's face was set hard in a lack of expression, as though he were one of the queen's guards in London. But there was some emotion brewing underneath, and she saw him swallow hard. "Thank you for saying that," he said. "It means a lot to me."

She waited, but he didn't go on. Each passing second felt like a knife to her heart. She fought back tears, forcing herself to take deep breaths. *You said it,* she told herself, thinking about what her therapist might say. *You came here and told him how you feel, and that was brave as hell. You can't force him to return your feelings. Stand tall. You've owned your part, and no one can take that away from you.*

Still, she waited another moment to give him time to respond. Just in case. But his expression was stoic, though she thought the corners of his mouth may have been twitching, holding back some kind of feeling. She couldn't tell what. But she would get no further answer from Dylan Burke today.

Gently, he prompted her. "And the second thing?"

She inhaled deeply, turning a page in her mind. *Move on.* "I need to borrow some money."

Even his expert control over his responses couldn't hide the surprise. "What?"

She sat in the chair across the table from him and slid the second notebook toward him. "Not borrow, actually. I need a donation. A big one."

27

A month later, Suzanne sat on an airplane bound for New York, feet drumming nervously. The man in the seat in front of her turned around and shot her a you-aren't-seriously-going-to-do-that-the-whole-time look. It was mid-October, just four weeks after she'd begun implementing her plan, and to her utter astonishment she had been invited to appear on the popular morning show *American Breakfast.* They had taken an interest in the Bonita Daniels Fallen Heroes Foundation, most likely because of Dylan's very public involvement with it, and Suzanne was going to have a minute-long interview the next morning.

Originally, they had asked Chrysaline to be there, too, but Mary had flatly refused, and Suzanne understood. She felt protective of Chrysaline, too, especially since her mom had died barely two months ago. It all felt fast and chaotic to Suzanne, and she was an adult whose grief was nothing compared with Chrys's. So she was going alone but bringing some of Chrysaline's best pieces with her, including a spectacular portrait of Bonita laughing at a family picnic, drawn from a snapshot.

The idea for the foundation was simple: filling in the gaps for kids who'd lost a law enforcement parent in the line of duty. Often, life insurance or collections from other officers helped these kids get their basic needs met, but things like college scholarships and special camps were still sometimes out of the question. And Suzanne wanted to do more than get them by; she wanted to help them find inspiration. To help them create the lives for themselves their parents had been working so hard to give them.

Even though Dylan never responded to her confession that she loved him, a pain that Suzanne was slowly beginning to tolerate, he had been immediately interested in helping Chrysaline and other kids. He woke Yvette up himself that morning on his deck and had her get a substantial check to Suzanne to get the foundation started, and by the end of the week he'd convinced six other young celebrities to do the same. He was even talking about getting some other singers to donate live recordings of their music for a fund-raiser album — a project the enormity of which had sent Yvette chirping in circles for days.

Suzanne herself had put together the foundation's board of directors, calling on the executives and managers whose parties she had planned for years, telling her personal story over and over, showing off Chrysaline's artwork over lunches and happy hours. Recounting her humiliation at the hands of Penny and Gunnar was painful, but what was her pride compared with Chrysaline Daniels's loss? Some of her old contacts were happy to help, and others had to be cajoled or shamed into participation, but at the end of the day, no one could say no to Suzanne.

They were planning a kickoff event for the foundation the following spring, putting Suzanne back in her old role as party planner, but this time with renewed energy and purpose. She had already made contact with 147 kids around the country, and there were many more she was trying to locate. The kids who wanted to do so could donate artwork, writing, music, science projects, photographs, and other items to be auctioned or used in the promotional materials. She also had the kids and their guardians working on lists of things they wanted, needed, and dreamed about, so that Suzanne and the board could begin establishing a process for helping them.

The project was a mind-blowing undertaking and, although she slept very little, she was happier than she had ever been. Even her parents were helping, and her dad beamed with pride when he'd report to her that he had secured a donation from an old colleague or convinced senator so-and-so to donate a flag flown over the Capitol Building. He also served as her informal legal advisor until she could recruit a volunteer as general counsel for the board.

As for Dylan, Suzanne saw him in spurts. They talked on the phone about the foundation, and once or twice he came to meetings of the new board to help. Suzanne was not in favor of exploiting his celebrity status, but she found it hard to deny that when he took time out to attend a meeting, the board seemed to take their tasks very seriously. Perhaps coincidentally, no one had to rush out of a room to get back to work when Dylan was there.

When they talked on the phone, he rarely volunteered information about where he was. She knew he had been in Los Angeles some of the time, probably in talks about doing more films, but she had only deduced this by passing comments about the time zone or the weather. Other times, he might be in Nashville or down the street in his Atlanta apartment — she could never be sure. Still, he seemed to think of her as a friend, and she did her best to accept it.

During the day, she accepted his friendship and help with a grateful heart. He had saved her life, and now he was making it possible for her to help others. To be in love was a gift, even if the person you loved could not return your feelings. She had friends: when she was lonely, she called Marci or Beth or Rebecca or Chad. She had occupation: the foundation kept her busy, and if she was sad or bored, she painted. She sold a few more paintings, enough to pay her rent well into the spring.

Only in the quietest moments did she allow herself to feel the pangs of love. Like now, when she was strapped into an airplane seat and had flipped through the *SkyMall* catalog a hundred times. Or in the middle of the night, when the bustle of the day had died down, when her paints were put away and she could no longer force herself to focus on today's meeting or tomorrow's to-do list. Only then did she allow herself to feel the hard, icy truth: this time, she would be the one left behind.

If he wasn't already, Dylan would be dating again soon, and she'd only be able to hide the truth from herself for so long. Eventually, his commitment to the foundation would have to wane, too, as his career progressed and a new Misty or Gretchen — or a more widely known conquest like a costar or duet partner — took his arm and pulled him back into the world where he belonged.

As the plane began its descent into New York, Suzanne wondered whether it might be time to start dating again. She didn't want to start her old pattern of running through guys faster than she went through shampoo bottles, but she couldn't pine away for Dylan forever, either. She decided to talk to her therapist about it next week.

She was awakened at 3:30 A.M. by an automated voice on the hotel phone. Suzanne rolled out of bed, muttering obscenities. She put Preparation H under her eyes like the beauty magazine she'd read had advised and took a taxi to the TV studio as instructed. In the cab, she got a text from Marci, who was due in two weeks, still not sleeping, and was now so big she could barely get comfortable at any point in the day.

Good Luck! We are Tivo-ing it just in case!

Suzanne hated the thought that she might miss the baby's birth while she was out of town, but Jake had told her confidentially that he thought Marci was being overly optimistic that she would come early. Suzanne's parents had wished her luck the night before. She had not heard from Dylan.

When she arrived at the studio, she was hustled to a chair, where hair and makeup staff fussed over her for a few minutes. The producer, a short man with light red hair who wore jeans, a blazer, and sneakers — and seemed far too young for this job — went over the plan. "You're in a segment called 'Meaningful Mornings.' All about people who have found their passion helping others. It's a short bit after the eight thirty news, so you have some time. Wish we could've interviewed the girl," he said wistfully.

Yeah, I'll bet you did. The tearful grief of a daughter who's lost her mom is far better TV than a rich blond woman creating a charity to help out. "Well, you got me instead," Suzanne sang in an artificially sweet tone. He

414

shrugged and left.

Suzanne nervously flipped through the artwork she'd brought and paced around in the tiny greenroom. A flat-screen TV on the wall showed the live feed from the studio just a few yards away from where she stood. Nadia Spencer, one of the show's two spunky female hosts, was cooking something with an excited little man who reminded Suzanne absurdly of a spider monkey. He jumped from station to station in the fake kitchen, mincing and shredding, throwing things into pans, pulling things out of the oven. *Not a spider monkey,* she decided. *An elf. On crystal meth.*

Nadia tasted whatever the finished product was that the elf had concocted, some kind of frittata, and looked at the camera with orgasmic happiness. "Scrumptious," she said. "And healthy, too! Check out the recipe on our Web site. And when we come back, country superstar Dylan Burke talks to us about life on the road and his latest charity project."

And there he was. They cut from the frittata elf to another part of the studio, where Dylan sat on what looked like a barstool, looking amazing in his jeans, crisp white oxford, and glasses. No camo hat. Behind him was a large window full of people waving into the studio from the street, some holding up signs or wearing silly hats. Suzanne noticed one of the signs said I "HEART" DYLAN in red duct tape.

Dylan smiled, half laughing, at the camera, as though the entire country had just said something endearingly funny. Suzanne smiled, too, at the TV in the greenroom. She was thoroughly confused by his being here, but his bemused charm was infectious. And she was, in fact, very happy to see him, no matter what the reason.

"You're up," said the producer suddenly, as the feed cut to a commercial for some kind of mop, which showed a woman in a ballerina outfit gracefully mopping her floors while classical music played in the background. "Follow me, please."

Suzanne trailed him numbly out to the stage, her mouth dry and her feet heavy. Dylan had moved to an oversized sofa and was chatting easily with Nadia while the latter had her makeup touched up and sipped water held up by an assistant.

"Suzanne Henderson," said the producer, bringing her forward to meet the anchor.

"Hamilton," Suzanne and Dylan corrected simultaneously. Then Suzanne continued. "It's a pleasure to meet you, Ms. Spencer."

Nadia eyed them both for a second and then extended her hand to Suzanne. "Nice to meet you, too," she said. "Thanks for being here. This should be pretty easy, so don't be nervous. Just answer the questions as though we're two friends talking in a coffee shop. Whichever camera has the red light on is the one feeding live, but try not to pay attention to that. Act natural, be concise. Easy on the Southern accent, though; we don't want people to think you're stupid."

"No," Suzanne replied. "We wouldn't want that." By this time, she had been seated next to Dylan, and he squeezed her hand lightly.

If the formidable little woman caught the sarcasm in Suzanne's response, she ignored it. "Kevin!" she shouted, and the red-haired producer jumped. "Are we coming straight from commercial, or is Anne doing the lead-in?"

"What are you doing here?" Suzanne hissed at Dylan when it seemed no one was paying them direct attention.

"It's a big day for us, Scarlett," he whispered back. "I couldn't let you do this alone. Now, just smile. And easy on that Southern accent."

She managed to elbow him in the ribs and make it look as if she was simply shifting to

417

adjust her suit jacket. "Ow!" he mouthed. *You deserved that,* she glared in response.

The commercial break felt shorter than Suzanne had anticipated. Suddenly, there was a blur of bright lights and people shouting and signaling, and then they were on. Nadia was talking to the camera about Dylan and his career. ". . . In the music business since childhood . . . Four multi-platinum albums . . . Highest number of downloads on iTunes in a single week . . . Just back from one of the most successful summer tours in the business . . ."

She felt as though he was a stranger. Suzanne heard the list of achievements and knew that she had read most of them in articles or press releases months ago, but they felt alien to her, as did the man sitting next to her. Here was the same feeling she'd had back in Jake and Marci's driveway months ago — like Dylan was two people. Only this time, instead of kissing Clark Kent in a driveway, she was sitting next to the untouchable Superman beneath the hot white lights of a television studio. She stole a glance as Nadia waxed on about his greatness and saw that he looked perfectly relaxed. *And why not?* This was his world.

Nadia was still talking. ". . . Two years ago, he was described by *Entertainment*

Weekly as one of country music's wild boys, and he has not failed to live up to that reputation, onstage at least. But today you're here to talk about something else." She turned to Dylan now and flashed a brilliant smile. "Good morning. Thanks for joining us."

"Thanks, Nadia," he said in his juiciest drawl. "It's always nice to see you at breakfast." It would have sounded seedy coming from anyone else, but in her peripheral vision she saw that Dylan was wearing his most charming, lopsided grin and that Nadia Spencer was genuinely laughing. The cameramen were also smiling, from what Suzanne could see.

"I mean, the frittata looks great," Dylan went on, and then in an exaggerated Tennessee accent he added, " 'Course, where I come from, we call them skillet taters."

More laughter, and Nadia reached across and jovially touched his hand. Suzanne could hear the blood rushing in her ears. Dylan began talking about their project and how he had always been committed to law enforcement and those who serve our country in uniform. On a personal note, he added, Officer Daniels had not only been a great mom and a great cop but also helped "someone close to me" in an hour of need.

He put his hand on Suzanne's as he said this.

Close to him, Suzanne thought. Her insides thrilled at the words and at his touch, despite her promise to herself to stay calm and emotionally detached in all their dealings. And then Nadia was speaking to her, and Suzanne saw the camera shift in her direction.

"I read the report Officer Daniels filed about your horrifying experience," Nadia said. *Great,* Suzanne thought, *if they dug that up, they probably dug up the thing at the High, too.* No way she could explain that in fifteen seconds or whatever they had. "It must have been so scary."

"Well, yes," Suzanne said, and then heard her father's voice in her head. *You own this room, darlin'. Run the conversation, and you rule the world.* "But I'm not here to talk about me or my experience. The fact is that Bonita Daniels touched my life and many others, and that's what law enforcement officers around the country do every day. They have a hard, dangerous job, and often sacrifice everything for our safety. Their families make sacrifices, too, and this organization was founded to honor those sacrifices. Mr. Burke has been instrumental in helping us get started, and we've had participation from many other artists and musicians, who have donated their time and resources."

A digital clock to the side of one of the cameras counted down seconds, indicating that there were only twenty-nine left. Suzanne was terrified that there was still enough time for them to flash a picture of her running half-naked across the lawn of the High Museum on the screen, but Nadia turned her attention back to Dylan.

"So, your summer tour is over and you're doing *meaningful* work in Atlanta." Nadia stressed "meaningful," Suzanne supposed, to connect it with the name of the segment. "What's next for Dylan Burke?"

"Actually," he said, and cleared his throat, "I've decided to take a sabbatical for a while. At least six months, maybe longer."

"Really?" a shocked Nadia replied. "And are you making this announcement exclusively here on *American Breakfast*?"

"Well, I guess I am, yeah." Dylan did not look at Suzanne, but she saw his Adam's apple bob up and down as he swallowed nervously.

"Dylan Burke," Nadia was saying dramatically, either for emphasis or stalling for time while she figured out what to ask next. "Taking a sabbatical in the prime of his career. Of course, everyone will be wondering why."

Dylan inclined his head as if to acknowledge the truth of this and said, "Well, to be honest with you, Nadia, I'm in love."

The perky host looked taken aback but quickly recovered her wit enough to say, "Wait a minute, you aren't going to go all Tom Cruise on me, are you? Because Oprah can afford sturdier couches than we have." She looked at the camera with a significant frown and raised eyebrow.

Suzanne thought she might faint. Only curiosity about what would happen next was keeping her upright, as though her own life was keeping her on the edge of her seat.

"Nah," said Dylan with his usual charm. "That's not really my style. But I think Tom could agree with me that love will do strange things to a man. Anyway, I don't know if the woman I love really loves me, or if she was just saying it because she got caught up in . . . a moment."

This last part had just enough innuendo to be endearing and funny all at once. Dylan was playing to the audience, per usual. Only Suzanne — whose heart was now pounding so audibly she was sure the microphones must be picking it up — knew that the moment in question had been a lonely sunrise on Dylan's mountain deck during which they had not so much as touched hands. "But I do know that my job scares her, and I'm willing to set that aside for a little while so she can figure out if she likes the real me enough to put up with . . . the me that everyone else knows."

And then he turned to her, still grinning. Suzanne realized he had taken her hand in his. She was too shocked to move. Her face felt frozen, like her mother's looked immediately after Botox. She glanced at Nadia, who seemed to be wearing the same lack of expression herself.

This seemed to bring the TV host's attention to the fact that they had a few long seconds left and were stuck in dead air. "Well, there you have it, America. Sounds like unless Ms. Suzanne Henderson — er, *Hamilton* — is completely out of her mind, country music's hottest bad boy Dylan Burke may be off the market. And off the stage, at least for a while. We wish them luck with that, and of course with their wonderful charity. Next up, workout secrets of a former supermodel."

When the red camera light went off, Nadia got up and huffed away without a word to either Dylan or Suzanne. "She doesn't like surprises," said Kevin, the producer. He smiled uncomfortably and raced after her, presumably to fix whatever harm Dylan's surprise had caused.

But Suzanne had no room in her flooded brain for concern about the fragile ego of a morning-show personality. She was staring into the familiar yet surreal face of Dylan Burke. The man she loved, who until this moment had never told her that he loved her back. Words failed her. So he spoke, gingerly. "Sorry if that caught you off guard. I figured publicly humiliating each other was kind of our thing, right? Anyway, I heard somewhere that girls like grand romantic gestures."

She was hearing the words, but they weren't sinking into her addled brain. "Dylan, I'm . . . your career —"

"Wait. Let's talk about this somewhere private. If you're going to shoot me down, I'd rather not cry in front of all these cameras. How about the hotel?"

"The hotel?" Suzanne had checked out of her hotel this morning, and her carry-on bag was waiting in the greenroom for her to take to the airport as soon as she left the studio.

"Yeah. I kept my room. Please, push back your flight. You can hear me out, make one of your cute little neurotic lists, and then go

424

home tonight if you want." Now it was his turn to blush. "Or we can stay."

We can stay. There's a *we*? *We* have a room? Try as she might, she could not get her tired brain to process what had just happened. So she nodded numbly and followed a chipper production assistant back to the greenroom to collect her bag, rescheduled her flight for later that evening, and followed Dylan out of the studio to the sidewalk, where he flagged down a taxi.

He held the cab door open for her. "What? No limo?" she said, grasping for a joke to break the tension between them.

"I hate limos," he said, not seeming to notice her anxiety. "If I'm going to be in a room on wheels, I'd just as soon it was an RV or a tour bus so I could at least go to the fridge and make a sandwich. Or to the bathroom. Just one of many things you'll have to learn about me."

"Okay, no limos. I'll add it to my neurotic little list," she said nervously, and he slid in next to her. The car pulled into New York traffic and drove just a few blocks before letting them back out again.

It turned out that Dylan's definition of a hotel room was actually a mind-blowing penthouse suite with damask draperies, exquisite furnishings, and views of the city on all sides. "So you hate limos but not all luxury accommodations, I see," Suzanne said as they exited the elevator into the massive suite. She was feeling more like herself now.

Dylan put her bag in a closet by the front door. *Easy getaway,* she thought instinctively, dropping her purse on a nearby table.

"Well, can you blame me? I am trying to woo you, so I thought it couldn't hurt to stack the deck in my direction, at least a little bit."

"Trying to *woo* me? Dylan, you —"

"Wait, me first," he said firmly, putting a finger over her lips. "You don't get to make *all* the speeches in this relationship. There's something I have wanted to say to you ever since you drove up to the mountain, but I have been trying to figure out how to say it. How to say it right, I mean."

"Okay," she said, holding her breath.

He drew her close to him, holding her hands down at her side. His body was inches away, warm and comforting, and she wanted to reach out and touch him.

"Suzanne, I love you, too." He said it in almost a whisper and then reiterated in a stronger voice, "I love you. You deserved to hear it from me sooner, but I'm an asshole about stuff like that sometimes. I'm trying

426

to get better. Anyway, I have loved you since the moment I saw you at the stadium in those ridiculous heels —"

"Hey!"

"— looking like the hot girl from a sexual harassment video. And then you showed me up and insulted my friend's batting stats in front of everyone. I sort of hated you for it, but I liked you, too. I can safely say you are the only woman I have ever loved, liked, and hated at first sight."

She felt herself smiling. She realized she could say the same about him.

Deflecting some of the intensity of the moment, she wandered over to the window, a gorgeous floor-to-ceiling view of what she assumed was Central Park. She gasped involuntarily at its beauty in the midmorning light. She wished she had her paints and a canvas.

"See?" he said, coming up behind her, as though he was continuing some point he'd been making before, gesturing out to the park below. "That's exactly what I mean. You appreciate things. You never seem to take anything for granted. I love that about you."

"It's beautiful," she said. An understatement, but her brain was too muddled to articulate it better.

"More than eight hundred and forty acres. Bigger than the average Texas cattle ranch, right here in the middle of the city."

Suzanne turned to look at him, astonished. The slight stubble on his chin gleamed in the morning sunlight. "How the *hell* do you know that?"

Dylan laughed. "Being on tour is boring most of the time. Once in a while, I get off the bus and look around."

She felt her face flushing with embarrassment. All this time, and she was still underestimating him.

As though reading her mind, he traced a finger along her jaw before grasping both her hands in his. "Scarlett, I know we don't seem to have a lot in common; I know you think our age difference matters. I know I'm not" — he hesitated, rolling the next words around in his mouth as though they had an unpleasant taste — "*William,* or somebody like him. Somebody whose parents know your parents and whose family isn't on the front page of the gossip magazines every other week."

"I told you I broke up with William months ago," she interrupted. He ignored her.

"I've been thinking for weeks about everything you said, about how you never wanted to get married and how you don't know how to bring kids into this scary world and my tour schedule and the women and Journey . . . and I want you to know I get it. All of it. And I'm not going to play games or try to be more relaxed than I feel. I'm as serious about this as I have ever been about anything. Cards on the table."

He dropped her hand and held up his palms to her in a gesture of surrender. "If you decide to leave this room now or" — his glance flicked behind him toward the open door of the bedroom — "*later,* then I understand. You can sneak out with your bag and add me to the list on your wall, and I won't resent you for it. I'll understand. Really."

Suzanne followed his glance to the bedroom doorway. She could see an enormous four-poster bed. It was impossible not to imagine herself there, with Dylan. She bit her lip, hesitating. "But . . ."

"But when I'm away from you, you're all I think about. Even when I was so pissed at you this summer. In fact, I haven't so much as touched another woman since that awful day in your apartment. Not the entire damn tour. And *believe me,* there were chances." He emphasized this and shook his head in a way designed to let her know just how hard some of those chances had been to pass up.

"What about Gretchen?" Suzanne demanded.

"Nope. Told her I needed a shower and stayed in there until she passed out." He smiled. "Got kind of wrinkly in there, actually. I think somebody had given her a Red Bull."

"But why?" Suzanne asked, curiosity mingled with jealousy. "You were mad at me. I was seeing William. You and I certainly weren't dating. You had no reason to —"

"I *know*," he said. "That was the frustrating part. I was so mad at you, but at the same time I wanted to be loyal to you. And that made me even more mad at you. It was a pretty ugly cycle for a few weeks there. Just ask the guys in the band. And about forty thousand people in Sacramento." He shook his head regretfully, remembering something.

"They probably all hate me."

"Nah," he said dismissively. "Sacramento is a pretty forgiving city. Though I did get a couple of bad reviews from that show."

She rolled her eyes.

"No, the guys don't hate you. Actually, Eddie convinced me to do this."

"To confess your love for me on national television?"

"Well, no. That part was mine. But to tell you how I feel — that was Eddie."

She nodded. She always had liked Eddie. "I guess you took that suggestion and ran with it, huh?"

"At first, I didn't know why I was doing it," Dylan went on. "Avoiding the other women, I mean. Well, avoiding and rejecting and, in a couple of cases, *really* pissing them off . . . Anyway, I think in a way I wanted to prove to myself I could be true to one person, even when I didn't have any obligation to you. I thought if I could be faithful to the *idea* of you, then maybe I'd deserve a chance with the *real* you. I know that probably sounds stupid, but —"

"No, it doesn't sound stupid." She interrupted gently, touching his arm. "It sounds sweet."

"When I was a kid, I used to think I'd marry the first girl . . . well, you know. And obviously that didn't work out, and since then —"

"I know," Suzanne said firmly. Even though it was all in the past and she had absolutely no room to talk, a sizzling pang of jealousy was cutting through the sea of other emotions like a hot blade. The image of Misty traipsing into her apartment like the cat who ate the canary was pushing itself to the front of her brain.

Dylan cleared his throat, looking at the floor. "Considering we're both . . . uh, *experienced* at this romance stuff, I wanted to do something that would make this thing between you and me different. I figured if I ever got to stand here and touch your face . . . your body, I wanted to know that I'd *earned* you in a way none of those other guys ever did."

Suzanne wiped tears, aware that she had cried more in front of Dylan Burke than any man she'd ever known, maybe including her dad. Seeing this response seemed to bolster Dylan's resolve. The words came out in a rush. "Suzanne, I love you. I've known that for a while now. I didn't want it to be true at first, honestly, especially at Kate's wedding. I was so pissed at you, even though I knew I had no right to expect . . . Anyway, the plain truth is: I don't want anyone else. We don't have to get married if you don't want to, and we can talk about kids; I mean, I think you'd be a great mom, but I have nieces and nephews I love, and I know life with a musician can be hard, but if anybody can handle it, it's you —"

"Shut up," she said.

"What?"

"Shut. *Up.*" Suzanne lifted herself onto

her toes and kissed him lightly. "You talk too much." She kissed him more deeply, allowing herself to believe the fantasy, just for a moment. If this was all going to disappear when she woke up, she might as well enjoy it now.

She wrapped her arms around his neck as they kissed. He was warm, and his body had a hard, sinewy quality. She imagined she could feel his pulse throbbing in the muscles of his arms and chest and thighs as they pressed against him. Or maybe it was just the echo of her own heart.

Dylan's hands traveled down her back and the back of her skirt, pulling her closer. She gasped as he devoured her throat, scruffy chin scratching the sensitive skin there. He tried to lift her, but his hands slid up the material of her skirt, causing him to growl lightly in frustration.

"Yeah, this isn't going to work," he muttered, tugging gently at the brown and pink tweed skirt she'd worn for her television appearance. "I mean, I love your business side, but . . ."

In one swift motion, he scooped her up and carried her toward the bedroom. Whatever tiny strand of resistance Suzanne had been clinging to snapped then, and when he set her gently on the edge of the bed, she pulled him down with her, kissing him like she had nothing to lose.

Suzanne could feel him getting hard against her, straining against his jeans in a way that was gratifying. Meanwhile, her unfortunate skirt inched higher against her panty hose and twisted, a little uncomfortably, around her. This making-out-with-their-clothes-on thing wasn't going to cut it for long.

Dylan realized it, too, because he pulled back from her and began unbuttoning his white oxford shirt. He lifted an eyebrow at her. "This okay?"

"So very okay," she said, breathless.

She was a little taken aback, then, when Dylan started to laugh.

"What?" she said, feeling some of the heat from her lower extremities migrate to her face.

"I was just thinking, Scarlett. This exclusive relationship is going so much more fun now that we're both in it."

She laughed, too, and covered her face with her hands while Dylan ran his hands up either side of her thighs beneath her skirt. He found the upper edge of her control-top panty hose, which she'd chosen on her mother's advice for the TV appearance — *the camera adds ten pounds, sweet-*

heart — and rolled them down to her ankles. In the fitted brown and pink suit she'd worn on the show, Suzanne felt like half temptress, half little old lady. She attempted to sit on the bed behind her, but it was too high to scale with her legs immobilized. Dylan gave her a crooked grin, lifted her onto the bed by her waist, and slipped off her shoes and hose. He rose to face her and kissed her again, starting softly and then building to something more forceful that eventually pressed her back onto the bed, with him on top of her.

Dylan continued kissing her — her face, neck, and collarbones — while he unbuttoned the sensible suit jacket and silky pink shirt she'd ironed hours earlier in her own hotel room, a few blocks away. Suzanne had had no idea, at three thirty this morning, that Dylan was even in New York. Much less that they'd be on TV together, he'd announce he was putting his career on hold for her, and she'd be in the biggest hotel room she'd ever seen, letting him undress her. And he loved her. She prayed her alarm wouldn't go off to end the dream.

With expert hands, he had her bra off in seconds. He cupped one breast and made an elaborate circle around the nipple with his tongue, smiling up at her. He gently bit down, sending a fiery thrill all over her. She gasped again, and he made an approving noise as he kissed the other breast the same way. She arched her back, and instantly his hand was under her, supporting her and pulling her in. With her suspended in air like that, his unyielding mouth traced the midline of her torso down to her navel, pausing there to hover deliciously over her belly with his hot breath. *Maybe it's not so bad,* she thought, *that we have a little experience.*

When he reached the top of the little tweed skirt, he lowered her gently to the bed before unzipping it with utmost care. Her body was buzzy with excitement, amplified by caffeine and lack of sleep. She willed herself to relax and stop quivering. She took deep, slow breaths as he shimmied the skirt down and off.

He stopped then and looked at her for a while from the foot of the bed. Suzanne, panting and nearly naked, thought she had never felt so exposed. Dylan seemed to be taking a mental picture in the unfiltered light of ten in the morning. He would be seeing the bags under her eyes, the wrinkles at either side of her mouth, spider veins on her calves. She felt squirmy and uncomfortable under his gaze, wishing he would close the curtains.

Dylan, on the other hand, looked fresh and boyish as always, still in his jeans and a white undershirt. He wore a serious expression, and Suzanne fought hard to hold back the anxiety threatening to overthrow her desire. Just when she was about to ask him whether anything was wrong, he bent to kiss the toes of her right foot, grinning at her. "You're so beautiful," he said, kissing her ankle. "Even more amazing than I'd imagined. And I spent a lot of time imagining. *A lot.*"

She lost focus as she felt his hot breath moving up her leg, to her knees, grazing her thighs, and then hovering over her panties — the one piece of clothing she had left. Through the lace she could feel the warmth of his mouth, and she wanted so badly for him to devour her, she could have cried. But he moved up to kiss her on the mouth again and then pulled his head back a few inches. She saw the serious look return.

"Oh, the things I want to do to you," he said, with a combination of a moan and a growl. His voice was gravelly, and sexier than it had ever been on the radio. He ran a hand from her shoulder between her breasts and down, letting it come to rest on the swell of her abdomen. She ached with desire. "With your permission, obviously. But I have one thing to ask first. A favor."

Suzanne had to admit, despite her constant goal of keeping the upper hand with Dylan, there wasn't much she wouldn't have agreed to right now. If only he would do those things he wanted to do. But she nodded, waiting.

"We can stay right here all day, and you can have your wicked way with me all you want." He gave her the lopsided grin she had come to treasure. "In fact, we don't have to leave for days or weeks — we'll live on room service if you want."

"Okay," she breathed, still trying to think of a clever retort or some remnant of their usual banter. Nothing came. His hand on her lower abdomen seemed to be clouding all her thoughts.

"Just please promise me one thing: if you're going to freak out and leave me here alone, go today. Or tonight while it's dark. It will suck, but I'm a big boy, and I'll deal with it. But if you're here tomorrow, I'm all in."

He was so sweet and sincere, part of her wanted to pull him to her and promise him that she would never break his heart. But in another part of her, the old hesitation was still there. She loved him now, but how long

438

would it last? Could she be trusted with someone's heart?

She chickened out and settled for their preferred method of communication. "I don't know . . . ," she teased. "Maybe a broken heart is good for your career."

Suzanne was angry with herself as soon as the words left her lips. For once, he was being sincere with her. How could she be so glib about it? She was confused: she loved him deeply, wanted him desperately, and was terrified of how out of control everything felt.

But her teasing comment didn't seem to hit Dylan the way it did her. "That's it," he said, with menacing playfulness. "You're in serious trouble now." He held her down and tickled her, and she writhed beneath him, making a show of trying to get away while they both laughed. Soon, his smile faded and they were kissing again. Suzanne sat up, pushing against him while they kissed, and found to her surprise that the shaky feeling was gone.

She lifted Dylan's undershirt over his head and admired his lean, bare torso and the tiny tufts of russet hair that emerged from the top of his jeans and under his arms. She let her nails linger on his skin, loving the way the flesh rippled slightly beneath her touch. He closed his eyes and groaned and then pressed her back onto the bed again with a long, deep kiss. His mouth resumed its roving across her skin, tenderly kissing and nipping at her neck and shoulders, following her midline down until he was removing her panties with his teeth.

Suzanne thought she would explode with excitement while his mouth danced around its goal, kissing her inner thighs repeatedly, and then the mound of flesh just above her pubic hair and back again, grinning up at her the whole time. She began to moan in pleasure and frustration, arching toward him, her whole body begging. And then, finally, he inhaled deeply and sank his mouth onto her, gently but fully, his warm breath finally connecting with its intended mark, along with lips, teeth, and . . . *oh!* tongue. At once, he was outside her, consuming her like a warm, comforting dish, and inside her, probing and exploring her to a titillation she had never before experienced.

Suzanne panted and moaned like she hadn't done since . . . ever. She knew how to make the noises men wanted to hear, and sometimes the noises expressed her pleasure, too, but never before had she abandoned herself this way. Perhaps it was the safety of the penthouse, where she knew they would not be overheard, or maybe it was just that she had no choice. She cried out Dylan's name as though it was the last word that would escape her lips, and he responded by making his movements more forceful. It felt like mere seconds until the pleasure overwhelmed her, sending her shuddering so violently into Dylan's mouth that she was worried for a moment that she'd hurt him.

But the lopsided smile said it all. He was proud of himself, she could tell. Or maybe he'd enjoyed it almost as much as she had, or both. "Damn," he said softly. She waited for him to say the standard things the occasion called for. *You taste so good,* or *I love watching you come,* or something equally bawdy. But what Dylan said next surprised her. "I do believe, Miss Scarlett, you could break my heart right now if you wanted."

She sat up to kiss him, and he kissed her back but gently pushed her hand away as she reached for his jeans. He eased her back down and lay half on top of her, kissing her deeply and massaging her with his hand. The second orgasm was surprising; the third, unprecedented. She was beside herself, and seriously expecting to wake any minute to find she'd overslept and missed

American Breakfast entirely.

Finally, looking pleased with himself, Dylan kicked out of his jeans, returned to embrace her, and pushed himself inside her as naturally as if they did this every day. He moved with a slow, regular rhythm, looking and feeling like something every woman would love to bottle and sell. To her shock, she felt herself moving toward climax again. "I love you," she said into his ear as she trembled once more beneath him, violating her own rules about professing emotion during sex.

Dylan let out a husky cry, and she felt him tense and then relax on top of her, kissing her neck and muttering something she couldn't understand. They lay like that for a long time, spent and happy, listening to the sounds of their own breath slowing to normal.

"Well," he said eventually, rolling next to her and wrapping her in his arms. "*That* lived up to my expectations."

She smiled and stroked his hair. The day's events were surreal, and now that her body was peaceful, her mind worked to understand everything that had happened.

"Are you seriously taking a sabbatical?" she asked after they'd been quiet for a while. "Or was that just the world's most dramatic pickup line? Which *obviously* worked like a charm . . ."

He laughed and turned on his side to face her, his elbow propping up his head. "Truth?"

"Have we ever done anything else?"

"Fair enough. Honestly, I was already planning to take a couple of months off after the tour anyway. The guys need a break. Eddie's wife just had a baby; John's dad has been sick. We're all a little worn-out right now, and if you keep that up, you get bad music."

Suzanne realized that, like most people, she had been seeing the glamorous side of his life, not the real-person side. Dylan was a musician and a celebrity in the press, but it was just now occurring to her that he was also a boss, the CEO of a company that floated or sank with him. Did he provide health insurance? 401(k)? Could the drummer in a rock band take family or medical leave? She supposed she would learn all of this, because this would now be her world, too.

The truth of it struck her. She was now in this, for better or worse, whether they got married or not. For an instant, the familiar sensation of panic tightened in her chest; her legs felt the first tingling of a desire to scoop up her clothes and run like hell. But she forced herself to take a deep breath and nuzzle closer to him, tracing patterns across his chest with her finger.

"So you were going to take a break anyway?" she asked.

"Well, a short one. I'd been thinking when we planned this tour that we'd start work on the new album at the end of this month — give the guys six weeks and then hit it again. We've done stuff at the holidays for the last couple of years, too, and then we were scheduled to record the album by the end of January. But then after your little speech at the cabin, I talked to Yvette and cleared everything through February. And we can push it back longer if you want. I said six months this morning just to cover the bases."

"That must have been some conversation," Suzanne said. She'd seen Yvette in an absolute tizzy over the wording of a press release; she found it hard to imagine the chipmunk-like woman after receiving news of at least a six-month setback.

Dylan shook his head, chuckling. "Yeah, she pretty much went supersonic on me. Dogs were barking for miles around. But I suggested it would give her more time to work on that charity album you've been demanding from us. Plus, I gave her a bonus and put her on a plane to Hawaii. She'll be all right."

This is how he gets you, Suzanne thought. *A little charm, a little pampering, and he's bending you to his will.* "She's probably happy, though," he went on, "making maps of all the places on the islands with cell service . . . rewriting my performance contracts . . ."

"So did you arrange all of this — the show and everything?"

"Well, kind of. Yvette's been trying to get me to go on those morning shows forever. Apparently, a bunch of country singers are doing more of that. Anyway, they wanted me on *American Breakfast,* and I told them only if it included you and we could talk about Bonita. The rest of it just sort of fell into place."

They lay silent for a couple of moments, lost in their own thoughts.

"I never got to tell you, did I?" Dylan said after a bit. "That I tried to find you?"

"What? When?"

"That first night we kissed. After I left Marci's house. I tried to come back to find you, but I got lost."

"You *what?*"

"I got lost in Alpharetta. Looking for

Marci's house. I drove around until, like, three in the morning." Then, seeing her face, he reddened and tackled her playfully. "Shut up! Everything looks the same there at night!"

"Really? I hadn't noticed." She laughed. Suzanne ran her fingers absently over a tribal-looking tattoo around one of Dylan's biceps. "So, what happens next?"

"That depends on you," he said. "If you feel ready, we'll do the album for next summer and do an abbreviated tour. Actually, Eddie and I have been talking about doing a small-venue tour for a while now — go play all the dive bars and garden parties we used to do. And I was hoping, if you're not too busy, maybe you'd come with me. At least some of the time."

"Won't that cramp your style? I mean, with the guys?"

"Did you know Paul and Linda McCartney only spent a few nights apart the entire time they were married?" he asked. "It didn't seem to hold him back. Besides, I'm the boss."

"You've thought about this quite a bit, haven't you?" she asked.

"Well, I did have some extra time on my hands this summer," he said. "I pretty much alternated between wishing I'd never met you and trying to figure out how to make it work. And cold showers, of course."

"At least you don't need one of those today," she said.

He rolled toward her, grinning lewdly. "Want to make sure?"

Suzanne shoved him away playfully. "Are you kidding? I'm exhausted. Besides" — she put on her most dripping Scarlett O'Hara accent — "when I was brought to this establishment, I was promised room service. And I expect you to keep your word to a lady."

He laughed, rolled on top of her, pausing seductively. He reached across her for the phone on the bedside table, handing it to her as he rolled out of bed on the other side. "Order anything you want. Literally, anything. They'll either make it or find it for you. I promise," he said. "I'll have a cheeseburger and a beer."

"It's not even eleven yet," Suzanne protested.

Dylan just laughed. As the concierge inquired in a professional, if slightly husky voice, how she could assist Mr. Burke today, Suzanne watched him cross naked to the bathroom and get into the shower.

"Hello? Mr. Burke?" the concierge asked. She had nearly hung up before Suzanne found her voice to answer.

Several hours later, Suzanne woke suddenly in the semidarkness. She felt the arm draped over her, heavy with sleep, and heard light snoring. It took a moment to remember where she was as the lights of the city helped bring the room into focus. Dishes were still piled on a tray near the bed; clothes and wet towels were scattered around the well-appointed room.

The bedside clock informed her that it was one in the morning, but she felt as though she'd had a full night's sleep. She pieced together her memories of the day: being on television, Dylan's announcement that he was in love with her and taking a sabbatical, making love to him for the first time (and three times after that), showering separately and together, talking for hours, falling asleep as the sunset gleamed in pink and orange through the massive windows. Now, with all traces of the sun long gone, the significance of the day and its events came back to her. His arm around her felt heavier the more she remembered.

Despite her best efforts to fight it, the familiar tightening in her chest appeared like an old friend. This panicked sensation, and the relief that running away produced, had been two of her closest companions over the years. They had outlasted every man she'd been with, propelled her through every door, protected her from hurt, and, until now, from love.

She turned to look at the man holding her. Dylan Burke — whose face had first become familiar to her through the pages of gossip magazines, whom she had insulted openly before their first meeting, and whom she had slowly come to adore — was sleeping soundly next to her. He looked happy. It was a kind of peaceful contentment Suzanne envied. Maybe, if she stayed with him, she would learn his secret to staying happy in the midst of the chaos.

If I stay with him. The tightness in her chest sharpened a bit, and she tried to push Dylan's arm discreetly up to relieve some of the pressure on her body. She had promised to stay and meant it, in the heat of their passion this morning. They had passed the afternoon in hedonistic abandon, talking, eating, and exploring the physical connection that seemed to culminate all their months of banter and confusion. The day had been near perfect, which made it easy to imagine that things would work out and easy to leave her promise untouched on the table like a peppermint from their last meal.

But now, in the quiet darkness, doubt was beginning to encroach on her. Dylan's arm, so comforting and strong earlier in the day, was beginning to feel like it was made of solid steel, trapping her. She remembered his words: *If you're here tomorrow, I'm all in.*

Suzanne understood what he meant. If she stayed with him, if she snuggled closer and allowed herself to drift off to sleep again, she was throwing her lot in with his. As consciousness slipped away, so would her freedom, the one thing she had always held dear, always kept to herself. There would be no looking back. And what real life would be like, after the dream in this room ended, she had no idea.

Or she could leave now, while he slept, and what they'd shared would be preserved and perfect. She would go back to the certainty of her own world, where she was in control. Dylan would be disappointed, but he'd forgive her, and she knew for certain that he would move on. There would be no shortage of young starlets and groupies waiting in line to nurse his poor, public broken heart. She would be sad, too; in fact, she knew that her own heart would be broken. But wasn't it better to break both their hearts now than the painful, public disaster this was sure to be?

Of all the men on her list, with *very* few exceptions, Dylan Burke was just about the worst choice imaginable for a boyfriend. He made his living being young and wild and loud; his reputation would continue to lure girls to his door for years to come, committed or not. In fact, she thought sourly, she knew that any public commitment he made to her might make him *more* of a conquest to some of those women he'd be meeting every night backstage. She had seen how some women flocked to men as soon as that little gold band appeared on their hands, eager to find out whether they could take someone else's treasure.

Worse, Dylan would be on the road half the time, living the life she'd seen firsthand at his mountain house. How could she compete with that? Would she have to be with him constantly? Follow him around like her mother did her dad, putting her needs last, trying to hold on to him? Plus, they would bicker constantly, she knew. They always did. What would happen when that stopped being stimulating and flirty and deteriorated into just plain bickering?

Suzanne glanced at Dylan's sleeping form, and her heart surged. She wanted to wake him and kiss him. She wanted to run away from the power he had over her and never look back. She squeezed her eyes shut, unable to see anything but the horrible list on her dining room wall. All the years, all the men, all the times she'd made this very same choice. It had never been so hard. She had never felt so lost.

Dylan sighed in his sleep and rolled away from her, settling once again into soft snores after just a moment. It was time to decide. Suzanne took a deep breath and willed herself not to cry. She eased herself out from under the sheet and out of the bed. Her hand trembled as she opened the front closet door, where her little suitcase stood waiting like a tiny, comforting sentinel.

28

The early-morning sun streamed through the giant windows. Dylan woke with the usual confusion he felt when he was not in his own bed, which was most of the time. In fact, he wasn't sure which bed he would consider his own at this point in his life, so often did he wake up in a new place. But as his eyes adjusted to the light, the view of the city below helped clear the fog and reminded him where he was, whom he was with. He smiled and rolled over, reaching for her, but the sheets next to him were cold and empty.

His heart sank. Suzanne was gone. Part of him had known this was still possible, and he had sworn to them both that he was protecting himself from it. Hell, he had seen the list of guys on the dining room wall firsthand and told Suzanne yesterday he might be added to it. But now that the moment had arrived, he knew he'd done a piss-poor job shielding himself. In fact, the whole concept was ridiculous. He had been in love with her for months. The minute he had allowed himself to touch her soft ivory skin, to kiss her throat and feel himself slide inside her . . . it was over. And he knew it.

A sudden sob rose in his throat, surprising him with its forcefulness. He willed it down, the way he sometimes had to will himself to hold a long note at the end of a show. But it escaped anyway, and all he could do was stifle it to a groan into the pillow. He punched the bed with a force that surprised him, causing his arm to ache and vibrate. How could he have misread her so completely? He had never really been in love before, but everything yesterday — the way she looked at him, the way they kissed, the way her body responded to his touch — had told Dylan that she felt it, too. *What a fucking chump I am.*

He got up, growling, and wrapped a sheet around his waist. He washed his face and brushed his teeth, scowling at himself in the mirror. *You look ridiculous,* he chided himself, looking at his bed-tousled hair and his face, one side of which was red with the deepest sleep he could remember. He turned away from the asshole in the mirror, threw on a clean pair of boxers, and started aimlessly picking things up to throw in his bag. There was no point in staying here another minute after making such an ass of himself. *I told her every damn thing,* he thought. *Never again.*

The towels they'd used were in a pile outside the bathroom door, and his jeans and boxers from yesterday piled next to them. The pink and brown suit was gone, of course, and her purse was missing from the table where she'd left it. Dylan knew if he checked the coat closet, he would find her suitcase gone, as well. The stupid, too-big penthouse was silent except for the muted sounds of car horns far below. He could still smell sex, sweat, and traces of her perfume. And coffee.

Coffee?

He followed the aroma to the penthouse's kitchen area around the corner, where a cheerful pot of coffee sat on the warming plate. *Did the staff of the hotel come in and make coffee? Or did she make it before leaving?* Both seemed ridiculous possibilities. He looked around for a note or something but didn't see one. The views on this side of the suite were equally stunning, though instead of the park they showed the bustling city and Hudson River in the distance. There was a seating area with a small couch and two overstuffed chairs, all empty, and a dining room table with space for six. The place mats and plates were untouched, exactly where the hotel staff had staged them amid candles and a floral-and-fruit centerpiece.

A glass door to the balcony was beyond the table. He had not noticed it at first, but now his heart leapt when he saw a long ivory leg propped on the balcony railing outside. She was wearing pink sneakers and khaki shorts more suitable for Atlanta than New York this time of year; even where he stood, he could see that she had goose bumps on her legs from the cool wind outside. She was facing away from him, sitting in a reclining patio chair and talking on the phone. He recognized the tail of his own white oxford shirt sticking out from beneath her. Her long blond hair flapped in the wind, not at all contained by the sunglasses perched on top of her head.

Without stopping to consider that he was in only his boxers, he crossed the room and went straight outside, letting the door close behind him. She turned in surprise but smiled, and he heard a woman's voice trailing off on the phone she now held out to the side.

"Hey, you," she said, ignoring the phone.

Her voice was as sweet as he had ever heard it. Relief washed over him. "Thought you'd never wake up. I made coffee and cleaned up a little. Didn't think you'd mind."

"Hey," he said, and then repeated dumbly, "you made coffee." *Me Tarzan. Jane make coffee. Idiot.*

"And I ran out for bagels." She gestured at a brown paper bag on the patio table, next to her own coffee cup. She stood and grinned at him, both of them knowing the significance of her still being here. With the wind whipping in her hair and the morning sun glinting off her skin, she looked so incredible that words seemed inadequate. "I borrowed your shirt. If we're going to be here for a few days, I might have to get more clothes. Marci can send some —"

He moved toward her, taking the phone from her hand. "She'll call you back," he said, and ended the call. He laid it carefully on the table, waiting for a protest that didn't come, and then took both sides of her pretty blond head in his hands and kissed her.

She kissed him back, and he felt none of the tension he usually sensed when he was with her. She melted into him easily, and he could feel her body relax toward his. "You're not going to run away? You're not scared?" he asked.

Suzanne looked up at him with clear blue eyes that matched the sky around them. "I'm terrified," she said. "But, no, I'm not going to run away."

"Does Marci approve?" he said, nodding toward the phone he'd just put down, expecting that he knew the answer.

"A qualified 'yes,' " Suzanne said, and Dylan raised an eyebrow. "She adores you; she's just worried about me losing myself."

"Are you worried about that, too?" he asked, letting his hands fall to her shoulders. He had to admit he had thought about that himself. Suzanne was so independent and ambitious, Dylan had wondered whether she would adjust to life while he was on the road so much. Would she come with him? If so, would she be bored and miserable? If not, would phone calls and e-mails be enough for them?

"Sure," she said without artifice. "But I figure we're a couple of smart people who love each other, and if you got me to stay last night, you must have a few more tricks up your sleeve. Or lack thereof." She glanced at his bare chest and arms.

"Anyway," she said. "We'll figure it out, right?"

"Yeah, I guess we will," he said, kissing her again. The wind was picking up. Even though the sun shone brightly, early fall was certainly in force. In only his boxers, the chill was starting to seep through him. He felt like a little boy asking her but did it anyway. "So you really love me? You'll really stay?"

She smiled at him, radiant. "Yes and yes."

"I love hearing you say that," he said, adjusting his shirt's collar on her shoulders. "I wouldn't mind getting a few more yeses out of you before today's over. And you should *always* wear this shirt. If you're wearing anything, I mean."

She shimmied closer to him, and he could feel her firm breasts pressing against his bare chest through the shirt in question. "I think that can be arranged."

Dylan turned with her hand in his to take her back inside and, hopefully, straight back to bed, to restart the day the way he had originally wanted. He remembered the hurt and anger he'd felt only moments before and felt ashamed of himself. *Will she always have this kind of power over me?*

He reached the doorknob, stopped abruptly, and faced her again. "Give me your phone."

"My phone? Why?" But she handed it over without waiting for an answer.

"I have to make a couple of calls." He

found the number he was looking for and called it. Suzanne stared at him, incredulous. "Mrs. Hamilton?" he said, when the lady answered. "Hello, it's Dylan Burke. Yes, ma'am. Well, thank you, ma'am."

"What are you doing?" Suzanne mouthed. He ignored her.

"That's very nice of you to say, Mrs. Hamilton. I'm very glad you enjoyed the album." He shot Suzanne a pointed look, and she rolled her eyes. "Well, yes, ma'am. I actually had two reasons for calling. The first is that Suzanne and I will be coming to Atlanta next week — next week okay, Scarlett? — yes, ma'am, we'll be there together, and I wondered whether we could take you and Mr. Hamilton out to dinner?"

In the ensuing pause, he could hear Suzanne's mother calling to her father somewhere in the background. In front of him, Suzanne rubbed her upper arms in a not-subtle hint that she was getting cold, too. He heard a brief, hissed skirmish, during which he was pretty sure Mr. Hamilton asked his wife who the hell Dylan Burke was and why they should want to have dinner with him. Then Mrs. Hamilton covered the phone, and he heard emphatic but inaudible whispering before she returned to the phone, suggesting Tuesday night would

460

be best and wondering whether there was any special occasion.

"Tuesday would be perfect," Dylan said. "And, yes, it is a special occasion. I know it may sound sudden, but I'd like to ask Mr. Hamilton's permission to date your daughter."

In front of him, Suzanne's eyes were wide, cheeks flushed with what he hoped was embarrassment and not fury. He covered the receiver with his hand and said with a grin, "Don't worry, you can always say no."

She flashed him that defiant but playful look he loved. He stuck his tongue out at her in response, and she rolled her eyes again. But he saw her move incrementally toward him, too. *That* was a good sign.

Dylan knew that Suzanne worried about the logistics of their relationship, and sometimes he did, too. But he had tested his own ability to be loyal to her and passed. Now she had chosen to be here with him when every man before him had gotten the boot.

Mrs. Hamilton was fretting and sputtering on the other end of the phone, whether in dismay or excitement, he didn't know. Or care. At least right now. The wind was making it both colder and harder to hear through the phone. "Yes, ma'am. We'll meet you at the country club at seven on Tuesday. I'm sure Suzanne can tell me how to get there. See you then."

He hung up and clicked on the browser icon, searching for the CityRock Hotel Web site while Suzanne looked on. He found the front desk number and dialed.

"What are you doing?" Suzanne mouthed.

He held up a finger in response just as the switchboard downstairs answered. "Concierge desk, please," he said. Then, to Suzanne, "just taking care of one little thing so we can enjoy the rest of the day."

She wrinkled her nose at him. Damn, she was cute.

"Hi, Daniela. It's Dylan upstairs. Um, well . . . Rhett Butler."

The concierge wished him good morning and asked how everything was going. "Great, thank you. Could you send a bellman up to the penthouse, please? Ask him to come right in and out to the balcony."

"What's going on?" Suzanne asked, her playful look turning to a worried frown. He tousled her hair and pulled her close to him, protecting her from the wind and her worry. He wanted to protect her from everything.

"Thank you, ma'am," he went on, almost yelling now so that Daniela could hear him. "And if you don't mind asking him to hurry,

462

please. It's getting a bit windy out here."

He chuckled as Suzanne pulled free from his grasp and tested the door behind him herself. When it wouldn't open, her eyes grew wide, and she smacked his bare chest lightly with the back of her hand. "Ouch!" he said, and shrugged helplessly at her.

He ended the call and pulled Suzanne into his arms again, for closeness and for warmth. "Well, this is embarrassing," she said to his chest. "The bellman will probably snap a picture with his phone and sell it to the tabloids for a million dollars."

"More like thirty thousand, probably," Dylan corrected. "But at least *you* look great. I'm the one who's in my underwear."

"I guess public humiliation really is our thing, isn't it?"

"I'm afraid so," he said.

"Dylan?" she asked.

"Mmm . . ." He breathed into her hair. *God, he even loved the smell of her hair.*

"If we're going to stay together" — she pinched him lightly beneath the ribs for emphasis on this point — "let's get a *new* thing."

He laughed and kissed her forehead. "Anything for you, Scarlett."

With a joy so bone-deep it almost hurt to feel it, Dylan Burke realized that he meant

463

those words, understood them, for the first time in his life. The woman in his arms wasn't perfect, he knew, and what he wanted to build with her wasn't anything close to what he had planned for this stage of his life. But he would do *anything* for her. Last night, Suzanne had given him her most prized possession — her freedom — and he would spend the rest of his life protecting that gift and the heart that gave it.

He sat and pulled her onto his lap. She put her arms around his neck and rested her head on his shoulder. The wind slowed a little, allowing the warm beams of sunlight to reach them in relief.

"Whatever happens next," he said, softly in her ear, "I'll be there for you." Once spoken, the words felt inadequate to their purpose. He wished he had his guitar so he could try again and again, until they were a song that she could hear and understand.

But maybe she understood already. "I know," she whispered back, her face buried in his neck.

Then she looked at him, her blue eyes brimming with tears. "Last night, I started to panic again, like I have so many times before. I started analyzing and listing all the things that could go wrong, all the ways that we don't go together. If I had a friend in this situation, I'd probably tell her to get the heck out of here. It's just so . . . explosive."

"Yes, it is," he agreed, remembering their throes of passion the day before and how angry she had made him before that.

Suzanne sighed deeply and looked at the city below them and the peaceful-looking river beyond. "But when I got out of bed and came out here and looked down at the world, I already felt too far away from you. I realized that I made my choice a long time ago and that not one person out there, anywhere, could make me feel the way you do. You are, *we* are, the only choice. That's why it never worked with William. Not because there was anything wrong with him —"

Dylan growled softly as a surge of jealousy hit him. But he said nothing.

"— but because he wasn't *you*. My heart knew it, and I'm pretty sure you did, too. Now I finally understand it, for the first time ever. So" — she licked her lips in that way that drove him crazy — "are you really sure you want to be stuck with me? This is going to be hard. And you certainly have a lot of choices, country star Dylan Burke."

He didn't hesitate. "You're the only woman I want to be stuck with, Scarlett.

On a balcony fifty stories up or anywhere else."

He kissed her again and would have done more, if they hadn't been out on a windy terrace and expecting company any minute. As it was, the bellman had to clear his throat loudly a few minutes later before either of them even noticed he had arrived.

They emerged, startled, from a long kiss, embarrassed together this time. The bellman nodded officiously as he held the door for them, as though this was an ordinary part of his daily duties, politely ignoring that Dylan positioned Suzanne directly in front of him as they stood, to hide how much he'd been enjoying having her on his lap.

Dylan held both of Suzanne's hands to keep her close to him, and they crossed the threshold together clumsily, laughing, fingers interlaced. The suite was warm and inviting, full of possibilities. Whatever the next steps, the wind, the world outside, and the past no longer mattered, at least for now.

They were rescued.

EPILOGUE

Mid-January 2016

Suzanne fidgeted with her pink cashmere sweater and brown suede skirt, assessing herself critically in the mirror as she did. A little plumper than she had been in the past but still acceptable, she decided. Between the holidays and Dylan's passion for Southern barbecue, she'd put on a few pounds in the past couple of months, and her body was threatening to burst out of the size 6 wardrobe she'd been able to wear since high school. *Back to the gym next week,* she promised herself.

"Dylan!" she yelled in the direction of the bathroom, pulling on boots and her mother's pearls. "Let's go. We're late!"

"Okay, okay, Scarlett," he said. "You don't seriously think they would start without us, do you? Ow!"

He grabbed his left foot, which was covered in a thin black sock and had just rammed painfully against a large cardboard box. Suzanne gave him an apologetic look. "Sorry. I'll unpack that one today. Promise."

"You've been saying that for a week," he said. "And there are, like, thirty of them still packed. I never realized how much stuff you had squeezed into that little two-bedroom condo."

"Some of us don't live on a tour bus with ten other guys," she countered, with the haughtiest air she could manage. "You're like the richest person I know, but your belongings fit in a duffel bag."

He came up behind her and put his hands on her shoulders, pretending to strangle her, and then softened at their reflection together in the mirror. "You're just lucky you're so damn cute," he muttered, burying his nose in her hair.

"Easy, cowboy," she said, turning to face him. "Marci will kill us if we're late."

"She might kill *you*," he said, pulling her closer. "But she *loves* me. I'm a celebrity."

Suzanne laughed and pushed him away, nearly causing him to lose his balance and fall over the same box he'd just kicked. He gave her a stern look. "Unpack it tonight. Seriously."

A couple of weeks before, just after the new year, they had closed on a three-bedroom townhouse in Buckhead, a little farther from the city proper than Suzanne's condo had been. Because Suzanne was not yet drawing a salary for her work with the foundation and she insisted on contributing equally to the cost of the house, they'd had a budget of exactly twice what she'd been able to get for her condo in November. Dylan had protested this arrangement at first, as he could have bought them any house she wanted. But then he realized that arguing with Suzanne was fruitless. She had, however, graciously agreed to let him pay the utilities and association fees until she was earning regular income.

And, of course, the mountain-sized diamond he'd slipped on her finger at Christmas had been all his doing, as well.

She toyed with the ring in the passenger's seat of Dylan's truck, watching the soft light of the afternoon play off the three-carat diamond with the same mixture of awe and giddiness she'd been feeling ever since her trip to New York in October. Though it was growing smaller each day, there was still a part of her that kept expecting to wake from the dream.

They pulled up to the little Presbyterian church Marci had attended since she was small, where it seemed she and Jake also intended to celebrate those family moments of life that called for religious rites. Now that she and Dylan were engaged, Suzanne supposed they would need to start thinking about things like that, too. *Engaged.* Her heart still palpitated at the word — mostly in excitement, only partly in terror — and she squeezed Dylan's hand on the seat between them to calm herself.

He smiled and gave her a kiss as he turned off the truck. "Come on, Scarlett. Don't want to make ourselves later than we are."

When they entered the crowded vestibule, Suzanne exchanged quick pecks on the cheek with Rebecca, as well as Beth and Ray, while Dylan followed behind, shaking hands. She waved at Chad and David, who were on the other side of the room talking to Nicole and Ravi, Marci's sister and brother-in-law. Nicole held their six-month-old son on her hip. Their little girl, Ayanna, now four, was hiding behind Nicky, watching shyly as Beth and Ray's children played with Jake's niece and nephews. Jake's sister, Leah, broke off a conversation with Marci's parents to scold her twin boys about something.

"Marci invited everyone in Atlanta to this thing," she muttered to Dylan under her breath. "I should've worn something nicer."

"You're beautiful," he whispered back, grasping her hand. "Smile."

Suzanne did smile. The friends, the parents, the kids. Everyone chattering and smiling, hugging and wishing one another well. She marveled for a moment at how two people became a family — both because of the people they brought into the world and the people they simply brought together. The happy chaos in the little church was all an extension of Jake and Marci, who at one point in time had been just strangers in the same freshman English class.

She felt a tap on her shoulder as Jake approached from behind. "They're in the back," he said, motioning Suzanne toward the sanctuary doors. "Dylan, let me introduce you to my parents. My dad's a huge fan, but he pretends it's just my mom who likes your music."

With that, Jake had confiscated her fiancé and sent Suzanne to find Marci and the baby. Bonnie Theresa Stillwell was having her dedication today, and Suzanne's job was to stand up and promise to be Bonnie's godmother. It was a heavy responsibility for someone who still couldn't figure out how to put on a diaper. She hoped she was up to the task.

"Hey," Marci said as Suzanne poked her

head into the pastor's office.

"Hey yourself," Suzanne said.

Marci was nursing Bonnie beneath a blanket but motioned with her head for Suzanne to come in and take a seat. She looked radiant as a mother. They had just seen each other for dinner a couple of days before — Marci's first night out without the baby — but today she looked different somehow. Motherhood had given her best friend a new kind of grace.

"Is it crazy out there?" she asked softly.

"Only in the best way," Suzanne said. "How are you?"

"We're good," Marci said, gazing down at little Bonnie. They sat quietly for a while, listening to the baby's soft suckling and the light rain that was now falling outside.

"So how's the unpacking going? You still driving Dylan crazy?"

"Yes. I know it's awful. I'm just a terrible procrastinator."

"No. You're not." The words might've been reassuring, except that Marci's tone was more firm than generous.

Suzanne hesitated for a second. "Um, what?"

"You're not a procrastinator. I've known you since you were a kid. You either do things or you don't, in my experience."

472

"What do you mean?"

"I mean, I'm wondering whether you're delaying putting away those boxes as one last holdout. Like your subconscious anxiety about living with Dylan and committing your life to him is manifesting itself by you not unpacking all those boxes."

Oh, great, she's back in Columbo mode. Or she's been reading Psychology Today *again.* "Come on, Marce. I moved in with him. I sold my condo. I accepted his proposal." She held up her left hand and wiggled her ring finger. It had a disco-ball effect in the low-lit office. "You really think I'm trying to keep a foot out the door by not unpacking a few boxes?"

Marci merely arched an eyebrow in response and handed a well-fed Bonnie to Suzanne while she rebuttoned her blouse. Bonnie was a lovely, pudgy little thing with wispy brown curls. She'd been born on Halloween, and Suzanne had already purchased a baby princess costume for her to wear trick-or-treating on her first birthday. She held the tiny girl close to her, cooing softly and saying a silent prayer that Bonnie wouldn't choose the pink cashmere as the place to spit up her lunch. Before she could challenge Marci any further, Reverend McClosky knocked to tell them he was ready when they were.

By the time they got back to the sanctuary, the crowd had tripled to include aunts and uncles and grandparents and cousins. Once the reverend had spoken, the blessings had been offered, and both Suzanne and Jake's dad made their speeches for the occasion, not a dry eye remained in the little church. The guest of honor, however, seemed oblivious of the whole affair, sleeping soundly in Marci's arms throughout the ceremony. They gathered again in the front room for punch and cookies, where Suzanne and Dylan hung back from the crowd.

"Thanks for doing this with me," she said.

"Don't be ridiculous. This is what we do now, right? We go to each other's stuff."

"Well, yeah," she said. *Of course.*

Dylan pulled out his phone and looked at it, a wide grin spreading across his face. "Anyway," he said, "you'd better get ready for more of this stuff tomorrow."

"Tomorrow?"

He held out the phone. "Just got a text from Jeff. Kate just went into labor."

"Oh!" Suzanne's hand flew to her mouth in excitement.

Dylan was still grinning. "Can you imagine my whole family at the hospital? They're not going to know what hit them."

"Definitely not," she agreed. "The tabloids are going to have a field day." For Kate's sake, she hoped she was wrong.

Suzanne had found that her relationship with the press, while certainly challenging, had not been as bad as she'd anticipated. Since Dylan's announcement of his hiatus back in October had formally launched their relationship, they had been the topic of gossip on and off as people tried to figure out who Suzanne was and why Dylan had chosen her. Several grainy pictures and a few shaky videos of the two of them on the hotel balcony had made the rounds — apparently at least a few people in New York still looked out their windows and knew enough about country music to recognize Dylan in his boxers.

And, of course, the pictures from the debacle at the High had reemerged, to her utter embarrassment. The press seemed to be spinning them differently these days, however, with variations according to media outlet. Some came close to reality when they speculated that Penny had spiked Suzanne's drink that evening, while one fringe tabloid claimed that Dylan and Suzanne were rogue members of the same nudist cult who disrobed in public whenever microchips in their brains were activated. Marci had sent a clipping of this particular view to Suzanne. "Yeah, I think I might be forced to write a song about that one," Dylan had said stoically when she read it to him. "So where do you want to go for dinner?"

She was learning from Dylan, slowly, about not taking herself too seriously. Suzanne thought this might be a longer journey for her than for some, but the last year had certainly forced her to make a start. She found that her work at the foundation was teaching her something new about character and love and loyalty every day. She was getting a makeover she had never realized she needed.

Chad and David approached, hands linked. Suzanne kissed them both and reintroduced Dylan to David, since her memory of their meeting at the High last year was more than a little fuzzy. "How's the new job going?" she asked Chad, with the air of an ex-girlfriend asking about someone's dating life.

David rolled his eyes. "Oh, you had to *ask*," he said. He rubbed Chad's back affectionately and turned to Dylan. "Gorgeous, you and I better pretend we have something in common pretty quick. This could be a loooong conversation."

Suzanne gave Chad a look of concern.

"What's going on?"

"Ugh, Suze. It's fine, really. It's just . . . so predictable. I mean, the money is great and I love working near David —"

"Not in the same department," David put in hurriedly.

"Right. My boss is a nice guy and everything, but it's just not —"

"Challenging? Fun?" Suzanne ventured.

"It's not the same as working with *you,*" Chad said. "Apparently, I don't function well with sane people. I am motivated by craziness. I don't know whether I need a job change or shock therapy."

Suzanne laughed. "Well, you know, the foundation is doing really well. We are looking at expanding some of our services by the summer. We might be looking to hire someone soon."

"Says the woman who doesn't even draw her own salary yet," Dylan muttered. Suzanne ignored him.

"The pay isn't great, obviously, and you might need to do some volunteering with us so you can get to know the board first and see what you're in for," she said. As much as she loved the idea of working with Chad again, it was probably a big step down for him in terms of salary and prestige. She didn't want him to be unhappy.

"Oh, Suzanne, I'd love to," he said in a rush. "I'll bring your coffee every day."

She smiled. He really *did* hate his job at the law firm. She felt the same thrill at the thought of having Chad back with her as she had nearly five years ago when Marci had moved home from Austin. But she tried to keep her emotions even so he wouldn't feel pressured and regret his decision. "Let's have lunch next week, okay?"

They said good-bye, and Chad kissed her cheek again, promising to call next week. David surprised her by throwing his arms around her in a farewell bear hug. "Thank you, thank you, thank you!" he whispered urgently. Apparently working in the same office was putting a bit of a strain on Chad and David's relationship.

That evening, Suzanne and Dylan sat on the couch together, she with a glass of wine, he with his phone handy, waiting for news from Kate and Jeff. The pregnancy had been difficult; Kate had often been overwhelmed to the point of tears by the misguided intrusions of her family. To his credit, Jeff had banned everyone — including their parents and Dylan — from the hospital until the day after the baby was born. Dylan had seemed surprised at first, but Suzanne had a hunch that he actually respected his brother-in-law for holding his ground.

A warm fire crackled — the first one in their new fireplace — and Suzanne looked through some work papers while Dylan watched a Tennessee Titans play-off game in his lucky socks, a ragged old pair of white tube socks with holes in the toes and paint stains on the bottom. He claimed the Titans won more often than they lost when he wore them. How he had kept track of this statistic, she didn't know, but it was one of the hundreds of endearing little things she had learned about him since October. These were the kinds of things she hadn't known about anyone before — except Marci — and certainly had never shared herself, at least not with anyone she'd dated.

But Dylan knew now. He knew that Suzanne still sometimes slept with a teddy bear she'd had since childhood, and by either great sympathy or great restraint he had not made fun of her for it. He knew she loved crime dramas and hated scented candles and was a tragically bad dancer. He knew she did her best painting after midnight and liked to sleep in at every opportunity but could also appreciate a sunrise if properly lured with a cinnamon latte and sweet words. He knew she'd spent the first half of her life so far afraid of letting her father down and the second half afraid of letting everyone else down, too. He knew all of this and more, and yet he loved her. For the first time in her life, she believed those words when she heard them.

They were still working on everything else.

So far, the news of their engagement had somehow not made it to the press — Suzanne didn't wear the ring in public yet — but it was inevitable, and she knew they needed to decide some things soon. The idea of planning a wedding right now was so far from desirable that she had suggested they simply go to the local courthouse on a Tuesday or something. She had a fantasy of getting married in jeans and a T-shirt on the way to the grocery store and then sneaking away undetected on a honeymoon in the middle of the night. Dylan had laughed at what he called an "anti-Suzanne" idea and suggested that even at the local courthouse they'd be unlikely to escape the press.

He didn't pressure her about setting a date. He also hadn't said anything about his career, but she knew that he was itching to go back to work soon. It only seemed fair, considering she had the foundation and her painting to keep her more than occupied. The three months they'd been together had been the longest break he had taken from his music career since middle school. In many ways, she could tell he was refreshed by it. They'd spent a few days here and there at his cabin — alone, amazingly enough — or down at the beach near Savannah. He'd caught up with old friends — like Jesse Mc-Creary, who Suzanne felt sheepish meeting personally after publicly criticizing his batting average — and he frequently went out to listen to small-time bands in bars and at little local festivals. When she could, Suzanne went with him. Occasionally, he'd introduce himself after a show and get a promising band's CD to pass on to his father, but he had yet to re-create their first dive-bar experience by singing James Taylor to her.

It had been an amazing three months for both of them, but Suzanne knew that if he stayed away from his work too long, he would begin to wilt and die. Not to mention everyone else who depended on Dylan for their livelihoods, too. She had been thinking it was time to talk about their plans for a while now, but there was always something else more pressing, or more fun, to do. She was waiting for the right opportunity to bring it up and, somehow, while he was yelling obscenities at a line judge on TV didn't seem like the right time.

This time, it was Marci's voice that came to her. You're delaying . . . one last hold-out . . . subconscious anxiety . . . committing your whole life . . .

No. This time Marci was wrong. "Dylan?" she said sweetly.

"What, babe?" he said, not taking his eyes off the screen, split into three parts. The two head coaches paced in their little boxes, waiting for a referee in the third box, who was watching a replay under a large black hood.

Suzanne hesitated. "Could we —"

"Aw, *dammit!* Come ON!" he said, throwing his arms up in exasperation. Apparently, the call had gone against Tennessee. He turned to her and composed his face into a semblance of normalcy, apparently with some effort. This was not a good time.

"Could you keep me posted, about Kate?"

"Sure, Scarlett," he said, glancing peripherally at the television. "You going somewhere?"

"Nope. Just going upstairs, and I don't want to miss the baby news."

"Everything okay?" he said. Now he looked concerned.

She crossed to him and gave him a soft kiss, tugging gently at his bottom lip with her teeth as they parted. "I'm fine. Just going upstairs." She gave him a grin. "Don't get all swept up in football and forget about me, okay?"

He growled slightly and leaned toward her. "What football?" Suzanne knew she'd never get tired of that lopsided grin.

The work took her nearly five hours. By the time she'd finished, it was one in the morning and she had lost all sense of time. She went downstairs to find Dylan asleep on the couch with the TV flickering. She shook him gently, and he startled awake, grabbing for his phone. They read the text together:

It's a boy! Adrian Burke Wendell, born 11:16 p.m. 6 lbs, 8 oz. Mom & baby GR8 :) Luv, Jeff

"We'll leave first thing, eh?" Dylan said, grinning.

"Definitely," Suzanne agreed. "They'll need your help controlling the rest of the family."

Dylan nodded and stood, stretching. His white T-shirt rose with his broad shoulders, leaving an exposed gap of perfect stomach between it and his jeans. The three months of relaxing had done Dylan no harm whatsoever. Tired and achy though she was, she felt the familiar longing for him rising in her lower abdomen.

"What were you doing all this time, Scarlett?" he asked sleepily.

"Huh?" she said, distracted by the desire to touch his abs.

"Upstairs. Were you painting something?"

"Oh, no. But I think you'll be happy to see what I was working on." She took his hand, his left hand, and pulled him upstairs by the finger that would someday wear her ring. When they got upstairs, she held out her arms in her best Vanna White impersonation.

"What?" he said, looking around. "What am I looking at, Suze?"

"It's what you're *not* looking at," she said.

Realization dawned. "All of them?"

"Every one," she said, and then squealed as he scooped her up in an embrace. He carried her up the additional flight of stairs to the master bedroom, where he enticed her to overlook her aches and pains while they made love. In their bedroom, in their house, where they were both all in, and every single box was unpacked. For good.

ACKNOWLEDGMENTS

Every novel has its unique joys and challenges; but I have to say that *Regrets Only* has been a favorite to write and edit, thanks in large part to all the encouragement and support I've had along the way.

My husband, Sam Turetsky, has been my biggest advocate and supporter, from the first word written and every step since. Our two sons are my littlest and best cheerleaders: they tolerate with grace many nights of mac and cheese, and many Sundays of trying *so hard* to stay quiet while Mommy is writing in her office.

As always, Nicole Sohl of Thomas Dunne, St. Martin's Press, and Macmillan Entertainment made the process of updating and editing Suzanne's story easy and fun. I'm grateful to Beth Phelan and Jenny Bent of the Bent Agency for their guidance and support. Thanks to Lee Morin, Paula Grothe, and Faith Williams for their continued advice and friendship.

To my critique partners and friends Becky Albertalli, Emily Carpenter, and Chris Negron, you are amazing and I love you more than guacamole. Almost. Thanks to George Weinstein, Valerie Connors, and the rest of the Atlanta Writers Club for great conferences and unparalleled support for authors, in particular the Roswell critique group.

This book was initially self-published as part of the *Marriage Pact* trilogy, and even though they are tired of being thanked in every acknowledgments page, I couldn't have done any of that without the support, feedback, and encouragement of these lovelies: Carla Birnbaum, Sarah Cutler, Jenna Denisar, Kristal Goelz, Marla Kaplan, Michelle Moore, Anna Turetsky Needle (and the entire Needle Clan), Patricia Reeder, Brenda Turetsky, Ryan Van Meter, and Rob Wade.

Finally, thanks to all the friends old and new who have read, reviewed, or recommended my books to others; and to those who follow and comment on my blogs, Facebook posts, and tweets. You make things possible.

— *MJP*

ABOUT THE AUTHOR

Manda (M.J.) Pullen is the author of complex, funny contemporary romances including *The Marriage Pact.* She was raised in the suburbs of Atlanta by a physicist and a flower child, who taught her that life is tragic and funny, and real love is anything but simple. She has a weakness for sappy movies, craft beer, gossip, and boys who talk baseball. After traveling around Europe and living in cities like Austin and Portland, she returned to Atlanta where she lives with her family.